Post-war Italy has been the scene of many important developments in film, art, and design that have had wide-reaching influence in many other countries. Italian literature, too, has had its share in this international fame. Unfortunately, however, only a few of Italy's best writers, such as Moravia and Silone, have been translated extensively into English.

This new anthology of modern Italian short novels, or novellas, is a representative selection of six of the top-ranking Italian writers who are immensely popular at home and deserve much more attention abroad. Each author was selected either because of his total unavailability to the English-speaking reader, or because of his prime importance to the modern Italian literary scene. Four of the writers have received some of the top Italian literary awards in the recent past (Strega Prize, Naples Prize, and Bagutta Prize), which are comparable to our own Pulitzer Prize. Five of the six novellas have been especially translated for this edition.

This edition has been edited with Introductions by William Arrowsmith, Ph.D., Professor of Classics, University of Texas, and a d̶ ̶ ̶ ̶ ̶ ̶ ̶ ̶ ̶ ̶ ̶ ̶ ̶ classical Greek̶ ̶ ̶ ̶ ̶ ̶ ̶ ̶ ̶ ̶ modern literatu̶ ̶ ̶ ̶ ̶ ̶ ̶ ̶

D1431486

Six Modern Italian Novellas

edited and with introductions by William Arrowsmith

A PERMABOOK EDITION published by POCKET BOOKS, INC. • NEW YORK

SIX MODERN ITALIAN NOVELLAS

A *Permabook* edition

1st printing .... January, 1964

ACKNOWLEDGEMENTS

Itaglio del bosco, THE CUTTING OF THE WOODS, by Carlo Cassola;
Oscar Pilli, by Mario Tobino; and *La speculazione edilisia*, A PLUNGE
INTO REAL ESTATE, by Italo Calvino are published in translation by
permission of Giulio Einaudi, Editore, Turin, Italy.

The translation of OSCAR PILLI by William Arrowsmith and the translation of THE CUTTING OF THE WOODS by Raymond Rosenthal are
reprinted with the permission of the *Texas Quarterly*.

Quel che vide Cummeo, WHAT CUMMEO SAW, by Domenico Rea is
published by permission of Arnaldo Mondadori, Editore, Milan, Italy.

Ricordi di un impiegato, JOURNAL OF A CLERK, by Federigo Tozzi is
published by permission of Vallecchi, Editore, Firenze, Italy.

La Garibaldina, by Elio Vittorini and translated by Frances Keene, copy-
right, ©, 1960 by *New Directions*, is published by permission of *New
Directions*, Norfolk, Connecticut.

CONTENTS

INTRODUCTION

THIS BOOK BEGAN AS AN ATTEMPT TO BRING TOGETHER A
representative group of what Italians, with amiable indifference, call either "short novels" *(romanzi brevi)* or "long stories" *(racconti lunghi).* With one exception—Tozzi's *Journal of
a Clerk (Ricordi di un impiegato),* completed prior to Tozzi's
death in 1920—all of these short novels (or long stories)
belong to the postwar period, roughly from 1945 to 1960.

Tozzi has been included, at the expense of chronological
neatness, for two compelling reasons. In the first place, though
almost utterly unknown in America and very little known,
outside a narrow circle of intellectuals and writers, in Italy,
he is indisputably one of the three or four major Italian
writers of prose fiction in the twentieth century. Verga and
Svevo are his peers, and this alone would justify his inclusion.
In the second place, he is also, however poorly recognized,
one of the major and decisive influences upon contemporary
Italian writers, particularly the young. And between Tozzi
and his "neorealist" successors and disciples, one can plot the
curve of Italian fiction for half a century. He provides, that
is, not only a standard and a model, but a point of reference:
the only novelist of genius between Svevo and the present,
and the only great master of realism in Italian after Verga.
As such, he is essential to this book, whose dominant narrative mode is, like Tozzi's, a highly formal realism.

The postwar (or so-called neorealistic) period in Italian
literature is now, there can be no doubt, a closed chapter.
Even by the mid-fifties the climate of poverty, misery, and
hope that had originally produced neorealism was visibly on

the wane; Italo Calvino's fine short novel *A Plunge into Real Estate* (1957) can, and should, be read as an ironic obituary on the whole postwar period; and by 1960 all but the most stubbornly doctrinaire of the neorealists were compelled to admit that the Italian reality in which they had hitherto found both subject and technique had totally altered, if it had not vanished altogether. The causes of this change were multiple, but by far the most revolutionary was the simple, overwhelming fact of sudden prosperity, the Italian "economic miracle," which, quickly gathering momentum in the middle and late fifties, was in full, exuberant swing by 1960. Poverty, real poverty, of course, remained, but it was no longer the incontrovertible *national* fact of the immediate postwar years; even the blinding, humiliating misery of the south and Sicily was slowly changing. Not unnaturally, given the terrible, millennial poverty of Italy, Italian realists had tended to assume that their preferred reality—the reality of suffering, oppression, and social injustice that everywhere in Italy had for centuries impressed itself upon the eye—was a reality with a future. That *that* reality should suddenly change, that Italy should suddenly become prosperous, was no more to be expected, at least in *their* lifetime, than the Second Coming. Hence the explosive irruption of prosperity caught Italian writers for the most part utterly unprepared. As one distinguished realist put it, realistically and irritably: "Prosperity caught us with our pants down." The irritation was only natural: after devoting some twenty years of his life to exploring and reporting what seemed to him the most evident reality of his time, he had now, in middle age and mid-career, to face all over again the whole, intricate, exhausting, compelling job of adjusting to a reality so strange and new that it seemed, in fact, formless. The decision which has been forced upon him—and upon so many other Italian writers—is, of course, the same decision that Verga and Yeats made for themselves, in middle age and mid-career: the decision that made them great writers.

At this point several elementary distinctions are in order. "Neorealism" (a term originally borrowed from the Italian films) is at best a clumsy rubric, and at worst a positive obstacle to understanding. As a literary term, it has the useful but limited value of distinguishing postwar realism (viewed as a *resumption*, after an interlude of forty years, of the *realistic* tradition of Verga) from the "traditional" Italian novel (Riccardo Bacchelli's immense Manzonian trilogy, *The Mill on the Po*, is a good example of the genre). But because the term was originally borrowed from the movies, it quickly became confused with the "neorealism" of such films as *Paisà* or *Umberto D*. Thus, while the writings of Pratolini, Moravia, Rea, Pavese, and even Vittorini are all, vis-à-vis Bacchelli or Palazzeschi, "neorealistic" in the first sense (a fact that shows the coarseness of the distinction), only the writing of Pratolini or Rea's *What Cummeo Saw* qualifies in the second sense. As a general rule, the (admittedly vague) term "postwar realism" is to be preferred.

In the second place, postwar realism was not a school, or even a literary movement (in the sense that Marinetti's Futurism was a movement, complete with manifesto, prophet, drums, etc.). It was rather a simultaneous convergence of experience, conviction, and commitment on the part of a number of writers, both amateurs and professionals. They composed no group; their ages, backgrounds, and origins were sharply diverse, and although they were basically Left politically, their color ranged from liberal to socialist to communist. Fundamentally they shared: (1) a loose and heterodox Marxism (many if not most of them started out as Communists and gradually drifted away); (2) a strong antagonism (basically Marxist) to "traditional" (i.e., Catholic and classical) bourgeois culture, and the "traditional" novel which it supported; (3) a profound conviction that poverty, exploitation, and social injustice (all summed up in Vittorini's phrase *l'offesa del mondo*—the world's wrong) were the glaring realities of the age, and that the only technique appropriate to them was some form of realism (*which* realism was held to be a matter of individual taste); (5) a hatred of Fascism, a direct (in some cases, a passionately vicarious) experience of the War and the Resistance, and a deep loyalty to the "Resistance feelings"; and (6) a commitment to some form of *nuova cultura* (another Vittorini phrase). They composed, in short, an informal league of committed writers. If the moral leadership belonged to Elio Vittorini above all, this was because, both as writer and as editor of *Il Politecnico* (1945–47), he articulated what so many of his contemporaries felt but had not succeeded in saying. But Vittorini never tried to become the leader of a movement (and if he had, he would probably have failed). Realism, after all, is either a democratic style or it is nothing.

Finally, if realism was the dominant mode in postwar Italy, it was not the only mode, or the only important one. The glaring exception is Carlo Emilio Gadda, by consensus Italy's greatest living novelist (a better writer surely than either Moravia or Pratolini, and one who, typically, has never been translated into English—admittedly no easy job). Again, Cesare Pavese may have shared realist convictions and experience, but his work stubbornly resists inclusion in the realist canon. So too, for one reason or another, does the work of Mario Soldati, Gianna Manzini, Elsa Morante, Vitaliano Brancati, Giorgio Bassani, Romano Bilenchi, Corrado Alvaro, and Italo Calvino (or at least the Calvino of the "fables")— all postwar writers of power and importance. Realists they may be in part, or now and then, or vis-à-vis D'Annunzio, but consistent, programmatic realists they are not. And meanwhile, the older, so-called traditional writers—Bacchelli, Palazzeschi, Moretti, Comisso—have gone their way, steadily writing—and just as steadily being ignored by the critics (in Italy, an unmixed blessing). Precisely because they are "traditional," they are little read in modish and intellectual circles, and they are often grotesquely patronized by the younger generation, and particularly by the more doctrinaire Marxists. In the case of Bacchelli, a good but extremely uneven writer, the neglect may be partially justified; in the case of Palazzeschi, it is a profound injustice. Not only is Palazzeschi formally far superior to most of his juniors, but he is also one of the most original and brilliant of Italian writers (he has still to be translated into English). Such injustices are unfortunately not uncommon in contemporary Italian literature. The reason is not merely modishness (Italians seldom seem to read any novel which is more than two or less than one hundred years old), but the unpleasant, sub-Marxist habit of indiscriminately applying polemical labels like "traditional" (i.e., "bourgeois") and "realist" (i.e., "Marxist") long after they have outlived their usefulness. Not only do such labels disfigure literature and distort the truth, but they embalm debates which were better buried. Culturally at least, Italy is still badly in need of a general amnesty.

But as a whole the postwar period in Italy and Italian realism need no apology. Although it has produced no writer with the stature and power of Camus or Faulkner, or any single work as good as Bellows' *Seize the Day*, it is, I am convinced, altogether the most solid body of narrative produced in Europe between 1945 and 1960, outranging in power and originality, if not in technical skill, the bulk of British, French, and German writing. This is, I suppose, a controversial statement, and one which will doubtless be discounted for that very reason. This would be a mistake. Italy has for centuries been the poor Cinderella of European letters, and her sudden claim to pride of place will not perhaps be readily accepted by those who are accustomed to think that her place is by the hearth, perpetually eclipsed by her cosmopolitan French and British big sisters. But the body of completed, rounded, committed work is *there*, a lively fact, and those who will read these *romanzi*, dispassionately and curiously, will see, I think, how serious the Italian claim is. It would, of course, be absurd to suggest that *these* six short novels will by themselves suffice to alter received opinion; but if they serve to enlist curious readers for the body of work they represent, they will have done their work.

Ideally, the reading of these *romanzi* should be supplemented by the reading of some fifteen or twenty more; for the best Italian work of the period is not the work of two or three, or even five or six, great writers, but of fifteen or twenty talented writers. Some of them, like Mario Rigoni-Stern (author of a remarkably powerful "documentary," *Il sergente nella neve*, 1954), have written only a single book. Some of the *romanzi* are not *romanzi* at all, but precisely "prose documentaries." Carlo Levi's *Christ Stopped at Eboli (Cristo si è fermato a Eboli)*, 1945, for instance, is not a *romanzo* at all (and certainly not a *romanzo breve*); and yet, both as a pioneering work and as fine fictional perception brought to bear upon social reality, it deserves a place as surely as Vittorini's classic *romanzo breve, The Twilight of the Elephant (Il Sempione strizza l'occhio al Frejus)*, 1947. But taken in their ensemble, these *romanzi* and "prose documentaries" compose, I believe, one of the most interesting and original bodies of literature in modern times, and certainly the most sustained, if not the most brilliant, Italian narrative of the twentieth century.

But why, it may be asked, a collection of *romanzi brevi* anyway? Why not simply a collection of the best prewar or postwar Italian fiction? For the simple reason that, in my judgment, the best of Italian postwar fiction has taken precisely this form, the *romanzo breve* or the *racconto lungo*, a prose narrative of between 60 and 150 pages in length. What is more, precisely because this form is an awkward one— too short to qualify as a novel and too long to be presented as a story—it has failed to fit American publishers' packages (and thereby, according to the publishers, has failed to conform to American taste). The result is that the best Italian prose fiction since the war has, in fact, been mostly neglected or ignored in favor of the novel of a more traditional size. Examples come easily to mind. Thus one reason why the reputations of Moravia and Pratolini loom so large abroad in the public mind (larger, I think, than their merits allow, though both of them are good and able writers) is not only that their work is fashionably modern and "European" (i.e., an adroit blend of Marxism, psychoanalysis, and sociology, cynical and aloof in Moravia, genial and cozy in Pratolini), but that their preferred form fits the common definition and sense of the novel. By the same token, equally (and sometimes more) deserving writers such as Gadda, Pavese, Tozzi, Bigiaretti, and Tobino are far less known abroad and much less translated.

Why these writers should so unanimously have preferred the *romanzo breve* is, I think, a question that goes far beyond coincidence or personal preference. In my opinion the short novel is a favored form because its size was more appropriate both to a certain kind of subject and a certain (curiously experimental) way of writing. That is, Italian writers, basically uncertain of their audience, their subject, and even their language (the gap between "spoken" and "written" Italian is still large and, for narrative, crippling), have naturally tended to prefer a smaller canvas. In the second place, they wanted a form that was, so to speak, "untraditional"; precisely because they were mostly in revolt against the "traditional" novel, they needed a form (akin to the *novella* but free of its traditional associations) that was different. The short story (and particularly the *terza pagina* story, restricted to a few thousand words—readers of Moravia's *Racconti romani* will recognize the genre) was too cramped for their ambitions, while the novel required either too sustained virtuosity or permitted insufficient concentration. In the *romanzo breve* they adopted a genre whose modest compass permitted and encouraged both a novelistic rhythm and a quite un-novelistic concentration. And for this very reason American readers, familiar with the relaxed pace of the large novel, may find themselves uncomfortable with the Italian *romanzo breve* with its tendency to lyricism or single-minded pursuit of its central "idea."

Which is merely a way of saying that, in its own way, the Italian *romanzo breve* is an experimental form. Experiment, as we know, is not a habit with which Italian fiction is often credited. But experimentalism in the Italian *romanzo* has necessarily taken forms which render it unfamiliar to Europeans and Americans, at the same time that, in its different economy and unconcern with "interior richness" or inner depth, it seems decidedly old-fashioned. Those Italians —and there are many of them—who join in the foreign chorus that condemns Italian narrative as unadventurous too easily lose sight of the very real experimental risks that their fiction has taken in recent years.

A word about selection. I would not claim that the *romanzi brevi* in this collection are necessarily the classics of their kind, though they are all, I think, both extremely good and appropriately representative. Selection was not easy. It would, for instance, have been possible to present two or even three alternate collections, each one completely different. But I was strongly swayed by the belief that, wherever possible, the material of this collection should be new in English; and of these six *romanzi*, five have been newly done. A number of other possible candidates—some of them my first choices—had to be eliminated for one reason or another (either they had been translated already, or the rights were unavailable, or the Italian publisher failed to answer inquiries).

—WILLIAM ARROWSMITH

Rome, Italy

SIX MODERN
ITALIAN NOVELLAS

FEDERIGO TOZZI

FEDERIGO TOZZI WAS BORN IN SIENA ON JANUARY 1, 1883, the youngest of eight children. A sickly and unhappy boy, his entire childhood was an unrelieved sequence of loss, convalescence, loneliness, conflict, and failure. Of his seven brothers and sisters, all died of meningitis in infancy or childhood; his mother, a chronic invalid subject to epileptic seizures, died when he was twelve. Between Tozzi and his father, the brutal and miserly proprietor of a *trattoria* in Siena, there was constant rancor and warfare; for long periods the boy kept himself isolated, eating his meals in his room and refusing to speak to his family. Later he revenged himself on his father's strictness by failing in school and ostentatiously refusing to work. In 1908 his father died, and Tozzi promptly married, sold the hated *trattoria,* and settled down to writing on one of the two farms his father left him. Six years later, overwhelmed by debts and the rejection of his writing, he gave up the farm and moved to Rome. Here he spent what seem to have been the three most miserable years of a miserable life. Finally, in 1917, with the publication of *Bestie* and a slender measure of success, he started writing with great speed (*Tre croci* was written in less than two weeks) the works that brought him his modest posthumous reputation. On March 21, 1920, he died of pneumonia. He was thirty-seven years old.

His major writings are: *La zampogna verde* (1911); *Bestie* (1917); *Con gli occhi chiusi* (1919); *Tre croci* (1920); *L'Amore* (1920); *Giovani* (1920); *Ricordi di un impiegato* (1920), probably a revision of an early work); *Il podere* (1921).

1

JOURNAL OF A CLERK
by Federigo Tozzi

translated by D. S. Carne-Ross

January 3

FROM FIFTEEN TO TWENTY I GAVE MYSELF FREELY, WILDLY, to the delights of idleness and irresponsibility: to turn my back on all that feels like an act of deliberate cruelty. It annoys me when people try to tell me that I must do what everyone else has to do: stop amusing myself and start to take life seriously. An intelligent young man, a young man in love—hasn't he the right to do just as he pleases? Love possesses my whole being, it seems the only occupation that accords with my own sense of myself and with my pride. There's nothing strange in the fact that I feel very ambitious too; it is precisely this ambition that makes me unwilling to take a job like everybody else. I am determined to wait from day to day, for a privileged fate to present itself: *my* fate. And no compromises!

January 5

My father has cornered me at last. By parading my brothers and sisters in front of me, he persuaded me that I ought to take the State Railroad exam. Half timidly, half suspiciously, I look at my mother—pregnant and still quite young—then I drop my head and start crying.

February 1

What I hate most, now that I know I've passed the exams, is leaving my fiancée. I'm really in love with Attilia and the thought of going away from Florence for some station God knows where strikes me as little short of odious. I pick up her photograph, and crying indulgently over it, I swear to her, as though she were there in the room with me, that it's not my fault. I swallow my tears with a greed that makes me feel even more desperate.

My mother comes in unexpectedly. The expression on her face suggests that she is absolutely against me—I read a kind of self-centered hostility there.

"So you want to bring your wife to live here," she says. "Don't you think there are enough of us as it is?"

I haven't the courage to reply, but with a nervous shudder that seems to penetrate to my very brain I show that I have no intention of giving in. With astonishment I realize that for the first time I have managed to disobey her. I look at her more closely, almost frightened at what I have done, but she takes no further notice of me and starts opening my chest of drawers to sort out the linen I will be taking with me. I have only three shirts, two pairs of shorts, no woolen vests, the handkerchiefs need marking so that the washer-woman doesn't mix them up with other people's or lose them, and my collars won't take starch any longer. When she has finished, she says:

"Your fiancée ought to see your wardrobe if she cares for you as much as you say."

Excited by the joy of defending Attilia, I take a carefully wrapped package from the drawer of a table that I use as a hiding place. With delicate haste I succeed in undoing it.

"Look," I say, "she's already given me this tie."

It seems to me such a fine tie that my eyes fill with tears again. Seeing the state I am in, my mother doesn't like to turn it over to look at the seam. But she doesn't think much of it.

"It won't last you a month. It's a cheap silk."

"And she's going to buy me a pair of shoes," I add, lying.

My mother turns pale at this. "Aren't you ashamed to let the girl dress you?"

I'm on the point of confessing that I lied. My chest heaves

as though it were going to burst. "You don't know her," I say. "How can you think badly of her?"

"I know more about women than you do."

"When have you seen her?" I ask, trembling.

"Her photograph doesn't appeal to me. Why does she fix her hair like that?"

More readily than before, I find another lie. "Because I told her to!"

"I don't believe it. You'll never tell a woman how to do her hair. It will always be the woman who tells you what to do."

"Do you think I have to obey her just because I'm in love with her?"

But my mother is looking out of the corner of her eye at the photograph lying on the table: the eyes of a pregnant woman, glittering, the lids lowered; she seems agitated, even her mouth appears to be thinking. Her presence is more powerful than the thought of Attilia; my mother has got to love her too.

"Will you promise to speak to her just once, before I go away?" I asked.

"I'll talk to your father."

I start blushing and feel humiliated, though with a sense of troubled pleasure.

Suddenly my three sisters, aged from seven to twelve, come in by the door, which was left open. I hardly have time to turn the photograph over, and my mother, drawing them to her and running her hands through their hair, says, smiling, "You're even ashamed of yourself."

Once I am alone again I try to make out whether it's myself I'm ashamed of or them.

February 2

They were dying to laugh at me yesterday evening at supper; my mother must have told them all about Attilia. Only my youngest sister seemed unable to stare at me ironically, though she looked around and tried to follow the others; she thought it was the right thing to do.

"You will write to us at least twice a week," my father said. "You must think of your parents before anyone else."

I wanted to tell him that the "anyone else" he referred to was my fiancée, but I didn't have the strength. I didn't even dare say I was in love. Instead I asked when I was leaving.

"I imagine you'll get your call at the end of the month," he said.

My two brothers opened their eyes wide and looked serious. The younger one said, "We'll send you some picture post-cards."

But my mother didn't approve of this. "You can add your greetings to the letter when *we* write to him," she told them.

When he had finished the main course, my father said, "You'll have to put your mind on the job and stop dreaming. If you go on playing around, you'll never earn a decent salary. And another thing—before you start making plans that are best left to people who've got somewhere in life, you'll do well to ask my advice. You write to me and I'll answer you."

My brothers started laughing, but stopped immediately.

"There is nothing to be ashamed of in obeying one's parents," he went on. "Everyone has done so. And if you want to go and marry while you are still too young—well, you won't get my permission."

My brothers and sisters began to shout and laugh, beating on their plates with their knives and forks. "Be quiet," my father told them, "and one of you go and get the dessert we're having in honor of Leopoldo's departure."

I wonder now why I ate the dessert and why I forgot about Attilia.

March 2, morning

The whole family came to the station. My father was nervous and kept his hands stuck in his pockets; his satisfaction in my having got a job made him behave quite rudely, bumping into people and not apologizing. My mother was frowning furiously and I was frightened all the time that she would find out where Attilia, who had come to see me off, was hiding. My brothers were yawning and talking about school; the girls were in their best clothes, the two oldest ones trying to attract attention. My spirits rose as the train started to pull out, but I didn't manage to see Attilia.

I am writing in the train, a notebook balanced on my knee. I long to take out of my coat pocket the tightly folded rose that she gave me. Touching it, I fancy it brings me luck.

March 2, noon

I'm distressed by the quarrel with my family that my engagement has brought about. Do I perhaps have to become hard and unfeeling if I am not to lose my own self-respect? Am I perhaps acquiring that hardness which they say you have to learn? Until now I've believed I could get on without it—for good. Is it so difficult to be kind? Everything seems fine when I manage. Nobody understands my love for Attilia. When I am with her, a miraculous sense of joy takes possession of my will and my senses. Time no longer exists, only an infinite space. When she speaks I take hold of her hands—to thank her.

I've been traveling three hours, thinking of her all the time; she seems to be there just outside the car, speeding along with the train—staying with me.

There are kinds of sweetness that hurt like pain. This spring I know that I have been a trial to everyone, unable to express myself, awkward, afraid even of my own laugh.

Sometimes when I'm asleep, astonishing sensations of reality come to me, but the reality I experience in dreams has the quality imparted to it at that moment by my soul. I measure it against my normal habits; it is perhaps no more than a vague sketch of something that lives inside me.

But now I feel the taste of death, which will come without my knowing how; will come because I have started to live.

March 2

It is after eight in the evening when I get to Pontedera. I pick up my heavy, awkward suitcase and report to the station-

master. He doesn't get up when I come into the office. He is
an elderly man with a gray beard; he is wearing a beret and
smoking a pipe. The electric bulb hanging over his desk gives
out a feeble light and I can scarcely make out the rest of the
station staff, who stare at me.

"Have you had experience?" he asks me.

"No," I tell him, turning red. "This is the first time I've
worked in a station. I took the exams a month ago."

He turns to the others, who look angry and disappointed;
then, making the best of it, he says, "Be here tomorrow morning at seven."

As I go out, I hear him cursing the regional office for sending him an incompetent clerk instead of someone with experience. I feel offended and exasperated, but in order to get used
to unpleasantness as soon as possible I give my bag to a porter,
whom I hear people calling Drago, and tell him to take me to
a café where they have rooms to let. As we go, he walks a few
steps behind, never taking his eyes off me; this annoys me and
I step out sharply. I pay him and sit down at a table. Drago
would have liked to stay and drink a glass of wine with me;
he is offended at not being invited and eyes me in an ironical
way that is meant to be offensive.

The proprietress, before coming to my table, stands leaning against the doorpost, taking a long, hard look at me. I can't
outstare her, so I look down at the table. When I raise my
eyes again she's gone, but I hear her bawling next door; that
hoarse whine is Drago—he is backing her up. But I stay where
I am: the weight of my body is too strong for me.

An engineer is eating a couple of eggs, one eye on a newspaper spread out in front of him, the other on me. I start to
get impatient and bang with my knuckles on the empty plate.
I hear the sound of chairs being moved and a confused noise
of voices; then a tall, imposing woman comes to ask what I
want. This is the maid.

I want something to eat, I tell her.

"Then I'll send the mistress."

She has been waiting behind the door; she shows up now
and the pair of them look at me in silence. The engineer stares

at me so intently that I am forced to turn my eyes away. Trying to make my voice sound pleasant, I ask what there is to eat.

But the proprietress is more irritable than the maid and she wants to let me know that I had better not throw my weight around.

"Do you want some soup, a couple of eggs, some steak . . . ?"

"Steak."

Plainly she is offended. "Don't you want any soup?"

"No."

"But the broth is delicious." And she looks at the engineer to get him on her side. But I stand up for myself and insist that what I want is steak. So then she says, "Yes, sir," her voice contemptuous, unforgiving. It's easy to see they don't like me; the way the engineer looks at me couldn't be clearer. I eat my meal and go to bed, but first I let the rest of the people there know that I am the new clerk at the railroad station.

I should write to Attilia now, but for the first time I feel that my mind is occupied by the things I have done and seen during the day. How can I write to her about them? I feel like a mouse trapped in a room suddenly full of people, and unable to get back to its hole in time. So although my eyes search the dark for her, I can't write her a letter. All the same, I get out of bed, and removing from my pocket the rose she gave me, I stick it in the frame of the mirror.

March 3

Up very early. I hear two or three steam whistles going off and I open the window. The Arno and the whole town are covered in mist, but I can make out a thin plume of smoke rising from one of the whistles. A train pulls in. Three girls, going in the opposite direction, walk in file along the bank of the river.

I get dressed and go to the office. My colleagues are breakfasting on bread and slices of cheese. I feel very uncomfortable and don't open my mouth. Meanwhile the superintendent comes in. If it weren't for his spectacles and the gold stripes on his black cap, I should take him for some burly peasant, with his blond mustache and cold, deep-blue eyes. I take off my hat and he asks me, half inquiringly, half maliciously:

"Why didn't you come and have supper with us last night? We kept a place for you."

"I didn't know where you were," I say.

He doesn't believe me and starts scolding me. "You could have found out easily enough. Look, there it is." And he points to a café on one side of the big square in front of the station. My colleagues wait to see what I am going to reply.

"I'll come today."

But the superintendent hasn't finished yet. "Have you found a room?" he asks.

No, I tell him.

"We arranged that for you. You can stay at Agostino's—he does the mail run between here and Pisa."

I thank him. Having made sure that I'm not on the side of his enemy, the assistant superintendent (I only found this out later), he rubs his hands, and turning to the others with an air of affected friendliness, says:

"Tell him what he has to do."

And out he goes. I am just wondering whether I've done something wrong when they start laughing. One of them picks up a chair and slams it against the chair of the booking clerk, who starts to swear. Their language embarrasses me and I go and stand by the outside door and look through the glass at the people in the station square. A few porters; a good many loaded carts with tarpaulins or red blankets over them.

Drago is strolling about; as soon as he catches sight of me, he spits. I tell the whole story to the booking clerk and he warns me that the man will go on like this until I buy him a drink.

After half an hour I manage to start working, but the ledgers are so full of corrections and illegible scrawls that I don't know what I'm supposed to be writing.

March 3, 2 P.M.

I went to look at the room after lunch. It's in town; to get to it I have to climb some dark, narrow stairs and pick my way through a room full of packages. Someone is snoring in a garret without either a window or door. A woman tells me it is a porter who does night duty.

My room has a window with an enormous grille. There is an oppressive smell; the air comes from a little yard belonging to the town jail. It feels as though the throbbing of some electric machine were shaking the very foundations of the house.

I feel like crying, but since I haven't got time to look for a better place, I agree on the rent and leave. Outside, everyone stares and the girls returning from work in the factories laugh at me.

"Ugly, isn't he!" one of them says out loud. "He looks like a priest."

I stop and look at her. She and her friends lower their eyes and she tries not to laugh. A few steps later and the wind whirls my hat under the wheels of the electric streetcar that comes clanging in from Pisa. The hat is covered with mud and the brim is cut away. The girls stop to watch and stand there rocking with laughter. Clearly I've got to get used to all this; I've got to show that I don't mind. But how it hurts!

I would like to stroll for a little beside the Arno before going to the office, but there isn't time now. I feel sad, sad.

March 5

Days of anguish, against which there is no remedy. My nerves are all in pieces. I am having difficulty learning the job. I've gotten into the habit of breakfasting on bread and salt pork; then a glass of red wine at the station bar. But I take no part in my colleagues' rowdy games; and I don't gossip.

Sometimes people who come to send packages ask the booking clerk:

"Is that the new man?"

"Yes."

And they look at me with an air of mock compassion and say, "Funny-looking guy, isn't he?"

"He's a good sort though," says my colleague, trying to defend me from their wounding hostility.

I suppose this expression means the same to them as it does to me, but the difference is that they don't believe it. They move away, still staring at me. If Drago is outside they return in two and threes. He comes in with them and they stand there talking about me in whispers. The last look they give me as they go is always an ugly one. Why do they think so badly of me? I look at Drago's ripe red nose.

All the same I managed to write Attilia a long letter. They don't know that I'm in love and that there is nothing they could do that would make her leave me. They can be as spiteful and rude as they like, but that they can't do! Attilia's kind, calm eyes will never change.

March 5, evening

Supper with the superintendent, Dante Brilli, and a young Florentine called Marcello Capri, like me a junior clerk. The man who owns the café has a job at a brick factory and finishes work at the same time we do. He doesn't do anything to help his wife, who has to do the cooking and serve at table with one of her two children almost always in her arms.

The other people at our table are traveling salesmen. We order the main dish a couple of hours in advance because the proprietress has so few regular customers that she shops especially for them. But for this system, we should find nothing to eat except hard-boiled eggs and salad.

Drago was there today; he ignored me and said hello to the superintendent, making it clear by the way he spoke how much he dislikes me; his voice takes on a kind of glittering edge. Why on earth don't I buy the man a drink and make peace? I don't because I know he's turning everyone against me. Things have reached such a pass that even the stationmaster isn't as friendly as he was at first. I hear that if Drago can get the assistant superintendent on his side, I may be sent to some station in the hills, miles away from Florence. Even the mayor of Pontedera is well-disposed toward him, because when a consignment of his wine is being dispatched, Drago keeps his eyes open and sees that not a single flask is filched.

He is sitting facing me. He orders a liter of wine and offers the superintendent a glass. But I can forgive him. He is dying to pick a quarrel with me and does everything he can to pull me into the conversation. Before he goes, he remarks:

"I can't stand a man without a mustache."

"Yes, why don't you grow one?" Brilli asks me. "You're not a bad-looking fellow, you know. What's the idea of going about clean-shaven? People at Pontedera don't like it."

I know that, I tell him, but I'm not going to give in.

The superintendent now decides to be sorry for me. "You'll regret it," he says.

But Capri wants to make a joke of it and starts a story to the effect that the assistant superintendent too is going to advise me to shave only my chin. At this point Brilli chips in and says, "He'd be better occupied thinking about his own shortcomings. I don't know how that man manages to hold down a job in a state organization." And he orders half a liter for the two of us, wanting to make us feel warm toward him. I can't refuse to drink now, nor can I keep out of the argument. The proprietress takes a hand at this point and asks why I didn't come to eat here the first evening.

"Perhaps you thought our place was a bit too cheap," she suggests. "You've got the wrong sort of habits, anyone can see that at a glance. But you will just have to get used to things like everyone else. Why, even Signor Brilli likes eating here better than anywhere else. And you're not as big a man as he is."

"Maybe he thinks secretly that I'm not as big a man as *he* is," Brilli says, laughing.

"I've noticed this about you too," Capri puts in. "You don't know how to treat us like equals. Why not? We're all equals here."

"Where do you get all these notions about me?" I asked them.

At this Brilli scolds me and says rudely, "It's the truth, and don't talk back to your superiors."

I feel fed up with them and I realize that it's best to hold my tongue. I can hardly swallow the rest of my meal. But since I don't have time in the morning, and at night I always go to sleep at once, I have gotten into the habit of writing Attilia a letter every day before I leave the table. It's usually a long letter, so I stop talking to them. The superintendent is annoyed and wants to know what I'm writing.

"Oh, he won't tell us that!" says the proprietress.

Trying to make Brilli like me a bit better, I explain to him that I'm engaged to a girl in Florence.

"What, *you* engaged!" the proprietress cries, crinkling her eyes at me. "I can't imagine you in love with a girl," she goes on. "You're such a gloomy sort."

I fancy this is meant as a confidential joke between us, but Brilli and Capri both back her up.

While this is going on, the older of her two children trips over a flask of wine; he falls down and starts crying. She looks at me as though it were my fault.

March 6

Attilia is ill. The letter giving me the news is written by a girl friend of hers, but I don't have any very clear idea of what the trouble is.

Sparagio, a porter who doesn't get on with Drago, has let me know that every Wednesday my room is being used by a dentist to pull teeth. I tell the stationmaster and he gives me permission to go and catch the man at it.

I find the door of my room is indeed open, with an announcement to this effect:

Giulio Boschetti, dentist, from Empoli, extracts and fills teeth from 10 to 12.

I go in, and thinking me a client, he nods and waves me cheerfully to a seat. I notice that my books and shirts have been put on the floor; the drawer of the table is open and full of shining instruments, spotted here and there with blood.

"But this is *my* room!" I shout at him. The man looks confused and I repeat my statement. "This is my room. You get out of here."

"I don't know anything about it," he says. "You'd better see the landlord."

I go and look for him, but can only find his wife. I'm really very angry. "Why do you allow such a thing? It's shameful!" I say. "Return my rent and I'll leave your house right now."

"What's the harm?" she says. "We've always made this arrangement."

"You ought to have told me. I would never have taken the room if I'd known."

"My husband will return your money."

"Where is he?" I shout at her, more violently than ever.

"I don't know. I don't know where he is."

I go back to the dentist. "Anyway, you get out of here."

My colleagues are highly amused at the story and find me another room on the spot.

But when I return to collect my stuff and the landlord gives me back my money, I find myself almost on the point of apologizing to him. The incident makes me regret that I left home before my father approved my intention of getting married. I tell myself that I ought not to make important decisions on my own.

I must take care to avoid unpleasant occasions like this because I simply don't know how to deal with them.

And yet at the same time I almost feel like involving myself deliberately in scrapes—in order to get used to anything. Let's say for instance that I'd been robbed. I would have gone to the police and reclaimed my property and then written a fine letter home about it. I am in a state of violent excitement and would willingly make it up with the dentist. How I enjoyed shouting at the landlord's wife like that! From now on I'm not afraid of anything; I hope I shall have some adventure in my new room which will set the whole town talking about me, envying me. Why shouldn't I have to defend myself against someone who tries to break in at night? And have the landlady praising my courage! To myself I repeat her name, which I have only just learned: Dina Calamai. Sparagio too will see what I'm made of. They will all be saying how glad they are that Leopoldo Gradi came to Pontedera. And if in due course I bring my wife here, what a welcome they'll give her; I can almost see the station hung with flowers!

Pontedera is the best place in the world. And Drago is quite right—I ought to buy him a drink.

March 7

The stationmaster has been transferred and for two days the junior clerks have to fill in for him.

His wife, who has had heart trouble for several years, is lifted into the train in an easy chair. He embraces us all, one after the other, from the senior to the most junior employees. The porters stand around cap in hand for a quarter of an hour.

The new stationmaster has six daughters and one son. He is a lean, elderly man, extremely nervous. He at once introduces some modifications in station procedure, and everyone is sorry that the other man has gone. The people working in the goods department are particularly active in stirring up discontent. He's aware of this, but feels that he would lose face unless he continued with his new methods.

But I would sooner talk about myself. It's strange the pleasure I take in reading the letters that Attilia—who is still ill—gets her friend to write me. When I see her big, elongated handwriting on the envelope (the letters look a little like almonds) I open it more quickly than usual—as though I did it out of respect for her. And I've noticed that although we don't know each other, her third letter does not seem to have been dictated by Attilia like the first one. Clearly she feels somehow friendly toward me. And since I know that she as well as Attilia reads my letters, I find myself writing more fluently than before—as though I had more to say.

My feelings are confused and I wish they weren't!

Heard a juicy piece of news today. It seems that the Calamai woman and the assistant superintendent are lovers. When Brilli learned that she was my new landlady, he screwed up his face and said, trying me out, "Look, without letting them

know what you're up to, you discover when they're together
and let me know. Can you manage this? I'll arrive on the scene
with one or two people who count here and we'll make him
decamp pretty quick! You just do your bit and trust me to
raise hell. I promise you he won't be able to show his face in
Pontedera again. From your own point of view, my dear
Gradi, it's hardly pleasant to be a party to this sort of thing.
Why, if my landlady weren't the very soul of virtue, you
wouldn't catch me under her roof, not if they chained me
down!"

Then, as the sheer pleasure of indulging his dislike took hold
of him, he gave a couple of puffs at his cigar and went on:

"Don't you see that you'll be compromised yourself if you
let this intrigue go on? Equally, if you're the one who puts a
stop to it, it will be a feather in your cap. It could be the making of you. I know what I am talking about. Oh, I can tell you,
I'll let him have it! I promise you I'll see to it the man never
looks me in the face again."

For my part I have half a mind to warn the woman and put
her on her guard. If I don't, it's because I don't want to give
the impression that I'm on her tail too. But just now, as I was
leaving my room, I saw Drago coming out of hers! The satisfied expression on his face and the way he walked on the tips
of his toes made it perfectly plain what he's up to: Drago visits
her too on the sly, at times when he knows that the assistant
superintendent is in his office.

My heart is pounding away and I have no idea whether or
not I ought to tell Brilli. Drago is at the foot of the stairs, waiting for me.

"If you don't tell a soul what you've seen up there," he says,
"I promise you my friendship. You can trust me."

"On the contrary, you simply want to get me to shut my
mouth and then you'll go on abusing me. But now that I'm in
a position to hurt you, you're afraid."

"May God strike me down this moment if there's any such
notion in my mind!" he cries. "Come and have a glass of wine
with me—I'll pay, and don't let's say anything more about it.

Heaven help me, you can do what you like with me—I deserve anything."

And he takes me by the arm and leads me out into the street. After we've had our glass of wine together, he goes off into town while I return to the station. I simply can't keep a thing like this to myself and I tell the superintendent at once, though it's rather difficult to talk privately there without someone noticing. He listens in silence and the blood mounts slowly to his face until it becomes unrecognizable. In his effort to decide how to handle the matter, he grips his lower lip between his thumb and forefinger. I can see he's not finding it easy. At last he lets out a great laugh, which attracts the attention of everyone in the station. I'm afraid he's going to compromise me, but he strokes my face and says:

"It couldn't have worked out better. Good for you, Gradi! Do as well as this in your work and you'll get promoted before the others."

My landlady, meanwhile, convinced that she couldn't find a tenant less inquisitive and less inclined to gossip than me, fusses over me like a mother. I have everything I want in my room. She lets me have two jugs of water instead of one. She has replaced the old basin, which was chipped, with an almost new one, striped red inside and out. The place is kept neat and tidy.

As a result, I confess that I feel less depressed when I'm alone in my room.

My window looks out on a neglected garden; running beside it are the two tracks of the Pisa-Empoli line. Next to the vineyard are a number of gardens separated from each other by low walls. Opposite the front door there is a well, from which they draw water by means of a long pole balanced on an upright prop. In the room under mine lives the woman who looks after the latrines at the station; I have the impression that one of the switchmen is her lover.

Today, happy in the knowledge that I no longer need to be afraid of Drago, I wore for the first time the tie which Attilia gave me.

March 9

Every time a man I don't know comes near me I'm afraid of him, sometimes even when he's a friend. It is not exactly the man that I'm afraid of, but rather of what may happen to me, deep inside me, when he starts to speak. For this reason there are certain people I have always kept away from. I remember I used to walk on a road just outside Florence; I had to pass by a green garden gate. Whenever I saw the gardener standing there by the open gate, I either turned back or passed by on the opposite side of the road. Anything to avoid having to come into contact with him.

There are people who would be astonished to learn what ineffaceable marks they have left on me. When I think that I am made up of as many bits of experience as I have lived days, I ask myself if I really exist or if it is the objects in front of my eyes that exist. What does it mean, I ask myself, "being alive"?

Why can't I ever forget the years I have lived—years scattered here and there like the moss that clings to stones?

How many eyes, how many glances I can still see which threw my very spirit into confusion!

There was the cripple with club feet; he used to spend the day sitting under the Lanzi portico. Propping his crutches against the wall, he sat there gossiping with a group of down-and-outs who took any odd job to earn a few pennies. Most often they were employed by the hotels to take luggage to the station in handcarts. Or when someone was moving. I remember three of them. One was something of a hunchback and he wore a black beard; another had a white mustache and tattoo marks on his arms; the third was a stumpy fellow with a black mustache and a suit that had turned green—he always wore the same one.

The man with the crutches, who couldn't work, used to look at me in a way that made me hate him. He stared at my feet as though he wanted to chop them off. When the sun shifted, he went to sit on the steps of the Palazzo Vecchio. And then there was a young fellow who was weak in the head; he used to pass by with a basket on his shoulders full of shavings. He was thin and he had a spiky chin; his eyes were dark green. He always got on my nerves and I remember once he took me by the arm.

There was a boy too who went to the same school as I did; he used to make my skin crawl. Imbecile, fat, with pig eyes, one arm paralyzed and the thumb missing. If he ever touched my hand, I had to shout so as not to start crying.

But the person who really oppressed me was a woman with chestnut-colored eyes that glowed with a kind of red light; she was all dried up and yellow. I don't know who she was.

And that priest, a tall man with black, glittering eyes—he made me feel quite hopeless. I used to get back home feeling so depressed that I wanted to die. Once, in spring, instead of going to school, I took a long walk in the country. It was so beautiful at one point that I can still remember it. A field of spiked corn, and shining through it a ditch full of clear, transparent water. The hedges were in flower and I liked the feel on my face and hands of the spider webs stretching between the olive trees. The vines had been pruned and were tied with thongs of fresh willow. I stopped to look at all the fruit and the cypresses over the roads leading to some cottages. I seemed to be able to see the earth turning into the fruit and the trees. The sun, very low down in the sky, was soft and gentle and it seemed to linger among the plants. Birds flew from the branches of the trees above the road away to the fields beyond, shaking down drops of dew; some of the drops fell on me. The windows of the cottages had shutters painted red and there was grass growing everywhere, even along the side of the road. I felt so happy to be alone that everything else went out of my mind. I wanted to run away and not go home again. The sky dazzled me.

As I was standing there, I turned around and saw not far away a man looking at me with a kind of sneer on his face. Tears came into my eyes. I have never forgotten those fields.

March 10

I tell the proprietress that I don't like the soup. Her eyes glisten with tears and the superintendent says that I spoke to her too roughly. So afterward when I have a free moment I go and see her, pretending that I want a glass of wine. She is sewing a large sheet and her children are playing with a chair.

"I didn't mean to hurt your feelings just now," I tell her.

She looks at me with those gentle eyes of hers, too gentle, and blushes. "Did you mind my not being able to help showing what I felt?" she asks with a sigh.

When I tell her that I didn't mind, she says, "Let's make peace then. Try this white wine; it's much better than the wine you drink every day."

And she pours out a glass of white sparkling wine. To please her, I sip it and smack my lips; and I thank her twice, the second time after I have gone out and closed the door with the glass window. She is very poor and yet she gives me credit for a whole month; she doesn't know how to write, and she trusts the reckoning I keep in a little notebook.

After supper I have to finish the fortnightly accounts, which are sent to the Auditor's Office in Turin. The stationmaster is not there and the assistant clerk is asleep on a sofa with his cap over his mouth. Toward midnight I go outside and stand under the station roof. The plain is misty and I light a cigarette.

I have the sense of something swarming indistinctly over the whole expanse; perhaps it is the mist dripping on the leaves and the grass; or the moist wind passing over. Even the stars must be wet. The solitude stuns and deafens me and I stop to look at the double lines of the tracks as though I were trying to make out what they are trying to say. I look at them but I can't understand.

Suddenly a sonorous mass grazes me, a speeding whistle is swallowed by the air.

The express!

Later I learned that it dragged a crossing guard onto the track and carried off his head, stuck on the catch of the headlights.

March 11

If it had been me who had died yesterday evening! But to-day there is the first glint of spring in the air and I want so much to live. How can I die? This station where I am chained like a dog in a kennel may be small, but the countryside stretches freely on all sides. Surely I shall get away from here someday?

At midday the cypress in the garden appears more weight-less than its shadow; the shine dazzles. I feel a kind of mad-ness and wonder if my hands are not painted red like that gate by the field.

When the light is like this, even the house seems new.

What do I care if the buds are swelling? What do I care if the fields are fresh, if my soul is fresher than they are?

Just now, midday enclosed me in the fields and the trees—there was no escape. And it seemed in that light as though all existence had ceased, as though there were nothing outside my own being.

Oh, how I longed to feel at ease under this roof covered by evergreens—almost as green as the gardens all around. These gardens that might have been made to contain the water that I can hear behind one of the walls (that one next to the wil-low) even though I can't see it, gurgling the way water gurgles when you scoop it up in the hollow of your hand or in a cab-bage leaf. And the other willows—how their pale green plays between the dark bluish-green of the cabbages. And yet the lettuce is paler still.

In my heart there are only coffins and the pains of death passing by one after another; and some poor garlands bought to grace the bier, which I dread will slip down between the jerking wheels.

And if I open the window I feel my heart contract, I feel it plunging headlong into the street below.

Poor rose that Attilia gave me, we are alone, you and I; alone in solitude, in the desert of reality, and no one thinks about us. Pressed between the pages of a book that I open now and then, you try to keep your color, which now seems like clotted blood. But we should tell no one about ourselves or about our story, a story so simple it would seem imbecile, for it consists only of this: you have been mine, I have loved you more and more.

The footpaths across the fields are hidden under the grass; a green so dark it seems almost black spills down from the hawthorn hedges. The shadows are as deeply blue as the sky. Perhaps even the old cracked fence is going to break into jewels and flowers.

I quarreled with the superintendent today and he doesn't speak to me, even though we still eat at the same table. He won't believe that I have had no dealings with his second in command except in the office.

I work on Sundays too, but today I left three hours early. I would have liked to take a boat and row up as far as the slender bridge that one can see down there at the point where the river crooks around and vanishes. But I can't find the boatman. So instead I start walking in the opposite direction. The banks are green, the Arno rather muddy. I meet a family and then two lovers. I go as far as Calcinaia, a little village whose gray image is mirrored in the water, and by this time evening is coming on. A ferryman calls from the other bank to ask if I want to go across, but it seems too late. I walk for a little while along the dry bed of the river, which is full of footprints.

The sun is setting fast. For an instant the hills are gold, the water glitters; then the reflections die away. I stop to listen to the sound of a guitar and the voice of a woman singing. A cheerful sort of song. Then everything is still except for the monotonous clatter of the water knocking against a rock as white as the moon.

I stay there until the whole countryside is lit up; when I set out again, I lose my way and a dog rushes at me. I shout but no one answers. I retreat as fast as I can and get back to the path along the bank of the river and walk there.

I feel bored, but the moonlight is beautiful. I stand looking at the fields for a long time and make out a few lighted windows here and there. I wait for the din of a passing train to die away.

When I go into the café there is nothing left except anchovies with ginger sauce and a plate of lettuce in which I discover a lock of hair. But this time I keep my mouth shut.

The superintendent is watching me.

The moon is slow as the weight of my fatigue; up and down it goes like a useless walk. And I do the same: I have nothing to say. But my thoughts are still out there in the road; as I approached I gradually began to lose them. It's funny, the sight of the moon sunk right down among the pools where the hemp grows.

March 16

Work is not going well. I'm always getting my figures wrong and I make mistakes in adding up the long columns in the ledgers. If I could only learn to telegraph, it would help. I wouldn't get so bored and it would make the work lighter. But I am never quick enough at reading the little strips of paper on which the messages are transmitted. I am sitting there, feeling as though my head were tied down to the table, when a clerk comes in with a message to send; he shoves me roughly aside and takes my place. The first time he did it, I was so humiliated that I thought I would never show my face in the station again. Then I had the notion of retaliating in kind and I sat down at the machine, all set to pick a quarrel. As he transmitted the message, he kept looking at me as though I were idling on duty. I felt even more humiliated at this and for several hours I couldn't get a word out. It was clear from my face what I was going through and everyone noticed. Yet that was the very time I chose to start writing to Attilia—and I used to write her good letters. She is still ill; apparently she has pleurisy. But I am sure that she will recover, because I love her. As for the letters that her friend writes to me, I now feel embarrassed to receive them and even more to read them. I take great care to think only about Attilia when I reply.

I forgot to say that almost every day now I go to see Signora Marianna and drink that white wine of hers. There was an attractive girl there today called Nèmora—I don't know her second name. She was wearing black because her mother died recently.

Raining today and thunder; the lightning looks damp; the rain all clarity under the gray clouds.

If only it would rain in my soul so that afterward I could feel the freshness that the olive trees have after it has rained. The leaves of the poplars quiver like the song of the cicadas in summer. Down the long furrows birds of some kind are singing; and my thoughts are moist. I have been a long way and on the way back I didn't dare to stop at any door, not even those that smelled of roses. And yet I might have found a gentle, welcoming smile there.

You see, it takes a lot of patience to get close to me.

Here is my hand then, you whose youth is as tranquil as the respect I claim. I accept your gaze, I go out to meet your friendship so long as it is as pure as my own intentions, as the things which I do not tell you. So: I let your shadow fall within my house.

But your voice is different from the alms I ask; your shoes are not washed by the rain. You have no need of me. You will not have my love then; not even my friendship.

I can see a roof under the rain—very low, very short, spanning the house which no one enters, which no one looks at except for the odd boy who breaks in. One evening, but only one evening, I saw two lovers resting in its shadow; they were quite still and every so often they looked up to make sure that no one could see them. One night a drunk fell down there and hurt his head. It is always quiet, quiet.

The walls are dead, the roof so weary that I feel like propping it up.

I saw a dead cat up there. First it decayed, then the body caved in as though it were nothing but skin, then it shrank till it grew into the tiles; the skin wore away and the bones showed through; last, the bones disappeared. There is still a blackish stain on one of the tiles, but soon that too will be washed away.

The church near my house is nearly always empty. The chapels are boarded up and on the high altar there is a huge oil painting of the Virgin, her feet resting on a snake and above her head a half moon. The candles are as high as the picture. Now and then a Capuchin friar comes out from the choir, crosses himself, and kneeling down before the Madonna, stays there to pray.

From the window one can see the tips of the cypresses moving, but the leaves make no sound. All one can hear is the crackling of an oil lamp. Outside, in a space let into the wall and protected by a grille, is the statue of a friar with a skull in his hand.

I am always meeting the beggar woman with no face; it is as though the red ulcers had little by little eaten away her head, leaving only her arms and legs. And yet, she can still move and walk about.

When I raise my head, feeling that my distress has passed, I realize that I am not alone; everyone in the room is looking at me. I can't move without someone looking at me!

As I turn the key in the office door on the way out, I have the sense that I am shutting in there a life larger than my own.

It is my fault, the trouble is in me. And of course it is I who finally suffer. I feel that so many fine things are reproaching me, things that come of their own accord.

So I have alienated myself from this kindly reality. Why, why? Why have I shut up my soul like this? Even when I was a boy I liked to be alone; I used to like standing at a half-open door and watching the people in a room talking. I regret what I do and yet I keep on doing the same thing.

I am hungry, but I don't eat; yet I like this sense of kindly reality that always returns as though it were in love with me.

And I like this sense of something reproaching me—so long as the day finishes soon, passes quickly through the tangle of my youth, leaving no trace behind it. Then I feel as though by hiding in my own depths I escape the power of death; I am afraid though, with a fear that stops my breathing. For its shadow passes through the spaces of my life and I close my eyes in order not to see it. Sometimes I am afraid that I will not be able to open them again.

March 17

Marcello Capri is playing around with the daughter of an engineer. She stands at a window that looks onto the station square; we get a good view of her from the office. She is a blond, rosy girl, and though she hardly looks sixteen yet, she is as plump as a fully grown woman. They have found a means of writing secretly to each other and the girl has fallen seriously in love. The letters she sends him are full of mistakes and when Capri reads them he makes a face and starts laughing.

"What should I do?" he asks me. "Do you think I should drop her? Heaven help her, she can't put down a couple of words on the page without making some mistake. Look at the way she's written this sentence."

I take everything seriously, and to persuade him not to leave her, I say:

"She'll learn. Isn't she still going to school?"

"Yes, trade school."

Capri is as blond and rosy as the girl. Half his attention is on the dirty cracks people are making in the office, half on her window. He works for a quarter of an hour, then asks me if I'll write her a letter for him.

"All right, if you'll check my figures."

"Bargain."

I take a sheet of clean paper and go through the motions of thinking. Capri is pleased, but when he sees that I'm not thinking any longer he says earnestly:

"You'll do your best, won't you?"

When I have finished the letter I hand it to him. He reads it and copies it out at once, altering a few words that he never uses. By way of rewarding me, at supper he tried to persuade Brilli to make it up with me, insisting that I was not in league with the assistant superintendent. Brilli was not convinced, but he is nervous of asking too much of me and so he gave way without a great deal of fuss.

Since I wrote his letter for him, Capri takes my arm and

tries to cheer me up, but in the end he grows bored and pretends he has to leave. When he goes, I feel really deserted.

Just now, when the superintendent made it up with me, I tried to take him into my confidence and told him about my family. But I realized that he didn't like it and that he positively disapproved of the way I spoke. With Capri I would never try to get on intimate terms: he is a couple of years younger than I am and too flighty. When he tells me that he had another girl at Florence, a music-hall singer, I shake off his arm and tell him to change the subject. He stands a few steps away, looking at me in amusement, then comes up again and begins speaking in the same way, only worse than before. He especially enjoys using dirty words.

"Why do you act like this?" I ask him.

"What about you—what's the point of being so damned virginal?"

"Look, Capri, I just don't like you."

"I don't like you either. No, what I mean is I can't understand why you don't go around with chorus girls too instead of going steady with someone. I just don't believe you. You must be smarter than you look. Perhaps you were a priest before you took this job."

I start to laugh, but he says, if not, then why don't I swear like everyone else. "Just listen to this lovely word you think is dirty," he says. "Try it and see if you don't enjoy using it too. And while we are on the subject, how about us two dropping in on your landlady and having a go at her too?"

To make him stop talking, I say that I don't fancy her—she's too old.

"Too old? That just shows how little you know about these things. Why, in your place I'd see that I had my bed and board free. Let the old girl foot the bill! But just tell me now, why do you want to go and get married?"

I don't know how to answer him and I turn my head away. I couldn't convince him, however hard I tried. The only course is to make him drop the subject for good, otherwise I shall just look silly, and I don't want that. If I didn't love Attilia truly, why should there be this sort of unvoiced quarrel between my family and me?

Attilia's voice grows out of mine; its inflections are soft and timid and to catch them I have to keep quiet.

When I say something, she understands me by the way I speak; she alone understands me.

She has been altogether mine only because I have spoken to her.

The parlor is empty, but there is a sense of tranquillity about the chairs and the couch, and I found myself saying, Hello, may I come in?

I am good, I am your friend, the couch announces. You have only to look at me to see.

The silence of the room is filled by the couch and the chairs.

March 18

A splendid morning, and I have to turn back feeling cloudy and dim. I was dreaming, and it seemed as though an invisible knife cut my dream in two. Oh, that fear of weariness! The pain of realizing the timidity of my dreams! To go home and to be afraid of never coming out again! My youth is like water, boiling, boiling, unable to keep still.

But do I really have to assume these airs of almost cheerful despondency? I feel as though I were freshly painted and not yet properly dry—like the gate next to the railroad track. Yet I dredge up from the past moments of delightful foolishness, like the occasions when you suddenly decide to rummage through a drawer without looking for anything in particular. A whole set of useless things (things you once used) fill you with a wild, restless discontent that makes no sort of sense. So it is with me when I go fishing in the past and come up with memories that claim an importance they don't really possess. In themselves they are nothing; what happens is that they try to fit in with certain states of mind that occupy me at present. Symbolic correspondences, you might call them; meaningless motions from the past which return without any conscious action on my part. And what is strange is that certain things that I was no longer thinking about should come so clearly into focus.

For example, two blind men were playing under my window this morning, one on the violin, one on the guitar. All at once my mind was suffused with moral clarity. This gave me a good deal to think about, but the point is that I thought about it instead of extracting from it some sensible conclusions that might have been of use to me; it seemed that this sense of clarity and freshness was like a day, a day in March perhaps, when I used to see the wind rising and falling like waves over a little hill all green with corn.

I was furious with myself afterward. How on earth did a purely moral experience turn into a pleasant memory? And a memory that in itself had nothing special about it. Certainly it was not related to my state of mind at the time of the original experience, for that would have been utterly impossible to recapture.

What would other people have thought of me? I was condemned always to be understood only by a very few patient people, while in the eyes of everyone else I was turning into a commonplace person in no way different from the common run. And all the time the wind kept rising and falling above that little green hillock; and I found myself having to resolve the problem on my own.

But my soul, which is very good to me, helped. What I had to do was retrieve my past and find many things there which I had not thrown away. My task was to retrieve them and scan them from the first line to the last like letters only half read and sometimes not even that. I was to discover many meanings there that I had given up, either through carelessness or because of some mistaken prompting of my will. (But then of course one always supposes one's will infallible.) Naturally it wasn't something that could be handled on the spot. On the contrary, I don't think I even started the job.

The main thing was to be much more sincere with myself, even to the point of becoming brutal with people who were not expecting such concentrated truth from me. I had to convince myself, at once, through an act of intuition, that my feelings were developed only in dreams and in moments of ecstasy, which had nothing to do with my everyday life.

This was the dirty trick the violin and the guitar played on me. I woke up feeling as though I had undergone some tormenting deception, and with the precise obligation not to stammer any more, but to talk: words had the force of law.

But why that green hillock? It may be, now that I come to think of it, that it is there standing out unmistakably as a point of departure, the point at which I am to start recapturing my past. It can't have any meaning; that it is a mere chance memory I am inclined to rule out. I don't even know what hill it is; in fact I don't recognize it at all. (This is the moment to cry a little instead of writing. Crying is nice, like laughing; the same gay feeling, but painful in a way, and bitter—like a sudden fanfare that makes the windows rattle.)

I went back finally to the poplars beside the Arno, because I feel myself grow lighter there, like the water, perhaps, that flows past and appears motionless, so clear it is and silent. I tremble with the tremulous motion of the trees and if I stand still I feel as though the grass is clustering around me. I feel that even the air is friendly.

I too have become like the grass: to be cut down with everything else in the field.

I like whatever Attilia writes to me. She is a living being who lives for me too; every word she writes moves in my room —I can feel it breathing.

But when I speak, I feel my silence growing greater. So that when I return home I can judge if I have behaved as I should.

How good it would be to stand beside a country church, with a bit of green in the hedges and the tall cypresses. How good it would be to make confession at the point of death and feel the presence of my soul. And suddenly to see a face that will never stop looking at me.

March 19

My father's brother used to live in Mugello and came to stay with us every three or four years. Just for a few days. The sound of his voice used to fill me with instant depression and I concentrated on his red eyelids, which suffered from some chronic inflammation. He would describe how he used to go and bathe them in a spring not far from where he lived, riding there on a donkey. The water cured his eyelids, but afterwards they were just as bad as before. My father told him that he didn't bathe them long enough.

Now I hear that he is dead, but all I can think of is his eyelids; as though somehow they were still alive.

I didn't like my mother telling me how often I had been ill. I want to be well. Now my uncle is dead; I no longer feel any affection for him! He should have been young and healthy!

A workingwoman from a nearby factory comes to the café every day at one o'clock sharp, just when we're all there. Without sitting down, she takes a plate of soup, never anything more. Then she goes and stands beside the door with the glass windows. She is thin and ugly. When the mail truck passes, bringing the packages from town, she starts to cry, soundlessly. Wide-eyed, she follows every movement the driver makes; he jumps down from his seat and walks around with his legs bent like billhooks. When the truck goes back to town, she says good-bye to Marianna and returns to work along with the other women.

Marianna's husband tells me that she had a child by the driver. "And now he won't even look at her!" he adds.

I take her side, but the superintendent can't stand her. "Bit late in the day now to be sorry for what she did," he says.

I don't dare contradict him, even if I knew how to, but I ask if he might not still marry the woman.

"Not a chance. He's treated two others in the same way before her. And that stupid creature knew what he was like as well as I do. But she had to let him have his way."

"I'm always scolding her," Marianna put in. "She upsets my customers. But she hopes to make him feel sorry for her. Oh, she's a damned fool."

"Doesn't he even speak to her?" I ask.

"Yes, when he has the notion to have her in his house on the quiet. But he sends her packing afterward."

"You'll see," the bricklayer says. "One day he'll meet some woman who knows how to get her own back."

March 26

I have seen Nèmora again and spoken to her. But why did I speak to her if I didn't have anything to say to her? And why am I always at the windows of the office, watching in case anyone should go into the café? When I saw her talking to a coalman a little while ago, I felt jealous and found myself clutching the handle of the door. Why at the first opportunity should I go and see Signora Marianna? Nèmora is making a dress for her and she is there from morning to night, except when we are there at mealtimes. Why didn't I pull a button off my jacket and go and get her to sew it on? Why does my heart beat faster than usual and why don't I want Nèmora to be sure that I like her? Why was she talking to that coalman? A girl isn't supposed to be seen talking to a man here at Pontedera unless she wants to get a bad name for herself. What's more, I feel sort of resentful toward her, because she makes me act badly with Attilia. There is no doubt that I'm attracted to the girl and I'd like her to be in love with me, but she's got to speak first. That way, I won't feel so guilty.

"What's wrong with living at Pontedera?" someone asks me. "You could marry the assistant superintendent's daughter— he's got lots of money. Or else one of the stationmaster's girls. You'd do all right."

I don't have the courage to tell them that I am engaged to someone in Florence and that if I were going to marry anyone from Pontedera, it would be Nèmora.

However, when I write to Attilia I forget all about this. I feel wholly sincere and quite without remorse, though I have made up my mind to keep quiet about Nèmora. I will never tell Attilia about her, I feel sure of that. Not because I'm capable of lying to her, but because if I were to leave her for Nèmora I would let her know and stop writing to her. Why feel ashamed; should I not rather compliment myself on my loyalty?

While I was writing this evening, the place was full of cheerful people singing. As a result, I felt more irritated than usual and sat there with my head in my hands.

I saw Nèmora leave as I came in; the longing I felt when I thought of her made me close my eyes. And there was another darkness in my soul, deeper and more troubling: Attilia. I must not forget Attilia! My hands, pressed against my face, felt cold and incapable of movement. But through the din I could hear someone ask, dislike audible in his voice:

"Why's he always so gloomy?"

They could only have been talking about me, and my heart closed up more tightly than before. But I kept quiet, waiting to hear what someone would say in reply. Half a minute passed, perhaps, then another voice said:

"I'll wake him up. I'll break this guitar on his head!"

Very deliberately I kept quite still; I didn't even want to protect myself. Then an energetic voice came to my defense.

"Let him alone. Everyone has the right to do what he wants."

I stayed just as I was until they had all left, not even troubling to find out who the man with the guitar was. When I raised my head, the first thing I saw was the light in the middle of the room. Then Drago, with a strange gentleness, said:

"You don't need to be afraid when I'm here."

But I was so deep in my thoughts that I didn't even thank him. Or perhaps it was rather that I didn't want to thank him. I heard afterward that Signora Marianna wants to get the superintendent to let me know that when I come to her place I've got to behave cheerfully, like everyone else. She is afraid of losing her customers; they come there to have a good time.

March 27

Almost midnight. I see home a woman whose husband has been in prison for fifteen years. She is afraid that the driver of the mail truck will try to grab her as he did last night.

I must either stop talking to Nèmora or I must marry her.

This is what Signora Marianna told me and I agree with her. But I don't know how to reach a decision, even though I have just mailed a letter to Attilia. It was a passionate letter—she is more ill than ever.

Marcello Capri is going to be transferred to Florence in a few days and as a result he has more or less given up working. I have to do his job for him while he spends the time making eyes at the engineer's daughter. They carry on like this quite openly now for hours on end. The porters and carters squat in the sun, laughing their heads off. A man fills his pipe and goes over there to smoke it while he enjoys the entertainment provided by the two lovers. The whole town knows what's going on and we are waiting for the engineer to show up at the station.

Without warning, a large, muscular woman appears at the window, and catching hold of the girl by the shoulders, pulls her behind the curtains, hitting her a couple of times. The porters get to their feet and go and stand under the window, swearing and shouting humorously. Capri is put out, but there is nothing he can do. He lights a cigarette and steps out into the square.

Every Sunday one of the daughters of the stationmaster takes a stroll near the office. Her brother, much younger than she is, walks beside her, his arm around her waist. They all point the girl out to me and encourage me to take a look at her. I got very red when, as I was standing there at the door, I caught sight of Nèmora crossing the track on her way to a house out of town.

The stationmaster's daughter abruptly put a stop to these Sunday strolls.

March 29

I have had to stay up two nights to finish a job they gave me. I drink my third cup of coffee, but even so my eyes won't stay open. I've taken the best lamp, but still I can't see clearly. The junior clerk has gone home; the telegraph clerk is asleep in his office.

Thanks to the racket the porters are kicking up, I make a mistake in my figures. A sister of one of the men is with them and they are having a kind of party. I could make them shut up, but instead I lose my temper. They sound as though they are falling over the trunks and boxes. More general laughter. The girl is swearing too.

Sometimes at night I used to look up at the stars and I felt as though I were losing myself; it was only a few steps home but they seemed like miles. A sense of anguish and dismay drove me out into those starry spaces. I traversed them one after the other and the clouds blew about my head. I was afraid of ceasing to be a man like other men; I was convinced I should never return. But then I saw myself stretched out on a bed in the country, a priest beside me reading from a book. And from that day on I have always felt I was a different person.

The thing is: to believe in your own thoughts.

Among the olive trees too, you can only see by starlight.

Insects stir inside the hedge; they make a rustling sound in the grass and the leaves.

A man who spends the day tilling the fields comes home. I have never made out his face clearly, but I see that he is dead tired and that he is dragging one leg. The evenings when he doesn't come by I look at the fields because they make me think of him—as though he were not made of flesh as I am but of earth.

March 30

A carter threatens to knife one of my colleagues who has had to enforce a regulation renewed by the stationmaster.

Market day today, with rabbits, hens, and geese in great supply. Every Friday the bench in the station is loaded with cages that have to be put on to the express trains. I don't even have time for a meal and when finally I do get to the café, people come plaguing me about their consignments.

But the porters have a good time. They hang around the cages and ferret the eggs through the bars. They use a long stick for the purpose; one old pro got as many as seven.

Oh, how I envy all those rich, well-dressed people who travel first class! This evening as a train was pulling out of the station, I caught sight of a couple standing in the middle of a compartment, kissing—the most innocently passionate kiss you could imagine. They must both of them have been oblivious of everything as they stood there mouth to mouth. They were enjoying the kind of happiness that only comes once or twice in a lifetime.

As I walk beside the railing along the track, I run into Capri's girl. She doesn't show up in town any more, and remembering that I saw her being smacked, she makes as though to turn back and looks half mad with shame. But when she is only a few steps away, she fixes me with her clear, shining eyes; then she makes off hastily and disappears inside the front door of a house.

I've made no friends here, and I have asked an inspector to get me transferred to a job in one of the larger towns—Florence, for example. It's impossible to live here.

At the café today I sat near a railroad man who has been tried for taking five hundred lire from the station safe. But thanks to the friendly attitude of the witnesses, he got off and he's hoping that the administration will give him back his job. He is all by himself and very poor.

I note the unembarrassed way he talks to us and how he manages to win our respect. Nobody despises him—and in fact he spends most of his time in our office, even though the stationmaster has forbidden him to do so.

He tried to justify himself with me by saying that everyone steals. When I objected that this wasn't so, he gave me a smile of pitying contempt. He keeps up an exaggerated tone of importance, even with the proprietress, to whom he is heavily in debt. He wants to be sent to some lonely station in the marshes. Obviously he is trying to rehabilitate himself. And all the time he's on the lookout for someone saying something bad about him.

No doubt I'm in the wrong, but I don't feel at ease with this misfit.

"Why did they have to keep me here?" he complains. "I

kept on asking to be transferred to some station where I could walk alone in the woods during my time off and spend hours without speaking to a soul. That's what I want."

Why don't I raise my eyes? The moon has already risen.

The darkness inside me fills me with joy.

Because I prefer this sense of sadness; it is vaster than the moonlight. I love this silence.

The moon will set without my having raised my eyes to it.

Its horn is twisted a little and worn away by these hours of wind; it gives me the same sense of pity as the wooden horses on a merry-go-round that bump into each other as they whirl around because they're badly made.

But at least the merry-go-round fills me with a kind of happiness—as though I had too much to drink, as though all my youth were making me knock my head against a wall without understanding anything. Those horses at least have their bellies and their mouths full of wood and don't feel hungry.

April 5

I can see the hills of Lucca from the office, standing out green against the houses and bridges and streets.

Signora Marianna is feeding her baby when I come into the eating house. Her husband stands with his hands on the marble top of the table where they keep flasks and cheese molds.

The older child, whose nose is running, breaks a plate. He is punished and they send him outside to cry. Signora Marianna has to put her little girl on the ground while she serves me.

"What do you want to eat?" she says, buttoning up her dress.

I ask her what there is.

She doesn't remember at first and makes a mistake. Then she says, "Spaghetti and sauce," getting it right.

"Hurry up," I tell her.

"You're always in a hurry," she says, smiling.

Meanwhile I rather lose my head as the superintendent asks if I intend to drink water.

"Yes," I say, "I don't feel well."

"Oh, come on, man," he says, "wine is what you need." And he pours me out a glass. It is redder than usual. He looks at me hard, then asks why I don't want to stay at Pontedera. I realize from the way he speaks how little he likes me, so I don't reply. Instead I listen to some customers who are starting an argument. Signora Marianna says to her husband:

"Why don't you hold the child for a bit? I have to put this meat on the fire."

"Hold her yourself. I've been sweating all morning counting bricks."

At this she starts crying, which makes him more angry still. "We're dead poor," he says, turning to us, "that's what's the matter. When we didn't *have* to stay here, we got on much better together."

She doesn't reply, but the superintendent nudges my elbow and mutters, "If I were her, I'd cut his throat with this knife."

The buds of the roses are like the points of red pencils; but I don't use them. And the wind doesn't seem to know whether it's coming or going.

I am waiting for better news of Attilia; and these cold shivers are more sensual than the sunlight.

April 6

Attilia's illness troubles me and I write to her with growing anxiety. If only they would give me a day off to go and see her in Florence.

I am munching a piece of bread left over from lunch when an inspector comes in, followed by the superintendent. Sudden silence. The inspector glances a little too casually at my ledgers and sits down at another table to look for the mistake which has been exercising five or six senior people in the administration for months now.

He is pale and seems to be in pain. The superintendent looks at him, then asks permission to leave. Another inspector now comes in, his face contorted by enormous wrinkles; his mouth is twisted to one side and behind his gold-rimmed spectacles his eyes are contracted to two points.

The silence thickens. The inspector doesn't look at anyone, but talks lightly to his colleague, who treats him with marked respect.

"Is the clerk who is to give his report here?" he asks after a while.

A man who has been standing by the door says, as unconcernedly as he can, that he is the person. And the questioning begins.

Midday sounds, but they are still talking away, multiplying, adding up. All the same, they haven't yet found the mistake. The inspector who came in first sighs several times and the other man looks more sour than before. The clerk is pale, but argues vigorously that it's not his fault. They don't believe him. At last they get up to go and instantly we all start talking.

April 7

Marcello Capri left yesterday. They gave him a farewell dinner, but I didn't go; I felt too tired. He promised he would call on my family.

I've seen his girl friend again. She looks as though she had been crying and affects an absurdly serious air.

April 9

It's starting to get hot. I am copying out the station inventory, but I feel exhausted almost before I've begun and have to stop and take a rest every quarter of an hour or so. I can't take my eyes off the fields.

April 10

Nèmora doesn't go to Signora Marianna's these days. Strange to say, I don't think about her any more. I have forgotten her altogether.

April 12

A ticket collector with a big, sick face is talking to a telegraph clerk about socialist propaganda. I make a copy of some letters on official paper. Over toward Pisa, big clouds are gathering in the sky.

A machine starts sending a message, tapping away against a strip of paper. A tiresome creaking sound. The clerk takes his pipe out of his mouth, stops listening to the ticket collector, and lets the machine go full speed. It makes a series of metallic clicks, quickly covering the paper with rows of blue marks. When he is done, he replies and gives an order to someone in the next room.

April 16

I got two letters today. One telling me that I have a baby sister, the other that Attilia is very ill.

I show the first letter to the stationmaster and he gives me leave to go to Florence for a couple of days. I have the feeling that I am not likely to be coming back to Pontedera, so I pack all my stuff. I say good-bye to everyone hurriedly and leave. The superintendent hardly answers me, but the assistant superintendent actually shakes my hand. Drago, too, is no longer friendly and if I go to say good-bye to Signora Marianna it is simply for form's sake.

As I climb aboard the train, I think how nice it would be if someone were there to see me off and shut the carriage door the way people do for someone they like. But there's nobody. The man on duty looks at me out of the corner of his eye in an unfriendly sort of way, and he doesn't respond when I wave as the train pulls out. Even so, before settling down and seeing who is in the compartment, I put my head out of the window. I was fonder of Pontedera than I thought; all the same, I'm determined not to come back, even if it means losing my job. I wonder where Nèmora is at this moment. The windows of the factories are already lit up and a woman looks out, but draws back again before I have the chance to see if I know her. The station is out of sight now. I put my bag up on the rack and sit there, hands in pockets, feeling very sad.

All that remains of these two months is a haze of tedium and distaste.

April 17

It is after midnight when I get to Florence. I feel as ill at ease in the streets as though I had never been there before. I take a room in a hotel since I want to see Attilia first thing in the morning without my family knowing. How much better I feel in Florence! I almost want to kiss the pillows on my bed. But I'd have liked to go and see Attilia at once.

In the train I asked an elderly man if I was doing the right thing in going to see her first; I told him about the two letters. But he didn't want to say what he thought and broke off the conversation. But right or wrong, I am at the hotel now. I shall be up very early tomorrow morning.

April 18

Attilia was already dead. I don't know why, but when I heard the news from a maid as I was coming up the steps, I wondered if I ought not to turn back. Her family had never met me; they didn't know anything about us. I felt as though Attilia wanted to frighten me and that I shouldn't see her. And I didn't really believe that she was dead.

I was standing there, as though they had stopped me from coming in, and I began to cry. I cried for nearly half an hour. When I was sure that I couldn't cry any more, I went up to the door and knocked, but I was all ready to go back down the steps again.

It was her mother who came to the door; I had seen her several times with Attilia. She looks at me without saying anything, her dark eyes soft with tears. Before I can get a word out, I start crying again; I am glad that she sees me crying.

"Do you want to come in?" she asks timidly.

I make a step forward, and she asks me who I am. I don't want to tell her that I was in love with her daughter, so I stammer out my name instead. Then, without paying any more attention to her, I come into the house; I look around and decide which Attilia's room is. As though I had been given leave, I walk toward it (moving on the tips of my toes), but before I go into the room I turn around and find Attilia's mother right there behind me. I had not heard her footsteps. She looks at me with a sort of frightened wonder.

I don't have the courage to tell her who I am, let alone go into Attilia's room. I sob violently and hide my face against the wall. At this point her father comes out of her room; he is already wearing black. I take his hand and cover it with tears. Once again I stammer:

"I want to see her."

A mad notion comes over me, that if Attilia could hear me crying like this, she would be glad. She would know that I love her.

It strikes me that I can't go in without explaining who I am; I would feel as though I were doing her a kind of violence. And I can't not see her any longer; I *must* see her.

So I explain everything to them. They don't answer, but her mother tells me to go in.

But I'm afraid of seeing her. I keep my eyes closed at first and open them only to avoid bumping into the bed; I look at a point above the place where she is lying. All I can see is the tips of four candles burning on the table beside her, and a rosary entwined in the bedstead above her head. I have to lower my eyes when they come to rest on her face. At once I bend down to kiss her; I am so close that my chin is almost touching her, then I see her hands crossed on her breast and I feel my head going around. Her hands are ice cold, her face pale and a little damp. Then, as though my head were being cut off, I bend down and kiss her lips. I am not crying now, but when I see that her eyes, like a misty paste, have kept the expression they used to have, my knees give way and I faint.

When I come to again, I search for that expression, which must have been meant for me, but it is no longer there. Death has washed her face clean.

I didn't have the heart to go home till late that evening, or rather I didn't want to go. I found my mother well and everyone in high spirits. I managed to put on an act and persuade them that I was merely tired and a bit bewildered. The baby was quiet and kept its eyes open, lying there in its swaddling clothes under the sheets. My father picked up the lamp and held it behind the baby's head so that I could see it without the light hurting its eyes.

At that moment, as though sensing the light, the little creature puckered its mouth forward so that the lips seemed to turn in. I got up and stood on tiptoes to get a better look at its eyes; I wanted to think of Attilia's eyes. My mother seemed to suspect something and asked why I stared at the child like that.

April 19

Attilia's father and mother simply wouldn't let me go and I spent half the day by her side. They are coming to take her away this evening. How quickly time passes.

But first I went home and said to my mother, "If you haven't already chosen a name, call her Attilia."

"Attilia? What makes you think of a name like that? I don't like it."

I don't want to tell her the truth because I'm sure that if I did so she wouldn't give the child that name. So I invent a story on the spur of the moment.

"I thought of it in the train," I tell her. "If you want me to love her more than all my other sisters, call her Attilia. Don't I have some say in choosing a name for my sister?"

"Well," she says, "since you came back to Florence to see her as soon as she was born, and if you promise not to go getting any more ideas about some girl, we'll call her that. But you might have chosen a name I liked better!"

And I went to see my fiancée to the cemetery; I asked her to forgive my mother.

April 20

I should be back at Pontedera by now, but my father has promised to go and see a friend of his who is a senior railroad official with the idea of getting me a job in Florence or some other large town.

April 22

I'm staying in Florence.

ELIO VITTORINI

ELIO VITTORINI WAS BORN IN SYRACUSE, SICILY, IN 1908 AND
spent his formative years in the period of emergent Fascism.
His father was a railroad stationmaster of lively curiosity and
a relish for rhetoric, whose influence seems to have protected
his children from the Fascist taint. After failing in business
school, Vittorini left home to work on a construction gang in
northern Italy. In 1927 he turned to writing and journalism as
his career. But an essay accusing Italian culture of provin-
cialism created a scandal and offended the authorities; attacked
by the Fascist press, he was forced to write for a small
Florentine journal called *Solaria* because the big newspapers
refused to publish him. In Florence he read proof for a newspaper and learned English by reading *Robinson Crusoe*.
Eventually he started to translate American novels, though
his first published translation was a novel by D. H. Lawrence.
Later Vittorini became known as one of the finest translators
of American fiction in Europe and Italy's most distinguished
Americanist (a role he shared in later years with Cesare
Pavese).

Forced to join the Fascist party as a student, he was sum-
marily expelled when he published an essay urging aid to the
Spanish Republicans. In 1941 he published his masterpiece,
Conversazione in Sicilia (In Sicily); banned a year later, it went
through seven clandestine editions. Later Vittorini was im-
prisoned in Milan for underground activities, and his books
and manuscripts were burned. In 1945 he returned to writing
and became the founder of the important literary and cultural review *Il Politecnico*. He is now a resident of Milan,

where he works for the publishing firm of Einaudi in an editorial capacity.

His more important works are: *Piccola borghesia* (1931); *Sardegna come un' infanzia* (1932); *Garofano rosso (The Red Carnation),* written in 1933 but not published until 1948; *Erica e i suoi fratelli* (written in 1936 but not published until 1956); *Conversazione in Sicilia* (1941); *Uomini e no* (1945); *Il Sempione strizza l'occhio al Frejus (The Twilight of the Elephant),* 1947; *Donne di Messina* (1949); *La Garibaldina* (1949); *Diario in pubblico* (1957).

LA GARIBALDINA
by Elio Vittorini

translated by Frances Keene

Part I

[1]

THE SUN WAS SETTING, IT WAS JUNE, THE YEAR WAS 19——, AND
a soldier, a *Bersagliere,* had just crossed the first two tracks of
the railway station at Ragusa in Sicily.

The train for Terranova, Licata, and Canicattì was waiting
on the third track just on the other side of the second platform.
It was loaded with people who were shouting a refrain dozens
of times, hundreds of times, their voices coming and going in
snatches. The *Bersagliere* looked the length of the train at arms
waving out of windows of carriages whose doors were shut
tight. He noticed the tattered berets some were waving, and
the yellowed, ragged bits of clothing others waved, and he saw
everywhere the dark, bearded faces of the region continuously
coming and going at the windows.

"What's the matter with them?" he asked.

He had turned to a brakeman who was walking back and
forth the length of the train, his whole body up to his hat in
the shade but his hat right in the bright sun. The brakeman
barely swerved enough from his course to glance at him and
immediately resumed his unhurried walk, tapping dryly along
on enormous hobnailed boots. He got to the upper end of the
platform, where white steam flowed in a long jet from the
lower body of the engine. And, as if he wanted to lean against
it, he touched the cast-iron pipe that watered the parched
coal in the tender. The soldier watched him from the place
where he still stood and saw the sun light up all the buttons
of his uniform and the shiny visor of his cap; he followed him
with his eyes as, little by little, the brakeman retraced his steps
along the platform.

47

The people inside the train hurled insults at him, or perhaps they were merely apostrophizing him or calling out to him. It looked as if a frantic tussle were going on from compartment to compartment, and the contestants were in desperate need of someone like him. But then the song would billow out again and it was always the same song, and the brakeman would not look anyone square in the face. Instead he answered the soldier.

"They're waiting for the train to leave."

He stopped suddenly, and stood with his arms crossed on his chest, exposing a rip in the elbow of his jacket sleeve.

"They've been waiting for an hour and a quarter," he added.

The soldier nodded vigorously; whether or not he remembered what he had asked before, he now looked more florid and smiling than ever. He pointed to the dark-green railway cars as they stood there in the sun that caught them squarely from the windows up, and to the ragged passengers overflowing every compartment. "Oh, of course!" he said. And he said that he hadn't wanted to bring even a box lunch with him. "You see how I've made the trip? Empty-handed! Just to be able to travel as comfortably as possible."

The brakeman, arms still crossed on his chest, was screwing up his face in an effort to catch the soldier's words against the clamor of what was going on in the train. But why was he putting himself through such an ordeal? One would have thought that talking to the *Bersagliere* would have made as little sense to him as walking back and forth along the platform. He looked ill. His color was greenish, as if he were suffering from malaria. Yet he went on standing there, even listening to the details of the three-day pass the soldier had managed to wangle. And it was only when asked if they were waiting for a connection that the brakeman started to move off.

"I thought I heard a bell ring," the *Bersagliere* added.

He saw the brakeman's arms fall, but this time he did not follow him with his eyes. There was an old woman who was signaling to him from the train, and a man who was calling to him amid a flag-waving of rags as he leaned far out his window. He ended by going toward them.

The passengers set up more of a ruckus than ever, and the whole carriageful yelled louder, then the whole train yelled louder. The soldier drew back hastily, repelled also by the furnace-like heat that burst on him from above. But he had not wiped the kindly smile from his face, nor the pleasant expression he had at the thought of going home for three days, and the brakeman, as he came back again from the rear end of the train, planted himself once more before the soldier and crossed his arms on his chest.

"There's a later train that's made up here," he told him gloomily.

"Does it go as far as Terranova?" the soldier asked.

"As far as Licata."

He told the soldier that the train that was waiting was for the riffraff, migrants who were going wherever there was a harvest to get in, men and women on their way back from the orange groves with their wages in kind piled up to the rafters —and hungry bums and vagrants, too many penniless vagrants.

Even when the brakeman was talking, he looked as if he were about to take off again. He rose on his toes and fell back on his heels, rose and fell, and said, falling back, that instead of this one, the train three hours later was just what a fellow needed who wanted to travel in comfort.

"Yes, but it's in three hours," the *Bersagliere* said.

[2]

The passengers had begun to stamp their feet rhythmically on the train floor so that hundreds together sounded like a single drum. Two or three words could be made out of the song they kept repeating—"lousy," "ground," "lousy," "ground"—and the soldier caught himself trying to make out the rest.

"Food's lousy . . ." he picked up.

He saw that a few young louts were pointing at him amid great bursts of laughter while the old woman went on trying to tell him something. The man was still there with the rags like

flags waving, and he had not stopped addressing him. A third
with a moth-eaten conical hat had decided to apostrophize him
too. What could he be wanting to tell him? The *Bersagliere*
seemed to realize that, at bottom, none of them had anything
very specific to tell him even if he did draw nearer, so he had
scarcely taken a step in their direction when he turned his
smiling blond face back toward the place where he had last
seen the brakeman; now a little old man stood there.

He too was a trainman but he was all oily and bare to the
waist, with a double flag, red on one side, green on the other,
tucked under his arm. He had just crossed the tracks and now
stood there watching him. "Having fun, eh?" he asked. He
winked and went on his way, waving the green side of his flag
in answer to a whistle which shrilled from a distance where
the tracks, beyond any shade, glared naked in the sun.

But now the brakeman was back a third time.

"I think I'll wait the three hours," the *Bersagliere* told him.
"I didn't want to take anything with me, not even a box lunch,
because of the long way from the station at Terranova to town.
I didn't want to be bothered with anything, have to think
about it, worry that someone might steal it from me. I haven't
been home since Christmas and almost all my gear needs
something done to it, a stitch here or there, but I preferred to
leave everything as it is until a long leave, just to have three
days without anything to worry about, and I wanted to start
off with the train trip itself completely free from worries of
any kind. You get worn out in the army. Oh, I don't deny the
fact that you have a hell of a good time, but you get worn out.
You sleep badly, you really do, and I was thinking that if I
could sleep on the train most of the way . . . That's why—if,
as you tell me, the other train leaves almost empty—I'll wait
another three hours and sleep those extra three hours in the
waiting room. . . ."

"You won't have such a long time to wait," the brakeman
answered.

Rising and falling as before, he showed him the station
clock.

"There's only an hour left," he added, falling back on his heels. "What with the time lost en route and the waiting time in the station, we're already a couple of hours late. . . ."

With a raucous cry, he walked away. . . . Already a couple of hours, already a couple of hours . . .

The *Bersagliere* was too pleased with his own lot not to admit a brakeman might want to make a cry like a peacock. He was only too willing to accept any strange possibility that might befall that train. For instance, he accepted the fact that blows sounded from within as if someone were beating against the doors with sacks of grain; that rumbling sounds could be heard; that a band of monkeys, for instance, might have been let loose inside the carriages to pull all the old women's hats off, and all the old men's beards; and that even in the midst of it all, the passengers found it possible to clap hands in time to their song.

". . . he sleeps on the ground," the *Bersagliere* made out.

The young wise guys who had pointed to him before were now hopping up and down at the carriage windows fairly bursting with laughter, and the soldier caught another word.

"Are they making fun of me?" he couldn't help asking himself.

The boys were now trying to make their voices harmonize but their efforts were continuously broken up by gales of laughter, and men and women interrupted them too, either from behind—within the carriages—or from the neighboring windows, from which they cursed the racket.

One of the boys was conducting, his arm raised. "No," he would yell at every false start, "no, no! Back to the beginning." And they would start in all over again, he beating time and the others singing in unison: "His food is lousy,/ He sleeps on the ground . . . His food is lousy,/ He sleeps on the ground."

The *Bersagliere* felt someone pull him by the sleeve.

"Having fun?" It was the little old man with the flag once more. "Don't take it to heart," he told him. "They aren't making fun of you."

And the train kept on singing what it's like to be a soldier.

Here's a soldier,
Still safe and sound.
His food is lousy;
He sleeps on the ground.

"But don't take it personal," the little old man said, and he
too burst out laughing. Still laughing, he pointed out that the
fellows who were singing ate badly too, and that they too slept
on the ground. "Like me," he said, laughing, "and like the
brakeman there." That meant that the youngsters were making fun not of the soldier only but of themselves, and of him,
old man that he was, and of the brakeman too.

"As far as we're concerned," the *Bersagliere* said, "we don't
eat so damn badly. . . ." He laughed along with the little old
man. "Besides, there aren't any wars we have to go to any
more; the wars come to us!"

[3]

While they were still laughing, they noticed that a
train had pulled in to the station. The locomotive drew in,
passed them, then one freight car after another passed with
decreasing speed.

In their perches raised above the cars, the brakemen could
be seen giving the last turns to the brake wheels. Their eyes
looked white in their smoke-tanned faces. They jumped down
as if alighting from a trapeze. A trainmaster, trumpet in hand,
ran the length of the platform. The red hat of the stationmaster appeared.

The *Bersagliere* climbed up the little ladder to one of the
brakemen's boxes, and stood on top of the great freight looking
at the bellowing train, at the roofs, still sunlit, at the gardens
and rocks, the windowpanes reflecting the last rays up there
on the crest of the city with its monasteries and churches.

Looking down at the platform between the two trains, he
recognized the brakeman with the malarial face. He called to
him gaily at the top of his lungs:

"Hey, colleague! Hey, *paesano!*"

But he could not make himself heard. He dropped down on the other side of the freight, crossed the last track still to be crossed, and went to plant himself on the threshold of the third-class waiting room.

There he found himself bellowing what the whole train had been shrilling. "His food is lousy. His food is lousy."

"So you've finally learned it?" the little old man with the flag asked.

He stood before him once more, having jumped down from the step of a first-class car which was now passing with its splatter of red plush; it was hauled by a station engine along the first track.

"Funny you should have to hear it from the peasants," he said, laughing. "What do you sing in the barracks nowadays? In my time, they used to sing that song."

On his way to attend to something, he added:

"Could be you eat better'n we did and you don't go to wars any more . . ."

Whatever else he said was lost in the racket and the soldier started to hum once more, "Food's lousy, food's lousy"; then suddenly he was aware that there was no more din coming from the far side of the freight train. The only sounds were whistles blowing and the banging of cars as they knocked against each other. And crickets chirping in the gardens that were scattered among the now sunless rocks.

When the freight pulled out not long after, he saw that its taillight was already lit. Did this mean that it would be dark before he reached his next stop? The soldier saw all the tracks empty before him and could not help fearing that there would be no later train for Terranova.

[4]

But the brakeman had not misled him.

There was a freight leaving at 9 P.M. in the direction of Terranova—and a duke who had holdings at Donnafugata, another with interests from Chiaromonte to the lower Mediterranean, a third whose castle was at Falconara, had pressured the National Railways into adding one carriage to this freight train, a first-class car with the inevitable red plush.

Further, they had gotten officialdom to agree to drive the train at passenger speed and not at that of the other freights. Influential people from Napoleone Colajanni's party and from the Socialist party hollered that it was an outrage. Protests rose from Caltanissetta to Girgenti, from Caltagirone to Modica. This train, they all said, should be hauling water cars to provide drinking water for some of the villages between Ragusa and Licata that had none. But moving at the speed of a passenger train, the "special" could not perform this service, and so the fountains of Comiso or Licata stayed dry until two in the afternoon, by which time they were flanked by long lines of women and boys who had come there to draw water from as far as seven miles away.

The carriage with the red plush served the fine gentlemen who had obtained permission for it, a convenience one of them might make use of as often as once a month, while it was a tossup if the others found use for it as regularly as once a week. But they liked to be able to count on its being there. Moreover, they liked to impress with their power the businessmen and lawyers who had occasional use for the train. "This is the way business is courted in our part of the country," the lawyers wrote the Palermo papers for which they acted as correspondents. And though the opposition ran articles on page one of the same papers telling what was going on around the fountains of Licata, the protests were in vain.

During the last pre-election rallies, they did use the comment made by one of the dukes in question: "But I always see the animals drinking troughsful . . ." he had said. And the Socialists picked up ten or a dozen additional votes when they explained to the long lines waiting at the fountains just what the duke had said. All the same, the train ran at its own privileged speed and according to its own privileged schedule.

And the railway workers on the Ragusa-Licata line, the brakemen, switchmen, linemen, men like the little old man with the flag, or like the malarial brakeman with the ripped sleeve, liked it better that way. Who knows what ungodly night duty they might have to face otherwise. And the *Bersagliere* liked the fact that at last he could climb aboard and walk the length of the car without running into a single soul. The upholstery on the long, facing seats promised an even better sleep than he had dreamed of, a comfortable trip, and the assurance that his three days without anything to worry him had at last begun.

"I was so right," he said to himself, "not to bring along a box lunch."

And he walked the full length of the corridor, looking into the compartments for the wooden benches he had gotten used to from all his previous train trips. Then, since there was nothing but plush to sit on, he sat on plush. It was already dark in the compartment; lights were on in the huddled brilliance of the city, and he leaned back against the armrest of the upholstered bench, looking out as the white setbacks of the mountains disappeared, fading gradually into the perfume of the jasmine, the song of the crickets, and the intermittent glow of the fireflies.

He fell asleep and woke. There were voices of people getting into the car and he woke only to fall asleep again. Then jerks and jolts broke the rhythm of "his" car and he awoke anew only to drop off once more.

[5]

His face was a peaceful blank.

They looked him over by the light of a lantern and saw the insignia on his military collar and shoulder tabs.

"But he's not a *carabiniere*."

"No. He's just a *Bersagliere*."

They shook him. "Sir, how do you happen to be here, *Signor Bersagliere?*"

He woke then with the light of the lantern full in his eyes. "Are we there?"

"Well," they said, "that all depends on where you're going." They asked for his ticket.

"But where are we?"

"In the Donnafugata tunnel . . ."

A wavering violet light came from the small oil lamp in the ceiling. But the only true illumination came from the lantern which now shed its beam on the hands of the two men who had wanted the ticket. Otherwise they were in stark darkness as they stood before the *Bersagliere* in the smoky air that came from the compartment windows. The windows had evidently stayed open all the time he had been sleeping, until the conductors' arrival.

"I thought we were already at Terranova," the *Bersagliere* said.

"You won't see Terranova tonight," they answered.

They had raised their voices a bit, talking to him in turn so rapidly that it seemed they were speaking in unison.

"You'll see plenty of Donnafugata tonight."

"But doesn't this train go to Terranova?"

"The train? Sure, the train goes to Terranova. The train can go there all right. It's you that can't go there."

"The train can go there but I can't?"

"The train has its papers all in order just so it can go there. Now, what kind of papers have you? You haven't the right papers to travel on this train and you know it."

The soldier stretched out a hand and touched the ticket the two of them held under the beam of the lantern.

"Isn't my ticket for Terranova?"

He heard an answer that implied there were two Terranovas, one toward which the yelling, crowded train he had passed up was headed, and the other, the one to which this train with its plush-lined compartments was going.

"On a military pass—get it—you've got to take the regular train," they told him. "This train is a special, and first class at that. You'd have to have a first-class ticket."

They went on talking, talking, but the long and short of it was that the *Bersagliere* had to get off at Donnafugata, spend the night and morning there, the afternoon too, and pick up—twenty-four hours later—the same screaming train he had not taken at Ragusa that afternoon. He moved a hand over his face.

"I should have figured that the idea of wanting to get there the easiest, most comfortable way was no good!"

Then he exclaimed:

"If only I'd brought my lunch with me! I'd have taken the right train if I'd brought me at least a box lunch!"

"What's all that crap about a box lunch?" they asked. They told him again that what he needed was a first-class ticket paid at the regular rate.

"It's all the fault of that brakeman with malaria!" the *Bersagliere* exclaimed. "He's the one that told me to take this God-damned train. . . . I didn't even know the train existed. I was as good as on the other one already."

Part II

[6]

MEANWHILE THE DOOR TO THE NEARBY COMPARTMENT OPENED a crack, then all the way, and a new face appeared out of the smoke.

"Who has that beautiful voice?" the face said. "What a beautiful voice!"

It came forward slowly, solemnly, one might say amply, as if it were somehow on horseback. The head of an animal came along with it. "Are we on the platform?" The face sniffed and coughed, yet managed to look up at the lone flicker of the overhead lamp which, showing the veils and wisps of hair, revealed that this was a woman of a sort.

The tone of voice in which she now sang out reinforced this impression. Pointing a finger at the *Bersagliere*, she said:

"Is *he* the one with the beautiful voice? An angel in the heart of a mountain . . . That voice brought back the young tenor I heard at La Scala."

She had pushed her way between the two trainmen by now, accompanied by the quiet animal which seemed perpetually mixed up in the fringes of her shawl.

"Let's have a look at him," she added.

And she seized the hand of the man carrying the lantern to raise the light to the right height.

"Why, he's fresh as a daisy! What a fine, frank face, in spite of the fright Don Carlos here gave him. . . ." Turning to the *Bersagliere,* she went on, "Don't pay any attention to him. He's only Don Carlos, he's no lion."

Then she discovered that her angel was a soldier.

"A soldier can stop armies! And there you sit, soldier, afraid of my great Dane. It's true he doesn't bark but then he doesn't bite either. He's absolutely useless. . . . You know, if you'd been born fifty years earlier, you'd have sounded the trumpet under the walls of Calatafimi."

At this point the trainmen tried to interrupt, addressing the woman as "Baroness." They wanted to tell her something, perhaps only that the soldier was just a *Bersagliere,* neither more nor less, but they didn't manage to say a word.

"And what were you doing to him?" she cut them off. "He was talking as if someone had insulted him. And as for you fellows, you sounded as if you were trying to play him one of your tricks. . . . What tricks? You can see perfectly well that he's innocent. What were they doing to you, innocent?"

The trainmen pointed out that it was "him" who had tried to play the trick.

"He?" the old woman exclaimed. "Can't you see his mother's milk isn't dry on his lips! What kind of trick could *he* ever play?" And she imposed silence on the two trainmen: "Let's hear what he has to say."

At this the *Bersagliere* blushed visibly even by the wan light of the lantern.

"Ah, God, what a rose!" the old woman cried. "He's blushing; perhaps he's afraid of my hoary locks, and here these heathen try to convince me he's played a trick on them!"

She broke off because of the smoke. "Can't you open the windows any wider in here? We're suffocating. . . ."

The trainmen pointed out that more smoke would come in if they opened the windows wider.

"Then let's get on with it," the old woman ordered. "It's because of you that I'm here," she said to the *Bersagliere.*

And she addressed her dog, which was now whining: "Shut up, you fool!" Then, turning to anyone else who might hear her on the train or over the entire surface of the earth, she said, "Will we never get out from under this mountain?"

A far-off whistle came from the engine; everything slowed down and once more picked up speed as metal plates seemed to fly open every so often to reveal iron doors spaced throughout the endless course of the tunnel.

"What if we were to go into my compartment," the old woman suggested. She said there was no smoke in there. "Let's go."

But only the two trainmen started to follow her.

"Hey, you," the old woman bawled, turning in the doorway. "Didn't you understand what I told you? There's no smoke in there."

"Well, I have to get off now anyway," the *Bersagliere* answered.

"You can tell me in there what they were doing to you. Do you want to get off at Donnafugata?"

"I'm not the one that wants me to get off there. . . ."

"Who else does?" the old girl thundered, taking a step back into the compartment. "You mean you don't want to get down there but you have to?"

"It's all because I didn't want to carry a box lunch," the *Bersagliere* answered. "I decided I wanted to travel in comfort, but instead I took the wrong train."

Then the trainmen explained the situation as best they could, piecing the story together between them and liberally sprinkling each sentence with "Signora Baronessa."

"Aren't you ashamed!" the old woman exclaimed. "This . . . this *innocent* here was good enough to give in to your tricks and threats. I knew he looked like a lamb ready to be led to the slaughter. I could see it in his face. . . . So, he can't ride on this train? This train is such a national disgrace that if Garibaldi were alive today, he'd get right up out of his grave at Caprera to protest. And you two dare talk about tickets, you dare ask whether they're in order or not! Why, if this train has ever been of the slightest real use to anyone, it will

have been tonight because it gave a poor soldier a ride. . . .
For whom do you two vote, anyway? The Bourbons? Do you
ever ask if *my* ticket's in order? Or Don Carlos's here? Do you
ever ask if my dog's ticket is in order? He should ride in the
cattle car, given his size—not even in the baggage car—but
instead he rides in the compartment with me and no one of
you has ever made the slightest fuss about that."

[7]

At this point, a locomotive's whistle sounded high and shrill.
Even the noise of their train's wheels seemed absorbed by the
other sound. The trainmen rushed one to one window and one
to another, dropping the casements open on a wooded night in
which a disk of light could be seen drawing nearer and
nearer. The men could not take time to answer the old
woman.

The train slowed.

The night was suddenly white with stones as they passed
a dried-up stream bed, and the train slowed still further.
There were the fireflies once more, and the crickets could be
heard, and the fresh scent of the hills covered with locust trees
rose to the nostrils.

The trainmen opened the doors now too, one on one side
and one on the other, and they leaned out ready to jump
down as soon as they could.

"So you're running out?" the old woman said.

One was swinging his lantern and a platform whitened the
night as passing acacia leaves brushed against the man's head.
He jumped down with a shout, landing between train and
high white cavelike wall of the station.

"Donnafugata!" he cried out to the desert.

The station wall was spectral white against the black
columns of the woods, and the *Bersagliere* searched in vain
for a more formal station either at his feet or under some
nearby roof; his eyes sought a light, some sign of life.

"Do I get off here?" he asked.

"I cooked their goose for 'em," the old woman answered.

"Didn't you hear me handle 'em? All they could do was run out on me. . . ."

"Then you'd say I could stay?"

"Obviously. As long as Don Carlos here can stay, you can stay. . . . They won't even come back. . . ."

"What about my ticket? If they don't come back, they won't return my ticket."

"Then they'll come back just to return it. What is it, a round-trip fare? They can't keep any part of a ticket you can still use."

But the *Bersagliere* was not completely reassured. "Let's hope they come back soon," he kept saying.

"Why?" the old woman asked. "Where do you have to get off? At Comiso?"

"I'm really going to Terranova, but if I can't stay on that long . . ."

The old girl snorted with satisfaction. "Terranova?" Then she cried out raucously, "You can stay on as long as you want to. I couldn't guarantee it if you had any further to go. But I get off at Terranova myself, and nobody's going to make you get down a minute before I do. Come on. Let's go. Let's close these windows out here on account of the tunnels up ahead. . . ."

And she flung herself about making all sorts of attempts to close the windows, but she was hampered by the black web of her shawls and veils and by the enormous dog, which always managed to get in the way, flattening himself against her on one side or the other.

In the adjacent compartment, where she wanted them to go because it was "hers," she kept nagging until the *Bersagliere* had opened all the windows, nor would she agree to sit down until he had stretched his hand out of each of them into the night to prove that actually they were open.

"You're here now to keep me company, and no one will try to put you off the train any more," she told him.

She settled herself with a squeaking of springs. "Aren't you going to sit down? Don Carlos here, he'll stretch out on my side of the compartment and you can sit opposite."

She worked herself into a comfortable position. "You'll see: they'll leave you alone and that's a fact. You can get ready to sleep on it."

"That's why I took this train instead of the other one. I wanted to sleep the whole trip."

"Well, in here," the old girl said, "you can sleep the whole trip. . . . It's ten o'clock now and they'll take at least three hours, what with the waits at every hole we pass. Then there's that other train that's up ahead now. We'll have to wait here till it leaves Comiso, though God only knows how they can tell when that'll be with this station that looks like the mouth of a tomb. . . . But you can be sure we won't reach Terranova before one. . . . You can count on that."

The *Bersagliere* tried to find the best possible position, placing not only his head but one cheek carefully against the velvet pile of the upholstery. By his smile he must have found things almost perfect. But at the mention of Terranova the old woman's voice had resumed its raucous tone of excitement.

"How does it happen you're going to Terranova? If you were born there, you must know who I am. I know everything there is to know about Terranova. And believe me, I'd remember having seen a face like yours among all those—those Carthaginians. Do you have relatives there or are you going back to your garrison? Well, in either case, you'll have figured out who I am. . . ."

"Really . . ." the *Bersagliere* said.

"Really what? You're not going to tell me you know my life from *a* to *z*, but I'm sure you know something about Italian history. Didn't you go to school? You must have finished the fourth grade. You must have learned about Cornelia, mother of the Gracchi. You must have learned who Lucretia was. You must have heard of Anita, who died during Garibaldi's flight to Rome. And that's why you must have heard of me, the one who followed her husband into exile! Now do you recognize me? Don't you recognize me?"

She threw herself forward with such vehemence demanding his reply that the *Bersagliere* was shaken from his position and raised his head. He readjusted himself as best he could in his former place, and repeated, "Really . . ." Then with more candor than wit he said that he could not guess who she was. "I just know they called you 'Signora Baronessa.' "

"That's a title the unimaginative vulgarians tack onto me," the old woman exclaimed. "It's my daughter that married a baron. Not me. I kept right on being a republican even after Garibaldi met up with that . . . scion of the house of Savoy."

Meanwhile the train had begun to move again. There was the noise and then there was the night air that came in in gusts. "Remember to close the windows when we go through the tunnels," the old woman cautioned him. But this was no more important to her than the gesture with which she adjusted her coils of hair during the black night ride, for she was waiting—and with no attempt to hide it—for the *Bersagliere* to give some indication that he had understood. She showed this if by nothing more than the pose in which she still held her head rigidly erect. And she now told him that in history she bore only her own first name "as a woman," just like Lucretia or Anita.

"Do you know what my name is in history?" she exploded.

[8]

But the *Bersagliere* had rushed to close the windows as smoke came pouring in.

"It's Leonilde!" the old girl shouted.

The soldier went back to his seat pleased at having been able to prove himself helpful, and the old woman, now armed with a pair of opera glasses, prepared to use them to probe the dark. It was on him, once more withdrawn into his shadowy corner, that she trained them.

"Doesn't the fact that my name is Leonilde mean anything to you?" she asked.

The *Bersagliere*, who continued to smile more or less, shrugged.

"I can see, I can see," the old girl checked him, "that much I can see without another word from you: Leonilde means nothing to you. But then Cornelia, mother of the Gracchi, means nothing to you either."

She plucked a confirmation from the *Bersagliere* that Cornelia meant nothing to him either.

"Perhaps Clelia? I mean the Roman virgin who fled with all the other hostages from the camp of the enemy! Does *she* mean anything?"

The *Bersagliere* indicated sleepily that not even Clelia meant anything to him.

"What about Camilla? She was that warrior maid who had something to do with Aeneas. Does Camilla mean anything to you?"

Not even Camilla meant anything to the *Bersagliere*. He murmured "Aeneas?" softly but gave no other sign that even Aeneas meant anything to him, and the old woman was appeased.

"Now I know why my name means nothing to you," she crooned. "*No* name means anything to you. You're as innocent as the angels the good Lord used to send to earth to punish us poor mortals with their flaming swords. I thought so the moment I laid eyes on you. That's just what you're like. And you have the same pure heart and unmarked mind as they, in order to be pitiless. . . ."

From the arm of the seat against which the *Bersagliere* was leaning and from the springs under him and at his back, squeaks rose in a steady crescendo as he twisted and turned in embarrassment. The train burst from—then re-entered—the mountain; its whistle shrilled down a gorge, and the *Bersagliere* leaped staggering to his feet to reopen the windows on the night. But the whistle was once more swallowed up underground, raucous still as it was stifled by the tunnel's gaping maw, and the *Bersagliere* dropped down again without having been able to open them.

"Not only do you have their voice and their face," the old woman went on, "but you're all pink and nice. Just like those paintings in which they stand smiling as they kill. And they're always blushing."

[9]

The *Bersagliere* interrupted, all of a sudden, to tell her that "those two" had come back into the car.

"Back again, eh?"

The *Bersagliere* reminded her that "those two" had not yet returned his ticket.

"Well," the Signora called out, "why don't you come in here?"

The compartment was a double one, with a corridor running along one side and aisles that separated the sections one from another. The trainmen were standing in shadow in the farther aisle. "Why don't you come in?" They didn't answer, but a streak of light passed under the seats, cast by the lantern they had placed on the compartment floor. Were they coming in or weren't they? They talked it over between themselves.

Don Carlos had placed one great paw on his mistress' black lap and this made it hard for her to get up. But she managed to heave herself to her feet and then turned, kneeling on the seat, and faced the two of them over the top of the back rest.

"Baroness—" one of them began.

"Don't give me that 'Baroness' business!" she interjected. "When you want to pay me a compliment, just remember I've worn the colors; I've been an officer. . . . Save those two-bit titles for those who enjoy 'em. Now, why don't you just hand over the ticket that belongs to the soldier here who's accompanying me?"

"The ticket . . . yes, of course . . . we can hand it over—"

"Can? You *must!* What's all the fuss about, anyway?"

"There's no fuss, Ba—"

"I've already told you, I'm no Ba! Now where's that ticket?"

The ticket passed from one trainman to the other to be examined all over again, turned and re-turned under the bluish light from the ceiling lamp. The old woman reached an arm across the seat backs to take it from them.

"But the soldier," they told her. "He'll have to get off at Comiso."

"The soldier is traveling with me and will accompany me as far as Terranova."

"*If* he pays the difference, he can do it, Signora."

"Difference? What difference? He's paid for his ticket. You wouldn't want him to pay twice, would you?"

The *Bersagliere* rose wearily. "Perhaps I'd better get off at Comiso."

"You're traveling with me," the old girl snapped at him over her shoulder. "You stay where you are."

The trainmen explained to her that they no longer questioned the difference between a military and a civilian ticket; they were now worried about the difference between a third- and a first-class fare. He must pay the difference or get off the train.

"I'll get off, I'll get off," the soldier said.

"Now what's got into you to want to get off here?" the old woman yelled. "I told you I'd take you as far as Terranova and I'll take you as far as Terranova."

She now told the trainmen they should be ashamed to make a poor soldier pay as if he were a feudal landowner, told them again their train was a disgrace to the nation, and mentioned Garibaldi, then Don Carlos once more. The trainmen could not get a word in edgewise, and the *Bersagliere* did not say again that he thought it best to get off.

Instead he opened a window.

"See, I fixed 'em for you once more!" the old woman said.

Soft clean air was coming in the window now, no longer the acrid stench of the tunnels, and even the trainmen were opening the windows on their side. The *Bersagliere* looked out and mentioned that he saw lights.

"Perhaps it's Comiso," he said.

It did not take much to restore his tranquillity; all in all, he was well enough pleased with the comfort of the trip, the soft seats, and the sleep he still promised himself with his cheek against that plush cushion. He felt Don Carlos push up against his back and turned to pat him. He was only a big dog, after all; he knew that from his smell. Like the smell of the night: you could tell just as surely that the train was running through countryside full of prickly pears.

Running? There was the screech of brakes along the tracks. The train slowed. Once more the two trainmen had disappeared from the compartment to the rear. Perhaps they were walking along the outer step, holding onto the handrails of the car. At last, with a croak like a frog's, the train stopped over a flat bed of gravel.

The old girl was still congratulating herself to Don Carlos over her latest victory. And Don Carlos gave as good as he got. The big creature was poking in among her shawls and she was chuckling to him over the things that had been said. She told Don Carlos all over again that the soldier had been all ready to get off, right here at Comiso. "Were you tired of keeping me company?" she asked the *Bersagliere*. And he found the question laughable. He admitted it.

He laughed with her as he had done with the old man who carried the red flag. He laughed as he told her now about the little old man who was so happy and the brakeman who was by contrast so gloomy, and he told her too about the train he ought to have taken. "The whole train was shouting and yelling."

He stopped to listen a moment to a sound that was not frogs croaking amid the frog noises. "What's that noise?" he said. It was not the rushing of a torrent nor the threat of an approaching thunderstorm. It was amid the frog noises, all right, as if it were the sound of other animals right in among them.

"We've caught up with it," the old woman answered.
"With what?"
"With the train you should have taken."

[10]

They were moving again, passing the three or four lights

which distinguished Comiso from the cactus-scented dark. The old woman was saying that they were lucky, as they would now be in the forward train, that they would no longer have to make long waits at the station stops, and that they could count on reaching Terranova by midnight.

"Because you must know our 'national disgrace' does things like this too," she cried. "I've been away from Sicily for the past six months and I'd come to believe they'd put a stop to it, but I see they still do it."

Suddenly she was indignant. The "national disgrace" should have considered it enough to refuse to carry the water needed daily by the towns with no water supply of their own. But the idea of catching up with and passing the work train of those poor devils and making it wait until the "national disgrace" arrived, that was too much. . . . Garibaldi would have withdrawn to Tierra del Fuego in protest, had he still lived.

"And what's happened to those two Arabs who wanted you to pay the difference between your ticket and the first-class fare?"

She added that the *Bersagliere* could consider himself lucky. "You were certainly born under a lucky star. . . ."

He said he thought so too, and the old woman told him that he would certainly be furious if he had taken the other train. It would be like having someone spit right in your eye, she said, to sit there and watch this train pass you by.

Then she asked him if he was always so lucky.

"I get good ideas," he answered.

They jerked to a stop and immediately heard the rumble of the first train, the train loaded with the people who had been shouting. The noise came from right and left, from above and below, yet they could see that the train had drawn up on the track alongside. In the dark, matches flared here and there.

The *Bersagliere* said something the old woman could not hear, and then she said something he could not hear. The noise that surrounded them had a distinct rhythm and the *Bersagliere* could pick out the words.

"His food is lousy," he recognized.

"He sleeps on the ground." He recognized that too.

Hadn't they ever stopped chanting that song? He yelled at the old woman that they were singing.

"What?"

"They're singing. I said they're singing."

His face was radiant, and he wanted to tell the old woman what they were singing. "They're singing about us."

"About us?"

He pointed to himself, touching various parts of his uniform. "About me. About soldiers." And he tried to make her hear the words they were singing.

The old woman nodded vigorously. She too had caught the rhythm and the words of the song, and it seemed as if at some near or remote period in her life she had sung it, and sung it again and again. Her strident voice broke in:

> Here's a soldier,
> Still safe and sound.

At this point the *Bersagliere* joined her:

> His food is lousy;
> He sleeps on the ground.

They wound up together.

Then he told her, as the old man with the flag had told him, that the people who were shouting that song had it in for themselves rather than for soldiers. "They don't have it in for me, for soldiers like me." And because of the noise, he pointed to himself again, touched his sleeves, his chest, and shook his head in dissent.

"They have it in for others. For themselves."

He was aware that his gestures and words, altogether drowned by the racket, did not convey his meaning and at first he gave up. But then he decided to try it again: "They don't mean to be offensive," he yelled.

He was interrupted by an impetuous rush of sound which

rose wildly, no longer rhythmically, in a whoop of triumph.

The old woman too had started to yell. She was shaking her fist out the window and yelling. What had come over her? But even before the *Bersagliere* could gather the facts from her words, he understood that the other train had started to move. This was what was happening. He was in time to see the last car disclose the empty platform on the other side as it pulled away into the night, and he heard the voice of the crowd fragmented by the distance which was swallowing it up as the train disappeared.

[11]

The old woman began yelling out the window.

"Now I suppose you'll keep us anchored here until that one reaches Vittoria!" she bawled.

That was why she was indignant. The shadows of trainmen with their lanterns in their fists now gathered beneath the window. They answered her, calling her "Signora Baronessa," and tried to calm her fury, but she would have none of them; she wanted the stationmaster.

"Baroness here! Baroness there! I'd like to see how you'd jump if Duke Armando had been here, or even that stuffed shirt Lillo," she said. "Then you'd have seen to it that this train pulled out first. But there's no one aboard worth taking a bit of trouble over, according to you. That's the point! There's only a poor old woman and a poor young soldier."

The men on the platform answered that this wasn't true, that there were other people on the train as well as themselves, and they mentioned Don X, Don Y, the son of Don Z. Meanwhile the old woman went on repeating that even if no one but that witless Lillo had been here . . . evidently extreme proof of the shortcomings of the trainmen.

Then she wanted the *Bersagliere* to express his horror of Lillo. The trainmen assured her in the interim that if her train had not taken precedence over the other it was only because the engine had to stop long enough to take on water. They would leave, the men said, without waiting for the other train to reach Vittoria. In five or ten minutes at most. The engineer would see to it that they did not pile up on the train in front of them. . . .

But the more the men on the platform tried to placate her, the more upset she became. "Irresponsibles! Irresponsibles!" she kept repeating. "Oh, what irresponsible minds! What Moslem irresponsibility! What typically irresponsible Moslem minds!"

At this she drew in her head, leaving the trainmen below on the platform shrugging their shoulders.

"Did you hear them?" she asked the *Bersagliere*. "Now they'll have us pull out before the other train has reached Vittoria. All I had to do was give them a dressing down and they've got us running off after the other one. Hurrah for the Moslem mind! Now mind you, I have nothing against Sicilians as such, and nothing against Arabs—in fact, I disapprove of our occupation of Tripolitania—but when they start stuffing all their nonsense down my gullet, that I can't take. Let 'em keep it to themselves!"

Once more she wanted the *Bersagliere* to express his horror of Lillo.

"Just think of that Lillo! You know who Lillo is? He's a dwarf, a regular dwarf about four foot high! His nurse dropped him; no, it was the midwife dropped him at birth and he hit his head and his tail. But the floor he went and landed on was that of the richest house on Piazza Armerina, all rose marble. That's why today you have the fine sight of that ridiculous dwarf receiving the judges who bow and scrape before him in open court, or being given a military salute by the commander of the garrison."

She asked eagerly what the *Bersagliere* thought of such goings-on.

"Doesn't it make you sick? All that for a fellow who runs to shut himself up in the broom closet when there's a thunderstorm! And he still wets the bed, though he's almost thirty years old! You know how we can tell when he's 'in residence' at Terranova? We can see the yellow sheets flapping in the breeze over his cousin's rooftop. . . ."

She heard a muffled snort of laughter the *Bersagliere* tried in vain to suppress. But the night was silent now all around them except for a sad humming that might have come from the telegraph wires.

"Makes you laugh, does it?" the old woman said. "It's nothing to laugh at, let me tell you."

But the *Bersagliere* looked as if he were laughing because of everything put together: the mix-up of the trains, the old woman who got indignant first for one reason then for another, then the Lillo business, and more because of the way she told it than because of Lillo himself. He was making manful efforts to keep himself from bursting out laughing.

[12]

As luck would have it, the train started to move just then. There was a short blast on the dispatcher's horn, then the splat and strain of the couplings from car to car, a screech of the wheels, an opaque flash of light washing in as they passed an open door; then the dark station dropped behind, and the dark water tower, and Comiso itself was swallowed up in the dark night, heavy with the scent of prickly pears.

"That's really too much," the old woman cried.

The *Bersagliere* saw her leap up and turn her head away. "Have they come back?" he asked.

"At 'em," the old girl hissed to Don Carlos.

It took Don Carlos quite a while to get on guard. He was in a half crouch and the old woman could easily hold him in. A frail voice could be heard addressing her over the top of the seat backs.

Perhaps someone asking alms? But why here? Not a word could be understood, but a hunched figure was outlined in the distant night light of the other compartment, shoulders bowed, head bent to one side, white hands gleaming bone-pale in the bluish light as they rested on the backs of the two seats that separated the compartments. Still, the old woman must have known who it was and what he was trying to say.

"You want to thank *me?*" she started to answer him.

She half addressed the cringing figure and half the *Bersagliere*.

"He thanks me for having got the train started again! A fat lot of work I did! And what if it piles up on the one ahead? Will you thank me then? The trouble is, nothing ever happens in this damned country! What's that? Speak up! Prospero thanks me too? See here, soldier, this old man holds all the hills in Butera. I mean he *owns* them. And he stands there thanking me in the name of three other big landowners sitting over there behind him. . . . What did you say you wanted? You all want to come in here to keep me company? You just tell them to excuse me. Excuse me! I'm already in good company. Tell them I can well understand their joy at seeing me back in Sicily; tell them I return their greetings but that they could have stretched their limbs enough to bring me their greetings in person. That's to say— What are you doing? Stay where you are! . . . I was saying, I admire the delicacy with which they sought not to disturb me. I don't want them in here, understand? Don Carlos and my orderly are enough. Stay over there. . . . Stay right there! Just put your rosary of thanks back in your pocket and keep it to yourself!"

Bent and ailing, the man withdrew his white hands from the seat back.

"Thanking me for having heard me sound off!" the old woman exclaimed. "For having got the train going again! It was I, perhaps, who gave a blast on that horn?"

And as the man meekly reappeared, trying once more to say something, the old girl reminded him of the harsh cold of the winter of 1908, of the cold of that January, of the cold of a certain Tuesday of that January.

"What can have gotten into you, Enrico, to come bother me?"

Shaking his meek old head, Enrico disappeared in a halo of faint blue light. The door back there could be heard opening and closing despite the noise of the rushing train. The old woman grumbled to herself. Even Don Carlos, who was still on guard, grumbled. And the *Bersagliere* could contain his laughter no longer.

[13]

"But . . . but . . ." he managed to get out between one hoot of laughter and the next.

"What's there to laugh about and say 'But . . . but'?"

"I said, 'But that Enrico—'"

"That's nothing to say 'but' about. He could buy and sell you ninety times over."

The *Bersagliere* tried to check his spasms of laughter.

"I just said . . . he talks . . . without saying . . . a word."

"Couldn't he have lost his voice? Couldn't he have asthma? Or bronchitis? What do you know about his hidden qualities?"

"Of course he could have hidden qualities," the *Bersagliere* said, merrier than ever. He was a little humiliated that he could not stop laughing, but not enough to help him check himself. "Of course . . . one shouldn't pass judgment . . . on a person one knows nothing . . . about. . . ."

"Are you blushing again?" the old girl asked. "I'll just bet you're blushing."

She gave him a kick in the leg and told him not to cross himself for what he must have been thinking.

"But I warn you it's no laughing matter," she went on. "He's quite capable of cutting a slice out of your side without letting you feel he's been near you. I had a holding, a mountainside at Butera, and he made off with it!"

"You certainly put him in his place though! That's why I was laughing."

"You were wrong. You were wrong. I don't spend my time putting people in their places. If they're out of place, let 'em stay there!"

A gurgle from the soldier told her that he had started to splutter with laughter again. The old woman's language, coupled with the admonitory tone she was trying to assume, was obviously too much for him to resist. It was as if she had tickled him and, despite his efforts, he had succumbed. Now he did not know which way to turn to find an acceptable object for his amusement.

"But . . ." he said again.

"But what?"

"But this train—"

"What's wrong with this train?"

"But we're really moving. . . . Oh! We've scarcely stopped a minute. . . . I mean we didn't have to wait . . . back there at Comiso. . . ."

He was completely sincere when he brought up this topic; a part of his amusement did indeed come from this source.

"Is that anything to laugh about?" the old woman interrupted. "Come, come now. Come, come."

At this, the *Bersagliere* burst out laughing more loudly than ever.

"But," he said from the depths of his being, "the idea of calling me your orderly! But the idea of being an orderly to a lady!"

The old woman was now laughing with him.

"You think I couldn't have had an orderly?" she managed to ask him. "There you sit hiccuping with laughter because, in your innocence, you know nothing of the world of man. If you knew the slightest thing about us mortals you'd know that I've had more than one orderly in my time. It's pretty tight-fisted of this socialist monarchy, let me tell you, that they don't give me an allowance for one now."

She laughed with an undertone of bitterness.

"And whoever called it 'socialist'? Just bamboozled with all the fandango they put on. They've failed to recognize my military rank, failed in every way to give me fair treatment, failed to pay me a double pension in the light of what my husband and I stood for. Son, you'd better know it: I've been everything, a soldier like you, then a lieutenant, a captain, a major, finally a colonel. . . . You think I didn't have an orderly when I was a captain? I had a bigger one for every rise in rank they gave me. And you, dear boy, descended from the right hand of God to play soldier in our socialist monarchy, you couldn't have guessed you'd also turn out to be the orderly of an old woman!"

Part III

[14]

THE DARK AIR ENTERING FROM THE WINDOW HAD A BRACKISH scent—of green grapes growing on a hillside covered with vineyards, of the far distant sea, and of the shore where a sandy hill ascends in a line of dunes to end in a flat sandbar.

The old woman stood up while the soldier pulled himself together after his irrepressible burst of laughter.

"And so we're about to reach the next town," she said, thrusting her head out into the black, racing wind. Then she withdrew it, rearranged her hair, and added, "I always liked the town of Vittoria. Nothing to it but houses in a row; still the town has something I always liked. Are you familiar with it? But to be familiar with it means little or nothing. It's the countryside. . . . The town with its overlay of roofs lies there in the midst of its countryside and not even the glow of a single lamp can be seen. Year after year, year in, year out, nothing ever happens here. You go to Milan and return, and nothing has happened. Once you get back to Sicily, you find nothing has ever happened. Nothing in Giarratana, in Ragusa, in Terranova. The era in which things happened is over. Finished. *Basta!* Gone when you were a baby," she said to herself, "not even a little girl, because after all you were only a baby in Sixty-nine. . . . Hey there, soldier! Leonilde was only a child when her name marked a page in history. Now she is happy if she can just manage to find something she likes as much as this village of Vittoria. . . . Something here, something there to be liked. . . . A little something everywhere."

She seemed happy, enjoying the invisible countryside spicing the air. The soldier too seemed happier listening to her.

The train slowed, then started to whistle as it slowed a little

more, and the air coming down from the black slopes of the
vineyards, and up and down from sandy slopes, from sea
slopes, entering the windows, left a little more of itself in the
compartment, and the smoke smelled as it does on top of a hill
when it plumes up from a railway valley.

[15]

The train stopped and started, stopped and started. In the
intervals between its whistles, a more distant whistle was
heard. A flash of another train could be seen. Then, at the
curve, the red lights of the other train were visible.

The other train, which had fallen behind again, now drew
up and the soldier could picture the faces at the compartment
windows, looking out into the black night: the boys laughing
at him, never tired of repeating their chant, the old woman
trying to say something to him, the man in rags like flapping
feathers, the other man, with the shabby, cone-shaped hat,
who had made a long tirade.

Whether he knew it or not, the soldier was excited; he faced
the window behind the old lady or turned to the one on the
other side, saying that this time no one would get away with
spitting at them as people had done at Comiso.

"Would you like to spit at them?" the Signora asked.

"It's not that," he answered, but he was excited just the
same and even more so when they passed the "chanting" train,
or when they stopped alongside it at the Vittoria station.

Scornful laughter came from the shouting crowd, the flares
of a match flamed up here and there. Then came the *tam-tam*,
the rhythm that the crowd's voice never loses, the same repeated chant, forever the same, a thousand times repeated
during the hours of travel in the sun near Ragusa, at sunset
near Genisi, in the night at Donnafugata, Comiso, Vittoria:

> His food is lousy;
> He sleeps on the ground.

The soldier tried once more to tell the old woman that they

were not singing against soldiers, not exclusively *against* them, not properly . . . and he took refuge in mimicry, but black figures in the night moved along their train on both sides, that of the narrow station and that of the chanting cars. The soldier was trembling with excitement.

"We fooled them, we fooled them!"

The old lady said he should be ashamed of himself and blamed both sides for the usual "Sicilian Moslemism." She could not be heard anyhow, and was interrupted by savage shouts, wild roars, and blows on the windowpanes, as people passed their compartment.

"Horned bastards, sons of cuckolds; cuckold sons of bastards, with a ribbon on your horns!"

It seemed to the soldier that the boys howled "cuckolds," that the old woman screamed too, and that the man with the shabby hat, and the other with his rags fluttering about like feathers filled the whole train with their faces, as many faces as there were windows.

It all seemed possible enough but it was also nonsense; even their insults were ludicrous; then the soldier laughed, but the old woman, interrupted in her last tirade, was now boiling as she listened to them.

"Oh, the scoundrels! Oh, the bastards," she shrieked, pulling at the soldier's sleeve. "Don't you hear them?" She wanted him to answer them man to man, answer them with a tough, commonplace insult, he who was a common man, but she herself answered instead, thrusting her head from the window before it was too late:

"Horns to you, and may you attach them to your babies' cradles! Attach them to your saddlebags, your packsaddles, you dogs!" The soldier, whistling with two fingers in his mouth, now joined her:

"Horns to you, and you!"

Soon nothing more was heard from the other train, for the railway switches were thrown, first one, then a second. . . . Their train was on the move again.

[16]

"I never met a man like you," the old woman said. "Didn't you resent their insults? It was *your* mother they insulted, after all. . . . Are you or are you not your mother's son? Have you a mother? I do understand and appreciate innocence but this goes way beyond a pure mind, at this point; it's like having fresh water instead of blood in your veins, or perhaps you really are what you appear?"

And she gave him a sharp little glance, trying to discern on his face the phosphorescent gleam of the divine sign, but the *Bersagliere* answered that he was simply happy. He was happy because he should have been traveling on that terrible train whereas here he was on this peaceful one. He should have stayed back yet he was now up front. He should have stopped at Donnafugata yet he was now running on well beyond Vittoria.

"And all this, thanks to you," he added.

The Signora had to admit he was a gem. "I *deserve* an orderly like you."

The *Bersagliere* was not so sure he deserved it; still, he had had the bright idea of trying for a comfortable trip and now he was having one. He had wanted to sleep all the way, and now . . . true, he hadn't slept yet but, since their train was ahead and they would no longer be harried by the noises of the other train at the stations, it was likely he could do so now. He had refused to take so much as a box lunch with him, nor had he shouldered his knapsack or carried even a small package—this had been the best idea ever. This impulse alone had given him luck for the rest of the trip.

As the old woman kept asking him to explain himself more clearly, he now started to describe the long walk at Terranova from the station to the town.

"Certainly," she said.

"It's a hard climb," he said.

"Of course it is . . . certainly is."

"Then, too, I'm not yet home at the end of the climb."

"Neither am I."

"I have to cross town and go down on the other side."

"Toward the sea? I have to cross the full length of the town too. I live near the Capuchins."

"So you can well understand. . . . I didn't want to bring a single thing along. On my arrival, I'll wake up and I'll have only a long walk ahead of me and nothing to carry."

"You're very lucky indeed!"

"That's so, don't you agree?"

The old woman said that his luck lay in being such a gem, in being her orderly, her squire, her protector, in being everything the socialist monarchy had refused to admit its obligation to give her.

But she made it even plainer. From her dark corner, she was searching again for a phosphorescent supernatural sign on that face whose features were scarcely distinguishable in the bluish glimmer of the compartment night light. And she told him that not only would he carry nothing but he would not even have to walk all the way.

[17]

"How come?" he asked.

"You won't walk!"

"But how will I get there?"

"You will go by carriage."

"In a carriage! Do you know how much a carriage costs from the station to town? Then down the slope to the big boats? I've never in my life ridden in a carriage; besides, there aren't any carriages waiting for the night train at Terranova."

"My carriage will be waiting."

"Do you own a carriage?"

"Oh, innocent boy, you think I don't have a carriage? I hire one for the months of my stay. My relatives have already been notified from Milàn, and again from Giarratana, and then from Ragusa; that's why we'll find their carriage, which I have already paid for. . . ."

"But, dear lady, what have I to do with your carriage?"

"Why not you? If I—and Don Carlos—can get in, you may get in too, as my orderly, of course. The carriage will be empty except for Lionheart on the box; my baroness daughter won't be there, nor my baron son-in-law, nor the other little Leonilde whose grandmother I am."

"And you'll take me by carriage all the way to town? After that it's downhill until I reach the Barconi district, the big boats, if you'll just drop me off at the square. But first I can accompany you home, if you wish. I can get to the Barconi from the Capuchins just as well. . . ."

"It is nice of you to offer . . . but you'll go home by carriage to your Barconi, you innocent, you. Innocenzo *is* your name, isn't it? I want you to have the best of luck tonight."

The lady asked him if he knew the fairy tale of a certain boy who had a certain cat.

"I want it to be that way tonight. I want to be for you what that cat was."

"Do you mean Puss in Boots?"

She nodded. "Well, I too have boots. I'm a female cat instead of a male, and I'm old, Innocenzo, an old cat, but I too have boots—a carriage, I mean. I'll have you jump aboard it, fold the steps, close the door, and there you'll be, inside with Don Carlos, a poor boy transformed as if by magic into another. I'll mount the box beside Lionheart. We'll climb the dusty road where there will be no light, no living soul, but if there were I'd shout to clear the way for the Prince of Donnafugata."

[18]

"What then?" the soldier asked.

"What then? Then we'll stop in front of your house. . . ." A full stop was called for at this point to imagine the scene of the arrival: she, descending in high boots from her box seat, unfolding the coach steps, opening the door for him as he, the Prince, was having it borne in on him that his home had not been changed for that of a prince.

"But I'll continue to do something for you. I can continue to do something. Nothing can happen to me, but it can to you. For you, things can be different. I can change something for somebody else, and I'll do it."

The tone of her last words conveyed her decision and the *Bersagliere* did not ask what kind of change she meant; perhaps he did not wish the "something" to happen, perhaps he even feared it. And he continued to stare into the dark corner occupied by the old woman, waiting in a state of suspense which may have been one of hope or diffidence.

"What's that?" said the Signora, suddenly vehement. "You don't care? Obviously, you can't care if you really are what you appear to be. How can you be interested in any change if everything is the same to you? I'll tell you what I think, anyhow. I like you in many ways, just as you are at this moment, without a trace of self-interest. It's because of your beautiful face . . . your beautiful voice. . . . Are you blushing? You certainly are blushing again. You wouldn't appeal to me if you didn't have this simplicity of heart which won't permit you to feel gratified by praise. But you mustn't think I want to seduce you. . . ."

She started to laugh in a submissive yet lamentably prolonged manner which differed from all the other laughs of the evening. Did it make her sound more like an old woman? Less like a lady? Or perhaps just the reverse: less like an old crone and more like a lady?

"Not that I never seduced anyone, mind you. I did seduce many! I really seduced them! I was quite an attractive girl, if I say so myself, both in my military uniform and in a simple skirt. I was a great temptress before I married and then again when I was widowed. You should have seen me at the turn of the century; what a whore I was. . . ."

"Whatever are you saying?" the *Bersagliere* exclaimed.

She went on talking, her voice quavering in the rush of her laughter. "Whatever am I saying? All the traveling men from your villages whispered it. All my lovers and all the others as well, those who only lusted after me; they all said it. What a hot whore she must be! And I was proud of it, I must confess, because I always knew what they call a real woman here in

Sicily. Elsewhere too. A real woman is a whore so long as she likes to go to bed. Isn't that being a whore?"

The soldier admitted timidly that it could be so.

"You see? You see? If a woman so much as shows, even a little—from the way she is made, say—that she *could* like it, then she's a whore. . . ."

The *Bersagliere* admitted yet did not admit it. Actually, she could seem to be one without having been; or be one, without seeming to be.

"What do you know about it?" the Signora muttered. "You can't possibly know anything about it with that blushing face of yours. . . . I know of some husbands who call their wives whores because they find them hot in bed. Shouldn't I be proud of being called a whore?"

"You weren't a paid prostitute," the *Bersagliere* interrupted. "You have no sons by men you don't even know. . . ."

"But I did like men! And I didn't confine myself to devouring them with my eyes from behind a shutter. Oh, no! I wanted to be a woman no matter what they called me. I took part in the war, crossed Italy on horseback, and filled a page in history all to myself by following my husband. I devoured the men with all of me, not just with my eyes—quite a few of them even before my widowhood. After I became a widow, one after the other, one after the other . . . Never heard of a woman like me? Well, you're young, let alone innocent, and Sicily is full of so-called whores who never leave the house. Have you heard of them? They have filthy minds, if you ask me; even go in for family affairs; they're worthless trash. Now you take me, I wanted to be worth something, dear Innocenzo, with the grace of God I had in my body! You should have seen the breasts I had until a few years ago! Are you raising your hands to heaven? You may well raise them. It was really a sight to raise your hands about; why, people would run and point me out to others. . . !"

[19]

Once in a while, the soldier would try to interrupt her:

"My mother, on the other hand—" but the Signora would not give him a chance to finish.

"You want to remind me that I could be your mother? I don't forget it, don't you worry. A woman like me may have done everything possible under the sun and still not have lost her pride. I never stayed with a man whose level I wasn't up to."

"My mother, on the other hand . . ."

"Your mother again! As soon as I knew I was old, I refused to go on. . . . Some attractions I still had; perhaps for a few years more; but I broke off my last love affairs right in the middle. In love I never wanted to be above them, but not beneath them either, if you know what I mean."

"My mother—"

"I've had enough of your mother!" And then she sighed. "Well, I buried the whole business, and now I'm alone; nothing more can happen to me in this world in which nothing ever happens anyway. . . ."

"Now, my mother . . ." the *Bersagliere* finally broke in.

"What's your mother got to do with it, in the devil's name? Your mother, your mother . . . are you trying to tell me that your mother was a saint?"

"No, ma'am."

"All you sons want to say your mothers were saints; even my own child, the one who's married to the baron. Little hypocrite! And even Ruggero, although the compliment's more justified in his case, given the little he knows about it. Doesn't it ever occur to you children that a mother may not take it as a compliment?"

"That isn't what I wanted to say."

"What then? You could even say it, for all of me. . . ."

"The fact is that my mother was more of a whore than that," said the *Bersagliere*.

"More . . . than that?"

The *Bersagliere* said that his mother was a real one. Not only had she given birth to him without any husband but she had abandoned him, turning him over to the convent by placing him on the wheel the nuns used for receiving packages.

"You never left a child of yours 'on the wheel,'" he said. "You have no children who are the sons of *things*. Yet that's just what you could call me, a son of a *thing*."

[20]

He said this with his usual good humor, in order to explain, not to recriminate. He wanted to say it because it was the truth.

Meanwhile, neither the old woman nor the *Bersagliere* realized that the train had stopped and started again. They were traveling, this much they knew. And they knew they were running through a world of vineyards, with the sea no longer so close as before. This much they must have known from the night itself.

They must have felt through the night the presence of tender hills covered by leaves upon leaves upon leaves. And further on, they would feel the hills turn moldy, then parched, reeking of malaria, stretched out there consumed by malaria, right up to the station at Dirillo, with its long, narrow slopes like the tombs of those whom malaria has killed.

The soldier, who had begun to yawn, was talking about the family by whom he had been adopted, his adopted father, mother, sisters, and brothers. He yawned as he talked on.

The Manina family?

Yes, the Maninas.

The Maninas from the Barconi district, the big-boat district near the beach?

His voice smothered by weariness, he was saying that all the Manina males were adopted like himself, boys left on the convent wheel, and all the girls were legitimate.

The soldier kept on talking and yawning, talking and nodding. People had come in and sat down in the rear half of their double compartment but the *Bersagliere* went on yawning and talking and it was the old woman who first became aware that the two trainmen were back there for the third time. She must have heard them some time earlier, for one of them kept clearing his throat. Still, she kept her soldier talking, asking him why he had joined the infantry to do his military service and not the navy. He explained sleepily that with the army he would be through a year and a half sooner than with the navy, and that old Manina would not have liked to do without his share of the work for an extra year and a half. She kept him talking whether he was yawning or not, nodding with sleep or not, and despite the presence of the two trainmen back there she told him something about herself, told him about what she called her own page in history.

She said that it had all begun when she ran away from boarding school, a flight that became the subject of a patriotic song. That was the period when rumors were rife that Garibaldi's *Mille*—his thousand courageous volunteers—were about to embark to liberate Rome, just as they had done in 1860 for the Two Sicilies. And she, Leonilde, had filled her page in history by searching for the *Mille* in Genoa, in Livorno, then in Palermo and Naples, until finally Garibaldi was ashamed of being sought out by a little girl who wanted him to do what he had always wanted and never yet accomplished.

Leonilde was Milanese. She spelled it out for the benefit of the two trainmen seated behind her: "Mi-la-ne-se"—from Milan. Eleven hundred miles away.

And her family had found her and taken her back to Milan after Garibaldi no longer wished to feel ashamed and preferred to do the deed for which Leonilde had sought him out. That was how she had filled her page in history, by encouraging Garibaldi to liberate Rome.

She said it, paying out the syllables one by one as she had when she told him she was from Milan. But once more she stopped to listen to the two back there, and she went on to say that she had further distinguished herself during the expedition that finished at Mentana, speaking as if Mentana had taken place in 1869, and repeating and repeating, and saying that she had disguised herself as a boy in order to be able to join up, that she had been first a private, then had been recognized as the Leonilde who had given her name to the patriotic song, that she had fought as a lieutenant, and had been discharged a captain.

Once her page in history had been opened, it did not close. All Garibaldi's expeditions—from Mentana to Aspromonte and Calatafimi—were jammed in between 1869 and '70. She spoke of them, addressing herself to the two who were still seated back there. She called out periodically, "Do you understand, you two?" Gradually it became obvious that she was addressing herself more to them than to the *Bersagliere*. She leaped to her feet at a certain point in order to offer them, swallowed up as they were in the shadow of the unlighted car, the supreme revelation that her page in history was not confined by national boundaries. Its scope was European, not merely Italian, and it was in France too that she had shone, on soil that was not monarchic, not under Bourbon domination. There she had fought side by side with the volunteers from the Vosges and the Garibaldi legionnaires from Dijon. Yet— and at this she turned back to the *Bersagliere*—she could be considered an historic figure more on the lines of Lucretia, Brutus' wife, than on those of Camilla, the warrior maid.

And she went on to say that it was above all as a wife that she had filled her page in history, that she had filled it by her wifely obedience when she followed her husband into exile among the—the Carthaginians of Terranova. Two years after the end of the Franco-Prussian War, he had wanted to retire, like Garibaldi, to his own equivalent of Caprera. Many men who had been among Garibaldi's intimates had wanted to do the same. Some found their Caprera by retiring to a villa in Venetia, some found it on a farm in Tuscany, some, by returning to the provincial cities of their birth. He had chosen to look for his in Terranova in Sicily, which he had never seen before. "Are you following me?" she rapped out. And she, Leonilde, had taken it "like an ancient Roman," who considered it her supreme duty to remain united to her spouse even in exile. Thus she had filled her page in history by supporting, at twenty, the decision of her husband of forty-nine, who may, yes, have found the repose he was seeking but in a place where Leonilde—especially after her French sojourn—had found only self-sacrifice.

[21]

Paris, Milan, Terranova . . . The war on horseback, and now only this sulky night train. The times of great events had flown by; all that could "fly by" now were these old tumble-down hovels called stations, like Dirillo. . . .

The old woman wanted to ask if they had already passed it. Whom should she ask? Those two back there?

The *Bersagliere?*

The soldier was asleep.

"Don't you know it's dangerous to sleep in malarial country?" she roused him. She had him get up and close the windows. "Never breathe the night air where there's malaria." And he might still be exposed to it for hours: after all, there were those two back there certainly plotting to have him get off the train at Dirillo. Then brusquely she asked him if he had slept well, if Leonilde had lulled him well with the rocking of her song.

"What song?" the *Bersagliere* exclaimed.

"My page in history, oaf!"

"Oh, I listened to all that—"

"You did not!" she screamed. "Watch out, soldier; I don't like to be cheated."

"But I did listen to it."

"Let's see, then: where was I born?"

"In Milan, ma'am."

"Did I mention what year it was that I filled a page in history?"

"You mean eighteen sixty-nine?"

"Of course. Eighteen sixty-nine. Now tell me, *how* did I make history?"

"In the Mentana and Calatafimi campaigns."

"You mean, first with my escape from school. But really, how did I fill my page in history?"

"You made Garibaldi feel ashamed of himself."

"I made history as a wife who followed her husband into

exile," the old woman exclaimed. "It's so simple! And I hope you won't tell me we went into exile in Paris."

The *Bersagliere* did not have to tell her anything about Paris or anything else just then, for people had arrived in time to cut off any further reply. Don Carlos growled.

"You back again?" the Signora said.

The cringing Enrico was once more trying to talk to her with his fading voice and his hands that resembled those of a corpse.

"What d'you want now?" she asked him. "I don't wish to give offense . . . but I never feel glad to return here, that's all. . . . And I don't like to see anyone until that state of mind has passed. . . ."

Don Enrico had no assignment to learn by rote, no questions of history to listen to and answer. He could wash his hands of the whole thing, yet he kept on fluttering his ghostly hands, excusing himself and blaming others. He stopped to answer Don Carlos' growl with something like a growl, then went back to excusing and blaming, pointing over his shoulder, and finally, turning to indicate others behind him, he brought out the name Prospero, and then another name, Filippo.

The voice of a young man said that many of them wanted to pay their respects to her before she reached her destination. "Well! Well!" she said. He went on talking and she said that it didn't matter; he kept it up and she said there was no reason to go out of their way, and he talked on and she repeated that she had meant no offense. And so it went until three or four of them were trying to make themselves heard over Don Carlos' growls and the old woman's comments, and they said at last that they were all planning to go to Butera from Genisi for the hunting.

The old woman shook her head when she heard him mention the hunt. They were always special in Sicily! In June the animals were always in heat, so no hunting in June. . . . But the Sicilians, always special, hunted anyway, the improvident fools, the dilettantes. . . . However, why should she bother her head about it? She didn't have to pay the piper. It was clear that she did not intend to be drawn into a discussion of the subject.

But then the men said they hunted only the birds that were using the flyways northward, birds of passage, in short no native strain, and above all no game. They were gentlemen. They knew enough not to fire unless there were quarry in season. That was why they were not stopping over at Genisi. They were leaving. And their only reason for going to all that trouble was that there were no migrating birds winging their way over Genisi. That was exactly why they were going to move on to Butera, to see if the big flights north had begun. The heavy influx was usually toward mid-June. The skies were black with birds heading north. And they wanted to look over the lay of the land to see which hilltops were best as cover.

"Yes, yes," the old woman was saying to each in turn as he added his word. "Yes, yes. Yes, yes." She spoke to them as to a bunch of children she was in a hurry to dismiss. She did not want to become involved. Still, at a certain point, she said that the flyways over Butera were not necessarily any more infallible than those over Genisi and that if she had been they, she would have gone to Piazza Armerina.

"Well, then, let's go there," the gentlemen said. "Come along with us," they said. And they even called her *Zia** in the local fashion. Enrico kept on gesticulating with his corpse-like hands, like a priest celebrating mass, and the names began to spill forth again, Prospero, then Filippo, then Michele, but the old woman said she had too many things to do to think of leaving Terranova and her own property just then.

"I'm not a lady of leisure, you know," she said. She grew more interested, though, and after protesting once more that she went hunting only at the right season and not at any old time of year like a savage, she started asking about guns, cartridges, hunting dogs, and which boys of the district would be used as beaters to start the birds. Were there good beaters at Butera? What about Genisi? Sharp eyes were needed for such a job. Still, she had her orderly, who could act as beater if she went hunting.

---

*Aunt.

She pointed her finger at the *Bersagliere* as she said this, and she added that his eye was infallible where such things were concerned. "That's true, isn't it?" He could see clearly even looking into the sun, she said, and he could sight a flight ten miles away.

The *Bersagliere* did not say a word about whether it was true or not. Instead he leaped to his feet. On the skyline he had seen where the stars began to be transformed, first one, then another, then a third, into quivering red lights as they steadied, then grouped on the summit of a distant hill. He lowered the glass in the compartment door. It must be Terranova.

"What are you saying?" she exclaimed. "It's impossible." They still had to stop at the Dirillo station. How could they see the lights of Terranova before they had stopped at Dirillo?

But she too saw the moving thread of lights far away in the night, stretched between earth and sky. And she rose to her feet as the gentlemen sought to kiss her hands. Once more they invited her to join the hunt at Butera or, if she preferred, at Piazza Armerina. Leonilde was furious with the trainmen, who had not forewarned her. "Quick, hurry, the small suitcase must come down; now the sack up, up here, the hamper, quick, out of that corner." All this while she was turning and twisting, trying to put Don Carlos on the leash. Everyone was helping her and joking about the amount of luggage.

"Don't bother, please, my orderly is here. Innocenzo, Innocenzo!" As the train slowed, the flash of a street lamp lighted a yellow wall. There lay the whitish reflection of a sidewalk, running before the already opened compartment door. The railway men jumped down and the wheels screeched under the pressure of the brakes.

"Good-bye, good-bye. . . ," "See you at the Butera hunt. . . ," The old lady tapped one of the gentlemen's arms to greet them all, as the soldier, about to take his leave, stood thanking her from the sidewalk.

"But I told you we have the carriage!"

Leonilde was standing on the step and looked for all the world like the statue of a saint, carried out of some church with all her shawls and necklaces about her. She even had flowers.

"May I help you?" asked the *Bersagliere*, as the railway men eased her down. Leonilde, standing there with her dog as big as a horse and the four pieces of luggage scattered about her, was still berating the two railway men because they had asked the soldier to pay a difference on his ticket. Finally she laughed at the nasty look they gave him as they jumped back into the open compartment of the already moving train.

The gentlemen were bowing and bowing, leaning far out of the compartment windows as the train passed. Then came the last cars, the baggage van with its red taillights, and the fading rumble as it disappeared. Only a little wind and some straw stirred by the train's passing were left behind. Terranova . . .

Part IV

[22]

THE ROOFS AND WALLS OF THE TOWN OF GELA, CALLED TERRA-nova for centuries, cover about two miles. The long plateau, elevated some hundred and fifty feet between the plain and the shore, divides the fertile tract of the one from the arid length of the other. This long plateau is a rock formation containing an admixture of both of its flanking elements: on the one side it is richly verdant where it faces the hills, on the other, the sea side, its soil is dry and sandy.

Desert is that sea, like Africa to which it leads; desert too the deep shore for twenty miles, plus another twenty on the other side. Desert, the interminable retaining wall that stretches for more than twenty miles from Terranova to Licata and for another twenty roadless miles, to the east, west, and north, with its tilled but empty plain, its undulating arid land, its land formless with malaria, dunes white with malaria, and the white valleys of the nearby hills.

Any traveler who ascends toward the village at night must

notice this phenomenon just as, later, he will become acquainted with the song of the wheelwright; whether you are coming or going, it runs through the Mazzarino road. Even if he remembers cities he has seen there—in days of winter light —crowning the hilltops at intervals some thirty miles apart with their wrinkled precipices all around their sides and their houses piled on top, the traveler knows that Gela rises like the ancient capitals of the first human races, the Chaldean city of Ur or the Hebrew city of Hebron. Those too were surrounded by cultivated fields and by their harvests; they had their steep pasture lands whence the closely kept, compact herds came down for the Monday fair. And on their far side they had the limitless circle—symbol of a world just born from God's hand —fluctuating vaguely between water and rock, united, empty, covered by thorn bushes with small white snail shells attached to them, and snake nests hidden under the stones among their roots.

This unfinished band of earth, called Dirillo and Ponte Dirillo from east to northeast, known as Uomo Morto to the north and as Serra Gibliscemi still farther north, called also Manfria and Mongiova, not forgetting Suor Marchesa and Serra dei Drasi, and known in its entirety as the Land of Buterese—unwound, extricated from the malarial slime—faces the seashore and at night forms with it an immensity of darkness on which the quivering lantern of a wheelbarrow gives the impression of armies of enemies or ghosts advancing for a last reckoning, until the traveler hears the creaking of the barrow's wheels.

[23]

Either the place in itself or some kind of memory of it seemed to please the old woman, for her happiness was clear on her face. The fact of finally having arrived made the *Bersagliere* happy, and this was just as obvious on his face.

The Signora's eyes were smiling at the dry scent brought in by the night where, here and there, the crops of the present season and the hay of the previous year were stacked together. The soldier's eyes were smiling too, round at the thought of three whole days without chores. He pictured a fountain, then saw himself among the dunes with the big boats pulled up on the sand, and he lying under the stern, under the smell of tar of the beached hulls, and farther down along the dunes near the mouth of the Gela River, near the Doric temple, there among the dunes and the bamboo of Betalem.

Their eyes met in secret communication as they silently congratulated each other on having arrived; then the soldier gathered up the luggage.

"What are you doing?"

"I'm taking them to your carriage. . . ."

The sidewalk was deserted under a breath of wind which flicked up the scattered straw. The feeble light coming from a street lamp and reflected on the yellow wall was like an ember.

"What about a porter . . . or a guard?"

"But what do you want them for, ma'am, when you have your own personal attendant?"

"We can make it in two trips."

But the soldier wanted to carry all four suitcases at once while Don Carlos dragged at the old woman, suddenly blocking her way in an impulse to smell the foot of a wall.

"And I was the one who didn't want to carry even a lunch box . . ." the *Bersagliere* kept on repeating as he hinted jokingly at the possibility that the lady had no carriage.

"Perhaps I'll have an automobile. An automobile would be even more appropriate than a carriage for a modern Puss in Boots, wouldn't it. And so perhaps they'll send a car."

By now they had passed the iron exit gate, still open for night passengers, and found themselves on the sidewalk, which was as feebly illuminated by its street light.

"As you see, there's nobody here."

"Lionheart is asleep on the box, I'm sure. Lionheart, Lionheart!" she called; then to the soldier: "Just be calm; he's bound to be asleep around here somewhere in the dark."

The *Bersagliere* searched the darkness, almost sniffed at it.

"Lionheart!" repeated the Signora.

"Be quiet, please," the *Bersagliere* put in, but in the sudden silence that followed, no sound was audible except that made by some straws which, pushed by the wind's fingers, were skipping about on the dusty piazza.

"Nobody here," said the soldier. There should have been a smell that was not there. There should have been sounds, and there were none. "We would have seen the carriage lights by now!"

[24]

The soldier put down the blanket roll, the expansible valise, the large suitcase, sat down on the edge of the sidewalk with her duffel sack over his shoulder and hid his face in his hands.

"This is just like the baron, my son-in-law. I should have expected this kind of trick from him, the calculating, blood-sucking vampire. Never satisfied, never ready to call it quits. . . . I should have known that he wouldn't send the carriage to avoid tiring the horses in case I shouldn't arrive. My son-in-law is like that; he uses the barter system with his peasants and pays them only after he has sold all his corn and tomatoes; that way, he avoids his peasants' competition on the open market. Naturally, he doesn't send the carriage to meet me even though it's my own, and I paid him for the horses, and I pay Lionheart's salary. The baron pays for the forage out of his wife's dowry so it's quite logical for him not to let the horses out to work up more of an appetite just to meet an old woman who may or may not arrive. After all, she's still strong. A woman who used to be a soldier and a *Garibaldina* obviously can walk. Don't forget, Leonilde, you are strong and you can make it on foot; you can carry those suitcases just as you once carried a knapsack. . . ."

As she talked, she struggled with Don Carlos, who tugged her from one side to the other until she finally released him from the leash. The soldier saw the great piebald dog running to and fro over the whitish dust of the piazza. Don Carlos was visible in the dark; behind him was the black outline of a hovel and, farther up, the whitish dust of a road—but way up, like the beginning of the Milky Way, like the Milky Way itself.

"I should have guessed it. A man like that, with a face like a delinquent moron, a man who looks like all his delinquent moronic ancestors hung in a row in the hallway! A man who hasn't turned those crooked noses and distorted mouths to the wall. . . ."

As she talked, the old woman examined the five black doors facing the piazza and several times attempted to turn the knobs, shaking them and rapping on the panels. Then she went on to talk about her daughter, the weakling, who may have kept her telegram from her husband in order to avoid a scene; she even mentioned her grandchild, Leonilde, the naughty brat, who may have carried off the telegram secretly to put Grandmother to all this trouble.

Meanwhile she continued to knock at each of the five doors, shouting loudly:

"Hey, stationmaster!"

"What do you want to do?"

"I want to leave the luggage with him."

"Do you think he can hear you? And will he come down to open the door even if he does?" The soldier, seated on the sidewalk surrounded by the suitcases and with her sack over his shoulder, shook his head.

"Why shouldn't he get up?" she exclaimed. Just the same, she left off calling at the top of her lungs and looked toward the end of the dusty piazza at the huddled dark mass of the houses where the Milky Way began, which marked the rise from the town. "But wait, wait, I have an idea . . ." and she flew across the piazza saying that somebody must have a handcart or pack mule.

"You think they'll wake up at this hour, much less get up?" the *Bersagliere* called after her.

[25]

The soldier heard her knocking and shouting, then talking with someone for a few minutes, growing angry, grumbling, and returning.

"Now what?" he asked, raising and hefting the large suit-case.

"I'll carry this one . . ." the old girl said as she took up the expansible valise. They started to cross the piazza, its dust and straw swirling around their feet, and they moved on toward the upward slope, which by now was turning as white as the real Milky Way; their goal was the row of five or six street lights that marked the far edge of town up there on top.

"A regular Puss in Boots . . ." the *Bersagliere* half groaned, "with a carriage . . . and maybe a car. . . ."

He dropped the phrases one after the other with gaps of silence between like the sound his steps made on the rock, the dust, the straw, and again on rock.

"What do you mean?"

"Nothing, nothing!"

"You said something, I heard you. . . . You don't believe I have a carriage?"

"I don't believe we're riding in one, that's all. . . ."

The old woman swore that the following day her carriage, with Lionheart in his gala livery, would come call at his door. She would put it at his disposal for his three days' leave and he would come to dinner every night; besides, he could have her husband's best suit and all of his underwear.

"It's better for you not to talk while you're climbing; you'll have no breath left."

On their right the road was flanked by a black abyss from which, every so often, a tiled roof emerged. The old woman seemed to be counting those heaps of tile as she struggled along. She was silent for the moment and her breathing was labored. She looked once more at the roofs, stopped, and suddenly moved toward a mound of tile and stone in which a door was vaguely discernible; she began to shout at the poor sleeping inmates while the *Bersagliere* continued his ascent. He heard her far behind him calling at each hovel door, and decided to stop and wait for her; he put the suitcases down on the walk and sat on them to rest.

The rustling of the skipping straw was gone and the Signora's voice came to him between breaks of silence.

"Hey, good people, hey, Christian souls . . ." Nobody answered but the dog howling from somewhere, then he suddenly reappeared and came galloping toward the *Bersagliere* on ghostly paws.

"Grrr," said the soldier. "Grrr," Don Carlos answered, and he continued his phantom gallop toward his mistress' voice.

The old girl had started to throw pebbles at the hovels as she went on calling intermittently, "Hey, good people, hey, Christians . . ." She was afraid of going down into the black ditches by the roadside and so flung pebbles instead of using her hands—or a foot—to knock on the doors. Finally a woman answered her from behind a tight-shut window.

[26]

"What do you want?"

"A porter, a handcart, or a mule."

"My husband has the mule with him and he won't be back from town until tomorrow evening. He went to Mirabella and Mazzarino. . . ."

"Well, you can at least store my luggage for me even if your husband has gone to Mazzarino, can't you?"

"I don't open the door at night when my husband's away in town."

"I won't eat you; I'm an old woman."

"My husband will kill me if he finds out that I open the door to anyone when he isn't here."

"Your husband will kill you if you open the door to a man, not to a woman. I tell you, I'm an old woman."

"But I'm a young bride, Signora."

"But I'm a woman, dear girl, just like you."

"My husband will never believe you're a woman. Don't tempt me, Signora. There's nothing I can do about it."

"If I were a man you'd do it all right. Who knows, perhaps you already have a man in your bed, someone who knocked before I did."

"What kind of manners do you call that? Do you wake people up in the middle of the night to insult them?"

"Everybody knows you're a whore; everybody knows when your husband's gone to town you open the door to any man who happens to knock. I'll tell your husband that you refused to open the door to me only because I didn't talk in a man's voice."

"You'll ruin me! And you said you are Signora Leonilde? A lady never calls a young bride a whore; you're no lady; you're the devil disguised as a lady. Father, Son, and Holy Ghost! What can this devil want of me?"

At this turn of affairs, the old woman changed her tune.

"If you open the door, I'll say nothing to your husband and show you a beautiful thing."

"Please don't tempt me."

"I have a beautiful soldier with me."

"Oh, please, please, don't tempt me."

"A handsome *Bersagliere*, my girl."

"Don't tempt me."

"Well, perhaps the man in your bed doesn't want it, eh?"

"Go away, demon! Go away!"

[27]

The *Bersagliere* had not been able to make out a word of all this. He only heard the old girl talking to someone, and he certainly hoped that she might come up with a mule or, failing that, that they could leave the luggage in someone's house overnight.

After all, he must have thought to himself, she's a fine, thoughtful person. It was on his account that she was going to all this trouble. But though he strained to listen, he did not hear a door open and in time the figure of the old woman came into view, black on the whitish road, bowed under the weight of the single suitcase which she shifted constantly from right to left, from left to right. The *Bersagliere* was still waiting for her.

"It was in the cards," he said.

The Signora, breathing heavily, uttered not a word, and for a long while they continued their climb toward the row of six lights not too far away now, toward the emerging outlines of houses with their black windows and doors. . . .

"You said your house is at the Capuchins?"

She hesitated but finally answered, "Yes. My daughter lives near the Capuchins."

"The long and the short of it is that that's where we have to go," he muttered, then sighed again that it was in the cards. They had reached the last stretch of the slope, where the road turns slightly and where, on the side of the rise, there is a sort of platform of beaten earth—of mud and ditch water when it has been raining, dust and straw leavings when it is dry—with a scale in it to weigh vehicles. They reached the first street light, haloed by a dusty glow which served to outline the vast shadows around it.

"Yes, it was in the cards all right," the *Bersagliere* repeated, and they looked each other straight in the face in the wan light, and as they looked they exchanged a wry grin.

"At least from now on we'll be walking on level ground, but I certainly . . . had quite an idea . . . when I decided I'd not carry a thing, not so much as a single parcel, not even a box lunch. It's all really funny"—he laughed—"to think I'd wanted to be able . . . to walk uphill, hands in my pockets!"

The old woman did not protest nor did she try to interrupt or try to alter the tenor of the soldier's lament. She walked beside him in silence. Let him add that it was time he got over the idea he was so damned lucky, got over the idea he was different from the others, got over the idea that he'd been well-advised to try what he had tried; let him say that she would stop trying what *she* had tried too, trying to get someone's attention at almost every house they'd passed. Perhaps after all it suited her better not to be without her things till morning. Otherwise, who knows, she might have run into someone more willing than the night watchman, or the cripple in the square. Yet, who knows, would she have found someone as willing as her good orderly, the *Bersagliere?*

She let him ramble on and laughed with him when he laughed. She had dropped behind a bit and now followed him, listened to him; then, suddenly, she whistled and called Don Carlos to her; the great dog appeared from one of the pitch-black side streets, the only living thing they had encountered uphill on their way to the main square and on the main road of the sleeping town.

Now it was the *Bersagliere's* turn to be silent. His step had resounded six or seven times before the old girl started to talk in turn, saying things in an undertone.

It was not true that he had not been well-advised, she said.

It was unkind on his part for him to say that his decision had been ill-advised; hadn't he met someone who could do a great deal for him?

From the very next day, he would be able to gauge how much she could do for him, and she repeated the promise about the carriage, with Lionheart in his gala livery on the box.

She repeated the invitation to dinner, and the suggestion of a dance. She added that there was a beautiful girl he would meet at the ball (it had now become a ball), a girl so lovely that he would be happy just looking at her, but that he would be allowed to do more: talk to her, pour out her wine, offer her bread.

Here he was, she said, lucky indeed to be walking beside, or almost beside, a person who held the warp and woof of his good fortune tight in her hands.

[28]

The tolling of a bell, whose tone fell suddenly, reverberating against the paving stones, reminded them both of the task they had in common, but it frightened Don Carlos, who ran out of one of the alleys. They looked back at the dark town, whose bronze throat had given voice. Was it one o'clock or did the sound mark a quarter after an unpredictable hour?

The town too had something that was indefinable. There were wide-open doors, dark wells of emptiness, wide-open windows, wells of emptiness too; and there were other doors and windows closed as if they had been blacked out for centuries upon centuries in a far distant age, before the flood.

The walls were covered with cracked dust and the northwest wind, blowing full strength, raised a yellowish clay of grit from the façades; even the houses with some sort of attempt at a style appeared shapeless, with their outlines frayed, their corners rounded, and their cornices nibbled away.

The town might have witnessed the coming of Abraham, the pilgrimage of the Three Kings, Roland's passage on his way to Roncesvalles, and Garibaldi's passing. . . . The soldier and the old woman were somehow reconciled. They stopped and decided to rest.

Trying to help the soldier free himself from the sack, the old woman realized for the first time that he was covered with sweat.

"But you're soaked, completely soaked! Don't take your jacket off; it's windy."

But the *Bersagliere* sat on the heap of luggage and took off his jacket; then he started to wipe the sweat from his chest by passing his handkerchief inside his shirt. The old woman said, "That isn't very good manners, I must say!" whereupon he hurried to put his soaked uniform back on. With little protestations and cries of alarm, the old girl made it clear that putting on a wet garment, all weighted down with dampness, was worst of all, and she kept it up, urging him to take his jacket off again. She too was wringing wet from the long effort and they sat there on the heap of luggage side by side, he saying that at home, near the shore, he was used to doing things differently, and that was a fact, he said; she saying at the same time that in wartime things had never been like this. First he would half listen, then talk at the same time; then she would half listen and break into her litany. Finally she pulled out a gold-colored cigarette case.

"Do you smoke?"

"Sometimes."

The old woman said that her preferred vice would have been taking snuff except that she didn't like to reek of tobacco; instead she limited herself to an occasional half cigar.

"Do you smoke cigars?"

"Oh, I have cigarettes too."

The *Bersagliere* took a cigarette and the old girl didn't have the strength to search for a half cigar in her things so she took a cigarette too. They lighted up and sat smoking, talking and smoking in the dark night on the main square seated on her pile of luggage.

"Certainly, I could never be a porter," he observed, laughing at his own sweat, at his fatigue, whereas she was still fresh and dry.

"Do you mean to say that I could be a good porter?"

"I mean to say that I am good at loading sand or pulling boats down to the shore, but that you would beat me at going to and from the station and the town."

"So I could stay down at the station and be a good porter?"

"You certainly could, if you weren't a woman and a lady."

They whistled for Don Carlos, who had once more got lost in the alleys, and started to walk again, the *Bersagliere* laden as he had been before, the old woman with her small suitcase, and they moved together from the darkness of the square into the sandy light of the main crossing.

[29]

They passed the massive building of the Mother Church with its sandy flights of steps, its gravelly columns, its sand from architrave to architrave amid channels of shadows up to where the pigeons and the bronzes that sounded the hours were fast asleep.

The right-angled roads to left and right appeared as a row of fires suspended in midair; on the right, toward the Capuchins, the fires faded to dwindling embers and the last points of light mingled with the stars at Capo Soprano. The old woman herself was stunned to see how far away it looked.

"But we aren't going to Capo Soprano; we're going to the Capuchins," said the *Bersagliere*, looking at the dusty, worn-out, rocky walls of the Municipal Building. Nearby, he felt in the darkness the presence of the invisible alley through which he could slip home in ten minutes.

"You could go directly from here and be home in ten minutes."

"Of course I could," but he didn't look into the alley; instead he counted the lights in front of him: one, two, three, four, five, six; one every two hundred yards. At the fourth light there was the public park, and at the sixth the Capuchins.

"Since I've got you this far . . ." he said.

The old woman started to look for a porter once more, a certain Leonardo, who was probably asleep behind an open door around the square somewhere, and she shouted, "Leonardo, Leonardo!" But nobody answered from the darkness; only Don Carlos reappeared.

"Don't waste any more time, ma'am. Leonardo is deaf and you couldn't wake him even if you kicked him. In order to find him, we'd have to search with a lantern behind each door on the square and in each niche of the Mother Church."

"Why not look for the night watchman then? Perhaps Galante knows where Leonardo is."

"We'll try to run into him . . ." but the *Bersagliere* wanted to get on with it, to walk fast, whereas the Signora, far to the rear, was trying to stop him, still looking for somebody.

As they passed the second light they suddenly heard a sound; thereupon the old woman dropped the suitcase and crossed the road, saying over and over, "This is where it came from, from up there. . . ."

"What do you think it could have been? Someone closing a door, going in or out. . . ."

"Doesn't this give you a ray of hope that someone may help us?" And she was off again, her short steps beating their tattoo, sure of finding help yet not knowing what kind of help she wanted.

"But how can anyone help us?" It could have been someone gone to call a midwife, or a midwife or doctor on the way home, he thought. "Signora . . ." he called. He got no answer, only a little scream. The Signora had once more disappeared.

The street lamps were separated by long stretches of dark night. The soldier stopped at the last light before the Public Gardens and waited for the old woman to reappear in one of the circles of light. Here and there, night was lifting a little and in the lessening gloom the two stone-faced, closed, unhearing and unheeding lines of houses could be seen.

"But Signora . . . Signora. . . ." he called, with no hope of
being heard, and he put down the suitcases once more and
sat on them as he waited for her to come back.

Part V

[30]

"SHE'S A REAL MADWOMAN!" HE SAID TO HIMSELF. "WHAT CAN
she be up to?"

And he said to himself he'd about decided to dump her
things there and go about his business. He reminded himself
that he certainly did not want to hang about with her until
dawn. He wanted to get a few hours' sleep this blessed night,
he told himself firmly. Furthermore, he wanted to get up early
in the morning of his first day on leave, he admonished himself
aloud.

"Ha, ha!" he heard someone reply.

Someone was chuckling up over his head, and the *Bersagliere* turned to see where the sound came from, and looked
up.

"She's a mad one, isn't she?" the voice went on.

It said, laughing, that perhaps calling her mad was going a
bit far; perhaps it would be more exact to say that she had a
screw loose.

"She has more energy than a town our size can cope with.
She does this, she does that, and she still has plenty left over.
That's why she's always getting the better of the rest of us.
What trick did she play on you?"

The *Bersagliere* kept searching for the source of the voice
from balcony to balcony, among the great arabesques of
shadow that the flowering wrought iron of the balustrade cast
against the façades of the houses. But nothing moved in all
that black foliage, nothing on the first floor above the street,
nothing on the second, nothing on the third, and the man
spoke with nearby sleepers in mind; he spoke so low that one
could not tell at what height he was standing.

"Well, I can see what she's done plain enough, after all," he went on. "There you are with her luggage! She always gets in at this time of day, or night rather, so that someone's got to tote them for her. And each time there's one more. And each time they get heavier. Doesn't it seem to you that they're heavier than they should be? She's quite capable of loading them with earth and stones. . . ."

The *Bersagliere* was not paying much attention to the meaning of the words. He was too busy trying to figure out the speaker's whereabouts. Yet at this point he thought he should intervene in some fashion or other on the old girl's behalf.

"After all, I offered to carry them," he said.

"Of course, you offered," the man continued. "Therein lies her cunning. . . . In inducing some—excuse me—poor bastard to put himself in a position that gives her a bit of amusement. And she doesn't do it out of meanness. It's because nothing happens in this world any more and one must help the time to pass somehow. . . . But if you offered your services with the idea you'd be rewarded, get it straight out of your head. She's the most tightfisted woman in the Two Italies and she'll never give you a lira. A lira? What am I talking about? Not a cent . . . not a red cent. . . ."

The *Bersagliere* protested.

"But I wouldn't have done it even for *ten* lire, if I'd been doing it for the money."

"So you did it out of courtesy, out of an impulse to succor the weaker sex, out of a spirit of compassion. . . . How perfectly she hit the mark! Would you have done it for a man disguised as a woman?"

"Now you're not going to try and tell me she's a man. . . ."

"How would I know? I'll go so far as to admit she's my cousin, or that she *became* my cousin, but as for anything else I could tell you, I don't even know if her mother was a dressmaker or a hairdresser. And she's quite capable of passing herself off as sixty, if it's to her advantage."

"You won't try to tell me she's twenty. . . ."

"Twenty, no, because as I remember she's been the bane of

our existence a bit longer than that. But anything is possible. In any case, however you may look at it, I'd refuse to carry four great pieces of luggage, even for a woman—a lady, if you wish—who's no longer young . . . luggage filled with stones at that."

This time the *Bersagliere* felt it was scarcely worth the effort to show his disbelief. By now it was plain as the nose on your face that the queer duck up there was making it up out of whole cloth! But he still couldn't get over not being able to see him, and he continued to look for him, throwing back his head and letting his eyes wander this way and that.

"I'm no ghost," the joker said. "I'm here, all right, I'm here."

The *Bersagliere's* eye was caught by something with a large shadow that seemed to be moving about on a first-floor balcony. What was it? He managed to distinguish the bulk of it from its shadow but he still could not be sure of what it was. It looked like the tail of a bird. "Here I am," the fellow continued, almost in a falsetto. And at last the *Bersagliere* saw the thing open and close, he saw that it was a fan, he saw the hand that held it, and he saw, farther back, the face of the man who had been talking to him.

It swung forward out of the shadows, with white teeth, a mustache, and thick eyebrows arched over two little, close-set eyes.

"Have you managed to locate me?" he said. "Now maybe you'll believe me. . . . I've never been a ghost. It's just that every night I like to chat a bit with the people who go by, provided they don't come from this hole-in-the-wall. Come again. It will always be a pleasure, and it will do something for you too. You'll learn, as we talk, as much as you would if you'd been to school with the Salesian brothers."

His tone indicated that the audience was over. To emphasize this impression, he had gotten up from the armchair or chaise longue on which he had been sitting and which he evidently kept on the balcony for his own convenience. And the *Bersagliere* saw through the thick, leafy shade that he was dressed in a garment he knew was called a Japanese dressing gown or kimono.

His mind went back to the old woman.

"Where the devil can she have gone?" he asked himself none too quietly.

The man on the balcony once more emitted his cackle of laughter.

"Where? You may well ask. Ha, ha! Didn't I tell you?"

The *Bersagliere* interrupted him because he thought he had heard something.

"Sssst! Quiet a moment . . . please . . ."

In fact, a kind of call could be heard. Did it come from the square? From farther away than the square? But the far-off bells of the Mother Church rang twice just then, and the man on the balcony insisted that must have been the sound.

"No, no . . ."

The *Bersagliere* wanted a chance to listen again. He heard whisperings more or less everywhere, stifled noises, as if from balconies and windows all along the Corso there were people spying on him as they whispered to one another. Then the voice that had sounded like a call was heard again, only stronger.

"It's up to you to get out of it . . ." the man picked up again.

"Please!" said the *Bersagliere*.

He heard the voice for the third time, stronger still, and strident.

"Whatever does she want?" he said.

"Ha, ha!" the man said.

The voice intoned its call the fourth time and now the words were plain:

"Are you talking to yourself?" they said.

[31]

The old woman had found someone.

"I've got Romeo here," the *Bersagliere* now heard, or thought he heard.

The man on the balcony bounced about in his flowered

dressing gown as if someone were tickling him. "Just listen to that, now!" he exclaimed. "She's unearthed Romeo."

The *Bersagliere* asked if Romeo was the beggar by the Church of San Rocco who moved about on his hands and the seat of his pants.

"The very one. The very one," the man on the balcony answered, and wriggled about some more.

"The one whose legs don't work?"

"That's the one."

The man was trying to repress a spasm of laughter, which he finally let out in a long, thin laugh. "That's the one," he repeated. The *Bersagliere* told him that as a child he had always been afraid of Romeo, and the man said once more, "The very one." Then the *Bersagliere* told him he had thought that one must be dead, but all the man said was, "That's the one."

"Can't you hear me?" The words penetrated the rush of sound that seemed to leap from one balcony to the next.

The *Bersagliere* gave no indication that he intended to answer. Instead he looked up, from one spot to another, at the dark façades and at those that received a little splash of light from the lamps strung along the street. The bulbs swung back and forth. A few wisps of straw moved on the ground beneath the nearest of the lights. There was a bit of breeze anyway.

But the man had jumped back and could no longer be seen or heard.

"God only knows what she wants," the *Bersagliere* said. "What's she calling me for? I can scarcely run back and forth with all these bags here. . . ."

"Ssst," the man on the balcony interrupted. "Speak low."

He reappeared above the shadows of the railing and, shielding his face with his fan, glanced to right and left at the buildings flanking his own. "After all, Gela was built of the stone from Dionysus' ear."

But he quickly regained his composure, took on all his former ease of manner, and repeated out loud, as if uttering a challenge, his dictum on the original sin of the city. He seemed amused by something his sharp hearing had managed to seize from a wrangle which had broken out a few seconds earlier and whose words had been deadened by the depths of the Corso.

"She's priceless," he commented. "Priceless, priceless. . . ."

Then, as if he considered himself blessed with perceptions which multiplied the effectiveness of his every faculty, he started to give the *Bersagliere* a play-by-play account of what he heard. "She's having a row with Romeo . . ." he informed him. "She wants him to rouse someone to take care of the luggage. . . . Or to carry it himself, just imagine. . . ." He spoke, then fell silent, spoke, then fell silent; listened and spoke and had a fresh burst of laughter, which he did his best to suppress behind his words and then behind his pauses. He seemed to find it irresistibly comic that the old woman sought "to draw even Romeo into her games," as he put it. But he said that there was little she could do about it: Romeo put no bridle on his tongue, and besides, he had seen she had a soldier in tow; he had seen them go by together; and she had him loaded down all right. What was she pestering him for if she had already collared a soldier?

"I know," the commentator went on, "that it's an ignorant prejudice to consider serving in the army as the lowest rank in the social scale. . . . But in these parts it's a prejudice they all hold. Even the porter, Leonardo, would consider it a kind of insult to be asked to carry luggage in place of a soldier. . . . That's why Romeo has got it in for you as well as for that old rogue. . . ."

"Got it in for me?" the *Bersagliere* exclaimed, incredulous and upset.

A recurrence of the distant squabble, which now sounded more like a hand-to-hand melee, had revived the murmur running from balcony to balcony like a sort of collective long-drawn-out whistle or sigh; and the man once more shushed the *Bersagliere*, this time stopping still himself right where he was, with a smile plastered like a slap across his face. His hand raised in a gesture which demanded continued silence, he cocked his head to follow for a good minute whatever was going on down there as well as the murmur which rose and fell every so often from the balconies; then he announced that a third character had come on stage.

It was Galante, he said, the night watchman so like a stone statue whose ghostlike tread stalked all murders, brawls, and breakings-and-enterings that took place in Gela without, however, his having prevented a single one of them. Just what was needed at night, he added: a statue gifted with omnipresence who could bestow the comfort of his company on whoever had been attacked yet who, at one and the same time, in no way inhibited the aggressor. He winked ever so meaningfully as he sang the statue's praises, then once more changed his tune abruptly—though how he could have heard anything in the heat of his own chatter was a mystery—to say that Galante had given a new dimension to the wandering inclinations of the old woman.

"Now we're in for it," he said. "Romeo has just reminded her that the seasonal invasion of the threshers began night before last. . . . They sleep in the square at Cappadocia behind the little house behind the Registry; there are a good three hundred of them, and *she's* asking for some reliable milksop to look after her luggage. . . . Yes, sir. . . . Going from here to Cappadocia would be like jumping from the frying pan into the fire with those three hundred sleeping thugs. . . . It might take from now till dawn but that's just what she's looking for, something to keep her busy, and I'll bet you my tomorrow's dinner that you'll soon have orders to wait for her here; she well knows all she'd get for her pains would be a laugh if she were to wake Giovinazzo to give a soldier a hand. . . . What'll you bet? I'll bet my beef-stew dinner. . . . Let's give her a moment to clear her throat and then we'll hear the trumpet blow: one—two—three—four . . ."

On the "four," in fact, the sounds of a voice could be heard calling "Don Carlos . . . Don Carlos!" It was clearly hers. Then she set to calling the *Bersagliere:* "Innocenzo, Fortunato, Innocenzo, Innocenzo, Innocenzo. . . ." A pause. "Can you hear me?" she went on yelling. "I'm just going over the hill for a moment. I'll be right back. . . . Now don't you move from where you are."

The man on the balcony was now up close to the railing. "You're surely not going to let yourself be led around by the nose all night, are you?" he asked the *Bersagliere.*

"Of course I don't want to waste the rest of the night waiting on her," the soldier answered.

"Well, you know what you've got to do if you don't. . . . You've said it yourself."

"What did I say?"

"That you'd put her things down and go on about your business."

The *Bersagliere* wearily inventoried the clutch of bags on which he was sitting. He asked, "Would you keep an eye on them for her?"

"I?" the man exclaimed. "I've never given a soul any cause to laugh at me: I'm a serious person. Besides, that's not stuff that takes looking after. If you come back this way at noon tomorrow you'll find it's all still here. Likely nothing but horseshoes in all four suitcases!"

The *Bersagliere* got up off the heap. "What are you talking about?"

He shook first one and then the other of the two suitcases, then lifted the big traveling case; last, he seemed to be weighing the rolled case with the plaid blanket inside it.

"I tell you what I'll do," he added. "I'll carry them to her house and leave them in front of the door for her."

"That'll be good for your health."

"Only trouble is, I don't know the number."

"Well, when you've reached the Calvary—"

"The Calvary?" the soldier exclaimed. "But the Calvary is in the other direction. The lady told me she lived near the Capuchins."

"If she lived near the Capuchins, she'd have sent you

toward the Calvary," he answered. "Do you follow me or not? It's because she lives east of town that she's sent you west."

[32]

The silver tinkle of women's laughter, quickly checked and all but stifled, raised louder murmurs and whispers from the balconies on either side. The man said precipitately that he must withdraw now, raised his clenched fist and shook it, muttering against something that prevented his taking a breath of air even at night, and after making a sign of greeting and farewell to the *Bersagliere*, disappeared.

The soldier, stock still, did not know what to do. He looked opposite, a bit up from the light hanging in the middle of the street, at the balconies from which the squeals of stifled laughter seemed to have come. They had roller shades of rushes, as well as the shadows of the black leafage. Most of them were pulled up high. Some, instead, were halfway down. One, which was directly in the path of the glare from the street lamp, had the blind dropped all the way so that it flapped out a bit from beneath the railing, and the *Bersagliere* centered all his attention on this one.

The fall of its tightly interwoven horizontal reeds seemed strangely like that tinkle of laughter. Then, too, the shade seemed alive with movement. The *Bersagliere*, not knowing what else to do, gathered his trappings as best he could and took them to the other side of the street just beneath this balcony.

"Do you want me to tell you what's up?" a voice began.

It came from the top-floor balcony, where a head now appeared and leaned downward.

"Leonilde is a rogue," it went on, "but that man is a worse one who tried to mix you up over there. Just go straight on toward the Capuchins. If she told you 'the palace,' it's because she lives there sometimes with her daughter; the first big building on this side just after you pass the convent. If,

instead, she'd told you 'the villa,' that's the place she goes
when she wants to be alone and weep for her dead husband,
and that's a bit on the other side, at Capo Soprano, but certainly not as far as the Calvary. . . ."

A murmur more or less of agreement seemed unleashed by
these words, running from balcony to balcony and even leap-
ing the adjacent dark patch to be picked up by those living
level with the next street lamp and across from the public
gardens.

"Niccodemo is so mean-minded in his resentment," the
voice now addressed the others, "that he'd really have had this
young man go to the other side of town to spite her. All
because he didn't get away with what he tried to pull off
with her. Am I right, Signora Eugenia? All because of the
iron he still has in his soul a good ten years after. . . ."

The voice of the one called Signora Eugenia now burst
forth from a nearby balcony as if the murmur, which had
become one of dissent, found its release there.

"Not right at all, Professor. You can't make a saint out of
Leonilde just because she turned a man down for once. Is it
to her credit that he didn't appeal to her? No thanks to her.
Niccodemo was a handsome man, into the bargain, and the
fact that she didn't know how to appreciate him is no credit
to her. And I don't think it's a feather in her cap that she
realized she might have to support him. Or has tightfistedness
become a virtue? From whatever point of view you wish to
look at it, no, I can't see where you're right."

"But the Professor," a third voice chimed in, "wasn't trying
to whitewash anyone. He was just trying to save the young
soldier a trip by not letting him go look for her where she
wasn't to be found. And he pointed out the malicious meanness of one who certainly has no more excuse for it than she."

It came from the balcony directly below the one from
which Signora Eugenia had let loose, and this voice was
weak, unaggressive in itself, almost spent, yet armed with
two shadows that climbed upward, the enormous silhouette
of two hands lifted toward the upper balcony as if to grasp
and shake it.

"For you won't tell me that Niccodemo is the more excusable because he lives over there, closing himself away in an entresol and agreeing to come out only in the hours when everyone else is asleep—all this with the aim of concealing what's going on between him and a certain lady who lives on the main floor. . . ."

The murmur from the adjacent balconies, visible and invisible, altered its tone depending on who was speaking. It had first been with, then against, the Professor. Then in complete agreement with Signora Eugenia. Then against the voice of the third person who had spoken. Now it agreed with the last words, and it was not slow to change as soon as a fourth voice made itself heard from a fourth balcony.

"Let's not stray from the subject," the new bell rang out. "I don't deny that what the lawyer has just said has an element of truth in it even if we have scant proof. But we are not talking about Niccodemo here. Here we are concerned with Leonilde. No question of the one who lives in the entresol, but of the one who lives up at Capo Soprano. It's she who has just arrived, she who ranges up and down the Corso, she who yells and storms about and sets the whole town by the ear. Aren't the suitcases hers? They are. So let's not talk about the wolf who's not there but about the wolf who is; thus the poor boy who's come within range of her fire may take timely warning. . . ."

[33]

The *Bersagliere* had a sort of road guide in those voices, in the talk passing from one to the other and from one balcony to the next. Fearing that his old girl might indeed live not in this part of the city at all but right on the other side, he sought continuous reassurance as to which direction he should follow. And the reassurance came from each new voice which led him along, a few yards at a time, toward the lights of the Public Gardens, which were now quite near; each move had him gathering up and depositing the luggage in a kind of relay.

A fifth voice, then a sixth, then a seventh and an eighth, a ninth, cut through the dark patch between the street lamps, running from balcony to balcony even where he could not tell if there were balconies, and each voice had terrible things to say about the old rascal yet each voice never managed to get them said. It seemed they were about to tell of murders, thefts, kidnaped children, and all they brought out was a phrase, perhaps, uttered on a certain occasion or in a certain fashion, which proved that she talked like neither a woman nor a lady. A phrase revealed her malevolence toward the archpriest, or lack of respect for the police lieutenant, or perhaps it was for the Bishop of Caltagirone, and so on and so on. Or perhaps she had done some task she should have left to her overseer or the keepers, instead of wandering around on muleback over her own land. . . . Then again, who had ever seen her embroider a stitch, or sew, or prepare a sweet or a rosolio, and instead who could not swear that she played *scopa* and went hunting? The *Bersagliere* laughed inwardly, recognizing in these comments the old woman he had met and as each one confirmed for the sixth, the seventh time, that at least she lived near the Capuchins in her daughter's palace when she was not in retirement at a villa she had up toward Capo Soprano, he kept on going.

Fantastic tales were attributed now to her openhandedness, now to her avarice, and, since these contradicted each other, he concluded that they canceled each other out. He heard it said that she was greedy, that she could outfast a camel; great wealth she had let her son-in-law, the baron, devour and, at the same time, she had devoured wealth from her baron son-in-law; hatred for her neighbor, pride, yet excessive familiarity, even intimacy with the last person she might have run into. This led him to believe that she was not lying to him when she had given him to understand that she was a woman of power, a real Puss in Boots, and the fact delighted him as he was indeed delighted to hear her called a regular trull, a first-rate old bawd.

What did they hope to accomplish by calling her such

names? A pity she wasn't on the spot to hear them and laugh with him about it. . . .

Of course there were things the soldier did not understand very well.

For example, what about the tenth voice's reference to "women of the wagon train," "camp followers," "women who —even today—manage to follow the regiment when maneuvers are scheduled," "the type who gives birth standing in the guardroom doorway while the trumpet shrills the leave call. . . ."

And what about the statements of the eleventh, according to which Leonilde must have been presented to Garibaldi at the time of her first communion? The General "as he grew old, liked 'em young" and "took his consolation prize from one after another of 'em for not having been made King of Italy in Vittorio Emanuele's stead." He had called the little girls *Garibaldinas*, hadn't he, just as she now called herself. . . .

The *Bersagliere* could understand well enough a person's being full of bile and he even understood that one might wish, or at least try, to inflame all the other denizens of the balconies with bile. But he could not assess how really offensive any of these statements might be, and it was only at the twelfth or thirteenth—when he heard himself called a "Maltese" and a "crazy Maltese"—that he began to realize it would be better to have been called a pig or an ass outright.

"Because, after all," he heard, "one should pay for one's own stupidity, and whoever manages to fall into a trap after all the warnings he's had from those who know what they're talking about has it coming to him. . . . He should pay through the nose. . . ."

"But I'm her orderly!" he protested.

From balcony to balcony on both sides of the street where it was dark and, farther along, facing the Public Gardens where it was light, a murmur arose in reply, a half-joking, half-indignant sound that grew as if the packed train with all its howling people had returned, drawing near, drawing in, to a

station. "Soldier . . . soldier. . . ." he heard over and over.
A new voice, the fourteenth or fifteenth, had already begun
its own version of "Now let's be reasonable." Yet the murmur
continued to rise with its refrain of "Soldier . . . soldier," to
right and left, near and far; and the *Bersagliere* (who might
well, at this point, have asked himself if he were not in a
strange city or if he were not a stranger in a city in which
he had lived until now with his head in the sand) had stopped
with the bags around him at that corner where the fence
surrounding the Public Gardens begins; his idea was to reply
in kind, as a soldier, as he had to the series of whistles
loosed against him in the Vittoria station; but just as he had
made up his mind to do this, he became aware that the
aggressive murmur was suddenly stilled, that it had ceased,
or rather that it had been canceled out and that the balcony
doors were closing their shutters one after the other.

[34]

"It must be the *Garibaldina* on her way back," the *Bersagliere* said to himself.

And he laughed instead of whistling, first of all out of contempt for those who ran for cover, and then because, hearing
the old girl call out, "Innocenzo, Innocenzo," and hearing her
tread, and Don Carlos thumping on ahead, he was glad that
she was like this and that he had guessed right.

But she was far from the winner this time.

"Nothing doing," she said.

Emerging from the dark with her hat in her hand and
strands of hair hanging lank on either side of her face, she
told him it was no laughing matter.

"I haven't a single one left."

"One what?"

"Not a single thresher, of course. . . . At first they wouldn't
stir, then some twenty or so followed me partway, and now
I'm just forced to depend on you again."

She plumped down on her luggage as soon as she had
drawn alongside. "Ouff!" she sighed, and took a moment to

catch her breath. Then she flapped open her fan to raise a bit of a breeze and clacked little strokes against the many chains and trinkets that adorned her breast.

"It's all that idiot's fault!" she added.

"What idiot?"

"That Romeo down at San Rocco. . . . He tells them I already *have* one soldier. And what a soldier! And what a soldier!"

"Shouldn't he have told them?"

"He said it as if he had been telling them I have a donkey. 'You got a soldier, Baroness? You got a soldier, *Garibaldina?*'"

"Well, if it's a question of *having* one, you've got one all right."

"Who tried to deny it? With that damned cock crowing and the whole bunch of 'em passing the word to each other, I couldn't get in so much as an explanation. 'She's got a soldier, so what use are *we* to the *Garibaldina?*' Just as if I'd asked them to carry the bags for a donkey. . . ."

The *Bersagliere* laughed. "Donkey or no donkey," he said, "I'm only too glad to finish what I've begun. . . ."

"You say that because you think we're nearly there," the old woman answered. "You say that because you think we're going to the Capuchins . . . because you wouldn't mind if I went to sleep under the roof of that baron son-in-law of mine on the very same night they refused to send the carriage to meet me. According to you, it would be perfectly all right for me to spend the night there, to knock on their door. You didn't even ask me if I had an alternative, some other house I could turn to. Let me tell you, I don't need to beg at anyone's door: I *have* another house, my dear, and that's where I'm going. . . ."

The old woman paused a moment to look him over and then finished what she had wanted to say, that she'd gone to look for another fellow to lend him a hand so that she could feel free to go where she damned well pleased.

"On the outskirts of Capo Soprano?" the *Bersagliere* asked, "or on the far side?"

The old woman looked him over once more and finally got

to her feet, saying that, at all costs, she had not wanted to have to impose on him again, but then she added, "Capo Soprano . . . midway." And she added, "Worse luck . . . too bad it's not on the far side . . . too bad it's not at Monte-lungo . . . too bad it's not at Manfria's tower," and she reiterated that, had it not been for her wish not to impose on him, she would have wanted to live far from the smoke of her son-in-law's chimney pots, in a part of the city out of his sight and thought!

"How many lights away is he?" the *Bersagliere* asked.

He had counted one more street lamp between him and the Capuchins and he walked, bags in hand, looking at the lights as they rose a bit before him, trying to count them from the Capuchins' on. He asked if it was the first after the Capuchins, or the second, or beyond the third.

"We'll see," the old girl answered.

She too was counting now, and she wanted to count the ones behind her, beginning with the farthest one she could see. But she could not decide if it was a first star or a last light and so reversed the count, beginning with the Capuchins.

In the distance, a dog started to bark. The old woman said, "That fool," and having broken her count, started all over again with the street lights, only to interrupt herself to snap out, "Perfect fool," or "What a numskull." Was it even Don Carlos barking? She snapped out that indeed it was Don Carlos, who had gotten to the palace. "He never barks," she explained, "except when he gets back home after a trip, and then he just sits and barks for a half hour at a stretch to inform the neighbors. At the palace, or the villa, or wherever home happens to be at the moment."

Now there were no more unbroken walls to flank the road, but dark masses of buildings of varying heights and degrees of formlessness, and the dog's voice singled out one of them repeatedly as if his bark had been a light flashing on and off. Although she went on saying "Ninny" and "Nincompoop," she seemed rather pleased. Her tone was increasingly lighthearted. "That's where it is," she said, her voice fairly bubbling. And she did not call Don Carlos to heel or whistle for him but

hurried her step like an old horse that still feels an occasional
spurt of youth, change of pace, an impulse to hear its own
bridle jingle and to feel its harness in place once more.

All the baubles she wore at neck and wrists rattled. "That's
where they live," she said. Her daughter, and that other Leonilde, who had made her a grandmother, her son-in-law, and
his eleven ancestors hanging on the walls of the main hall,
each with his nose out of joint. They'd all be hearing Don
Carlos now; they'd hear him bark and they'd know that she
had come back and been able to get as far as the palace, and
beyond. "That's where we're going," she added, "just beyond
the villa of those English people; see, up there, after the
second light; that is, the third—well, let's say between the
third and the fourth. . . ."

Part VI

[35]

AN HOUR LATER THE *Bersagliere* WAS RETRACING HIS STEPS
from one to another of those lights with the springing step of
one who—all things considered—had not had too rough a
day of it.

He said to himself, "It must be at the third street light!"

And he said to himself, "It must be between the third and
the fourth street lights."

But he said it laughing, and he ended up by believing—he
said to himself—that he was going to his own home now just
as he'd hoped. Wasn't he about to arrive without so much
as a lunch box? Hadn't he been right to leave without a
thing to load him down? Otherwise he'd have been walking
along now with packages in his hands. As for the chore he'd
just accomplished like a beast of burden, it was over and
done with. To make up for it, he'd traveled much more comfortably than if he had taken the other train. And that
wasn't all: he'd seen so much he would never forget, learned

so much, things that would be useful later on, so much he could tell others. . . .

He said all this to himself and much more, with Don Carlos' bark still ringing in his ears as if the villa itself, on its lonely ledge of rock and behind its iron grillwork, were barking after him from farther and farther away.

"What a character!" he said to himself.

The longer he walked, the more easily the sound of his footfall drowned out the bark of the dog. That was why he would stop every so often and say to himself, "What an old woman!" as if it were she barking after him in the night.

By the time he reached the Capuchins he was whistling. Now, he could have taken a short cut at this point but he chose to continue along the road lit by the street lamps, on the paving that, after all, he liked to feel under his feet. He whistled, then he broke off to say something to himself; he chuckled about it, then he began to chuckle again. "And what an old skinflint!" he said to himself. "True! I wouldn't have taken anything. All the same, she could have offered. . . ."

Laughing, he said to himself that she had probably thought she'd paid him off with the lees of the marsala and the cracker that smelled of camphor she had urged on him in her dining room where all the furniture was covered with dust sheets.

"What nerve she has though!" he said to himself. "How can she live in that lonely house without so much as a single maid? It's plain as the nose on your face, she'd sleep in her husband's tomb rather than give her son-in-law the satisfaction. . . . Think what Mama Manina would do if she were all alone in a big house like that! Why, she'd think the very doors—painted white like that—were ghosts."

Starting to whistle again, he found a strong, lively tune on his lips.

The air was fresh as if that point of daybreak had already come that wakes the animals—the donkeys waiting to be harnessed to the carts, the cocks in the courtyard, the host of rustling warblers in the trees—when he thought he heard "Hsst! Hsst!" He had gone from whistling to bellowing words. They came out in a warm, resonant voice in time to his step.

"Hey, there . . . blon . . . di . . . na, tea . . . sing Ga . . . ri
. . . bal . . . di . . . na . . ."

But just at that point he was sure he had heard "Hsst!"
and that it wasn't a bird he was hearing; all in all, he was
sure someone was trying to catch his attention. Could the
story of the balconies be beginning all over again?

He kept straight ahead, his song muzzled, and he heard
"Hsst!" behind him, above him, ahead of him.

People were trying to catch his attention from at least
three places at once. He kept on going beyond the point of
the third "Hsst!" but there was a fourth, then a fifth, and a
sixth. . . . He could not turn off the damned Corso until
beyond the Public Gardens. He hurried his step. But there
was still a stretch to go, and he could not keep on pretending
that nothing was happening when from every damned balcony
visible or invisible there came the shrill undertone of calling.

He stopped. "What do you want?"

One of the reed blinds on one of the balconies moved ever
so slightly. "Do you have to yell?" a barely audible voice
hissed at him.

"But you're all calling me!" the *Bersagliere* said.

"Just come on over here and talk to me. Don't pay any
attention to the others. Will you tell me something in strictest
confidence?"

"I'd always spit out anything that could be helpful."

"Sssh! Quiet down," and the voice behind the blind went
on in scarcely distinguishable tones.

"What?" the soldier asked.

The voice repeated a little louder the words it had already
uttered.

"What? What?"

The voice repeated for the third time, "What have you been
doing with the baroness all this time?"

[36]

The *Bersagliere* heard a twitter of laughter run from bal-

cony to balcony. He answered sharply, "With Signora Leonilde?"

"With her. With her," the voice said. Then, in a tone so
different that it might have been a different voice, it went
on, "What were you up to all this time?"

"All what time?"

"Almost two hours. . . . I saw you both pass by at two-
twenty and now it's past four."

"But I took her all the way to the villa at Capo Soprano.
Not just to the Capuchins."

"What of it? You could go there from here in twenty
minutes."

"Not if you were loaded down as I was, you couldn't."

"Well, let's say half an hour. Two-twenty plus thirty makes
it ten to three."

"Then there's the half hour back. . . ."

"The way back is downhill and, besides, you weren't loaded
down. You know what time you should have reached this
spot? Well, I'll tell you: three-fifteen at the latest."

"Well, what with one thing and another . . ."

"That's just what I'm asking you. With *what* thing and
what other?"

A fresh wavelet of laughter rippled along the balconies,
and the *Bersagliere* did not know how to get out of standing
there trying to justify himself.

"Well, between the business of the key and the business of
the light bulb, and with that dog . . ."

"What business of the key?"

"The Signora couldn't find it and we had to open the suitcases to see where it was while the damned dog kept poking
his nose into everything, even snatching things right out of
our hands . . ."

"And may one ask what was 'the business of the light
bulb'?"

"Same thing. The Signora sent me in ahead of her to turn
on the light, up on the first floor, she told me, but there
wasn't any light bulb and the light wouldn't turn on so I had
to come back downstairs to rummage through her suitcases

where she said she had one, and that meant opening up everything all over again. . . ."

"And what about the dog?"

"I've already told you. He went on scattering all the things from the suitcases up and down the street the second time we had to open them and I had to run after him to liberate a slip he'd run off with. . . ."

"The slip belonging to the Signora?"

"One of them. That's the way I lost most time, running after the dog."

The voice behind the blind recognized the fact that the *Bersagliere* might well have spent all the time unaccounted for performing these acts. *Might* have, yes. And they might equally have taken up ten minutes instead of forty-five, or three hours, for that matter. He'd passed his time to no good purpose, in any event, and who could object to that?

"There, you see?" said the *Bersagliere*.

He could go on his way, pleased at having answered calmly instead of having worked himself into a rage even if he heard the voice laughing behind his back and talking with the other voices from neighboring balconies, all of the voices laughing now.

"Hsst! Hsst!" the signals continued thick and fast, coming from invisible beings facing the path he traversed between the two sides of the street.

"Who are you, anyway?" he heard someone ask. "Are you Maltese? Are you from Malta?"

But knowing what they wanted, he could afford to ignore them and concentrate on getting out of the pickle by turning, immediately after the Gardens, down the dark little street where there were no more houses with balconies and no more nosy people who called themselves ladies and gentlemen. He joyously burst out whistling the *Garibaldina* theme again. And why shouldn't he sing it? He reached the Public Gardens in full voice and passed them, still singing despite the guarded catcalls that followed him, through the very trees, despite the birds that the morning freshness had by now awakened and who awaited only the light to take flight from their nests.

[37]

But as the lights went out, all of them at once right down to the end of the Corso, you could see that the sky was no longer black. The Corso itself, the asphalt paving, looked blue between the high walls. And together with the sounds one heard, a cock crowing some little distance off, carts creaking into movement still farther away, one could see shadows of men coming steadily uphill with metallic reflections glinting at about head height.

The *Bersagliere* soon ran into five or six men walking in line, their black hair curly, their cheeks all but black, their eyes flashing; by their yellowed rags and moth-eaten berets he could recognize them as the screaming people from the other train or men just like them, who had now become—as if by magic—quieter than ghosts. They barely glanced sidewise to look him over as they passed and they made no noise, not even with their feet, which for the most part were bare, though a few had theirs bound with rags.

Their sickles were over their shoulders and these were what gleamed now and again whenever a reflection struck them as the men shifted their weight. The last in line jiggled his sickle up and down as a sort of greeting. The gesture was repeated by others in the next line and in lines still to come. The calls from the balconies had stopped; the signs the men with the sickles made as they passed were characteristic of the Sicilians, although a little on the mysterious side, and the *Bersagliere* no longer felt any urgency about turning off down one of the byways. He continued along the Corso, making in his turn certain small negative gestures which were meant to have the same slightly derisive undertone as those of the reapers.

Was it because he was a soldier? The mocking signs made at him from the windows of the train as it stood in the Ragusa station were more or less the same kind. In any event, he was not intimidated by them; he gave as good as he got but with decreasing emphasis, decreasing frequency, and finally he went back to whistling his *Garibaldina* theme.

He whistled on without giving a thought to the foolish remarks he heard from some voice in the line.

"Mmmm . . ." he heard.

And "Prrr . . ." he heard.

A loud fart that he heard distinctly provoked only a change of one note in the motif he was whistling between his teeth. And a few laughed at his response. Then came a howl from the steps of the little church where the cripple Romeo huddled night and day.

"Hey, there!"

Was this aimed at the *Bersagliere*? It would seem so. Otherwise, who *was* it aimed at and why? The soldier did not turn down a dark lane that opened off the Corso a bit before the church. He was about to do so as the call echoed and re-echoed with stubborn insistence, taken up from afar. But then he decided against it and resumed his rapid stride, resuming too his whistling air of the *Garibaldina*. As he drew level with the façade of the church, he saw Romeo's face with its round eyes fixing him from under the tattered brim of a conical hat.

[38]

In the faint rosy light of dawn, the *Bersagliere* saw little groups of men gathered along the two sidewalks that flanked the Corso from Romeo's church to the piazza. The men had the black whiskers appropriate to reapers but their hands were in their pockets. Just the same, you could tell they were reapers, that is to say, migrants, by the strange clothes they wore, which no regular hired hand would consider wearing. There were the vivid blobs of color from women's blouses or skirts which they did not refuse to use for patches, and the triangular or circular bits tacked here and there on their clothing to transform their mends into ornaments. Then the braid or strips of cloth with which they had bound up their cuffs, shirts, or pants. Or the gilt cord with which a few of them tied back their wild, uncut locks at the base of the neck. And some wore a single gold ring in one earlobe as proudly as they wore their great mustaches.

Going from place to place in large groups for the sowing, the reaping, the threshing of the grain, for the picking of the cotton, they paid no heed to the impression they might make on others wherever they happened to be, just as an outcast, a Romeo, one who has gone beyond any concept of trying not to displease his neighbor, dared flout the permanent residents of the place. But though Romeo or Leonardo, the porter, might take salacious pleasure in noting the wildly varied condition of the reapers' rags, those who came to overrun the city two or three times a year—some boasting ostrich plumes, a piece of red canonical cloth, the trappings from a discarded police uniform, the bells and trim of a worn-out harness— were known simply as "the sowers," "the reapers," or, generically, "the Calabrians," though most of them came from the northern mountains of Sicily, and the townsfolk let it go at that.

If the *Bersagliere* had reason to notice that they all more or less resembled Romeo, it was because he sensed the understanding that existed between Romeo and them, or rather between Romeo and those groups of men who stayed seated or lounged on the sidewalks, hands in their pockets, leaving it to others to wend their way up the Corso, sickles over their shoulders, in a single line of march which started at the piazza, all black and noisy and marked by a continuous furling and unfurling of the doves, which rose, circled, and swooped to settle down again in constant rotation.

The sickles of the loungers were stacked nearby with their sacks and cooking pots. There were sacks of rotten mattress ticking, with red-and-black, red-and-yellow, red-and-brown stripes. There were pots and pans, all sooty on the outside but shining copper inside. And the sickles were stacked against the wall with their cutting edges down.

The *Bersagliere* caught a glimpse of a man urging his comrade to get in line and give up his spot among all those things. In another place there was a woman squatting on her heels. The scene took place almost directly opposite the church, near the still-closed hotel where Romeo offered his services as casual bootblack or laundry hand. But at that very instant Romeo repeated the cry.

It was not the *alluli* the people of Terranova use. It was his own version of the north Sicilian *alluca*, which has a certain mountaineer's defiance, even if they mean the same thing: "That's what's at the bottom of it." In any event, it seemed more mocking than necessary, and the *Bersagliere*, turning around all of a sudden, saw that Romeo's face was flushed as a turkey cock from the effort.

He walked by him, looking at the narrowed eyes that followed him and the wide mouth that seemed to stretch from one ear to the other, closed tight on its own hurtful laughter. Without stopping, he said, "Have you got it in for me?" And, aware of the excitement that Romeo's cry in its sharpest form seemed to have roused among the threshers on the sidewalk, he added over his shoulder, "You may be drafted some day—who knows?"

Then he heard the bird-call laugh burst out behind him and saw Romeo, turning, turning, bumping about on his ass and waving his arms. He was laughing, and pointing a finger at the *Bersagliere*, telling him that he would be the one to reap a harvest of blows.

The soldier found himself surrounded by the brutish faces of the threshers.

[39]

They were not laughing, not joking. Only black, with a dogged expression or with that look beyond doggedness that bespeaks grim boredom.

"Was it you?" a tall man asked, facing the *Bersagliere* with flashing eyes.

"Of course," Romeo cried, hitching himself upright on the steps. "Who do you think it would be? Of course it was that one. We don't have any other soldiers wandering around here.

I saw him with my own eyes, and the *Garibaldina* told me so, and he himself'll tell you. . . ."

"Let him tell us then," cried the reapers. "Let him tell us."

Meanwhile a man on horseback rode up from the piazza, opening a way for himself as the doves rose about him with a whir of wings. The *Bersagliere* looked at him as if, in some way or other, he were coming especially for him. He was an old man dressed in corduroy hunting clothes, one of the best-known hunters in Terranova, who roamed the woods of the great estates; his teeth were sparkling white, and the gun barrel, pointed downward, was slung behind him from shoulder to saddle.

"Giovinazzo!" he called.

He was searching in the crowd of reapers gathered around the *Bersagliere* and he rode right into their midst, nor did he rein in his gentle horse with its mule's ears until he had opened the circle along one entire side. "Well, then?" he asked. He was addressing the tall reaper who had questioned the *Bersagliere*. "Well, then, are you going to Settefarine? Or you and another squad can work Ponte Olivo as far up as Sparacogna. But don't forget, it's almost five. Will you come to terms with the other squad leader?"

The reaper, Giovinazzo, was holding the soldier by the front of his jacket. "I come to terms with nobody," he answered.

"Then take your men to Settefarine. . . ."

"Haven't I already told you, I'm not going!"

"Don't I pay you just the same as the *Garibaldina?*" the man on horseback asked. "It's a lira a head we pay. That's the going price here."

"It's not the price," a grumbler muttered from behind Giovinazzo. "It's the treatment that plays its part."

"You won't have me believe," the man on horseback answered, "that that skinflint treats you better than I. She gives you a two-pound loaf and we give two and a half. She gives half a flask of wine and we give a flaskful. . . ."

"Well, from *her*," the grumbler went on, "it's a half a flask sure enough, and you can thin it as you want. But with you others, those that are giving a flaskful have already thinned it good or they give us water and vinegar. . . ."

"Here's something new," the man on horseback interrupted. "We all know that the wine given the reapers is watered, from the time of Noah, because its purpose is to quench your thirst, not to get you drunk. But since you've brought up water and vinegar, it must be with vinegar that the *Garibaldina* thins hers. Otherwise why would *you* thin that 'sure enough' half-flask? You wouldn't thin it! You'd drink it off just as it is and you'd get drunk and fall asleep, and get a touch of sunstroke. . . ."

He was speaking now with irritated condescension, looking at the *Bersagliere* instead of the persons he was addressing. "What's happening to me?" the *Bersagliere* might well have asked himself. He saw the man was looking at no one but him, was staring at him with increasing attentiveness, and he might well have asked himself if what was going on between him and the reapers was not pretty serious.

By now he had shaken himself free of Giovinazzo's hand. He had even managed to draw a bit back from the center of the circle, and Giovinazzo too had raised his hands along with the others to protest with outcry and gesture against the implications of the man on horseback. "As if we . . ." he cried. "As if we . . ." the others cried.

The man on horseback, his eyes still on the *Bersagliere*, said that he did not wish to stay there indefinitely discussing and cajoling, as if there weren't plenty of able-bodied men in the piazza to call up. He said he had lost enough time already. He said he'd be on his way. The soldier saw the man take his eyes from him just at the moment a reaper turned to cry up to the mounted figure that there was no need to take it like that, and that if Giovinazzo wouldn't go, *he* would go, and with him the eight men in his squad.

"What?" howled Giovinazzo. He asked one reaper after another if it wasn't true that they had all been present when the *Garibaldina* had let it be known she would pay twenty-two soldi that season. But the man on horseback cut in with a re-

minder that his offer had been made to Giovinazzo, and that
he would pay a lira a head for a squad like Giovinazzo's,
adding that for men like Tremestieri he could pay only
eighteen soldi.

At this, they all set up a howl. The men of Trimestrieri's
group wanted to know why they were worth less than
Giovinazzo's. Giovinazzo's men were sure they had this and
that advantage over Tremestieri. The latter group hurled
insults, used rough words. But Giovinazzo's men let them roll
off like water from a duck's back—after all, they'd had
quite a triumph and all they said was that it certainly served
Trimestrieri's men right.

[40]

Romeo was laughing from the top of the steps.

He was enjoying the scene, laughing, flinging himself about,
and he marked the hours when the five strokes sounded from
the piazza, underscored by the thick whir of hundreds of
wings as the doves wheeled into the air. Then he commented,
laughing, on the departure of the man on horseback. And
he cried out as he saw the soldier start to take off.

The *Bersagliere* was caught by a sleeve and brought back
into the group.

But Giovinazzo's men were only in a mood to sneer by
now.

"What have you got against me anyway?" the soldier asked.

The reapers nudged each other, winked at each other
broadly, asked each other what, after all, they had against
that particular soldier.

"What have we got against him?"

"There's no doubt we've got something. . . ."

"But what?"

One of the men, with a red bandanna with white polka
dots on it tied around his head, began by asking what a soldier
does.

"He sweeps out the barracks," they answered.

"He cleans the latrines," from someone.

"He washes the stewpots," from another.

He answered by telling them that he went on marches, carried a knapsack, but the interlocutor continued to ask the same question while Romeo, hunched down on the top step, twisted in contortions of laughter.

"His food is lousy . . ." someone added.

"He sleeps on the ground," another said.

The reaper with the bandanna no longer needed to repeat his question. All he had to do was raise his hand as a signal to elicit a fresh answer from the circle of his fellow reapers, and the answers soon became nothing more than "His food is lousy" and "He sleeps on the ground"; in due course the rhythm was established and they picked up the beat, and they all hammered out the chorus.

The *Bersagliere* might have believed himself in the midst of that bedraggled group on the other train, with the young boys and all the others, with the brakeman too, and the two conductors who wanted him to get down at Donnafugata, but the reaper with the bandanna now turned to him as well to get his answer to the question.

"That's just the way it is," he answered. "He goes to war . . . and . . . he sleeps on the ground. . . ."

"And you wanted *us*," the reaper hurled at him, "to carry your bags for you?"

A great roar went up, in which Tremestieri men joined.

"Just take a look at him!"

"He's not a general!"

"He's not even a noncom!"

"He's only a soldier. . . ."

"And *we* were supposed to carry a soldier's bags for him?"

The *Bersagliere* tried to say that the luggage had not been his, had never been his, and to say all the rest that he could have said, but he did not manage to say any of it, for the reapers drowned out his voice with their noise, and they pushed him from one side of the circle to the other, and from one man to another, and then there was Romeo, who was choking out from the top of the steps:

"I . . . I . . . I . . ." he was saying, all red in the face.

Halfway up the steps, below Romeo but above the reapers, the mug of the night watchman, Galante, came into view. He was thin, small-boned, with that grayish cast to the skin and enough white at the temples to make even a man in his fifties pass for old. Just the same, he looked spry and sharp, rather gnomelike, as only those along in years can look. He reminded the *Bersagliere* of the little old trainman who had appeared with a red flag in his hand at the Ragusa station, and that was why the soldier kept on trying to tell his story, directing his gestures to Galante, there on the steps.

He kept on talking and talking, as if aware that he could not be heard but wanting to begin again anyway. Nor was there any dearth of reapers seeking the same thing: five or six of them were, in the same manner, asking the little old man to hear their side of it. Then there were seven, then eight, then nine, and they all were aware of the difficulty of being heard and would stop a bit only to begin again, louder than before. The old man looked at the soldier and shook his head, looked at the reapers and shook his head, but as if he'd already made up his mind what to think about all this. He never stopped smiling, his face sharp and alert, and he made a few gestures to first one and then another to calm down. "Don't take it personally," he finally managed to say to the *Bersagliere*.

Giovinazzo and the reaper with the bandanna on his head were talking to each other in whispers interrupted by great guffaws, and the old man told the *Bersagliere* that it wasn't with *him* they were annoyed. "It's because the *Garibaldina* doesn't want them after all," he said.

He kept on wrinkling up his face with cunning glances and told him that he should try to put himself in their shoes and pity them. Since they had always reaped and threshed the *Garibaldina's* grain, they had come back to do the work again this year, and all of a sudden she'd turned them down. They didn't know which way to turn. "I don't know if I make myself clear, but they don't know what to do with themselves. . . . They're out of work, see."

[41]

"What?" the *Bersagliere* asked him.

He could scarcely hear. But behind the little night watchman Romeo's voice now rose too.

"Whose fault is it, I'd like to know," he cried, "if they're out of work? Whose fault is it if the *Garibaldina* doesn't want them any more, if she's turned them away? Whose fault is it that they made her angry . . . that they had to turn her down? It was just so's they wouldn't have to do the bidding of that good-for-nothing soldier and carry his bags for him, so it's plain as the nose on your face it's his fault. Whose fault is it? Whose is it? No one else's but that soldier. . . ."

The old man was shaking his head, smiling. "But they're all over that now," he said. "They aren't offended any longer. It's only that they're out of work, and he must take all this with patience, and feel for them."

He had turned back to the *Bersagliere*, who still could not hear him clearly, and was urging him not to take offense, while Romeo, behind him, was imitating him in a falsetto voice.

"Feel for them!" he repeated in falsetto. "But it's those fellows," he cried, "who feel for *him!*"

Meanwhile the reapers, between one guffaw and another, one snort and another, had found a new game to play with the soldier.

"Let's salt him!" was the new proposal.

Giovinazzo and the reaper with the red bandanna had worked it out between them, whispering in each other's ears, and now they loosed it, and the others took it up.

"Let's salt him! Let's salt him!"

Grabbing the *Bersagliere*, they threw him down; the idea was to hold him motionless, unbutton his trousers, and rub his genitals with salt or street filth.

The *Bersagliere* tried to fight back.

"They're salting him!" Romeo howled. And he heaved him-

self about, imitating grotesquely every twist and turn of the
prone *Bersagliere*, and the rags with which he was clad flew
around him like ruffled feathers. "And you," he said, turning
to the night watchman, "what do you say now? Shouldn't he
take it personally now?"

The old man did nothing more than shake his head under
his watchman's cap. Of course he disapproved of what he was
witnessing, yet he kept on repeating that it was nothing and
underlining his words with certain slow gestures which meant
to convey the same thing.

But the reapers had neither salt nor street filth at hand.
They reached in their pockets, then imitated one another by
running to the nearest unpaved lane to pick up whatever
they could find, and one of their number had the idea of
running to their knapsacks, but by then the reaper with the
red bandanna had come up with a third proposal.

"Let's have him carry our knapsacks!" he proposed.

They all considered this the best and most appropriate suggestion yet. "Let him carry our knapsacks! Let him carry our
knapsacks!"

Only Romeo was against it. He cried that this was a foolish
prank, without any kick to it, that "salting" him was a worse
punishment. "At least, salt him first!"

But the reapers were already dragging the *Bersagliere*
across the street toward the pile of knapsacks. Red Bandanna
was following in their wake and directing them with his
hands, as if he were an orchestral conductor. "What does the
soldier do?" he asked.

"He carries the knapsacks," they all replied.

Their voices were trying to hit the beat as before.

"The soldier?"

"Goes to war."

"The soldier?"

"Sleeps on the ground."

"The soldier?"

"Carries the knapsacks! Carries the knapsacks!"

This last response, though thundered out, was each time

interrupted here and there by splutters of laughter, and when they tried it a third time it trailed off into a murmur. A horse was coming; the sound of its shoes could be heard, and all the reapers stopped and looked toward the middle of the Corso.

[42]

The *Bersagliere* turned around too. All of a sudden they had loosed their hold on him; he could shake himself, stand up straight, and rearrange his clothing, and he saw a white-and-black horse shaking its head in the air and all the reapers gathered around. He saw that the figure, though covered by a cloak, seemed like that of the old woman; then he heard a voice he recognized, and he saw that it was indeed her figure moving toward him, that it was "his" old woman on horseback.

"Never in my born days," she exclaimed, "would I have expected to see you all here at half past five in the morning! Giovinazzo, what's our agreement? From sunup to sundown . . . This evening you'll stop the minute the sun drops below the horizon. But meanwhile you're not at the Bruca, getting ready to start work. Perhaps it's your idea that you'll go to work when lawyers go to Mass?"

Giovinazzo, cap in hand, kept on repeating, "Well . . ." Tremestieri too. He held the horse by the bridle and kept on saying, "Well . . ." They certainly wanted to say by that "well" that they must have misunderstood that she had let them go, or that she had expressed herself unclearly, or perhaps had changed her mind at the last moment, but they got none of these things out. They just stood there looking at each other and kept on repeating, "Well . . ."

"Well, what?" she exclaimed. "I watched from the window to see which squads were passing: Marzapane, yes; Dardanello, yes; you, here, no. So I had to come all the way down here to see what's got into you."

"Well, you see . . ." they said, and the reapers' faces were red. And not just Giovinazzo's and Tremestieri's, those two had already managed to stammer out, "You see, *Garibaldina* . . ." That much they had managed to say.

"Well, for today," the old woman went on, "you won't get your twenty-two soldi. Take it or leave it: you'll get one lira."

The reapers were consulting each other as if they did not consider this at all fair. But the confused sense of well-being that had spread over their faces had not been wiped off. If anything, it seemed to grow.

"Well, then, *Garibaldina?*" Tremestieri asked.

And Giovinazzo: "You want us to go to the Bruca?"

And Tremestieri added, "To the Bruca? And us too?"

The old woman answered that they should know where they were to go from all the years they had been doing the job, sowing and reaping and threshing for her. Dardanello was working the Mautana fields, as usual. Marzapane, Cappellania. There was no reason that she could think of why they two, in squads of thirteen and nine, could not work the Bruca as usual. Or did they want to make a change? But then they should have got together with the other two to work out the change.

"And how much are you paying Marzapane?" Red Bandanna asked.

The old woman said she had seen him pass with his squad at four-thirty, as she watched from her window. She would keep her promise to them and to Dardanello. They would have their twenty-two soldi.

"And why not us?" the reaper asked. "Why're we getting only a lira?"

Each reaper uttered a little sound of protest, but vague and formal as if part of a ritual.

"How often do I have to repeat it for you?" the Signora exclaimed. "Had I seen you pass at four-thirty, as I watched from my window, I would have given you people twenty-two soldi an hour too, and I wouldn't have had to come all the way down here. I could have stayed home and rested a bit after the strain of my journey. . . ."

The reapers were murmuring among themselves, "True enough," and "That's fair enough," but there were those who wanted to say something else and one of their number got as far as trying to say it.

"But, *Garibaldina* . . ."

He stopped, silenced by the black looks he caught from some of his comrades. A few nudged him, others tried to kick him, and this left the way open for Red Bandanna to take over once more. "From tomorrow, at least," he half stated, "it's twenty-two soldi you'll be giving us?"

"Listen carefully," the *Garibaldina* told them. "You go up to the fields now, do as much as you possibly can, and at sundown I'll come by and look things over. . . ."

"Ahhh, *Ga-ri-bal-di-na* . . ." the reapers chanted, paying out the syllables one by one.

"And if what I see . . ." she went on.

"Ahhhh, *Ga-ri-bal-di-na* . . ."

". . . satisfies me . . ."

"Ahhhhh, *Ga-ri-bal-di-na* . . ."

The reapers did not try to drown out her voice with a cheer. Instead, each one had put his arm around his comrade's shoulder and they were all swaying in unison and moving their heads from side to side, repeating "Ahhh, *Ga-ri-bal-di-na*," with the long, slow syllables scanning as they fell.

[43]

And the scraping of the horse's hoofs began again.

Surrounded by the reapers, who kept up their chanting and swaying, the old woman rode off in the direction of the piazza. She was decidedly old, got up in men's clothes, with a little hat on her head trimmed by a long veil, and with her heavy cheeks flabby and a black weariness about her eyes, her hair in disorder, her clothing flung on every which way despite the baubles. But she was wonderful just because she accepted the fact of being—and in no way tried not to be—

old, beyond any single thing that recalls youth yet far from beyond the things that make for life. She called Don Carlos, whistled for him, and turned to look back to be sure he was following when she saw the *Bersagliere* following the train, a little behind the others.

"Hey, Fortunato," she cried to the *Bersagliere*.

His eyes were shining. He saw her in her gray veil, and she was as attractive to him as a young girl. And it was just because she was old, not because of some residuum of youth.

She was a lot older by daylight than he could have believed during the night he had just spent with her. But alive in her old age, alive in the same way a young girl is who is on her way, for example, to a wedding. "Now do you believe," she called back to him, "that I have a carriage?"

And she laughed. If she had a horse, he could have no possible doubt that she must also have a carriage. "Besides, I'll send it over for you," she added. "I promised I'd make your fortune and I will. . . ."

One last time she turned back to ask him again where he lived. But the horse had already broken into a trot, the reapers were falling behind one by one, and the *Bersagliere* wanted to cross the street.

He walked faster.

He kept on walking faster, almost started to run, and reached the piazza in the midst of men talking to one another, some on horseback, some on the ground. From the cupola of the sandstone church, already touched by the sun, the two bronze bells rang out, one long, one short, summoning people to the first Mass of the day. At every two strokes of the hammers, the doves flew out of the bell tower or rose from the cornices, from between the columns, from the steps, but they rose only to settle down again, rose and returned, as if it were they sounding the bronze bells each time they circled into the air.

The *Bersagliere* turned down the street that led to the sea. It was all downhill now, with the bells echoing all around him, and from every terraced level he could see the sea on the horizon. Above the terraces, the doves wheeled gleaming in

the sun with the heavy old breeder leading the flight of males
and females. And the *Bersagliere* broke out strong and free
once more with the song he had been singing earlier:

> You—are—the—bright—star
> Of—us—poor—sol—diers;
> Hey—there—blon—di—na,
> Teas—ing Ga—ri—bal—di—na. . . .

DOMENICO REA

DOMENICO REA WAS BORN AT NOCERA INFERIORE, NEAR NAPLES, on September 8, 1921, the son of a poor bank employee. Almost completely self-educated, Rea spent his childhood at Nocera; as a young man he spent years drifting from country to country throughout Europe. At one time he even considered emigrating, but finally he returned to Italy and settled down in his native town, where he still lives. He maintains himself as a creative writer by teaching school and contributing articles on the problems of the Italian south to *Paese Sera* and other newspapers. Very much the engaged—but not the provincial —southerner, Rea has consistently tried to keep aloof from literary politics and fashion, quietly cultivating his vision of the world, which is Naples from his vantage at Nocera. Despite this unfashionable withdrawal, Rea's work has received general and handsome recognition, winning the Premio Viareggio in 1951 and the Premio Napoli in 1959.

His chief works are: *Spaccanapoli* (1947); *Formicole rosse* (1948); *Gesù, fate luce!* (1950, Premio Viareggio); *Ritratto di maggio* (1953); *Quel che vide Cummeo* (1955); *Una vampata di rossore* (1959, Premio Napoli).

143

WHAT CUMMEO SAW

by Domenico Rea

translated by William Weaver

WHEN HE WAS A LITTLE BOY, HE WOULD WATCH FOR HOURS the young couples who came love-making in the Chivoli forest. He and the rest of the gang gathered stones and loaded their slingshots to attack the lovers, and as soon as a couple was sighted, a first volley was fired from the treetops. The stones would hit the young man in the head or the behind or the hand or the foot, or in all these parts at once. He would turn around, angry, then the couple would walk on. But from the other side of a clearing, a stone would land on his foot. This was the signal for war. The young man would advance, his chest out, and ten more stones would hit him, as a terrible roar of laughter went up all around. A boy would drop from a tree. With a shout, the man was off after him, forgetting his girl. The other boys swarmed from the trees to surround her, with slings and clubs, crouching as they advanced, shouting, putting their faces on the ground to have a look up. . . . And she would start crying. Then Biase, the leader, ordered, "That's enough now. She's crying."

Cummeo, sitting on a big branch, never hurled the stone they put in his hand. Spell-bound, he watched the pretty young lady and the man, still young, who was already dressed like Cummeo's father. Cummeo was calm—"born without a sound," his mother used to say—and he would go out with this gang or another, with anyone who wanted him. Usually they made him carry messages, or the sling, or else he was the sentry. And whatever silly cap of feathers or branches that they put on his head, he was satisfied.

He liked to gather spiky chestnuts, grass whips, which he

145

presented to his mother for brooms, and the first spring flowers, tender and white, which dripped milk when you broke them off. Once he brought a bunch home to his father, that man of few words and much anger, who accepted the flowers and said to his wife, "He's been pulling at my coat for half an hour. I thought he wanted to fight."

All this happened when Cummeo wasn't yet six, before he began the first grade, when Giovanna, his sister, was repeating the third grade for a second time. Unable to read, he would leaf through the ragged mass that had once been his sister's first reader. Until then his toys had been things he had been able to construct himself, with his own imagination: the bottom of a box with some wooden wheels, his "wagon"; a broom handle with carving and colored streaks, his horse; an iron slingshot with inner-tube strips; two or three ball bearings, which he kept greased and shiny; boxes of various sizes that he found along the street; and the animals and flying machines he imagined as he fell asleep in a corner of the courtyard among insects and butterflies.

But when he discovered the reader, with its colored illustrations, half ruined with damp, he laid it out in the sun, dried it, bent back its worn ears, glued in the loose pages, and repaired the torn ones with transparent tape, knowing he wouldn't be given a new one next year, because every object, item of clothing, or toy in that house was handed down to the smaller child, then the next, and the next, and only Giovanna, the oldest, ever had new things.

But that reader, which he knew page by page and letter by letter, having used it before, not as an instrument of knowledge but as a richer, more varied and colorful toy, was a great comfort to him in the first days of school. Many of the other boys cried, called for their mothers, and tried to run away from their desks. It was a game for him to learn the vowels and the other letters. He had drawn them so many times in the dirt of the courtyard, or carved them on the wooden table. Before they became letters for him, they had already been fantastic forms, free and useless, like his childhood.

New facts, of a different nature, came to the surface of his innocent consciousness, and suddenly illuminated it, darkening it, too, with the first fits of sadness. He would have gone to school with greater pleasure if he could have worn a smock, like his sister. His mother explained to him, "Giovanna has a smock because she's a girl. Men don't wear them."

But that wasn't true. Many boys at the school—Marasca, Fioravanti, Tebo, Gigliotti, Balestra—had smocks with collars and cuffs of white lace. They had shiny shoes too, and neatly combed, gleaming hair; so they were called to sit in the first desks. The teacher sent him to the back, among the boys without smocks, with dirt-streaked faces, their hands kept warm by old cotton stockings of their mothers'. There were as many as three of them to one desk, scratching and hitting one another. Often the others put flies in his bread, the single slice his mother gave him every morning.

He fouled his pants twice, for fear of the teacher, who sat at a desk decorated with two or three whips, including a long one, like an antenna, which touched the opposite wall. This was to recall the attention of the absent-minded with a whack on the head. Another whip was broad, like a saddle strap, for whacking open palms; and the third, a proper lash, was taken in hand by the teacher, when he came down from his desk, to whip the delinquent scholar on the spot.

In the spring, Cummeo always brought the teacher daisies, or a rose if he found one, or clumps of wisteria. As he went past the desk toward his seat, he would leave the flowers there. The teacher never asked who had brought them. He gave them to the lady teacher in the next classroom, with whom he would linger for a low-voiced talk as the boys worked in their copybooks, or whenever he pleased. And it so happened that on the very day he had thoughtfully brought flowers, Cummeo received his share of whacks on the palms. He jumped up and down, shaking first one hand, then the other, to shake away the pain and to cool them off. The whole class laughed. He laughed too.

One day the teacher came in a new suit and found the classroom clean, straightened up, and adorned with flowers offered by the boys in honor of his name day; on that day he had an argument with the young lady. He shut the door (always a bad sign), went to the blackboard, and wrote out a problem, shouting, "Gigliotti, go to the blackboard."

Gigliotti, all neat and clean, went there, and after holding the chalk in his hand for a while, trying to raise his hand up to the numbers, he burst into tears, saying, "I can't do it, I can't!" He spoke proper Italian; he didn't come from Nofi.

"You know what you are?" the teacher said. "Don't you know what you are? You're spoiled, and I'm going to tell your father this evening. Balestra."

The next boy ran to the board and, as usual, said with his superior smile, before working the problem, "I know how to do it."

"Good," the teacher said, with no confidence. Balestra went through the motions of working the problem. He traced over the numbers with the tip of the chalk, retouching them to make them more beautiful to his way of thinking. But the numbers simply became larger and more threatening.

"Well?" the teacher said. "Can you do it, or can't you?"

Balestra smiled as if he were the teacher's friend. But the teacher took his whip and came down from the desk, while silence fell over the room. Balestra lost all his courage and crouched under the board, crying and wailing, "I'll tell my Papa!" even before the teacher had whipped him. Balestra was driven to school in an automobile every morning. He was the son of the owner and operator of Balestra and Company, and after him came Gigliotti, whose father, the Captain, had an orderly who accompanied the boy to school, then Sgherro, who arrived between two maids, and Forio, who, when he came into the entrance with his father, was caressed by the teachers, figuratively caressing the father. All went to the board, failed, and went back to their places, frightened.

The numbers on the blackboard meanwhile had grown fearfully large. Even those who could work the problem suddenly were afraid that they couldn't. Cummeo was shaking like a leaf, and felt somewhat calmer only when his deskmate leaned toward him, with a smile on his little face.

The teacher said, "Now let's see what you back there can do." He chose a name at random. "Caprioni," he shouted. Caprioni didn't stand up, as if to say: He goes and picks me, when everybody knows that I can't do it.

Caprioni was repeating the first grade for the third time, and he was always laughing. He was a child of the manure man, an old man with an old wife; they went around barefooted, picking up dung with their hands from horses, donkeys, and mules. With a little cart they used to run after the cavalry stationed in town, so as not to lose a single pat. For that reason, no one wanted to share a desk with Caprioni; and the teacher sometimes, as a punishment, ordered one of the boys to sit next to him.

"I called on you," the teacher repeated, raising his whip. Caprioni, without hurrying, daring to smile at the others and even at the teacher, left the last desk and, in his flapping shoes twice the size of his feet, went to the board. He didn't bother to pick up the chalk. And they all laughed. But the teacher shouted, "You fool!"

The boy looked at him, half frightened and half smiling. He received the first lash, impassive, with a shadow of his former smile. The lash came down a second time. He took the chalk, then replaced it, turning toward the class, hard and defeated. The whip came down a third and a fourth time on his cold, bare legs, as if the teacher were whipping a tree trunk. Then the boy looked at the man with his wide animal eyes.

The teacher shouted, "Don't try that again, you little wretch!"

The silence was absolute. Caprioni's legs were bleeding. The teacher threw away the whip, went back to his desk, and ran his hand through his hair, staring absently at the faces of the boys. Where his eyes passed, heads were bowed. Caprioni slowly went back to his place, took up his scrawled notebooks, tied them with string, and paying no attention to the teacher, who said in a hoarse voice, "Go back to your place," he left the room, dragging his feet. The boys could hear him shuffling over the stones in the courtyard.

[2]

Their father took little interest in the children or in the house. At night he came home from work and they all ate. At midday, the children and their mother ate bread with something or other, but in the evening there was spaghetti or bean soup or *pasta* with chick peas or lentils or cauliflower, depending on the season. They drank water in abundance. After the meal, the family went to bed.

Cummeo spread out a mattress of corn shucks on the table where they had eaten, and there he slept. Opposite the double bed, Giovanna and Rosaria slept in a cot; and on the left, in an iron crib, slept Micuccio, who was three. Mario, a year old, slept between his father and mother in the big bed. At five in the morning, the father got up and went to the sawmill. An hour later it was the mother's turn, when Mario started screaming. She put the baby in Giovanna's bed, where Micuccio would have already snuggled in, and then the children all started laughing and playing. Cummeo would have liked to join them, but Giovanna wouldn't let him, saying he was too big. And he grieved at having grown. When their mother came back, they all crouched on the floor around her while she sliced the bread: a thicker slice for Micuccio and for Rosaria, a little less to Giovanna, and the thinnest slice to Cummeo.

"Because you're a man, and the oldest boy." To make up for it, Cummeo was given a pinch of sugar on his bread. Then he went off to school.

He never had a smock or a book bag, but his notebooks filled with good marks were envied by many a boy who did have smock and book bag. Gigliotti often gave him jam tarts in return for the privilege of copying Cummeo's arithmetic. And when the copybooks were returned, the teacher said, "Gigliotti, excellent. He's the only one who worked the problem. He and Cummeo. But Cummeo copied, and this is the fourth time he's done that." Cummeo stood up to tell the truth, but he promptly sat down again, looking at Gigliotti, who smiled sadly at him. The jam tarts!

Once Gigliotti said, "Do you want to come to my house? We can do our homework together and then we can play."

Cummeo shouldn't have gone, but he couldn't resist. His mother had a lot of clothes to wash that day, and he was supposed to take care of his little brothers. Giovanna had already started going in the afternoon to see Signora Sberi, a lady who had helped their mother. She ate at this lady's house and wore different clothes, because "the Signora loves her like a daughter," as their mother explained to the other women in the courtyard. Giovanna resembled her father. She was thin, with big eyes and thick lashes. She was the passion of her parents, and Cummeo had to do his sister's work. But Gigliotti's invitation was too fascinating, so he didn't go home.

At three o'clock he went into the great building, with many cars parked at the entrance. The concierge, an old man in his shirt sleeves, his suspenders hanging down, shouted, "Where are you going?"

"Gigliotti." Cummeo started up the steps. The concierge, with a big head and even bigger ears, came after him and said, "What are you going there for?"

"He's a schoolmate of mine."

"We'll see how true that is." He telephoned up to the Captain's apartment, then said, "You can go up. The open door."

Gigliotti was waiting for him in the doorway. They went through a corridor along a bright veranda, then out on the terrace. Cummeo headed straight for a little red automobile with real rubber tires, a brake, headlights, and horn. He wanted to sit in it, but Gigliotti pushed him away and sat in it himself, driving around the terrace two or three times, blowing the horn as he went past. From behind the blinds of a window that opened on the terrace, a man's deep, hoarse voice was heard. "Franco, stop it. You're perspiring. Go and study."

"No, Daddy," Gigliotti answered. "I'm showing a friend how the car works."

"I saw how," Cummeo was saying meanwhile, running after him, stopping, looking for a moment at his schoolmate's apartment, then running after him again, with a sad smile. Franco got out. Cummeo, thinking his turn had come, wanted to get in.

"After our lessons," Franco said, stopping the car with the brake.

"No, now. If you won't let me, I won't show you how to do the problem."

Cummeo caught on to the pedal at once, and would have liked to have the car to himself, to enjoy it all afternoon, go down into the street and arrive at his home, blowing the horn, packing his brothers in with him, then driving on and on forever. But Gigliotti had different ideas, and wouldn't give in. He wouldn't let Cummeo drive fast, as he had, and after half a turn, he said, "That's enough now." For Cummeo, who kept pushing the pedals, held back by Franco, the fun turned into work, a struggle against the strength and the dead weight of Gigliotti's body. They looked at each other, Cummeo unsmiling, realizing that there was no hope, as Gigliotti said, "Afterward."

Cummeo, disappointed, got out and said, "Let's do our lessons. I have to go home."

Going back into the corridor, Cummeo saw the tiny leg of a warrior sticking out below a door. He opened the door. It was a closet, the place where Gigliotti's toys were kept: a train with a little string of coaches, another larger train, balls, balloons, swords, a rifle, sabers, pistols, warriors' plumed hats, one toy on top of another, and Cummeo touched them all.

Franco said, "They're old toys." And since Cummeo didn't want to let go of the tiny warrior, in armor, Franco said to him, "You can keep it, only hide it in your pocket, and come with me to do our lessons now."

As they were opening their notebooks, Gigliotti's father came in, the Captain, a big man, wearing saber and pistol. Franco ran up to him with all kinds of simpering expressions that Cummeo could never have managed. The Captain told his son to do his lessons well and kissed him on the mouth; to his wife, who had remained in the doorway, he said, as if Cummeo didn't exist, "Who is that boy?"

"A schoolmate."

"Hmph," her husband exclaimed.

The door was shut, to be opened again two or three hours later. This time a young woman in a white apron came in. She also spoke Italian rather than dialect. She carried a cup on a little tray.

"Franco, your egg."

"No!" Franco cried, in alarm. "Not today. I don't want it."

The mother than ran in and went straight to Franco, pulling his ear and shouting, "If you don't eat that egg you can't go to the movies tonight."

Cummeo sat there, holding his pen suspended in midair.

"If you don't eat it I'll hit you today." Then, to Margherita, the maid, "Give it to me, girl. You have to handle children with affection."

Franco took a little sip of the raw egg but he didn't swallow it and ended by spraying it over his mother in disgust, weeping and running off to the terrace.

Finally the Signora said to Margherita, "Nothing doing today, I see. Perhaps his schoolmate would like it."

"You want it?" Margherita asked Cummeo. "Don't you want it?"

Cummeo drew back, his head hanging, his pen still in his right hand. He drew back to the wall, and without raising his head, he took the cup and sipped slowly, glancing up, and sipping very, very slowly.

[3]

That evening, by pure chance, he didn't get a beating. In the afternoon his mother had gone to see his father at the sawmill, and her sister-in-law, who was very fond of Cummeo, had taken her place.

"His father is a captain of soldiers," Cummeo narrated. "He has a saber and a pistol. And he said I was Franco's schoolmate. Franco's mother hit him because he wouldn't eat a raw egg."

The little warrior was in his pocket, and he held his hand over it. He didn't dare display it, because his brothers would have cried and made a fuss until they had got it away from him. He would hide it in a hole under the door, where his other toys were kept.

"The cup was full of raw egg, and he didn't want it." At Cummeo's house a raw egg was a reward for a child who was ill. Cummeo didn't say that he had drunk it, from the same instinct that led him to enjoy the warrior by himself rather than display it proudly.

It was October, and it was cold in the ground-floor room, which had only a door and, over it, a little window with an iron grating. The children sat, two to a chair, around a brazier and listened to Cummeo with wide eyes, aware that their brother was telling of things—pistols, sabers, warriors, guns—worthy of the maximum attention. Even their aunt, with Mario in her arms, was listening carefully. Giovanna came home and she listened too; then she in turn described the marvels of her Signora's house. She talked about it every evening, omitting only the description of what she had eaten.

Their parents came home, laden with packages.

"There's something for everybody," the mother said, on this happiest of days for her. "Here are shoes for Cummeo. Try them on. And here are the socks and this is the shirt. You'll have the jacket at Christmas."

Cummeo clasped these gifts in his arms and huddled down on the chest to gloat over each item in turn. The others also went off by themselves, like animals. Only Giovanna received nothing, but she didn't complain. In those days she was already completely dressed at the expense of Signora Sberi. Her aunt and the mother busied themselves with the children. Father would receive his new suit the next day, Sunday. He had been promoted to the position of skilled worker at the sawmill, and that day he had been given a bonus, some back wages.

"Thank God, thank God," the aunt kept saying at the table.

Listening to her husband as if an oracle were speaking, and happy to see him so carefree, Cummeo's mother said, "That'll take the wind out of his sails; he doesn't believe in God."

When they ate, the children used a spoon and their hands.

After the macaroni with melted cheese, they ate meat, and then pickled eggplant, nuts, and ripe persimmons. Like Christmas! Their father began to tell the whole story carefully, as the little children crawled under the table or on the beds with their presents. Cummeo and Giovanna preferred to listen.

"He sent for me and I went to the office, and he said, 'From now on you'll work at the square. You're in luck,' he said. 'And what about the pay?' I said. 'Don't worry. Take this for a start.' And he handed me the envelope. 'It's my personal contribution, for your children,' he said. 'It's extra.'"

Then he took the stub of a carpenter's pencil from his pocket and calculated on a piece of paper how much more he'd be making per hour from now on. He was pleased with the total, and his wife said again, "He's always getting depressed."

"Depressed?" the father answered, looking at his wife. "It's just that there's never enough money. We ought to get out of this hole here. We ought to be living on a second floor, at least, with some sun for the kids. You see," he said to his sister, "the state we're in? Look at the damp." He pointed to the huge stains on the walls, black with mould. Cummeo was in the crook of his father's arm. One of the smaller boys was delicately working the warrior loose from his brother's pocket. And the father went on, "Take Giovanna. She's all right. She eats. She has red cheeks. But who is this Signora Sberi?"

"Don't you know her?" his wife answered. "She's the sister of Professor Sberi, that man who's so religious. A fine lady. If you can keep on her good side," she added, turning to her daughter, "you'll be the luckiest of us all. Then, when your father is making money, you can come back home. I can't go on alone any longer."

So it was a beautiful evening, in love and harmony.

The next day the father's suit arrived. His wife helped him dress. She knotted his necktie for him, put a handkerchief in his pocket and opened it like a rose. He held her tight in front of the mirror and said, "I love you too." And she said, "You say that, and like a fool I believe you."

At noon another big meal: macaroni, cutlets, nuts, fruit. The children in their clean clothes. Giovanna with her hair in

a knot, against her wishes. But after the meal the father said
to his wife:

"I wanted to take you to the movies tonight, you, Rosa"—
his sister—"and the two older ones"—Giovanna and Cummeo—"but I have to go to Sarno with the boss. I met him on
the street. We have to look at a load of wood."

"Another load of wood. And on Sunday again, too. This is
the third time in a month," his wife said.

"Even if it was the fifth or the tenth," her husband answered, losing his temper, "or the thousandth, he's the boss
and it's a matter of money."

He said it in such a tone of voice that anybody would have
believed him.

[4]

Ever since the night before, Cummeo had been gazing at
his shoes, without tiring of them, and the socks and the shirt.
He went to bed, and for the first time in his life he didn't fall
asleep at once. Usually, putting his head on that lump of a
pillow and going to sleep were two actions that became one.
He put the shoes and socks, the latter still in their shiny paper,
under the table, so that he had only to glance down and he
could see them; and he gazed down as long as the little flame
lasted under a tapestry image of saints over his mother's bed
table. As time passed, he was overcome not so much by sleep-
iness as by a stupor that was never free of an anxiety to
awaken, and only in this way did he manage to live through
the hours that preceded dawn.

But as soon as he heard some of the familiar noises of the
courtyard, still uncertain whether it was day or night, unable
to resist, he jumped down from the bed and went to touch his
shoes, the objects which—even more than the socks—represented for him the end of an era, the time when he went barefoot or in a pair of battered old shoes that, even at his tender
age, told him how humble his station was. It was lower even
than a blade of grass, which at least is what it's supposed to
be.

Hearing Cummeo moving about, his father said, "What's this?" and the boy climbed back on his corn-husk mattress, making a noise like a donkey when it throws itself down on its straw. These were the most anxious and exhausting moments, as he closed his eyes to think of all the things he would do in the great Sunday now being born in the sky, or as he peered at every crack in the door, anxious not to miss the first, watery spreading of the dawn's light. The noises in the courtyard became more frequent and more distinct. He heard Spanzano's voice saying good morning to somebody, and Vito the cabby saying "Ah!" to his horse, meaning "Hold still," and the horse's hoofs and the tinkling sound as he shook his head, and the drip of water from the freshly washed hack.

If he hadn't feared his father's wrath, he would have lifted the latch and gone out into the courtyard in the cool, open air to see for himself how close they were to the end of that long night. Finally he received the signal of liberation from his father, who—workday or holiday—had the hour of rising in his blood. Sitting on the bed, his father recovered from his sleep, rubbing his hand over his face, sighing, holding out his arms, and saying, "Well, another Sunday."

Cummeo said to him, "I'll open the door." His father didn't answer, and for the boy that was enough. His father paid no attention to this unusual request, nor was he surprised at the early rising of the boy, whom he always left asleep when he went off to work. The father was too shut up in his own little world of difficult matters, concerning not only their daily bread, and he gave no sign of appreciating the basin of water that Cummeo prepared for him, with soap and a clean towel. Cummeo performed these favors in order to put his father in a good humor and to take advantage of this humor to put on at once his shirt, pants, shoes, and socks. Before Giovanna and her mother were up, Cummeo was all ready; his hair was even combed and shiny with oil. He started going in and out of the house, and was impatient for everyone else to be up, his friends and the grownups, on this, his first day of glory.

The little shoes of shiny black leather fastened at one side with a single little button. The short pants grazed the tops of his knees and were very loose, exposing his thin, olive-skinned legs and thighs. The collar of the shirt was also too large for him, but Cummeo's appearance was, in general, neat and clean, no less humble than usual, but not absolutely poverty-stricken, not torn and dusty as he had been on weekdays and holidays in a long tunnel of years preceding this Sunday. He began to walk around in front of the already open doors of the one-room houses like his own in the courtyard. Everyone paid him compliments. Here and there he stopped and allowed them to look at him. Other boys, still in bed, stood up on their mattresses and stared, incredulous. The first schoolmate he ran into, after measuring him with his gaze from head to foot, said, "Those pants are your father's. You see how loose they are?" He called the other boys and said, "Look! Cummeo's wearing his father's pants!"

Cummeo accepted this accusation in silence, and went off elsewhere, roaming in search of compliments. But another boy said to him, "That stuff's not yours. You stole it."

Cummeo rushed over to hit him, but then he sensed that he might end up with torn clothes, and he gave in at once.

He didn't realize that the others behaved with contempt because of human envy, and for something even more subtle than the word "anger" can describe. Because his mother said to him, "They're just angry. That's why they talk like that."

"But are the things mine?" he asked her. "The pants weren't Papa's?"

"Don't be silly."

He hung around their door, careful not to allow himself to be touched for fear of being soiled, and not sitting down until he had unfolded a newspaper. Finally, after supper, still dressed, without a spot or a wrinkle, he fell asleep on his chair, his shoes and his hair still shiny. His mother had to undress him, and she put him to bed without Cummeo's even being aware of it.

[5]

Because of his many forced absences, Cummeo failed his

exams at the end of the fifth grade. His father was seldom at home, and fought with his mother so much that she slept in the bed with Giovanna and Rosaria. With the bad exams as an excuse, his father took him out of school. And they talked no more about it. But he wasn't even apprenticed to a trade, as had been previously decided, because in the house, husband and wife were divided in soul and body, and their poverty grew worse day by day.

The mother was forced to enlarge her circle of customers, and she washed clothes ten hours a day. Giovanna, then about fourteen, started coming home very late from Signora Sberi's house and fought with her mother, who used to say to her, "If we all only had your luck."

Giovanna refused to touch food. She said that Rosaria was dirty and she didn't want to sleep with her any more. She walked on tiptoes with her hands in the air, so as not to touch anything or be touched, and she begged her mother to make her father permit her to stay day and night at Signora Sberi's.

"I don't talk to him even about important things," her mother said, "so why should I talk to him about your comfort?"

Then the girl gave her some money, which the mother pretended she didn't want to accept, but it always ended the same way. The mother took a knotted handkerchief from her bosom, undid it, tied the money inside, and put it back in her bosom, saying, "He'd even steal it for that Sarno bitch. Just wait till things are a little settled between me and him, and then I'll talk to him."

And Giovanna, with this hope, would change her clothes and mind the babies a while.

Cummeo thought that it would have been better if he had been born neither a man nor a woman, but like Giovanna. If she told him to do something for her, he refused. He refused to accept her money. He even resisted the chocolates, eating them later when his mother gave them to him. He looked at Giovanna grimly, with the same gaze that followed his father's movements: dressing, undressing, beating their mother, snoring in the bed, or saying, "I'd be a young man still, if I didn't have you and these children."

Their father would say a word or two to Giovanna, who, like him, only came home in the evening. She was the bridge between husband and wife, but she didn't like the role and only wanted to go and stay at Signora Sberi's. Because of this new situation, Cummeo had to mind the children and couldn't leave the building, not even the courtyard. As he watched the babies, his mother washed and talked, unburdening herself.

"When you're bigger, we'll throw him out. You'll take care of that. When you're grown and he tries to hit me, you know what you should do?"

"What should I do?"

"You'll know. You'll learn, by yourself."

It all seemed so far away now, the times of the Chivoli woods, and Gigliotti in that house with that lady and the raw egg. He too was changing in appearance. Pale flesh was stretching over his frail bones. Only his hair grew abundantly and strong, becoming downy on his cheeks and hanging over his ears, which he scratched all the time.

He and Lucia, the girl who lived opposite, daughter of a beggar woman, scratched each other with both hands. Lucia's mother went out every day to beg, and by then she had stopped dragging the girl with her to make her sing. Lucia was even poorer than Cummeo, and often Cummeo's mother, as she gave the bread to her children, held out a slice to Lucia, saying, "You too."

When Lucia woke up, she would come straight to Cummeo's house, and since they were the same age, they were always together. They would go and hide behind the building, in the cool grass, doing "dirty things," as she said.

When Cummeo's mother went off, Lucia would say to the boy, "Let's go," and he could never resist her. For that matter, he had no wish to resist her, because he had been waiting for that moment all day, or for several days; and if Lucia went out with her mother, he acted grumpy, and felt a strange fire in his body as soon as he saw her again.

Soon he was the one who said, "Let's go," if he saw her

playing with the other boys in the courtyard, "and if you don't, I'll tell." If he didn't want to go, because some new game was interesting him more deeply, she would be the one to say, "I'll tell your mother."

They touched each other, looked at each other, locked themselves into the latrine of the courtyard. They felt more secure within those fetid walls. Meanwhile, all the other children played in the courtyard outside, hitting one another, and playing war, digging holes, killing lizards, stoning dogs, among the chickens and cats and dogs and the rats that came up from the sewers. Women argued or sang or combed their long hair with iron combs. Buckets of dirty water were hurled from doors on the second, third, and fourth floors. The police arrived, armed, to arrest somebody that none of them had seen for a week, and priests came, in red or in black, and horses with the great crystal box to receive a dead body that had been dressed in Sunday clothes since morning, with children waiting for the funeral candy. There were about seventy children, plus their fathers, their mothers, the old maids, the grandmothers sleeping on chairs outdoors with flies sucking at their faces like carnations, and the peddlers of soap, combs, mirrors, trinkets, and laces, who came in under the arch and shouted their wares.

Only when the landlord arrived suddenly, in a fury, was the courtyard deserted, and the children ran off to hug their mothers' legs.

[6]

One morning, waking up, Cummeo saw that his father was still in bed. He hadn't gone to the mill. He was awake, smoking. Beside him was Mario, with his notebook open. His father said he had got the answer wrong, and the little boy started to cry. Then his father half sat up in bed, and began to copy from the textbook. The children ran to the bed and gathered around him. Cummeo looked over and said, "You're wrong too," and his father accepted the correction. Bored finally, he said to Cummeo, "You show him."

His father stayed in the house all day. He sat by the door. Not far away, the mother was washing, but the two still didn't speak. The air in the house was changed, however. They ate hot food at noon. The father sat among the children. Cummeo, his hair uncombed, sat in his place, opposite his father, serious and a bit grim, but pleased at his father's presence. It was as if the man had come back after a long absence, and all were content. The mother sat on a chair, by herself. She wouldn't sit at the table. But as her husband had his back to her, she looked and looked at him and her expression relaxed. She hung her head when he said to her, "You, I suppose you never made any mistakes. . . . Come here."

After the meal, the little children went out into the courtyard, and the mother, as he pinched her behind and kissed her hair while she washed the dishes, said point-blank, "Out with it. Have you been fired?"

He hadn't been fired exactly. Hard times were beginning for Nofi. One after the other, when the euphoria of the war was over, two tomato canneries had closed down, for lack of foreign orders; two big basket factories and seven mills had also shut. Only a few little concerns were still going, and the powerful, impenetrable ones were locked and barred like insane asylums. But even these had fired shoals of men. Unemployment was spreading. The sawmill had gone bankrupt, with a deficit of twenty million lire. From that day on the father stayed at home.

At first he was in a good humor. He would dress up, go out, and join the other unemployed men. Later he began to stay in the house with his wife, who spoke to him now and had forgotten about the children. She washed sheets while the father boiled fat to make soap.

"He's a man in a thousand," the mother would say. "He can't stay idle. He helps me make soap." He even thought of opening a laundry. But nothing came of the idea.

Weeks went by, and months, and now he didn't shave every day. He tried to make each twenty-five-lire razor blade last as long as possible, saving the last in the pack for a special occasion. What occasion? He allowed the inch or two of perfumed shaving cream to dry up in the tube, and the half-empty bottle of toilet water to evaporate.

He had bought these luxuries the day they raised his pay, a day he had believed would last. It was the end of a period, a single season of hardship, a dark and ever narrower cavern where he had spent and lost his childhood, adolescence, and youth, giving up everything: first because he had been born poor; then because, half-grown, he had had to contribute to the expenses of his family; and finally because, once he was a man, he fell in love with his wife, married her, and love lasted a single night. The morning after the wedding, as that love began to beat its head against the wall of daily life, it was despoiled of every residual passion except the act that helped strengthen their growing family. After two weeks his wife for him was also a sister, a mother, and love with her was freed from all desire and reduced—or elevated—to a way of living together.

Clelia, the Sarno woman, on the other hand, had come into his life on that day when he had more money and had therefore begun to ask something more of life—"toilet articles," for example. He had never felt this adultery of his was a betrayal; indeed, this love seemed so beautiful that he would gladly have talked about it to his wife-mother-sister. It was the first time he had ever made love simply for pleasure and amusement, and he couldn't see where this new sensation might take him. He had always scrupulously given his wife a pair of stockings, since for that matter she agreed with him that their money should buy necessary objects. But he couldn't go to Clelia unshaven or dirty or empty-handed, even if she had never given him time to explain his situation to her. And this heedlessness of hers fascinated him, because it distracted him and made him believe that he had escaped from his fear of toiling on and on forever, without reward.

When Clelia had to be abandoned, the shaving cream, the perfume, and the razor blades became the useless symbols of a past which was only chronologically recent. Clelia never knew how fast the beard grew on the face of the man who had been so affable and heedless when he was with her. But even if she had known, she would have agreed that it was time for him to go back to the wife-mother-sister.

The rare days of hope were followed by weeks of dejection, vain hunting for a job, boredom that he tried to escape by working hard around the house, washing dishes or repairing a chair or fixing his wife's washbucket or patching the children's shoes. But woe if he didn't find the pliers or the right nail or screwdriver when he needed it. The children went to earth like rats, because their father's fury had no limits. These days were followed by others of total idleness. He would get up when his wife had already been bent over the washboard for hours and Giovanna had already gone to Signora Sberi's.

Often Giovanna brought home things left from the Signora's table—loaves of bread or a couple of eggs or oranges or some cigarettes for her father. At times she brought old pieces of cloth, which her mother sold, or if they were unsaleable, adapted for Rosaria or for herself. The following year Giovanna began to bring money too, and her father was happy to talk with her alone. He wanted to know what they did at Signora Sberi's house and he listened spellbound. Finally he would become angry and beat Giovanna, saying that the whole business wasn't clear to him, that she was getting into bad habits; and this to the great delight of Cummeo, who couldn't stand Giovanna because she didn't seem like his sister. He couldn't speak to her or look her in the face, because her clothes stopped him, as did her terrible perfume, and the fine Italian that Signora Sberi taught her to speak so that she would become a lady.

For better or worse, nobody took any interest in him. He had his plate, his bread, his share of blows. Often all the children cried at once, in fear, as their father chased them around the room with a stick. But not Cummeo. He didn't cry any more. He let his father hit him; he lived only for evening, when he went to the Chivoli forest with Lucia, for now both of them knew what they were doing. They went there and came back by different paths.

One evening after having been with Lucia, he came home late. His brothers and sisters were in bed. His mother was sitting in a chair darning some socks, and his father sat with his elbows on the table, idle and grim. Cummeo came in, barely saying good evening because of his fear. His mother set his supper on the table. Beans. And the boy sat down to eat. His father lighted a hand-made cigarette and, without taking it from his mouth, stared at his son. And in a low, almost sleepy voice, he began, "I want to know how this is all going to end. Our little gentleman. We've made a little gentleman. At your age, I was earning money to bring home to my mother."

Cummeo tried to eat in haste, to escape from his father's eyes. But as if he had suddenly seen a glaring truth, the father started shouting, "Sponger! Bum!"

Cummeo stopped eating, his spoon still in his hand. His father knocked it away. And they both stood up, the boy to escape, and his father to catch him. Cummeo didn't want to go out into the courtyard, knowing that he would be pursued and beaten before the eyes of all, including Lucia, who at that moment was the only reason he wanted to avoid shame. He jumped on the bed, waking his brothers, who saw their father with the stick in his hand, laughing as if it were a game, and their mother in the doorway, imploring people to help. The children burst into tears, innocent and terrible.

At this point people invaded the room. To the mother, slumped on a chair, they said, "Poor woman." She didn't speak. She stared into the void. Her face was pale, with two great furrows of terror. Cummeo had disappeared. The father regained his composure in front of the other men. He ran his hand through his hair, saying, "It's nothing. A man loses his temper."

"That's right," a man said to him.

"I'm sorry for her sake"—indicating his wife. "The children are killing her."

The mother should have shown some emotion at these words, but she had the strength to say to him, "The children, the children. It's him. He's turned into a devil."

"It's nobody's fault," the first man said, looking at the whole room, the whole situation. And the father, to find an explanation for his fury, started saying, "You see, he's never satisfied with what he finds," inventing out of the whole cloth, knowing that he was inventing but beginning to believe it. "He sucked the blood out of me, and now he's doing the same to his poor mother."

Cummeo was hidden under the doorway, ashamed. He wept in silence. The warmth of the tears on his cheeks comforted him. He felt helpless. And he felt that he loved his father and his mother. He sensed that all this wasn't his father's fault, but the fault of something more mysterious, something he couldn't touch or strike. His father was talking with the other fathers, his mother with the other mothers. Even Lucia's mother, who was lame and who preferred to stay on her knees or in the center of a circle of people, was now listening, fascinated. Lucia stood awkwardly along the wall, unable to go to Cummeo, but looking at him from the distance, without saying a word.

Then Giovanna came. She was coming home on her high heels, with her hair on top of her head, and her shiny leather purse. They all looked at her, all thinking the same thing, and mentally saying the same words: "Lucky." She drew back and said, "My God, nothing but fussing in this house."

It was very late.

[7]

After this scene, Cummeo decided to get up at dawn so as not to encounter his father.

He started going to the market, keeping his distance from the other porters, who had little pushcarts. He saw the money in the wholesalers' hands; saw the peasants, who didn't want to accept a small sum and went off, then came back, and because they had gone away, now received an even smaller one.

The wholesalers were a pack of thieves and they had the nerve to put thirty lire in his hand for a load of four hundred pounds, saying, "You're just a kid. That's plenty for you."

So Cummeo preferred to go with the peasants when they asked him to lend a hand. They didn't give him any money, but in return they let him do as he pleased in the country, and they never failed to commiserate with him and give him some wheat cakes or a salami or a stalk of broccoli. His real pleasure was simply to be in the country, where he felt free and happy, to forget the world he was in. He often found a place on a cart going down to Nofi, drawn by a filly hung with bells; and the peasants, standing in the wagon going from farm to farm, called to one another and talked.

Nofi, seen from the high fields, was all different colors; it was hard to imagine that inside it there were houses like his, men like his father, poor women like his mother. Everything was simpler in the country. Here rows of broccoli, there a hundred orange trees, here clumps of lettuce opening like immense flowers, and there a cluster of piglets and a rooster moving along the furrows. Good things to see and to eat, the pleasant voices of the animals, the cool, fresh air. For this pleasure, Cummeo bore even the jokes of the peasants, who said, to tease him, "You're just out of the hospital! You're only good to make axle grease."

The peasants rarely asked for a hand, so he had to make up to Marianna, the oldest fruit vendor in Nofi, who went directly to the market at dawn to buy. Afterward, since she was lame, she wanted to be pushed on the pushcart, behind the baskets of vegetables and fruit that she had bought. On these occasions Cummeo went along the Corso, where there was nothing to be seen at this hour except a little café or two with steam coming out of the door. At home, he gave his mother the few lire he had earned, and sometimes some fruit or vegetables that had been rejected. He told his mother that he could earn more if he had a pushcart of his own. They would have to save up for five or six months. His mother wouldn't hear of it, because she counted on those few lire every morning.

If Cummeo hadn't earned anything, he didn't go home. He'd go and eat at the monastery, along with Lucia and her mother, but without waiting in line like the other beggars. The two women would bring him a bowl to the field, behind the insane asylum, where there were always ten or so mad people at some window in the immense façade of the hospital, hanging onto the bars, shouting greetings first and then insults at anybody who went past.

He, Lucia, and her mother ate with the metal pan between their legs, swallowing huge spoonfuls of the congealed food, while at the arsenal, in front of the ten or twelve gentle hills of the landscape, the soldiers' helmets gleamed as the men had target practice.

Cummeo would have liked to be there every day with Lucia, to explain to her the great exploits of those people. He told her that a captain—and he was thinking of Gigliotti's father—had allowed him on the parade grounds, as they called it, and he had seen and touched everything. They went as far as the fence, their ears filled with the commands of the captain, who shouted as if there were enemy troops in front of him. On the deep, dusty path behind them passed patrols of mounted officers, the horses rearing up to free themselves of their riders, dropping flecks of saliva, and disappearing finally behind the little houses where the ladies stood with their parasols. For Cummeo it was an exciting vision, and for Lucia too, who believed what he said and what he would do; both forgot their native sadness, their guilty games, lost now in those eyes pure with childish light, peering through the fence.

Little by little the sun faded, and the soldiers, mounting strange wagons with weapons and monstrous wheels, abandoned the field. On the meadow of purplish grass, Lucia's mother sat in Indian fashion, still eating, taking crusts of bread and leftovers from her begging sack and watching the sun disappear. An inexpressible sadness came over Cummeo, so strongly that he suddenly stopped as he was running. He followed Lucia mechanically to the courtyard; he went past his house, peeping in to see if his father was inside. If his father was there, Cummeo went and sat down at the end of the courtyard, envying Lucia, who had a good mother, as he waited for things to change and favor his re-entry into the house.

Seeing the families eating all around the courtyard at their tables under a naked bulb—some bulbs weaker than others, some with candles, some houses closed and barred, their poverty lighted only by the moon—and his playmates freely making a racket around their parents, he would go over to one of those doors and look inside. They offered him bread, and he didn't refuse it, but he was even happier if they let him come inside and share in this freedom between father and children until the lights went out around the courtyard, the doors were all barred, and he heard his mother's voice saying in a whisper, "Come."

[8]

He would have liked to have long trousers to cover his hairy thighs and legs, a real pair of shoes, money to go to the movies, a real suit to wear along the Corso. Many of the other boys from the courtyard were already able to have these things, and now that in July he would be old enough, he'd go and work at the tomato cannery if he could get in.

His father had the same idea, but they didn't like him and wouldn't take him on. Cummeo was hired as a porter. He started on July fifteenth and stopped at the end of September, when the tomatoes ended.

And what did he get out of it? Food, a pair of shoes, a sweater, trousers—all bought at the market, like when he was a little boy, and according to his mother's taste. Not a cent went into his own pocket. His mother, on his father's orders, went to the office to find out what wages her son was earning; and his father, later, ordered his mother to draw the pay directly every week, because Cummeo was seventeen and still a minor.

When the work ended, the other boys had suits, winter overcoats, a little money, and afterward shared out the winter unemployment allowance with their families. Cummeo's unemployment concerned his parents only. He only went to draw the money. And he started rotting in the courtyard again.

"Need makes man a thief and turns parents mean," his mother said to another woman. "Thank goodness Signora Sberi has taken such a liking to Giovannina. But what can she bring us? It's enough that the Signora has brought her up. We have to slice every penny as thin as a communion wafer. Him"—she pointed to her husband—"he's out of work. He's turned into an old man. And he's one in a thousand. He makes soap for me. He goes to pick up the washing and delivers it afterward."

Cummeo listened to this talk and in his heart he was convinced that if his mother had more money, she would have been more generous with him. She came from a good family. Her brother, a sergeant, had died in the war. A sister was living in America, rich, but they didn't know her address. Cummeo had his mother's thin lips, her hands, her teeth, the warm color of her eyes, and her instinct for resignation. He was content when his mother said, "I know. You're right. Better times will come for you too."

But their poverty was intense, filthy, and unrelenting, like the cold that year, and in their one room, father and son were two caged beasts.

"You act big because you're my father," Cummeo dared to say. "But don't worry. I'll join the navy. I want to see what all of you will do without me."

"Are you throwing those few pennies you've given us in our face? I clothed you and gave you food, I created you—and you're reproaching me now?"

His father really couldn't see him with any pleasure. In this son, who was now as tall as he, he recognized himself, unoccupied and helpless, and if he ever forgot that he was jobless, Cummeo reminded him. He became a real father only when a child was ill. Then he was all over him, driving away flies, preparing a raw egg, going into debt to buy him a slice of roast meat.

"Sickness is undernourishment," he said. "With eggs and meat, even the dead rise again."

[9]

In July the factories reopened, and Cummeo went back to work. At the end of the first week, handing his wages to his mother, he said, "I'm going to work overtime, but I'm keeping that money."

His mother repeated this to his father, who concluded, "What's fair is fair."

Cummeo gave up swimming on Sunday at the Vietri beach. He gave up movies. He didn't buy even a soft drink. He spent all his time at the cannery. For days and nights he didn't sleep. He was thinking of the coming winter. He would buy himself an overcoat, a suit, shiny black shoes, a real shirt, a thousand-lire necktie, a raincoat. He worked and thought of the colors of the cloth, the shirt, and the rest. The suit would have to be one that would do in all seasons, an overcoat with a belt in the back, the kind he had once seen Gigliotti wearing. He would try to have a little money left over, to keep in his pocket, for a movie, for an occasion. He calculated everything again, and he realized that he would have to choose: either the suit or the overcoat.

"It's bad, going around with no overcoat," he said to a friend. And the friend answered, "If you look at it that way, you should have a raincoat too. For myself, I'd take the suit. That's what I did last year, and this year I'm buying the coat."

He no longer thought about the marvelous overcoat of Gigliotti; only the suit, the shoes, the tie, the handkerchief, as he said to himself, "On cold days I'll stay home." He was already happy. He would be able to go out of the courtyard, he could even go to the Corso, to the Bar Oriente, the best bar in Nofi, mingling with the respectable people without being looked at like a dog. "Clothes are everything for these bastards," his father always used to say.

With this fixed thought he bore nearly three months of work, and at the end of September, when the shutters of the cannery were drawn down, he went to Faraone, a fine tailor, who understood the young man's wishes and saw the cash. He made a splendid suit, narrow around the hips, broad across the chest, the trousers tapering at the ankles. Cummeo could just barely pay for the shoes, and he had to be satisfied with a second-class shirt. When they saw him at home, they couldn't restrain their pleasure at having such a gentlemanly looking son.

"Just like my brother," his mother said. Giovanna promised to introduce him to Signora Sberi, and Lucia burst into tears, saying, "Now you won't want to marry me any more!"

"You're crazy," Cummeo said. "Even without the suit, I wouldn't have married you."

And they didn't see much of each other for some time.

[10]

After the first reception was over, his mother asked him how much he had spent for the suit and the shoes.

"Fifteen thousand lire in all," Cummeo answered. It seemed a lot to the woman, who, driven by her curiosity, questioned the cobbler, the shirtmaker, the tailor, and discovered the true amount: thirty thousand. She came back home disconsolate, her deepest affections betrayed. The father was out, and she began to slap herself, to weep, to writhe, and slump on a chair.

Cummeo was afraid his father would arrive, and he said pleadingly, "I'll sell it all, and I'll give you the money. But don't make him hit me now."

In vain. As the other women of the courtyard arrived, her grief turned into a performance. But when the father appeared in the doorway, a woman said, "It's nothing. She only fainted, that's all." And the mother forced a kind of grimace and deceived her husband, who never learned of the thirty thousand lire. Fifteen thousand was bad enough for him.

Cummeo's suit was out of place in that half-dark, spent, cold room, occupied by seven lurid phantoms, and any occasion served as a shortcut to bring the conversation back to that suit, which the father attacked with fierce lamenting and terrible precision.

"With those fifteen thousand lire, we could have faced Christmas without any fear." He would calculate the pounds of pasta or bread, the oil that they could have bought, and Cummeo felt it was all his fault. His father could make him visualize that bread, that pasta, that unbought oil. "How can you have the nerve to go around? What must people think of me, with a daughter who walks along the Corso on high heels, an egoist like you, and a son who's always at the bar, drinking coffee as if it was water?"

Cummeo would have liked to stay in the house, to keep them company, but he couldn't stand the torment of this same speech, the reproach for sins he hadn't committed, because he had done his duty. His father had definitely lost his nerve; he went to the market now, to pull carts. Now it was Cummeo, torn and dirty, who didn't shave for a week and let his hair grow for months down over his ears and neck. For some time Giovanna had been staying day and night at Signora Sberi's and even her presence, the symbol of salvation that she represented, with her aroma of a better world, was lacking in the evening. From time to time she sent Signora Sberi's real servant, old Serafina, with the left-overs, to which even Cummeo wasn't indifferent. The mother divided the bread on a little scale, and the children hid it. Who could eat, ate. And at the table, the improvident brother looked at the frugal one. They stole the bread from one another and hid it. Almost every evening their father was obliged to give some of his own to one of them, but before he did, he would yell at Cummeo. At the table, lighted by a little candle on a piece of tin, the filmy handkerchief in Cummeo's pocket was an insult. And his father would start saying again, "We would have plenty of bread now. . . . No-good! You could at least keep out of our sight. That, at least!"

Cummeo tried putting on his old things, a handful of tatters; he felt unrecognizable in them. But his greatest sin, the suit, was also his salvation. He could leave the house, go to the Corso, the Bar Oriente, without anyone feeling sorry for him, without being noticed. And this helped him live his solitary life.

Clean and neat, before his father came back from the market, he would go on an empty stomach to the Oriente, where the chairs to the right were occupied by a group including the ex-sergeant of the local military headquarters, who hadn't

been able to save enough to buy a suit to replace the uniform
that he now wore without insignia; an ex-sawmill worker, a
companion of his father's, gossipy as an old woman; the
ex-foreman of the Altieri factory, who preached revolution,
and by another twenty or so idle young men, ready to listen
to anything.

They took up half of the bar, and they only went out when
nature drove them, as Turolla, the owner, said. In the back
was the card room, and they could hear cards being slammed
down, people shouting, more cards, and between one card
and the next, often as much as twenty minutes of silence
went by before a diabolical laugh would explode in the air.
Turolla sat hunched over the cash register with his fat, beard-
less, woman's face, moaning over the ruination of his bar,
"worthy of the Lido of Venice." But he couldn't drive them
out because he would have lost the money they owed him
for what they had drunk, and he would have made dangerous
enemies in the town. Anyhow, in the event of one of the
factories' reopening, "this bunch of bums would become a
flock of customers."

Cummeo happened into their midst, greeted with cold,
hostile antipathy, only because of that suit, which would not
look out of place on a factory owner's son. From the first
day, he lacked the courage to sit down in the more numerous
group, and he stayed in a corner, to one side, sitting with
his shoulders erect, not crossing his legs so as not to spoil
the crease in his trousers, patting the handkerchief in his
pocket or his tie, then resuming his immobile position, like
someone who has sat down only for a moment, but is being
kept waiting.

"Who's that young man?" the ex-foreman asked. And the
man from the sawmill answered, "You know him surely. He's
Gerardo Cummeo's son. Don't you remember the father?
Used to work at the sawmill. Scum. The daughter is one of
Sberi's girls."

"Ah," the ex-foreman said. "His sister keeps him well-
dressed."

"I wouldn't want to be in his shoes," the other man observed.

The foreman knew what kind of man the other was, and what he would have done to be in Cummeo's shoes, ambitious as he was and vain above all vanity. The carpenter had never left Nofi, not even for military service, and he talked of Turin and Milan and Rome as if he had been there, surrounded by women. Ciccio Borro, the broker, who was well off now and had a mistress who was ugly but spoke proper Italian, talked about Venice as if it were his own street, but he had already been there once, "in transit," as the ex-sergeant said. In an hour's layover in Venice, he had worn his hands to the bone sending postcards to the whole town; and he had been living for half a century on the memory of that hour. The others listened to him, so that they would also be listened to. What else had they to live for? A couple of hours were dedicated to criticizing the women who went past. The men guessed at their fornications. A couple of hours went by in calculating the money of other people, and half a day was dedicated to football, despising or admiring "the eleven parasites of the team," as the sergeant put it.

"I'd whip them," he added, "I'd make them run barefoot on ice. By God . . . I, who after all . . . I, who . . ."

Cummeo took his seat at eight o'clock, almost as if he were going to an office. When the radio signaled one o'clock, he got up, along with the others, waved to an acquaintance or two, and disappeared. When she could, his mother prepared a plate of something for him, and he tied a handkerchief around his neck to keep from spotting his clothes before he devoured the food, whatever it might be, whatever color or smell it had. Immediately afterward, he went back to the bar, still empty. Arnaldo, the relief barman, a reader of comic books, would give him the latest. Often Cummeo found nobody at home, and he went off to wander around the monastery, waiting for Lucia. Then they went to the field. Lucia often purposely kept him waiting. Since she had started wearing high heels, a pair of shoes costing a thousand lire given her by God knows whom, she even dared to refuse herself to him, saying she was busy. And Cummeo, who had always felt he was doing her a favor, condescending, was now eaten by jealousy and thought of her with deep bitterness.

Her attachment for him returned whenever Cummeo began to talk about his probable imminent departure as "a sergeant in the navy," in which he believed firmly. He said, "Anybody can go. Your birth doesn't matter; it's the military spirit that counts, and I have it. You travel all over, even in America. That's the career for me."

As he waited for the tomato season to return, he began to think seriously about the papers necessary to enlist. He considered it as good as done, but then, sudden and insurmountable, appeared the obstacle: the money required for the documents. There was a remedy: the certificate of poverty. With that, he could have all his documents gratis. But this meant going to the town hall, taking his father there, and witnesses, who would have to testify that the Cummeo family had become officially destitute. Cummeo didn't have the courage to bring the subject up with his father, who thought only of the present and considered as an illusion anything that took more than twenty-four hours; and in addition, Cummeo's shame grew on him like leprosy.

On the other hand, the navy, with its distant lands, seemed constantly more real and vivid to him, a physical and moral salvation, which in any case would help him find a path, either if he stayed in as a noncom—he would distinguish himself, be liked by his superiors—or if, in desperation, he jumped ship in America and stayed there, even becoming a gangster, so he could send money to his mother and father, because this was the chief thing on his conscience.

He began to confide in his mother. She saw things in as rosy a light as he did. The word "America" reanimated her visibly. Because she was related to so many emigrants, it held a hope that had slept but not died in her blood. But when it came to the question of the documents, she said, "Is that what you were getting around to? You're out of your head."

Cummeo stopped, but when he was alone with her again, he took up the subject of America once more—because now it was only America they talked of—of the documents and the necessary money. Otherwise the whole plan would collapse, for want of those few pennies.

Even his mother began to think about it seriously, and finally she told herself that the boy was right, that this was truly the only possible way. Cummeo sensed this maternal attitude in his favor. Though he knew that soon the family wouldn't even be able to go out of the courtyard because they had debts with the grocer, the baker, the candlemaker, and the oilman—and perhaps they wouldn't even be able to look out of the door, because all their neighbors were also creditors by now, some for a loaf of bread, others for a bit of tomato paste—for the first time in his life he invented a whole story. He said that he had talked to a man in the navy, who had told him there was nothing to jumping ship in America; this one and that one had done it. All he needed was the few lire for the documents.

"All right then. I hope it's true. Tell me how much you need. And not a word to anybody. We'll tell about it the day you leave."

Cummeo never knew how his mother managed to collect that money, where she squeezed it from, since they had nothing left to squeeze. When he had collected the documents, he started waiting. He waited, and so did his mother and Lucia. From time to time they met, knowing that they were waiting. And finally the postcard came.

The day of the medical exam, which was to take place at the town hall, Cummeo's mother persuaded her husband to go out early, with the excuse that if he delayed, he wouldn't find the women at home and they wouldn't give him the clothes to wash. When he disappeared, the others went to work at once. The mother took the wooden washbucket, rinsed it well, and filled it half full of cold water. She heated other water over the brazier. Naked in his bed, Cummeo waited until all was ready. His little brothers were in the courtyard, saying pensively, "Cummeo's got to take a bath."

Then his mother opened the door, brought in the bucket, and said to her son, "Hurry up, before it gets cold. It's just right now."

"Go outside," Cummeo said to her.

"Just look at him. I made him, I've kissed him a hundred times when he was a little boy, and now he's ashamed in front of his mother. Come and wash. How can you wash your back by yourself?"

Cummeo went and lay down in the water, and as his mother washed his back with soft black soap, Cummeo scrubbed the rest of himself. The water soon became greasy and bluish. It had been years since he had washed himself, since anyone had washed himself in that courtyard. If anybody tried it more than once, what with the drafts and the cold of the place, he could catch pneumonia. Finally Cummeo stood up; as he dried himself, his mother said, "Sailor? Why, you could be a royal guard. You should have seen the man your father was. . . . He was a marvel."

"What am I going to put on now?" Cummeo said.

"Wait," his mother answered, going into the courtyard for a moment. She came back with a little bottle of perfume.

"Don't waste it all." From the other side of the door came the voice of the woman who had lent it.

"What did you lend her?" another woman's voice asked.

"Perfume. Her son's going for his medical exam."

His mother gave Cummeo his father's only decent pair of underwear, the Sunday ones, reminding him sternly, "Afterward, you come back and take them off."

No other boy set out for the exam as sweet-smelling inside and out. But when he had to undress in the midst of all those young men, peasants and workers, friends and strangers, gentlemen and beggars, seeing the others, who may not have washed, but who had flesh, big muscles, and hair on their legs, their arms and chest, he lost heart. He went through it all, to one side. When he was naked, the others started teasing:

"Where do you think you're going?"

"You're in the wrong building."

"Look at Mr. Bones over there."

Already defeated, he prepared to face the medical officer, who didn't bother to take Cummeo's measurements. Cummeo's chest was striking; there was a hollow in the midst of it. Thighs and legs were equally thin. He was a living example of what hunger can do.

"Your shoulders are broad enough," the doctor said, "and you might fill out. But there's no hope for this year at least."

After this, Cummeo became a figure of secondary importance. He was able to dress again without being disturbed, slowly, now that he knew there was nothing to be done, that they wouldn't have him as a *carabiniere* or a policeman or even a traffic cop. He didn't speak for two days. His mother, all by herself, wept over her son's body, and he said nothing to Lucia, for fear she would make fun of him.

He started going back and forth again, between his house and the Bar Oriente, with terrible punctuality. The thought of the cannery, his only sure hope, lay in the depth of his heart with a deep torment. But since it was his only hope, he began to caress it and love it. But then the troubles began, the riots of the older unemployed men and the veterans, including even the sergeant, who insisted that the army should be expanded.

Cummeo rushed to see Balestra's father, the owner and manager of the cannery, and managed to speak to him.

"Are you a veteran?" the man asked brusquely. "Are you married, do you have children? What's your position, in other words?"

Cummeo wanted to say that nobody had ever allowed him to have a position, but he only said that he had been to school with the director's son, Eugenio.

"Glad to hear it," the man said, assuming a hypocritically familiar tone. "I'll make a note of your name, just in case. But for the moment, there's nothing I can do. Not only are there too many of us already, but I also have to deal with the union. See what you can do there."

At the union there was chaos. Too many people. Too many fathers. Too many unemployed. Above all, he had to persuade himself that he was alone in the world. His father was there too. And he came away, because his name had already been on the list for two years—he couldn't even remember the number.

Cummeo tried, in vain, to explain the situation to his mother. She remained silent, almost angry. She didn't dare to say that she couldn't keep him any longer. But he understood her, without words.

So Cummeo began to be ashamed to wander around the courtyard. He came back when he was sure his father wasn't at home—and he didn't know where he was—to wash his face and his feet in the bucket of water. He couldn't change his underwear. His suit was heavy, and the summer that year was hot, like all the summers. He smelled the odor of sweat rising from his skin, from his chest. Perhaps that is why many people kept their distance when they spoke to him. He had to be careful to walk in a certain way, not raising his worn shoes too high. He pulled his ragged socks under the soles of his feet, so that the holes didn't show. The crease in his pants had vanished; he seemed to be wearing two pipes.

Like it or not, at one o'clock he had to leave the bar. Turolla, who felt himself in a strong position with Cummeo, would say, "Can it really be a whole year you've been sitting here without buying so much as a cup of coffee? And now you bend to pick up cigarette butts? Go to your sister. . . . Let me have some peace at lunch hour anyway. . . ."

For Cummeo the bar was still an illusion. He liked the smell of ice cream that came from the shadowy interior, the long aluminum counter, the fresh, ceaseless hum of the refrigerator, which contained the soft drinks, the beer, the ices that he liked, which, sometimes, Arnaldo secretly gave him a taste of, in the bottom of a glass. He observed the pleasure with which a gentleman put a spoonful of ice cream into his mouth. Cummeo didn't want to watch, and yet he kept looking back. At least once he would have liked to live like a gentleman; to have a normal family, a sister who was a sister, a girl friend he could talk to. And he wasn't consoled by the words of Arnaldo, who in the summer afternoons sometimes sat down beside him and said, "You think the boss lives any better than we do? He's stingy with himself, won't spend money on medicines. He never buys a coffee outside, because it costs too much."

And Cummeo said, "Maybe so, but he has the money . . . so it's as if he had all the things he doesn't buy."

That afternoon he had gone home and had run into his father. He had rebelled against the man and had hit him, so that the whole courtyard, woman by woman, had reproached him. Even a child, seeing his mother raging at Cummeo, had given him a kick. They took his father to the other side of the courtyard and gave him something to eat. They forgot about Cummeo.

He wandered for a couple of hours around the monastery, but he didn't see Lucia or her mother. He decided to go in himself. He was stampeded by a horde of beggars, left without food, as he was. He wandered around some more, thinking of his hunger, until he found himself in front of the Bar Oriente, literally empty, with Turolla among the tables, as if waiting to drive Cummeo away. He pretended to retrace his steps, in the hope that the owner of the bar would go away, and he retreated to the corner of the street, picking up a long butt that caught his eye, with a kind of smile of thanks. From the house opposite, two stories, with shutters and terraces of flowers and plants, a young man came out, wearing a white sports shirt, navy-blue pants, tennis shoes, and carrying underwater fishing gear. It was Balestra, his former schoolmate. He hadn't changed a bit since the days when he sat at the first desk in school. Then everybody knew that a light slap would knock him to the ground, but not even the teacher dared to take the whip to him. Now he was still thin, worn and haggard-looking, but—as in the old days—his clothes made these defects into splendid virtues. Turolla greeted him in a loud voice.

Cummeo had a moment of great confidence: to go over to him, explain his situation, tell him that he hadn't eaten for several days, take off his coat and show him how his shirt only covered half his chest, a rag, and he had no underwear, and ask Balestra for a pair of socks to hide his dirty, knotty ankles when he walked, so that nobody would have to feel pity for him. But the vision of Balestra as a child, striking the others, much stronger than he, at the teacher's orders, suddenly made Cummeo lose his instinctive trust. Now, as then, Balestra was better dressed than he; now, as then, Balestra seemed to belong to another race.

"He was always like that," Cummeo said to himself. It was a thought that took immediate and complete possession of his mind. He took two or three steps along the wall and sat down furtively at the first chair in the bar, completely alone. The square in front of him was a sea, mobile and thick with sunlight, not to be crossed; and he was happy, because he could have explained this to Turolla, if Turolla wanted to drive him away. Staring into nothingness, he felt his inborn silence spreading through every vein, every feeling. Mechanically he leaned this way and that, to make sure the hole in his socks was invisible, to adjust his jacket, his handkerchief, running his hand through his disheveled, dandruffy hair, to arrange it over his ears, listening to the idle undertone of the refrigerator as if the continuity of his life depended on its steady hum.

[11]

He woke up—because it must have been a kind of sleep he was in—when the sun had almost left the square. The little tables of the café were filled with people who had come out to enjoy the cool of the evening, and the town's sprinkling machine, wetting the street, raised the pleasant odor of damp earth. Saying nothing to himself, he got up and went across the square, along the street toward the country and the So-calla bridge. He didn't know what to do, where to go. He was no longer aware of his hunger pangs. He didn't see the cars coming back from the beaches of Vietri, or the boys and girls in their light clothes going off to make love in the nearby forests.

Then, in one of the automobiles, he thought he glimpsed his sister, sitting between two young men. She must have been swimming. But his sharpest impression was the usual one: Giovanna was his sister only in a manner of speaking, a false affirmation of his father and mother. She was too different, even physically, with her beautiful mouth, her strong arms, her free, young movements; almost aristocratic with her indifferent nature, her absolute lack of interest in what was going on in Cummeo's heart.

He would have liked to feel jealous of the two young men with her in the car; to say to her, "Go home. Our mother needs your help." But his body preferred to go on at its slow pace, with its dirty, dusty ankles. He went over the Socalla bridge and sat down on a patch of grass near the railroad. It was the hour of the express trains, the ones that rattled the pebbles of the tracks; the fast train going to Calabria and the other that, as he believed, went to Naples—and no farther, because over there, where the sun was now glowing red, the known or imagined world ended for him. He looked with pleasure at the grass and the yellow wild flowers that peeped out of it. He was comforted by the loneliness of the spot, and decided that he would spend the night lying on the grass, with the noises of Nofi, like the dull sound of a seashell, in the distance. He stretched out, his eyes on the sky, not moving as the trains passed, allowing himself slowly to start thinking again of Giovanna, who would never imagine that he was only a few feet from the Signora's little villa. Perhaps she was now having an ice on the terrace among the colored tables and the tile porch, as he had once seen it. And because of this curiosity—to see if he could see her, though not to speak to her—he stood up. There was the villa, deserted, with its balconies and windows wide open to allow the evening air into the rooms. In front of the gate stood the young men's car. He crossed the stretch of flowering grass, and was under the villa, waiting for his sister to appear. Or rather, he was there because that was what his legs had decided, his eyes and his head.

A little later old Serafina appeared with a pitcher of water in her hand. And he was immediately distracted by the opening of the door, from which came Giovanna and the two young men. At the same moment, the Signora appeared above the terrace in a dressing gown and wearing a hairnet, to add her good-byes to the young men. Cummeo couldn't help uttering a name which still meant something to him; because he had played and slept with the person bearing that name so many times, and because that girl, no matter how transformed, must still have another memory and another life in her spirit.

Giovanna understood at once that it was he. She thought that he could wait until the boys had gone; she was a good sister, but she didn't want to be disturbed. Without turning around, she said, "Wait," as if to say: Keep behind those bushes, or you'll spoil things for me.

Cummeo waited without bitterness, with sympathy, realizing his sister's situation. They summoned each other, they answered in such a way as if it had been telepathy, and the two young men paid no attention to that "wait" of Giovanna's.

When the automobile had gone, Cummeo came out on the lawn, and Giovanna said to the Signora, "It's my brother; he has something to tell me." The Signora barely looked at him as she entered the house.

"What do you want?" Giovanna asked him.

"Did you know Mama's sick?" he invented.

"What do you want from me? I never exploited her. No, I was the only one who ever gave her a hand. I sent her a thousand lire yesterday, and some things."

Seeing this brother, filthy dirty and defeated, there was no doubt as to what he was and how he lived. She said, "You shouldn't come here. None of you. The Signora is terrible. She'll make me pay, you'll see. . . . It's a menace. Papa was hanging around here yesterday. What does he want? He never did anything for us, except beat us."

Cummeo listened in silence, his eyes on the ground; he had no intention of answering. It was Giovanna who said, "Have you eaten?" Then, shaking him, "Haven't you eaten?" She took him by the wrist and drew him behind the villa, to the little garden gate. She went back into the house, and then came and opened the wooden gate. She led him into the barn, where there was an old carriage, some dusty packing cases and other things, the washbuckets and the mangers that had been used for the Signora's horses in the old days.

"Wait here. I'll go and get something for you."

He waited at least an hour, which seemed only a short while to him. He liked the horse smell that had remained in the barn, he liked the carriage, which had a long, soft black cushion, and all these old country things, shovels and hoes, the things that had always excited him. When the Signora had been young and thin, and they called her "the American," she drove her own bay horse through the streets of Nofi, a symbol of sin and fascination. He would like to have been the coachman, driving the coach and especially caring for the horse. He would have been willing to sleep in the barn, not bothering anybody in the villa. It would have been better than staying at the tables of the Bar Oriente. He thought of saying this to his sister, but he realized that this wasn't the moment, and that probably the Signora would be more willing to have him than his sister would, because Giovanna would be ashamed of him, which was a way of being ashamed of herself.

He heard the door of the upper floor open, then the heavy main door slam, then his sister, coming down the bright-colored steps. Once, as a little boy, he had gone inside that house, and he remembered it as a magic world, with the odor of good cooking. Giovanna said to him, "Eat here, on the chest."

Cummeo wanted to ask for a candle, but he was afraid of going too far.

"I told her," his sister said.

"And what did she say?"

"Nothing. She wanted me to bring you a whole dinner, in fact."

Cummeo ate. He couldn't see very well, but he knew it was as if he were eating for the first time. He touched half a loaf of soft, white bread. He wanted to sniff it. He lifted macaroni and meat balls to his mouth.

"There's a party tonight," his sister said. Cummeo was coming to life again. He put meat stuffed with egg to his mouth—one, two, three, ten forkfuls—and a mixed salad, some fried potatoes, a sip of cool wine. He ate and thought: This is what Giovanna eats. That's why she's young and plump and pretty. "Good food makes pink faces," his father used to say.

"Another time I'll have you try the chicken," Giovanna went on. "There wasn't much in the house tonight because we were at the beach all day."

His mouth full, Cummeo looked at his sister and approved, feeling himself affectionate, without rancor, ready for anything. He wanted to ask her if the Signora needed a handy man, a gardener, a man to do the shopping, or somebody who was all these things at once, but he was afraid of making a bad impression.

"You're right, maybe you're ashamed of me . . . but I think that, if you wanted, I could stay. . . ."

"Hurry," his sister said.

"You know why? To help them." He had only just thought of it. "You could say: If you don't help my brother, I'll go away too."

"Fine. Then I'd be another dead weight at home," she said, with a sad and sinister laugh. "What could you do here?" She asked him why he hadn't gone home, why he didn't obey their father—as if she had ever obeyed him—and she concluded, "I don't like the whole bunch of you, always hitting each other and making scenes, like no-goods."

She's like a foreigner, Cummeo thought, but then he too felt an aversion for his father, and with growing enthusiasm went back to daydreaming about staying in the Signora's stable. He concluded, "Isn't there anything she could have me do? I'd be satisfied with anything. I'd never go upstairs. I'm in too bad shape, and half this amount of food would put me in shape again."

"I know," Giovanna said, annoyed at having taken him in

this evening. If she had only thought of giving him two hundred lire that would have been the end of it. "I know. You think I wouldn't like to? But it's her. She isn't nice, like she seems."

The next morning Giovanna said nothing when she saw him in the garden; at noon she came down with the Signora, in person, to speak to him before going to the beach. The night before, not knowing where to sleep, Cummeo had pretended to go out of the gate. Then he had retraced his steps, climbed over the wall, and shut himself into the stable. He took the cushion of the buggy and stretched out on it. Dazed by the small amount of wine he had drunk, sated and without a worry, he had fallen asleep at once, missing a fine chance to see the people at the party that was held in the Signora's house. He woke up in the cool, disordered garden. The villa was still all shut up and solitary in its restful surroundings. No regrets for the courtyard, none for his mother or his brothers and sister. As if he had always led this life, he no longer remembered the recent past, even yesterday, Turolla, and the rest; he was willing to forget it all forever.

He thought of throwing himself at the Signora's feet, asking her to have mercy and give him something to do. He promised himself that he would never go upstairs into the rooms, he would sleep in the stable, and do exactly what he was told. He spent the morning with these thoughts, until Giovanna and the Signora came to him.

"He's just a boy," the Signora said.

Cummeo didn't say a word, and his sister had to remind him to say thank you. He didn't know how.

He would have liked to run home, tell his mother, now that he felt a love for her he had never felt before; but the Signora gave him his first orders: he was to go to Nofi for the carpenter to replace a broken window, and after that he could go upstairs and eat. The maid would take care of the rest.

He ran off toward Nofi, did everything properly, and ran

back, without the carpenter, but with the glass, because he had a talent for repairing things.

The maid said to him, "Are you the carpenter or are you Giovanna's brother? I have orders to feed only Giovanna's brother."

Cummeo replaced the pane beautifully, and afterward he sat down in the cool kitchen, which had a big window overlooking the garden. Serafina did her chores, saying, "Don't think you're all that lucky, staying here. The old woman has a long tongue, and she throws her kindness in your face afterward. Ask your sister. Your sister lets the old woman make a fool of her though. If she only had what she ought to have . . . But she's satisfied with a dress or two, and cigarettes. . . ."

Cummeo didn't know his sister smoked.

"What's your name?" Serafina asked him. "That's an ugly name. The old woman'll make you change it, you'll see. She calls everybody Lily, Daisy, Carnation, if they give her money. You know what she says to me? 'Serafina, my name is Madam Money.' "

There was a knock at the door, and Cummeo stood up to go and open it.

"Stay where you are," Serafina shouted. "That isn't your job." Then he heard her saying, "You can't now."

"But I'm a friend of the Signora."

"I have orders not to let anyone in if she's not here."

"But why not?" the young man insisted. "I tell you, I'm a friend of hers."

"The rooms are all occupied—every one."

And when she came back into the kitchen, she was muttering to herself, "They're all like soldiers. They're not ashamed in front of an old woman like me."

Cummeo couldn't believe that it meant what it did. Giovanna had always said that the Signora treated her like a daughter, looked after her with a real mother's care, that she was going to give Giovanna a dowry and perhaps even the villa when she died.

Cummeo wanted to ask Serafina who the man was at the

door, but the old servant began to say, "My boy, you're right. If you start acting dumb in this house, if you don't see and don't hear, you've found a gold mine. . . . We needed a helpful boy. I do everything here, you know. The Signora gives me plenty of kisses and talk, but nobody lifts a finger but me."

He went down into the garden to the stable, took a sickle and began to trim the flower beds, restoring them to their heart-shaped pattern. From time to time Serafina looked at him from the big window as she dried the dishes. Then he was alone. He worked until his sister and the Signora came back, flushed from the sun, the Signora with half her bosom exposed and a good part of her back. Both of them had forgotten about Cummeo.

"Who's that young man?" the Signora asked Giovanna. "Oh, how silly of me. It's your brother. . . . Did you have the pane put in? . . . Good for you, and you can garden too? At last I'll be able to come into the garden and read my newspaper."

A little later, Giovanna called him from the terrace and sent him to buy some strawberry ices. When he came back, Cummeo went into the house again, and though he stayed in the kitchen, he realized that there were people in another room, some men and two young ladies. They were chatting and laughing. Serafina came in and out of the kitchen, with her centuries-old expression of disgust. The Signora also came in for a moment, and as if she were discovering Cummeo for the third time, she said to him, "Back already? Why, you're like lightning!" She put some cups under the faucet and added, "You'll have to wash your neck. You should wash all over, in fact. You can do it in the garden. Then this evening you'll eat with Serafina. Are you all settled?" Suddenly addressing the maid, "Serafina, a little faster and less talk. . . ." Then to Cummeo again, "I'd have had you sleep in the house, but there's no room."

Cummeo had seen soft couches and easy chairs everywhere, and each seemed like a private living room. He ate even better than the night before, drank more wine, then went down

to his place in the garden. Upstairs they must have been
dancing. Somebody came and looked over the back terrace,
and Cummeo heard voices, laughter. He kept thinking what
he was thinking, what anyone would have suspected, and his
curiosity got the better of him. He came out of the stable,
and went to the back of the garden and hid. His sister was
sitting with Don Pasquale Altieri—just as the sawmill worker
had said—in a big red armchair, and they were drinking together, with two straws, from the same glass. Another girl,
in a corner of the terrace, was in a man's arms, a gentleman
too. Only when Cummeo had had his fill of watching them
did he notice an intermittent red glow at the large kitchen
window. It was Serafina, who was passing the time smoking a
pipe. Slowly and softly he went back to the stable—they
had given him a sheet, a blanket, and a pillow—and thought
of going away. The men in the café had told the truth. But
as he thought of them again, and his house, the terrible
poverty, his mother, ill in the stink of their room, he was
nauseated. He sank back without thinking any further, without wanting to, and on his back, his eyes wide, he thought
of the horse and how he could ride it happily into the country. . . .

[12]

The next morning the Signora sent for him, to tell him
she was giving him a suit. She was a woman of sudden likes
and dislikes. They had to fit the suit to him. She also gave
him a shirt, saying, "All my dead husband's things. Better
than letting the moths eat them."

Giovanna said nothing, as if the object of this charity
weren't her brother, and she heard the Signora say to her,
"You're going to be my ruination, that's what. You shouldn't
have done it, not to Don Pasquale, who has done so much
for you."

Giovanna answered her violently, and they went into the
Signora's room and shut the door. They yelled and screamed,
and perhaps did even worse. A girl whom Cummeo didn't

know came to sit in the kitchen and smoke. And in a low voice, as Giovanna and the Signora continued yelling, she said to Serafina, "I don't want to take sides, but I think that this time the Signora's right. A girl shouldn't act like that."

"Giovanna has too high an opinion of herself," Serafina said. "I'd like to see what would happen to her if she really quarreled with the Signora. You're all too young to know the meaning of protection. In our day, it was war, war in the streets, in doorways. Nowadays it's parlors, like palaces, and nothing but gentlemen and aristocrats! . . . Don Pasquale Altieri! . . . Why, just the name is enough, isn't it?" she asked the girl, and the girl nodded. "Don Pasquale means money and protection," Serafina added, going on with her housework, her face wrinkled with wisdom.

At this point they heard the Signora sobbing. Giovanna was silent; a heavy, concerned silence also fell over the kitchen. They distinctly heard the sound of every object that Serafina moved or touched, the sighs of the girl who was smoking. And Cummeo became sad. A moment later the girl went and knocked at the closed door, and Serafina followed her, worried and sympathetic, with a glass of cognac. Cummeo heard the two of them comforting the Signora, saying that everything would turn out all right, that it was a misunderstanding; and he saw how they neglected Giovanna, who came into the kitchen in the other girl's place, a lighted cigarette hanging from her mouth, smeared with lipstick. She looked at Cummeo as if he were an object. Cummeo didn't know what to do or say. He felt useless, an outsider. Then, hearing the Signora shout again, insulting Giovanna, he said to her, "What are you doing here? Why don't we go home?"

"Don't bother me," Giovanna answered. "That's all I need. If you want to leave, you know the way; nobody's keeping you here."

He wasn't expecting this answer, and to soften it, he added, "But the Signora mistreats you. Can't you hear what she's saying?"

"Naturally. And at home they pet me," Giovanna answered

with harsh irony. "Besides, I don't like being questioned. I'm all right here, I'm fine, and nobody's moving me. Those who want can go; the door's unlocked."

For the second time, Cummeo ignored the clear invitation. He saw the failure of his attempt to penetrate his sister's heart, to tear a confession from her, a moment of tenderness or confusion that would have shifted their blood relationship to another plane. Then his sister said, as if to herself, "Now they've got a watchman for me, I'll bet. . . . I knew it. . . . I knew it. . . ."

The other girl rushed in and said to Giovanna, "Come on and make up, or she'll have a heart attack. Come on, you know how she is. . . . You're right, I know, but what can you do? You want to go away? . . . We all say these things . . . but where would you go?"

Giovanna allowed herself to be dragged in to the Signora, and when peace was made, Serafina exploded her pandering, wrinkled joy, and the house, with all its machinery, seemed to be set in motion again. The Signora, borne in triumph into the kitchen by the two girls, having really won, seemed to forget the whole argument, as if what had happened had been only a necessary explosion to release the joy which would follow, free from any impurity. Tranquil, touching her hair as she looked in a framed mirror on a marble table, she said, "What are we having for lunch? Ah, our old Serafina—she's the only one who really loves me. How much did they charge you for the chickens? It doesn't matter; today we're celebrating. You like chicken, you two? Do you want some fresh cheese?" she asked Giovanna. "Didn't you tell me you weren't feeling well? Come on now, don't be sullen. I suppose you even want me to say you were right. Now then . . ." She turned to Cummeo, still sitting in his place with a foolish smile on his pale lips. "Run and buy two packs of Laurents, four bottles of beer, and some cheese for your sister. Tell them I want fresh mozzarella, from Battipaglia. And run! The change is yours." With a sigh she repeated a favorite adage: "Do good and forget it, do evil and regret it."

"I don't care whether you give my brother money or not," Giovanna said, still cross about the argument.

The Signora, with a resigned attitude of sainthood, went on chanting, "Do good and forget it, do evil and regret it."

Cummeo went to buy the cigarettes, wearing his new suit, shoes, socks, handkerchief, and underwear, with a five-hundred-lire tip in his pocket. His immediate benefits freed him from any scruples. The world seemed simple and acceptable to him. He felt even more courageous. Now he wasn't noted as that bum he had been until the previous evening. He couldn't keep from going to the Bar Oriente and ordering an ice cream from the amazed Turolla.

"I'll have it at the table, outside," he said. He ate the ice cream, with no bitterness toward anyone. Life was beautiful. To have a home, good food to eat—this is what he believed he wanted, he had always longed for. His sister could really help him. By now she was already in the arms of Don Pasquale Altieri. And Cummeo would be able to detach himself from that house, to step onto solid ground, to begin his honorable life, with a nice girl. He could go back to the villa now. He considered this an obligatory stay, during which he would make himself useful. The next day he agreed to go to the beach with his sister, the Signora, and the other girl, along with the two young men of the first day. The Signora wanted him in the back, with her, and she explained to them all who he was, his qualities, the things he knew how to do.

"Oh, really," said the young man at the wheel, with Giovanna at his side. Cummeo had to pretend to welcome all these attentions. He had to pretend not to see that Giovanna and the driver were touching each other, and from the front seat, the other boy leaned back and grabbed the other girl wherever his hands happened to fall. Cummeo had to look out of the window, thank them for including him in the party. The car was an Alfa Romeo . . . but Cummeo's position didn't give him a moment of calm.

At the beach the Signora had rented a cabana at the most fashionable bathing establishment, where the ladies and gentlemen went. The cabana was a brick room, with broad shutters, a sink, a table, and a thatched roof. All three women had sunglasses. Cummeo didn't know how to swim; he stayed on the beach, under the umbrella, to keep the Signora company. She sent him to buy a paper, or cigarettes, or an iced coffee, or some beer. She wanted everything, that woman, and always ice cold; Cummeo was in perfect agreement with her about that.

His sister, the other girl, and the two young men came back and stretched out in the sun around the umbrella, so that the Signora seemed like their mother, and Cummeo, a delicate son who had to take a cure at the sea.

Lunchtime came, and they went to eat in the restaurant there on the beach. Cummeo boned his fish carefully, as the others did, but he left a good part of his spaghetti in the plate because he couldn't wind it on his fork without the aid of a spoon. And he had to leave most of the delicious mullet, after tormenting it with his fork. He filled up on beer, but he kept feeling that it was all stolen. He would have liked to be here, but without Giovanna, or else with only Giovanna and the Signora, without the young men.

It was at this point that he glimpsed two companions in scant bathing suits, bony and thin, two serious-minded boys with whom he had talked often of his situation and theirs. Cummeo felt comforted and he greeted them, but his friends didn't answer, pretending not to have seen him. They slunk off, and they couldn't have expressed better their contempt. Those two companions had never made the slightest reference to his sister's conduct. And no woman at the courtyard, in a futile argument with his mother, had ever let a word slip. His father was also supposed to be unaware. He had no doubt about this. And yet there was something, an invisible signal, an atmosphere of silence when he appeared—this he seemed to recall, and the more he returned in his memory to the past, the more he discovered, visible and tense, that signal, which now suddenly became concrete. He lost his appetite as something began to take shape within him, something that wasn't exactly anger or jealousy or revenge, but an immense bitterness, a desolation in this life with no exit, without even the help of another person like his sister. He saw the collapse of all his plans of yesterday, when he had gone to buy the cigarettes, and he understood finally and completely the bitter weight of every spoonful of that ice cream, the only ice cream he had ever eaten, the day before at the table of the Bar Oriente. It was exactly then, at the same moment that he was making plans for the future, that he had felt more alone than ever, more neglected and abandoned.

The Signora said to him, "Eat a banana. A banana's as nourishing as an egg."

Giovanna had stood up and walked off. Giving a look almost of amazement at the Signora's face, so simple and plump and fresh, like a respectable lady, he took advantage of the moment to stand up. He wandered among the cabanas. He went past the establishment and looked over the railing of the "City Beach" and saw his friends.

Gioacchino Fiore, who had a withered leg, had buried himself under the sand, and Maria, his girl, was brushing the horseflies away from his face. Rosa Gambale and Mario del Bene were also nearby. The two friends he had seen near the restaurant were playing ball; and then, all together, the girls included, they started playing the slapping game. From the distance, on the dusty sand, the sea glinting behind them; they seemed happy to him. There was Rosa Gambale's brother down there, diving from a rock, showing off his body, like a Negro's. With these friends, he had come swimming at Vietri the year before; in the train as far as Cava, which was uphill, and on foot from Cava to Vietri, downhill, happily teasing and playing and telling tall stories; and coming back, in the train uphill from Vietri to Cava, and on foot down from Cava to Nofi, red from the sun, tired, breathless. They had stopped to drink something, to rest and to air their feet. Under the darkening sky they came to Nofi, singing in concert and solo, separating as they reached their neighborhoods—at the Camerelle bridge, or the San Clemente bridge, the Pucciano bridge, Socalla—until Cummeo reached his courtyard alone, and already half-asleep.

He thought of going down to his friends. He went as far as the line of cabanas built on stilts out into the sea. . . . Lucia was there. Lucia and Mario Benevento. She was wearing a red suit with a gold chain around her neck; a thin girl, she seemed beautiful to him—and he immediately thought the worst as she sat beside Benevento.

"Cummeo," his friend said. "What's wrong with you? Come and sit here. Here's Lucia."

Cummeo allowed himself to be led, and he sat down with them on the planks of the boardwalk, his feet hanging down in the air.

"Alone?"

"Yes."

"Why?"

"I'm with my sister, at the place next door."

"Oh. Is anything wrong?"

"I don't know myself."

"I didn't find work this year either. And neither did Lucia. Anyway, being a girl she wouldn't have made much."

Lucia remained absent, silent, looking elsewhere. And Cummeo asked Benevento, "You mean Lucia works at the cannery?"

"Didn't you know that? For two years now. . . . We had her mother put in a home. They amputated her leg and . . . we hope to get married, Cummeo. Poor together, or poor apart. . . ."

Lucia remained silent, her history in her body, the childish history of the woods of Chivoli, the park, the parade grounds, looking emptily at the vast, wrinkled, blue cover of the sea with sails stuck to it.

"Don't you see Cummeo?" Benevento asked Lucia.

"Of course I do," she answered.

"How are you?" Cummeo asked her.

"All right."

"I'm glad."

"So am I," the girl answered, calm and serene.

After a while, Cummeo excused himself and went off. He was losing Lucia at the moment he had found her again. He could not hear or see; he felt that he couldn't bear so much bad luck, he who felt after all that he was a good boy. He was in front of the shower, and he stepped under it, moving out on the other side into the fashionable cabanas, a more silent, harmonious, and orderly atmosphere. He reached the Signora's cabana. He wanted to dress, comb his hair, and go away, alone. The cabana was locked. He rapped on the door and Giovanna answered, "Who is it?"

"Cummeo."

"I can't open the door now."

He waited, then started knocking again.

"Who is it?" his sister asked again, in a muffled voice.

"Cummeo."

"What do you want?"

"I want to come in. I need my comb."

"Borrow the Signora's."

"I want my own."

"I can't open now. And that's that. Go away."

The Signora had come up. She asked him, "What are you doing there?"

"I'm waiting for Giovanna to open the door. She's inside."

"She can't now," the Signora said.

"How do you know?"

"She must be getting dressed, that's what I know."

"But she's been in there half an hour."

"Your sister is slow."

He started knocking again and shouting, "Open the door or I'll break it down. If you're really getting dressed, put on a robe. But let me in."

The Signora immediately thought of the other people around them and said, "Come, don't behave like this. We've had such a nice day, and now you want to spoil it. You know how fond I am of you. . . . By the way, where are the cigarettes? Do you have one?" she asked the second young man, who pretended not to have any. "Would you go and buy me some?" she said to Cummeo, as if the cabin weren't locked up like a tomb.

"She's got to open the door first," Cummeo insisted.

"Oh, you're impossible!" the Signora said, annoyed.

But Cummeo wasn't listening to her. With a kick, he broke open the door of the cabin and found his sister with the other man. Giovanna darted toward the door, but he held her fast.

The other man hid because people had begun to gather around. Cummeo began to slap Giovanna. He pushed her out on the sand and slapped her.

The Signora was saying, "The shame of it!" But the second man didn't rush up to defend Giovanna because though he was a gentleman, he was still a young man of Nofi. With blood on her lips, Giovanna said only, "Stop, stop," in her sisterly voice.

He left her on the sand, then calmly went back into the cabin, took his clothes, and went away.

He walked from the beach up to the town of Vietri. Here he found his friends, waiting for the train to Cava. He went over to them, without saying a word about what they had seen and approved. They all talked happily to one another, and since the train was late, they began to play and shove one another gently, including Cummeo. It was a way to restore his confidence. Cummeo tried to smile, and shove the others too, but he couldn't shake off his inner turmoil.

He was still too aroused, excited, nervous, and thoughtful. Finally the train arrived, rattling along the tracks that had been laid between Salerno and Pagani thirty years before. Painfully, the train began to crawl upward toward Cava. The friends sat inside the car, but Cummeo preferred to stay on the back platform, like a little loggia, which moved among tall, thick hedges. A single friend stayed to keep him company, still saying nothing about what had happened. He offered Cummeo a cigarette, talked about his work, and a dance that was being held late that evening, if he wanted to go too. Cummeo hinted that he wasn't well, he preferred to go straight home. The train reached Cava, and now, without brakes, it galloped down the three steep slopes that took it to Camarelle, where the Nofi country begins.

From that moment on Cummeo felt safe. Seeing those fa-

miliar, homely places again, he had the impression that he
was returning not so much to his town but to himself, and he
felt welcomed with concern and love. He didn't think even
for a moment of going back to his place at the Bar Oriente.
To him that bar seemed connected to the story of his sister
and the Signora. The entire city of Nofi seemed a distant
world to him, definitely alien. That is why he felt safe, because in his house, poor, but his, made for him, to hide him
or support him, everything was familiar: houses and stones,
names and faces. Only among these things and people could
he regain his courage. When he came home, if his father
wanted to throw him out again, he would talk to him, make
him understand the situation that both of them were in, what
they should do instead of fighting and cursing the day they
were born.

But when he came into the courtyard, he saw that people
came to their doors to greet him, and when he headed for his
home more people ran up to look at the face of this boy who
had suddenly become a man. The news of what had happened at Vietri had reached home before him. It was in
the evening air, like a symbol of festivity. Cummeo glanced
at once toward the door of his house. It was ajar. He went inside, saying good evening. His father and mother were already in bed. And his father, for the first time in his life, returned his son's greeting.

Without saying anything else, Cummeo went to his little
bed and found it already prepared, the pillow plumped up
and swollen with fresh husks. A shudder ran across his back.
He took off his shoes and set them under the bed. He took
off his pants, folded them carefully, and set them on the chest.
He removed his shirt and hung it around the back of the
chair, and then he got into bed, lying on his back, his arms
along his sides, his eyes on the little barred window over the
door, beyond which flowed the cool and dimly glowing air
of the summer night. He began to think. He thought that
he was at home and was happy to be there, that he was lying
on his mattress of fresh corn husks and he was comfortable
on it, relaxed and without fear. He was a few feet away from

his father—his friend—and his mother, who was weeping silently and who couldn't have said whether she was weeping for Giovanna or for the peace that had been made between her two men. In the heavy silence that reigned inside and outside the house, the mother's weeping had the continuity of the domestic peace that had returned. But it was the silence of the things around them and of the two men that moved the mother and gave her the courage to weep openly. Neither the father nor Cummeo dared interrupt her. Later, much later, when all three had thought out their whole story, the father said, "Let's sleep now. It's two o'clock. Tomorrow I have to get up at five. Spanzano called me. He's put together a motor and an electric saw, with money from all of us, to make crates. He told me to bring Cummeo too. Spanzano's a good man."

MARIO TOBINO

MARIO TOBINO WAS BORN IN VIAREGGIO ON JANUARY 16, 1910. After finishing secondary school, he studied medicine at the University of Bologna and took his degree in psychiatry. Until the outbreak of the Second World War, he lived and practiced in Florence; during the war he served as Medical Corps psychiatrist on the Libyan front. At present he lives in Lucca, where he is director of the Psychiatric Hospital and a specialist in neuropathology. A frequent contributor to such reviews as *Il Ponte* and *Il Mondo,* his reputation rests largely upon his fiction, and particularly upon *Il Deserto della Libia* (from which "Oscar Pilli" has been taken). Among his other works are several volumes of poetry, some fictionalized case studies, and several volumes describing his travels in France, Spain, Germany, and Italy.

His chief works are: *L'Angelo del Liponard* (1951); *Il Deserto della Libia* (1952); *Le libere donne di Magliano* (1953); *Due italiani a Parigi* (1954); *La brace dei Biassoli* (1957); *Passione per l'Italia* (1959). None of his writing has yet appeared in complete English translation.

OSCAR PILLI
by Mario Tobino

translated by William Arrowsmith

I AM A PSYCHIATRIST, AND ONE EVENING IN MARCH, 1940, I
was, as usual, at the mental hospital in V——. I had just
finished checking some files when—that same March evening
—a man arrived at the gate of the hospital. He was a man of
average height, somewhat heavy-set, who swayed from left
to right as he walked. His mouth was large and toothy, his
cheekbones fleshy, and his blue eyes small and restless. He
wore the uniform of a captain in the Medical Corps* and
his shins were encased in two stiff polished boots.

He entered the porter's lodge and asked for me. He wanted
to see one of the patients. They telephoned me that a captain
in the Medical Corps was waiting downstairs. I went down
to meet him. Together we went to the ward to which the
patient had been assigned.

As I stretched out my hand to the Captain and murmured
my name, he immediately said, "So *you're* Dr. C——! Ah,
you're a saint, sir! A saint! You're all saints here, sir. As I love
you, sir."

Somewhat startled by these words, I pointed out the ward
to him and suggested that I escort him there. We walked
over together.

My guest's name was Oscar Pilli, Captain, Medical Corps.
He talked continuously.

After visiting the patient, the feeble-minded son of a major
in the Veterinary Corps, in whom Pilli took only the slightest
interest, we walked back, and I offered to show him the more
typical parts of the hospital.

Sanitá, which means both "Medical Corps" and "sanity."

203

Meanwhile he talked about everything under the sun. In between extremely frequent interjections—"As I love you, sir," "You're a saint, sir," "My *dear* sir"—he told me that he was a district doctor, that it was his duty to examine recruits, and that he was under pressure from every side, especially from superior officers, to reject recruits with special influence as unfit for military service; that that very morning two of his superior officers, at dawn—"my *dear* fellow, as I love you, sir, you're a saint to spend your life in a mental hospital, you're all saints, sir"—anyway, at the crack of dawn, two higher officers had come to his room to put in a word for a recruit who was scheduled to be examined later that day.

In the meantime, while walking, while entering the observation ward, while talking to the patients (with whom he conversed as though they were absolutely normal), while telling the attendants that they were saints, calling them his "dear fellows" and pointing to the ribbons on his chest as though offering proof of what he was saying, while alluding, briefly but sadly, to the black mourning band he was wearing in memory of the death of his "heroic" father—while he was doing all these things, continually swallowing, pointing out, indicating, asserting, he also managed to tell me that in case of a general mobilization, in case of war, he had seen, he *knew*, that we would be in the same division together, he as a captain and I as a lieutenant, and this division was a line division, a first-aid section, and dangerous; and as he announced this, Oscar Pilli had commented that we might die together; and he repeated that he had seen the mobilization orders—"Together, in the same company"—he hoped not, and yet . . . we might die together.

I accompanied him to the door. He continued to chatter. We said good-bye; he called me his "dear fellow" once again and went off, swaying from side to side as he went.

A month later the mobilization order arrived. I was to report to the military hospital at V—— on the 25th of April.

The Colonel said to me, "You have been assigned to a hospital group in Libya. You will leave in a few days."

Oscar Pilli, Captain, Medical Corps, made his second appearance.

We went to Naples on the train; we crossed the sea. The ship docked at Tripoli.

From the boat a gangplank leads down to the dock.

In front of me was Oscar Pilli. As he started down he seemed terrified of the abyss beneath him. In his hand he was carrying a suitcase. I told him to give it to me.

His legs spread wide; convulsively clutching the railings with both hands, panting heavily, he started down the little gangplank. I followed him. His terror was almost animal. His legs, shaking, groped for nonexistent purchase. At last he reached the bottom, and we stepped out in Africa. I gave him back his suitcase.

The next day they loaded us unceremoniously into seven trucks. They unloaded us by dumping us out in the oasis of Sorman near the Tunisian frontier.

In Libya, Pilli always dressed as follows: a light cloth jacket of a faded pea-green color, a souvenir of the war in Spain, and beneath the jacket, a peasant's vest; beneath the vest, in the lining, pinned with huge safety pins, were his Postal Savings Book, little packets of thousand-lire notes, his savings bonds, his banknotes. This mass of paper made two little humps on the front of his vest.

The vest was never removed, day or night.

He was wearing the same boots that he wore in Italy, big, stiff, and buffed to a shiny gloss.

On his head he wore a cap, smaller than regulations provided for.

Before arriving at Sorman, Pilli and I met with a slight mishap. We were abandoned in the desert. The trucks in which we were traveling were stretched out in a long column, one behind the other. Pilli and I were in the truck at the head of the column. At a certain point the driver believed that he had overshot his destination. He turned off the motor and expressed his doubts. Behind us the whole column came to a halt. Until then a sandstorm had been blowing. Now it was night.

On one side of the road, less than half a mile away, there was a light. Pilli and I walked toward it to ask for directions. The others were to wait for us on the road.

We stepped into the light to ask questions. It was the headquarters of the artillery regiment of our division. The officers were eating. Pilli and the Colonel recognized each other. Pilli brightened up. "Quite, quite, quite," he began, stood at attention, smiled, and then snapped to attention again. "In eastern Africa, wasn't it?" and he pointed to his chest with the East Africa campaign ribbon. Finally the Colonel asked him what he wanted. Pilli glowed all over. At the same time, flights of ideas were pounding through his head. He described our arrival at Tripoli, our journey to find our headquarters, *any* headquarters, and how no headquarters wanted us, no one recognized us, no one knew anything about us. He described how the vast amount of sand-covered Medical Corps matériel was loaded on the trucks, and how the sandstorm had made us feel as though we were sailing through a world turned yellow; he talked about the Major in our company. And in every sentence he dropped insinuations against someone; then he retracted them, restated them, all this with extreme rapidity and precision. He also asked for the information he wanted.

Everybody listened intently to what he was saying; they had almost stopped eating.

When we got the information we wanted, we left. Once again we reached the road.

The trucks were gone.

"Incredible!" Pilli exclaimed, bellowing into the darkness. He took a few exploratory steps toward the right and then toward the left. He did this over and over, incapable of reaching a decision. "Imagine, the *Major!* The *Major* of our own company! Incredible."

Since there was nothing else to do, I suggested he go back to the Colonel of artillery and ask him to tell us this time where we could find the division headquarters. They would know there exactly where our company was supposed to be and we could go directly there.

Once again Pilli descended upon the artillery mess hall, and as he went in he became extremely vivacious; he pointed out, he described, he smiled, he added "My *dear* fellow" and then "Quite, quite, quite, quite"—an endless line of them. He explained that when we reached the road the column of trucks that should have been there wasn't there at all. And while he talked, he ate what they gave him (hastily inferring that they would not make him pay for it), and between mouthfuls he started dropping insinuations against the Major, against me—when I left the room—but always speaking as "your humble servant, sir" before a colonel, "Yes, sir."

When we finally found out where division headquarters was, we left and at last arrived where our company had been unloaded.

Pilli reported to the Major, snapped to attention several times in front of him, obsequious, festive, and gay.

Our company was camped in a sandy stretch of the oasis. On one side was an Arab house.

Arab houses are roofless; they are only four walls with the sky above them. When you enter an Arab house, the sky is overhead. The walls are about seven feet high. Naturally, if someone standing outside should throw something over the wall, it would fall inside, since there is no roof.

In Libya there is a wind called the *ghibli*, a wind that lifts the sand and carries it everywhere.

In order to protect our field kitchen from the *ghibli*, we put it inside an Arab house. Being roofless, the sand could be blown in from above, but the four walls nonetheless kept some of it out.

Enclosed by the four walls, the cooks confronted their pots and pans.

One morning near their pans the cooks found two little packages, elegantly wrapped and tied with string. Since they did not know what they were or where they came from, the two cooks came closer, bent down, and picked them up. Then they untied them, opened the wrapping and looked. The contents lay open in the light and it was: feces.

The cooks reported this lurid discovery to an officer. The news about the two little packages quickly spread through the company, but a few days later it had been forgotten.

But one morning the cook discovered two more little packages and the morning after that still another two. The affair of the packages once again became the talk of the camp.

The following day it was discovered that the author of the packages was Pilli. At dawn he would leave his tent (he was observed by several soldiers who were spying on him) in his underwear and his vest stuffed full of banknotes, approach the wall of the Arab house, and gleefully and happily, one after the other, toss his two little packages over the wall. And because the house was roofless the packages landed inside, close to the ladles and pots that took up most of the room.

It is worth stating that the soldiers who were watching, despite their inexperience in judging states of mind, noticed that Pilli was extremely gay while doing what he did, that he laughed and seemed almost to be singing an operatic aria, although he never opened his mouth, seeming to suggest a singer by his every gesture, with his whole body, by the expression on his face and the way he moved.

Pilli's story falls into two periods. In the first period—the present one—there was a major in the company, a superior officer; and because Pilli had a terrible idolatry of rank, he revealed his full personality only in a muted and subdued form, as though he were muzzled; not quite gagged, but muzzled.

In the second period he was in absolute command of the hospital company, and in this second period he loomed to enormous size, lasciviously, happily, uncoiling his dragon's tail to its full length.

We are now in the first period.

In both the first and second periods our company was in reserve, abandoned to idleness on the edge of an oasis, which frequently happens to various detachments in time of war.

There were a number of pairs of sunglasses in the outfit—expensive sunglasses and cheap sunglasses. Oscar Pilli was a thief.

The finest glasses, the flawless, restful, glare-free glasses were Zeiss.

The Major who commanded the detachment was an oculist; his glasses were Zeiss.

The Major was an amiable man, serenely convinced that he would spend fifteen days in Libya and then return home, a conquering hero, to the loving arms of his beautiful young wife.

It happened that a certain lieutenant in the artillery was temporarily the guest of our detachment.

He too had Zeiss glasses. Which disappeared.

Other glasses, ordinary glasses, had previously disappeared. And nothing happened.

When Pilli came ashore with us at Tripoli, his baggage consisted of several boxes, half empty.

Many men are naïve, many good; but all men are greedy.

And so it happened that the Major's glasses also disappeared. The Major got angry. It would be hard to imagine a more energetic major in a crisis like this. But he did *not* say that his glasses had been stolen; he said that he had lost them and that the finder should bring them back.

Pilli had struck boldly. Kleptomania eclipses the brightest blaze of glory. He had cut down a higher rank than his, he had dimmed the Major's brighter light by an act of daring.

It was "in*credi*ble!"

Here another character now made his entrance: Capone. The longer a man lives, the more mysterious men become. Capone was a soldier devoted heart and soul to Pilli. He saw Pilli's faults, and loved him with a selfless, loyal love. He was Pilli's spy and factotum, and he was hated for it by the whole detachment, without the slightest advantage to himself.

And so the Major's glasses had disappeared.

It was a test of Pilli's courage. Which he did not have.

Someone advised the Major what steps to take if he wanted

to recover his glasses. He should state explicitly that the man who had dared to steal his glasses—the Major's glasses, the C.O.'s glasses—would be mercilessly punished, punished for a military offense.

The Major was not the man for making threats, inhuman threats, but the thought of his glasses made him discover just the right tone, and at dinner, in the presence of the whole company, he repeated as an absolute order what he had said the day before in a very general way.

While the Major was shouting the threat he had been advised to make, I was watching Pilli. His head was dangling, giddy but attentive, and there was a little dry spittle on his lips. In that moment the thought of his superior officer, of a higher rank than his own, loomed to such gigantic proportions within him that it shattered his kleptomania.

Not that I was certain that Pilli was the thief; but logically he must have been and everybody suspected him.

We finished dinner and the company scattered to its various tents, wrapped in heat as though it were cotton batting.

The next day the faithful servant Capone made his entrance on the scene.

Capone reported to the Major. After making his salute, he handed him the glasses, saying that he had found them in the lining of the dispensary tent. Because he knew that the Major had lost them, he had brought them back.

Since the Major had made his threats at dinner, twenty-four hours had elapsed.

One might infer that Pilli had shown a certain strength, that he had not let himself be cowed, that he had not handed over the glasses immediately but had held out for twenty-four hours.

This is what had happened. After Pilli heard the Major's strict orders to return his glasses, he went to his tent, opened one of those trunks stuffed with every sort of object, all laid out as though for inspection. Then he picked up the Major's glasses and contemplated them.

It was at that moment that the splendid blazing orb of Military Hierarchy rose up against Kleptomania. For twenty-

four hours they battled with changing fortunes, until finally
the pure abstract glory of higher rank won out, as happens
so commonly in human history, and the Oculist Major got
back his beloved glasses.

Pilli had a passion for rubber stamps.

As soon as we reached the oasis—despite our being in
reserve—Pilli ordered the 9 x 11 first-aid tent set up. Rubber
stamps suddenly became all the rage; in Pilli's hands they
became living, feeling flesh (and later, when he was C.O.,
downright sacred, like the consecrated host).

Soldiers, like robots, unconsciously understand everything.
And they began to handle rubber stamps gingerly and with
respect, perhaps divining the future.

Everywhere stamps went flying through the air, landing on
the backs of envelopes, covering every line of the sick-call
book, every space that could be stamped.

Once—it was nearly noon—Pilli had spent the morning
fretting about nonexistent patients; he had handed out punish-
ments, examined, re-examined; in many cases he had written
in the sick-call book "Malingering, to be punished severely!"
and he had underlined these phrases with two strokes in ink
and a thick stroke in blue pencil. At this time Pilli was in
shirt sleeves, wearing, of course, his pea-green vest. It was the
hour in which he started to curse, turning to the soldiers as
though beseeching justice against the other officers, who were
not working; and these complaints alternated with his per-
petual complaint, that he was still only a captain in the Medical Corps, and his anxiety about getting married so that he
could get promoted; and he kept asking the soldiers if they
knew of a woman who would marry him. At this moment Pilli
had a line of spittle on the edge of his lips. He had talked
continuously for four hours and he had created a furious hub-
bub within the first-aid tent, at regular intervals growing
angry and finally screaming, telling some soldier that the
soldier was an impostor, that he had insulted him, a captain,
ridiculed his rank; and then raising his voice even higher,
shouting in the face of the soldier, who was standing at atten-

tion, silent, white, naked, bewildered, he had said to the soldier, "I'll have you shot! I'll have you court-martialed!" Pilli had just reached the climax of the noon hour, preceded by four other hours, when, smiling and officious as always, the postman appeared at the door of the first-aid tent.

Pilli was signing something, repeating his complaints about not being promoted, about the inefficiency of the other doctors, etc. And just at this moment, raising his eyes, he saw the postman standing in front of him. And suddenly he glowed all over, like a diabolic cherub. He picked up the round rubber stamp, the holy of holies, and standing up, he moved closer (and at this moment his lip muscles twitched as though touched by an electrical current) and he said, "Quite, my dear fellow. Quite, my dear fellow," and—*pam!*—he stamped the postman on the forehead, a perfect round print in which every letter was visible.

Immediately after this, Pilli, whose every muscle expressed his joy—the soldiers were laughing—Pilli, in a flash of lightning suddenly saw the specter of the Superior Officer Who Was Bound to Find Out. Then, overflowing with a joy that knew no limits, he tried to undo the damage; putting a hand on the shoulder of the postman, who stood there dumfounded, and turning to the clerks and attendants, Pilli began, "Yes, he's a *good* boy, yes, he's a good boy, what a good boy." Then, turning directly to the postman, Pilli said with emotion, "My *dear* fellow, I love you like a brother. Like a brother, quite, my dear fellow." But already the shadow of absent-mindedness fell upon his last words; already flights of new ideas were racing through the mind of Oscar Pilli.

Two women, one helping, the other with hydroadenitis of the armpit, an abscess ripe for lancing.

They came to our company, and one of them said that she had an abscess under her arm, that she didn't trust the "doctor" of the district. Would I lance it for her? I said that I would. The woman was already stretched out on the table, I had the lancet in my hand; she raised her arm, the abscess under the light, the abscess swollen to a head, the head already oozing.

Enter Pilli. "Yes, my dear fellow. Quite. You're a good man. You're a great doctor," he said, "but you know my experience in these matters, my training, my education. *Please.* By the love I bear you," he said excitedly, his nostrils flaring like a foal's. And he took off his jacket, standing there with his vest buttoned up.

I stood there with the lancet raised; I had already swabbed the abscess with iodine. "You know, my dear fellow, I love you like a brother," and his eyes filled with tears, his mouth went dry. "You know my talent for this sort of thing. Of course, my dear boy, I'll do it. Don't you worry about it. You're an angel, sir."

I stood there not moving.

And he: "Yes, dear boy. Here I am, my dear fellow. Quite, quite," he murmured, his eyes already glued to the abscess.

"Here I am, dear lady," he said, turning to the woman, "here I am. Here I am, at your service. Ahh, dear lady."

"You don't mind, do you? You don't mind, do you, dear boy?" And barely even looking at me, he added, stretching out his hands like the Discobolus, "I love you like a brother."

The woman was waiting, trembling all over. He fulfilled her wish. And in that instant that separated her from the knife, the woman thought that he was the captain, I a lieutenant. That sudden burst of "My dears" had instantly convinced her; she hoped that with a captain she would feel no pain.

He cut the abscess. Her wishes were fulfilled. He drained her armpit. He grazed her arteries. He was generous (he was panting as he worked with the knife in her flesh).

The woman's rosy image of the captain and his "Dear girl" withered away. She looked at me beseechingly, like a woman in love, betrayed.

In the privacy of their tents the soldiers talked about him obsessively. Out of the tents came guffaws, silences, descriptions. At last the people had a theater.

Pilli could obliterate the desert. And that is an impossibility.

Only a fantasy soaring like a distracted bird toward the heavens can compete with the desert, walk side by side together with it like two horses in a harness, and around their necks the straps with their jingling bells.

Other sections like ours, in reserve like us, were subject to drowsy homesickness; but we were wide awake, intent on Pilli.

It was at this point that I, as psychiatrist and spokesman for the others, officially notified the Major that Pilli was mad. But the Major gave a vague reply, and when I persisted, answered irritably that this was military life and we had to obey.

Pilli's diction was flawless. His syntax was excellent too, but the words, simple ordinary words, poured from his mouth precise, harmonious, elegant, incisive. Indeed, the more his madness pushed him to talk, the more rapidly his words flowed, saying precisely what they were designed to say.

And when he talked about the past, the best moments of his life, his words expressed precisely that tiny perfect space that lies between the tragic and the comic, lightly veiled by a touch of tenderness for himself, tenderness for Pilli, their author and protagonist, and as he spoke, he stole attention even as it wandered, a little cherub laughing at himself with an indefinable sadness.

But these were Pilli's better moments, quickening between one episode and the next like a blessed rain from heaven, and lasting as long as our company still had an officer higher in rank than Pilli. But his diction never betrayed him, neither in the good moments nor the bad.

Every officer had an orderly. Orderlies are usually loyal to their officers.

The greater the orderly's loyalty to his own officer, the more Pilli disliked him, because Pilli wanted all the soldiers to look at him, to turn to him, and because he feared that the orderly and his officer might be plotting against him.

And so Pilli was suspicious of orderlies.

Pilli's commonest phrases were these: "As I love you, sir," "my dear fellow," "dear boy," "I love you like a brother." It was these phrases which he periodically inserted into his conversation and which, although spoken almost automatically, usually seemed fresh, minted in the very moment in which he pronounced them. In fact, these phrases—"As I love you, sir," etc.—had by now spread through the camp. You could frequently hear a soldier, a peasant from the country near Bari, saying to another soldier, "Listen, dear boy"; and the other, a peasant from Anghiari, begin his reply with, "By the love I bear you, sir." Naturally, these imitations took place out of Pilli's hearing.

One afternoon Pilli came to my tent. My orderly was standing at the door, and he rose when he saw Pilli approaching.

Pilli was in one of his calmer moods; he had the relaxed face of a man who has had a good night's sleep.

He raised his finger to my orderly's face, waggling it in vague threat, as though somehow piqued, and a second or two later began, "As I love you, sir—" and he stopped his sentence in mid-career as though suspended on a white cloud.

Up to this point, it had been the usual phrase, so well known that it had become a byword among the soldiers. But Pilli, as though touched by some uncontrollable happiness, now added, "I don't love you any more." And he smiled, perhaps at himself, perhaps at some other thought that had occurred to him, and strolled away.

My orderly immediately joined a group of other soldiers (there was a group of men from Arezzo who were wonderfully successful in doing imitations of Pilli's phrases) and recounted the brief scene with Pilli and what Pilli had said to him: "As I love you, sir, I don't love you any more." This phrase seemed magnificent to some of the soldiers; they were rookies, enjoying for the first time the pleasures of high style (besides, they were alone in the desert) and they repeated it among themselves a few times, hoping to polish it by dint of repetition into a jewel of language, a plaything for themselves.

And before long, this new phrase was running gaily from tent to tent, and it was night, and the soldiers were off duty, and the heat of the day had vanished and in its place the night air was like a breath of spring, and soldiers are the biggest children on earth.

In the quiet of the afternoon, in a corner of the first-aid tent, I surprised Pilli in the act of writing a letter to his mother. He read the letter aloud to me. In it he described himself as a child abandoned in the desert, a prey to poverty, incurable diseases, and desolation. But above all he spoke of his sense of loneliness, the loneliness of a child lost at the bottom of an abyss.

While he read, I stepped closer and examined the letter. It was written in his usual precise penmanship, but what startled me was the underlining. While drafting his military reports, it was Pilli's habit to underline the more important words for emphasis. Then he reread and underlined some new words, also important. After a third reading, he scored still more words, adding a second line, more heavily drawn, to the words he had previously underlined. In the end everything Pilli wrote was composed entirely of underlined words since, in his eyes, they were all important, in fact "of the *utmost* importance," as he used to say, being fond of superlatives and super-superlatives. Like his famous "In*cred*ible!"

The letter to his mother was also underlined, and during his reading he kept scoring fresh words until every word in the letter was completely underlined. He did the same with the address. First he underlined his mother's name, which was obviously important; then he scored her surname, the street, and the number. The city was underlined twice in blue and red pencil—items that were, together with rubber stamps, in constant use on Pilli's desk.

On the back of the envelope Pilli wrote his rank, name, surname, and return address, and promptly stamped it with a rubber stamp that said exactly what he had written out by hand. But the envelope was wrinkled and the stamping took badly on one side, so Pilli stamped it again, this time successfully. Then he gazed with satisfaction at his work.

It still lacked a postage stamp.

Pilli opened the drawer of his table and pulled out a number of letters he had received in the last few days. He placed them on the table and examined the canceled stamp on the envelope of each letter. He picked out one that was only slightly soiled in cancellation, moistened it, waited, drawing his sweaty face close to the stamp (his face at that moment was the face of a long-suffering man unjustly and continuously afflicted). He pulled the stamp off and applied some fresh paste, since the old paste was gone. Then he stuck the stamp on the new envelope, which was now ready. He sighed— either because he had finished a demanding job or because afflicted by pain, I don't know—and said, "Isn't it incredible, the life we lead? And they talk about convicts? Eh, what about us? Saints, we are." And he looked at me "like a brother."

Then the unexpected happened. Pilli became C.O.

The Major had been transferred.

The company was called together because the Major was leaving.

Weak men become emotional; a torrent of words broke from the Major's lips.

A second unexpected event was that the Major, who had several times conceded that Pilli was morally and mentally unstable, turned to him and publicly thanked him, said that he was grateful to him, that he was leaving the section in his hands, that he would be its leader, etc.

Everybody—the soldiers, the officers, the noncommissioned officers, and Pilli himself—was listening.

The Major left.

Pilli ascended the throne, and sat down with unaccustomed buttocks. And as he sat, his whole face shone.

As C.O., Pilli accompanied the administrative officer to Tripoli to pick up a million lire in company pay. The sun was shining as always. The two went on the bus, both nervous as the flies of Libya—Pilli nervous in the delirious light, the administrative officer nervous because he was next to Pilli.

They received their money at Tripoli. When Pilli saw it, he puffed himself up as he did when he saw a general. He wheezed. And his thoughts raced on ahead, blazing like the African sun. He walked through Tripoli with the administrative officer, who had a million lire in his pockets. In Pilli's eyes danced myriads of thousand-lire notes.

The thousand-lire notes that they had received were crisp and new, printed with perfection; they seemed like sheets of delicate metal.

Pilli walked for a while close to a million lire, then said to the administrative officer, his throat dry, "Yes, my dear fellow, I am the C.O., and by rights, my dear fellow, I ought to keep the money."

The administrative officer made no objection and handed him the packets of thousand-lire notes. Pilli, with a sudden swift storm of flying images, walked through the city with— yes, my dear fellow—a million in thousand-lire notes.

But other images also arose in his mind: images of loss, robbery, responsibility, a trial, false accusations of theft. At first he resisted; then he said the administrative officer was responsible, that *he* was in charge of the money.

The administrative officer told him to give the money back to him.

They sat down to eat. Pilli alluded several times to the money in the pockets of the administrative officer.

When the administrative officer went to Tripoli with one of us, it was his habit and pleasure, as a wealthy, older, and kindly man, to offer us a meal. He did not offer a meal to Pilli because he was exasperated. He paid for his own meal only. Then Pilli asked the waiter to bring him his bill too.

The waiter brought it and waited. Pilli was talking; he made no immediate move to pay the waiter. The waiter went away to another table. He returned to be paid when he saw the two of them about to leave. Pilli said, "But I've already paid," and turning to the administrative officer, he said, "You

were there too, you saw me pay him. You can tell him." The
waiter did not wait for the administrative officer to corrobo-
rate Pilli's story nor for Pilli to say anything more; he replied
immediately that he should pay him because he hadn't yet
paid. And he began to raise his voice. Pilli suddenly became a
circus juggler. He wriggled. He said, "Yes, my dear fellow.
You didn't believe us, did you? How much is it? Couldn't catch
you napping, could we?" And he laughed affectionately in the
waiter's face. And he paid, although he sighed as he paid him.

When they left the restaurant, they decided that it was time
they returned to the oasis, a long way from Tripoli.

On the way, Pilli talked and talked; the administrative officer did not, because it irritated him to be with a man like
Pilli.

When the bus stopped, they were in the oasis of Sorman in
front of the company tents and it was night. Except for one
sentry, everybody was asleep.

The administrative officer went toward his tent but Pilli
stopped him, saying, "Look here, my dear fellow, I ought to
keep the money. I'm the C.O. I'm the C.O. and I'm responsible. I'll have two sentries stand guard in front of my tent."

Angered, the administrative officer hesitated, then gave him
the packet of bills and the strongbox containing a few thousand lire. Pilli carried everything into his tent.

He woke up the camp, and a little while later there were
two sentries in front of his tent. The canvas walls of his tent,
tightly shut, glowed because the light was on inside. Then the
light went out. In a short while it went on again. Then Pilli
came out and told the sentry to go with him to the administrative officer's tent. When he reached the tent—the administrative officer was asleep—Pilli opened it and said, "Forgive
me, my dear fellow, you're right. As I love you, sir. Yes, sir.
Quite. You're right, sir. My word of honor. I was wrong. I'll
put it down in writing. You're right. You ought to keep the
money. The strongbox is yours; I've brought it back. You keep
the sentries. They'll stand guard for you. You're right, my dear
fellow. You know it, sir, I love you like a brother."

He returned to his own tent.

Next morning, the administrative officer requested Pilli to come in person and verify the money in the strongbox in the presence of three officers, the customary procedure before paying the soldiers. Pilli came. The sentries set the open strongbox on the administrative officer's bed. The administrative officer, whose civilian occupation was a similar one, began to count the money, carefully, quietly. When he reached the end, he said that one thousand lire was missing. He recounted. A thousand lire missing. Pilli kept murmuring, "Quite, my dear fellow." The administrative officer became suspicious and angry, something he had never been before. He took up the money again. He counted each packet separately—what had been in the strongbox before, and the new money, the million lire in thousand-lire notes. The thousand lire was missing from the million lire. When he had received the money from the army bank, he had counted the bills; there were a thousand of them. Now there were nine hundred and ninety-nine. He looked at the serial numbers. The bills were numbered in sequence; they had left the treasury for the first time in packets of one hundred. Number 059519-V II was missing from the third packet.

At this discovery, Pilli exclaimed, "Oh! They were numbered!" His mouth was dry. Then he began to repeat, as though walking in his sleep, "Quite, quite, quite." Then suddenly he shouted toward the administrative officer, "It's *you*. *You're* responsible."

The officers present looked at him in astonishment.

Pilli now had in his voice, in his eyes, in the aggressiveness that showed in what he said, in the whole expression of his face—all crowded together as in a bunch of poisonous flowers —avarice, kleptomania, sadistic pleasure in making a thief of an honest man, the consciousness of being the commander, the terrible splendor of the superior officer to whom he might be reported, but above all, in every inch of his face, gleamed his morbid delight in evil.

The three officers, the sentinels, saw then, in that moment, as though in a transparency, who Oscar Pilli was.

2 P.M. While the sun hung motionless, its wings spread wide over the oasis, and everybody else had sleepily taken cover in the tents, beneath the shadow of the shrubs, Pilli emerged from his tent and gave a furtive and mischievous wink to the two men who were waiting for him. They strode off, crunching the scorching sand underfoot, in the direction of the Arab house. At that hour the house was deserted since the cooks, after cleaning up the kitchen, had gone off for their siesta.

He went in. The two men stood inside. He shut the door. All three of them stood inside, the sun overhead. Flanked by his two henchmen, Pilli dropped to his knees, knelt there for a moment, and then straightened up, holding out his hands to heaven like some saint in a sacred painting, all the time winking mischievously with his blue eyes. Then, as though eager to finish these preliminaries and get down to serious business, he abruptly pulled out the key to the small storeroom in which the medical supplies were locked away. The padlock sprang open and they entered. The two soldiers pulled out the large container of quinine extract from its hiding place behind a row of cartons. Then they filled a smaller bottle with the quinine. Taking the bottle and glasses with them, they left the storeroom and returned to the central room, flooded with sunlight. First they sampled the quinine. Pilli, holding the bottle, filled their glasses. The two soldiers drank greedily.

Then Pilli turned toward the rear wall and begin to recite the Mass.

His voice was deep and resonant but subdued so it would not be overheard, and he made guttural little trills in the line of the chant, accompanying them with little motions of his arms, which he frequently flung wide, and held them there, extended to the full.

The two soldiers knelt on the sand and made the right responses, since they had assisted at the Mass when they were boys.

The Mass had its periodic culminations, and at these moments Pilli stood stock still, not saying a word, facing the heavens and the rear wall, his arms extended wide. After this he would make a pirouette, turn toward the kneeling soldiers, and fill the glasses that they held out to him. Then he would take a drink himself and smack his lips loudly. Once again he filled the empty glasses. He resumed the chant. Once again he poured the liqueur into their glasses, raising the bottle high so that the liquid fell through the air like coagulated sunlight.

When the moment for the consecration of the host arrived, Pilli's every gesture was performed in total silence, while his lips spasmodically wrinkled and twitched with words, laughter, solemnity. Then the benediction. The soldiers rose, returned to one side, and now knelt again. As the Mass proceeded, the bottle gradually emptied.

When the Mass was finished, Pilli made a great variety of bows, both solemn and burlesque, to the two soldiers, meanwhile holding the bottle up to show them that there was still some extract left. The soldiers held out their glasses. Finally the bottle was empty.

The soldiers left quietly and cautiously. Pilli followed them. The Arab house, the camp, the oasis were flooded in silent sunlight.

Our midday meals, which took place around a chest under the scanty shade of a wild olive, were eaten without nostalgic remarks, discussions about the war, calm conversation. They were obsessed by Oscar Pilli.

He started his meal, eating and drinking—he ate a great deal—by complaining that he was a victim, a man of misfortune, and he also told us that we were poor suffering wretches, but wretches with a hint of the heroic, like the veil of heroism he threw over himself. This at the beginning. We waited in silence. Slowly Pilli took another tack and then he began to quicken his pace. Above us the leaves of the wild olive hung pale and motionless. The sun was blazing down as always. The flies buzzed over our dishes and clung to them, and when brushed away, immediately returned.

Suddenly the C.O. loomed up enormous in the sun; he became a horse that rears up on hind legs, huge, with the animal paunch above us, the eyes blazing with fire.

Pilli had begun to tell a story; he turned to one of us in particular. He was saying, for example, that one day the Major's sunglasses were missing. Everyone thought that he had stolen them. "And what happened? Capone found them in the first-aid tent. Good old Capone! He promptly restored them to the Major."

We listened.

Pilli continued, turning to one of us in particular.

"Yes, my dear fellow, and I suppose you think I stole them because the glasses were found in the first-aid tent?"

The horse reared up on its hind legs.

"You think *I* took them, do you? Me, Oscar Pilli? Look at my chest, my ribbons. There's your proof of courage. Oscar Pilli is a soldier," and his eyes flared, his face went red. Now he was looking directly at one of us. "Ah, so you think I took them? You say that I'm a thief! Me, Oscar Pilli, a thief! Say *I* stole them, will you? You say I stole them! You say I steal! You dare call me a thief in front of everybody! Your own superior officer! You insult me in front of everybody, your own superior officer! There's a court-martial for things like that. A thief, am I? You called me a thief!" And turning to one of us, he said, "You heard him? You're my witness. You'll testify. There's the firing squad for that. Court-martial. I'll have you shot!" And then, after a long, pregnant silence, he said rapidly, clipping his words for emphasis, "I have in my pocket an *extremely* important letter, a letter of *supreme* importance, to one of the *most important men* in Libya. He'll see justice done."

And so the crisis passed. From this point on Pilli was normally more tractable.

Of course nobody had said that Pilli was a thief, and we "witnesses" had not heard or seen anyone speak.

We had seen and heard only Pilli unfurling his glistering power as our commander and chief.

And at this point the reader is requested to consider that we were in military uniform, in a war zone, that Pilli was in fact our C.O.—the officer who is never questioned. And above all the reader should take into consideration the Italian military bureaucracy, which, once started on its way, proceeds blind, dumb, insensitive as an engagement book; and the fact that no one dares to intervene and bring the truth to light. Military procedure was an engagement book that moved with a negative but enormous momentum. The only momentum in that Italian army.

Pilli used to act as follows.

The soldiers were required to take typhoid shots. The inoculation is made in the chest, which swells at that point.

Standing in a line, the soldiers offered their bare chests; the doctor inserted the needle.

About noon Pilli's mind was a beehive swarming with—the heat, blood, bare chests.

Energetically he drove the other doctors away from the first-aid tent, saying, "I'll do it, my dear fellow. Go take your siesta. I *order* you to go take your siesta."

The doctor—or doctors—left.

He delighted in being alone.

He raised the hypodermic syringe in the air, displaying it to the remaining soldiers.

The soldiers looked at Pilli and the syringe in dreadful suspense.

His blue eyes twinkling like a diabolic cherub's, he began his chant.

The two clerks, the same two clerks who assisted him during Mass, accompanied him.

The chant was low.

The soldiers, their chests exposed, were forced to kneel.

Pilli approached the chest of the kneeling soldier, and bringing down his arm, plunged the needle into the white flesh, working it up and down in the young man's chest.

With trembling, excited fingers, he prepared to inoculate the next soldier.

The hushed hieratic chant hung suspended on that razor's edge that lies between the comic and the serious.

Pilli used large needles for the inoculations.

As soon as he became C.O. he enforced the bugle calls. At dawn the bugling began.

Buda was a quiet, reserved lieutenant, not given to talking. He lived alone with his own thoughts. For the rest we knew nothing of his past, nor did he allude to it.

The company was held in reserve, abandoned to a life of idleness in a part of Tripolitania.

Pilli was continually in a state of exalted, useless activity.

As soon as he became C.O. he enforced the bugle calls. At dawn the bugling began.

One morning when all the other officers were still sleeping, Pilli was awake. He winked at the bugler, nodded in the direction of Buda's tent, indicating that the bugler should put his bugle next to Buda's ear and blast away.

The bugler executed his orders.

Buda immediately went up to the bugler and asked him why he had waked him in that manner. The bugler replied that he was acting on orders from Pilli.

Buda went to Pilli and said, "I'll put a bullet through your head."

At this Pilli went pale with terror and said, "But no, I love you like a brother. It's not true. I swear it's not true. Here, we'll ask the bugler. You'll see it isn't true. I give you my word of honor."

And he called for the bugler.

The bugler replied, "But you ordered me to, Captain," and he spoke with the incredulity of an honest boy.

Then Pilli said angrily to the bugler, "That's a lie. So. Call me a liar, do you? You accuse me, you insult me. You've insulted your superior! Insubordination to your C.O." And, white with rage, he shouted, "Get inside. You're under arrest. It's the firing squad for men like you, all of you!" And utterly beside himself, he shrieked, "Criminals!"

Pilli immediately called for two corporals who took the bugler by the arms, as ordered, and carried him off to a tent that Pilli had designated as the guardhouse. Two armed sentinels with fixed bayonets were stationed at the door, as though the bugler were to be shot at dawn.

The company was as tense as a ropewalker. The company was as tense as a stalked deer. So also the wet leaves move, tense and uncertain, in the still air after a storm.

The soldiers had eyes in the backs of their heads, eyes everywhere. They crouched in their tents, watching Pilli from a distance. Like dumb crickets their eyes danced about him.

And an alliance between the soldiers and the officers was born. A friendship was born which lasted our whole time in Libya.

Pilli created this friendship because he was incapable of creating a tyranny.

The tyrant has his spies whom he rewards and protects, whereas the man who played Pilli's spy found himself in prison a few hours later.

For this reason, those whose natures disposed them to be spies—one meets them everywhere—distrusted Pilli and took care to keep their distance.

And so officers and soldiers were compelled, as human beings, to form an alliance, and this produced an effect very rarely encountered in the Italian army. From this time on officers and soldiers actually protected each other, were mutually loyal. For instance, in other companies the officers—who fought the same miserable war in Libya that we fought—managed to escape to Italy, either through intrigue or influential connections, abandoning the soldiers in the desert. But in our company, no. On the contrary. Several of our officers—or rather, one of them—succeeded in getting several soldiers in our company transferred back to Italy, while he himself remained in the desert with those who had not been so fortunate.

And so, because of Pilli and the military bureaucracy which protected Pilli, a friendship was born.

The military bureaucracy declares that an inferior must obey his superior, especially at the front; and the Italian bureaucracy declares that it wants "no nonsense" and that everybody must "play ball"; and because it is inconceivable that a superior should be accused by an inferior, the inferior must grin and bear it, because that's the way it is.

No regular officer in the Medical Corps—the officers at headquarters—would have taken steps to get rid of Pilli, who was himself a regular officer in the Medical Corps.

Our putative English enemies, who were planning encircling actions—often perfect ones—against us in the desert must have thought that Italian soldiers were stupid.

The Italian soldiers had to cope with encirclement in their own circumstances.

When soldiers heed the call of amusement, everything else is forgotten.

The other officers had gone to lunch at Mahmud's. Pilli had been left alone with the soldiers. He took a bath. He sent for one of our milk containers—a tub that held three or four gallons of water—and ordered it set up in front of his tent. He pulled off his trousers and stood there, his legs and thighs nude, and wearing nothing but his shirt and, over the shirt, his vest, stuffed full of banknotes.

He set a stool in front of the tub, stuck his bare feet into the water, and sat down. Pilli's flesh and skin were white. He paddled with his feet and then started calling to the soldiers who had the tents next to his to come and listen to his jokes. He was, in fact, "alluding," in a pointed and common manner, to sexual jokes. The soldiers formed a circle around him where he sat with his legs in the tub.

He talked, and in the instant between one obscene sentence and the next, the soldiers laughed like a chorus. Pilli was happy. There was a harmony, a precise, perfect dependence. In that moment he was truly the leader. An absolute spontaneous discipline prevailed. He raised his swagger stick, delivered his line, and the laughter came gurgling up like the gurgle of water when one pulls the chain.

Happily and naturally Pilli spouted his bawdy lines until eventually they carried him and the soldiers into that free and anarchic world, that joyous world which perpetually, for a few brief seconds, appears and will appear in this world, and is then swiftly annulled by the bigotry of life.

The soldiers formed a circle around him, he himself a soldier who happened to be an officer and commander of the camp.

Because he was sitting on the stool in front of the tub, his very white and flabby behind was hidden by his shirttail. But he rose, and just as a dancer at the end of her dance turns her back to the audience and flips up her petticoat so that you can see her behind, so too if Pilli had done as dancers do and flipped his shirttail up, then the soldiers would have seen Oscar Pilli's behind.

And because he was extremely excited by his words and the laughter, this is what he did, and the soldiers saw Oscar Pilli's behind.

After this, sticking his feet into the tub, Pilli gave the signal for the dancing to begin.

Now he was no longer C.O. He was one of those winged cherubs who flutter, free and happy, about the head of the Madonna in sacred paintings.

The afternoon in the oasis unfolded candidly and freely, outside of any law. Pilli and the soldiers were human creatures who were amusing themselves.

That man who sets himself to judge with black and sullen looks—that man is wrong.

He was Pilli, Oscar Pilli, he was a sadist, a maniac, he was mentally deficient, he was subject to flights of ideas, insane impulsiveness, he was likeable, he was happy, he was genial, he was instinctive, he was a thief, he was pursued by phantoms, he was a cherub with blue eyes, he was a Tuscan in corruption; his physique was strong. He was greedy, he couldn't reflect, he couldn't think, he was ignorant of morality, he was a stranger to love, he had no friends, he had no heart, he was infantile; he forgot, he forgot and he had a memory like iron, which wasn't his, which wasn't his; he was a Tuscan, an ancient Tuscan, a Catholic Tuscan. He didn't think, he didn't reflect, he couldn't, he didn't love, love is thought, life is love, men are brothers. Pilli was cowardly, Pilli was a coward. He didn't know how, he didn't know. He was an idiot, he was a sadist, he knew Italian, he was a Tuscan, he was a Tuscan gone rotten; his physique was strong; he had never felt dejected. He was always flying, he was always running, his ideas were always flying, flights of ideas, always flying, they were not his. Pilli was crazy, everyone knew it, he was a regular officer, a career soldier, he knew the rules and regulations, he didn't love, he had no heart, Pilli was a Tuscan, Pilli was crazy, the colonels could see it, Pilli was, was Pilli, Oscar Pilli, a Tuscan corrupted, a Tuscan gone rotten, a Catholic in corruption.

We thought of eliminating Pilli, because if fighting broke out and the casualties were brought to our company, what would a C.O. like Oscar Pilli do?

But Pilli could be eliminated only by going through Medical Corps headquarters. This was the course we took.

One of us went to Tripoli.

He got the ear of one of the secretaries at headquarters and told him the story of Oscar Pilli.

The secretary at first doubted our story, just as a grownup might doubt a fairy story. Then he laughed at it and accepted it. And the following day he passed the gossip on to his superior officer, who was incredulous and then amused.

The route which we had followed was the customary one, the route which they had taught us. We made no official outcry, we avoided exposing ourselves, we whispered. Unobtrusiveness succeeded.

And so the rumor spread through Medical Corps headquarters that there was a captain by the name of Pilli who chanted Mass in the desert, tossed elegant little packages among the kitchen pots, and kicked his heels like a wild goat in rut.

We conducted ourselves like professional bullfighters.

First we had to create the gossip; then the gossip would breed of itself.

At first, during dinner, the colonels found it amusing to discuss Pilli's antics. But later, when they were alone, the question arose, unbidden and terrible: if Oscar Pilli, in his madness, in a forward unit, at the front, committed some colossal,

catastrophic blunder, who would be responsible? We know
about him now. Not only we; all the officers know about him,
from lieutenants up to us colonels. The story is general knowledge; the entire officers' mess knows what Pilli has done. If he
commits some horrible blunder, who is responsible? We have
been informed about him, even if not officially informed.

It was at this point, troubled and irritated, that the colonels
found themselves while they undressed in the silent room before getting into their soft beds.

"These junior officers think it's funny, but we'll be held responsible." And the more they considered the fact, the more
irritated they became.

We had managed this much then: rumors about Pilli had
been started at headquarters. If we had Pilli on our minds, so
did they. Even if unofficially, the senior officers *knew* that a
captain, who was in some sense insane, was the C.O. of a
medical company, through whose hands in time of war the
wounded of a whole division had to pass.

There were some who thought that, once the rumors about
Pilli gathered weight, the brass would be compelled to put
matters straight. Which was what happened. And they would,
of course, put matters right, not for justice's sake, or for the
good of the army, or because it pained them to see soldiers
suffering the excesses of a lunatic; no, they would put matters
right solely because they were afraid the consequences might
be unpleasant for them personally; because in the eyes of
headquarters, they, as the ranking officers, would be held solely responsible for anything that was irregular or out of line.
And Pilli was out of line. And so it happened that the two
colonels (who were jointly in charge of Medical Corps forces
in Tripoli in Pilli's time) put their heads together and discovered—predictably—the only, the time-honored solution:
they made an inspection of the company.

What did they expect to find? Soldiers walking around on
their hands, in those stereotyped cartoons of the inside of insane asylums?

They arrived in the cool of the morning, when the fog of
Tripolitania begins to lift, dispersed by the sun.

They arrived in a car and got out. Both of them had paunches, which were emphasized by their uniforms. One was flabby, shy, bright-eyed; the other was dark, a Calabrian.

As soon as they stepped out of the car, the company was alert. All the men had spent more than a year and a half in the army. They knew what had to be done when top brass and politicians visited the outfit.

They all saluted briskly, tidied up their tents in great haste, smoothed out their uniforms. Those who were unpresentable at the time got out of sight. A hush fell over the camp.

By the time the colonels reached the center of the camp, everything was in order.

The soldiers had sensed that there was something in the air, that somebody had taken steps to put a stop to Pilli. They were alert. And now that the two colonels had put in their appearance, they were even more alert. Give Italian soldiers a motive for being alert, and they will outdo themselves. Which they now did.

The two colonels inspected to see if the area was policed, if the first-aid tent was in order; they particularly inspected the sick-call book, the inventory records, papers, notations, comments.

Everything was in perfect order. Pilli had not forgotten a single stamp. Pilli had a passion for paperwork, notebooks, underlining, rules and regulations, and his passion appeared in those documents. The two colonels were almost in ecstasy over those bulletins, files, etc., kept so scrupulously but above all so painstakingly worked over, so countersigned, read and reread. The colonels were familiar with only one profession: paperwork. This was perfect. Who then had dared to call Pilli a madman? It was a contemptible slander. Why, Pilli could have become a colonel, a colonel like them. So, in private, the two colonels began to think.

They might instead have asked merely: Is it true that the Captain chants Mass? Is it true that he steals sunglasses? Is it true that he raves all day long, alternating fraternal embraces with threats of the firing squad? Is it true that his baggage, which arrived half empty, is gradually being filled up with the most unlikely objects?

But none of these questions occurred to them. The two colonels inspected to see if there was dust on the furniture, not caring the slightest whether the furniture was bandy-legged, worm-eaten, useless, or even if it was furniture.

Irritated to find no dust, one colonel interrogated Pilli, while the other colonel—he of the bright eyes and the flabby flesh, the colonel with the large white rump—walked over toward the officers, who were standing to one side in a small group, waiting. In a thin, icy voice, he asked us who was responsible for spreading all those rumors at headquarters. One officer stepped forward. He looked at him malignantly, as though he had discovered a petty thief, and told him that he would be punished, that he had clearly acted as he had in order to remove Pilli and get himself appointed C.O.

This was our second failure.

Our first had been with the adjutant of the division. In the early days, one of us had gone to him and reported on Pilli's antics. He had listened in silence, with severity. We thought that he would take action. At the end of a month the only reply was still silence.

For this reason we decided to take the matter directly to Medical Corps headquarters.

The result was negative.

One of us, however, stubbornly persisted in prodding. He returned to the same secretary at headquarters, and flatly pointed out, indicated precisely where the two inspecting colonels had made their mistake and (here he merely alluded) their logical and moral inadequacy. In short, he acted in such a way that the secretary, without resenting it, was given a lesson in the ABC's of the case. He mastered it and, as foreseen, when all the medical officers were gathered pleasantly and complacently around the dinner table, he repeated our arguments as a means of parading his acumen, and once again those present were amused and this time understood, and even the colonels slowly understood, and once again they rose to the same conclusion as before: to wit, if Pilli committed some gross blunder, they—and they alone—would be held responsible, and something had to be done.

Pilli received orders to report to Tripoli for a medical examination, because he was ill.

Without his knowing anything about it, the colonels had requested an examination for him.

Under the hot sun, a motorcyclist rode up with a letter. Pilli read the letter in front of the tent. "In*cred*ible!" he said. According to the letter, he was to report the following day to the military hospital in Tripoli for a medical examination.

"But, my dear fellow, I've never felt better," he said to the motorcyclist, who was getting ready to leave.

"Wait," he added. "There's been a mistake." And while he was rereading the letter, he muttered, "By the love I bear you, sir . . . it's in*cred*ible. . . ." And the word died on his lips. His enormous head changed color, his skin flushed red like that of a newborn baby fresh from its bath. In that instant Pilli seemed to have just issued into the world, thunderstruck. And he added, "There's been a mistake, my dear fellow." But the motorcyclist was already gone.

So, standing there in the hot sun, he found that he had requested a medical examination, when he was in splendid health.

With the letter in his hand, he went back inside the first-aid tent, and approaching the soldier who was standing there naked, waiting for Pilli to finish his examination, he said, "There. Look." And handing him the letter, he said, "Read it, dear boy. Go on, read it. It's in*cred*ible!" And ripping it from his hand just as the mystified soldier was starting to read God knows what and handing the letter—that is, the orders to report to Tripoli—to the clerks, he said to one of them:

"Read it. Look at it. I tell you, look at it," and he waved the letter (by now almost completely crumpled) in the air without handing it to anybody, while the naked soldier and the orderlies looked at Pilli expectantly but, knowing Pilli, not surprised.

A ray of light, however, was shed when Pilli said, "But I'm in perfect health. It's incredible! Asking for a physical for *me!* Here, look at it. Read it." And at last he shoved the letter into a clerk's hands to read, but because the clerk had to read so hurriedly, interrupted by Pilli's usual exclamations, he understood almost nothing. Anyway, Pilli had already snatched the letter back and then, like the girl with the plate who wanders along the street soliciting money for the organ grinder, Pilli wandered through the camp soliciting the soldiers' approval of his argument: that it was monstrous to send him off to Tripoli so unexpectedly, that *he* should have to report to that hospital, he, Oscar Pilli, who had never felt better in his life, never more than now when he was in absolute command, and that it was to *him* that they send a message saying that he was a sick man.

But while he was zigzagging like a bolt of lightning through the camp to deliver his news, he managed to interject—with his customary miraculous quickness—the suspicion that it was *someone,* that *somebody* had informed, *somebody* on the inside was the instigator, and as he proceeded in his circuit, he now and then stopped speaking altogether as his suspicions loomed larger.

And in the pauses that followed his fulminations, he began, "You know who it was," and jerked his thumb in the air in the direction of the officers' tents.

At suppertime, the whole camp was still buzzing with news, and Pilli sat there at the table, his face ruddy as the moon, with the letter still clutched in his hand and the words pouring out of his mouth like white flour pouring from a slit in the sack.

The next morning the faithful Capone drove Pilli to Tripoli in the company pickup.

He reported to his superiors—this time they were Medical Corps officers and hence his *direct* superiors—snapped to attention a thousand times, suppressed his fraternal phrases (but when he was left alone with the orderlies, they spilled out like water from a dam). But oh, the flights of ideas! With lightning swiftness, as never before, those shining associations darted through his mind, shattering as they collided, no single thought completed, each alike flaring into vivid life and just as quickly snuffed, as other ideas came crowding forward, each imperiously demanding its place in the sun, and then in turn trampled down by its desperate successors.

They examined him from head to toe while he kept saying, "with all respect, sir," that he was in the best of health, that he had never felt better in his life. They X-rayed him, they examined his throat, they gave him a blood test, a urinalysis, they tested his reflexes.

And that evening he returned to camp, his head ruddy with the mental storms that had broken there during the day.

He said, "They told me I was a bit run down. 'Captain, you're a bit run down. You need a little rest.' What could they mean, my dear fellows? That was all. That was all they said. 'Captain, you're a bit run down.' The Colonel—it was the Colonel—a harsh colonel, a very severe colonel. 'Strip,' he said. And when they tested my reflexes, I couldn't hold still, when they tapped me on the knee, I kept laughing, and he said, 'Stop laughing,' but I couldn't stop, what with that little hammer, I was completely naked. 'Strip completely,' he said. A very stern colonel. Very, very severe. What could he mean? 'You're a bit run down.' Eh, dear fellows? 'Yessir, but I'm in perfect health.' A colonel. And his eyes—stern, very stern."

And Pilli, like a racing motor, like the shining wake of a ship, drove on and on.

The next morning a messenger on a motorcycle drove up with a message which said—in*cred*ible!—that Pilli had been granted a two-month sick leave.

· Let us analyze these two months of convalescent leave.

What went on in the minds of the two colonels?

They had reasoned as follows: Everybody knows about Pilli now. If he commits some horrible blunder, we can't say that we didn't know about him before. Very well, we'll send him away. Let him be a burden to somebody else. We'll send him to Italy. Let them take care of him in Italy.

Consider for a moment the two colonels' argument.

If they had wanted to act for the good of the army, they would have been compelled to remove Pilli altogether. They would have had to discharge him from the army. They knew with complete certainty that he was mad. How can a madman command a company of medics, or anything else for that matter?

But they had no intention of acting for the good of the army; they had acted in their own interests, that is, to relieve themselves of all responsibility on Pilli's account.

To achieve this, they had concocted the physical examination and the two short months of convalescent leave. Two short months, with the result that, at the end of those two months, Pilli would be sent—which actually happened—to another sector and, because of his rank, would once again assume command and create the same problem he had already created in our company, and so the story would repeat itself as it had been repeating itself for some time now. In fact, before coming to us he had been in Spain, where something of the same sort must have happened, since he was shipped home; and before that he was in Abyssinia, and before that in his own district, where his sadism had found good opportunities, and so on.

They granted him only two months of leave. It was utterly obvious that Pilli was incompetent and a menace to the army. But the colonels granted him two short months of sick leave.

The reasons for treating him in this way are these:

Colonels are regular officers; Pilli was a regular officer. They belong to the same caste. Whatever may happen, members of this caste do not injure one another, they protect one another.

In the second place, it was the custom in the Italian army to evade responsibility by dumping it on others, to postpone every problem, never to make a final or unequivocal decision. At V—— Pilli had been a continuous source of trouble, so the colonel decides to get rid of this embarrassment by transferring him to Libya. In Libya Pilli creates problems, so the colonels in Libya transfer him back to V——, and the colonel at V——

will promptly bounce him somewhere else. Nobody removes
him; everybody transfers him to someone else.

Meanwhile Pilli's chest is covered with campaign ribbons,
since he spends three months—the period required for making himself known—in every war that comes along. And whenever he leaves, he leaves like a casualty; he travels on the hospital ship or the hospital train; he is a gallant casualty, and
during his months of convalescence, of course, he draws his
disability pension, and, of course, since he has completed three
months of active duty, he is entitled to the campaign ribbon,
and his gallant chest is dotted with various-colored ribbons,
which in turn will make him even more respected in his next
campaign, and on his next sick leave he will be treated with
the even greater regard which is due such a man, a veteran
of so many wars.

For these reasons, therefore, the two colonels who were in
charge of Medical Corps operations in Libya slyly pawned
off on Pilli two months of sick leave, and the customary messenger on his motorcycle brought Pilli one last dispatch, which
contained the findings and decision of the examining board.

It was the last night, Pilli's farewell.

He was no longer C.O. The command had passed to the
highest-ranking officer after Pilli, that is, to a lieutenant.

We took our evening meals inside an Arab house.

Over our heads stretched the stars of heaven.

Silence and fragrance in the oasis.

Pilli was, as usual, the first to arrive, and when he entered,
the messroom orderly, following our instructions, respectfully
informed him that his place was no longer at the head of the
table. That seat was reserved for the C.O., and he pointed
out his new place, on the right of the company commander.

"Quite right, my dear fellow. Quite right, my dear fellow."
And he took his seat. No one else had yet arrived.

But before long, by twos and threes, the others drifted in.
They barely even nodded to Pilli, but stood quietly waiting
for dinner, as though Pilli didn't exist or weren't worth the
trouble of noticing.

The C.O. was still absent.

He made his entrance.

Like a monarch.

The space between the door of the Arab house and the dining table was illuminated by a number of kerosene lamps.

The instant the officers saw him, as though startled from sleep by a blaze of electric light, they leaped to their feet, snapped to attention, and stared in front of them: they were saluting their superior officer.

Slowly the C.O. approached.

Pilli was still seated, but his head was rigid, his eyes staring. He was watching that glorious ritual as though enchanted.

The C.O. drew near, benevolent. He stood at the head of the table. His manner became severe. He seemed to be waiting for something. There was an enormous silence.

Pilli was uncertain. He pulled himself from his chair. His body slowly straightened, as though it didn't quite know why. Then suddenly Pilli saluted, stood rigid at attention, his eyes probing empty air.

The C.O. returned the salute and then nodded. The tension died and dinner was served as though nothing had happened.

Pilli, still stunned by what he had done—he, a captain, saluting a lieutenant, saluting *first!*—found himself seated once more and said shyly, like a boy confessing the secret of his first love, "What discipline! What extraordinary discipline! Before I've even left!"

But the soldiers—who never change, who do not even want to understand—now that Pilli was no longer C.O., vented their anger on his past excesses.

Suddenly from every corner of the room the barrage against him began: "Hey, Pilli! Hey, Pilli, why'd you do it? You did it, hey, Pilli!"

Utterly overwhelmed, like a small boy who is made to abandon his games and compelled to walk along a deserted alley, and suddenly the doors, the crumbling masonry, the windows and the bricks assail him—utterly overwhelmed, he turned to each in turn and answered with a sob in his throat (for the first time, and not grief, but the sob of stunned terror), repeating to each, "Quite, my dear fellow . . . but no! . . . but no! . . . like a brother . . . I regard you as a brother." (And they did not realize that Pilli had no memory, that he lived solely in the present instant, an instant that appeared and vanished).

But at last they stopped, since dinner was finished too, and they left the Arab house, and Pilli was already forgetting what they had said. And suddenly one of us, a man who must have known every track of Pilli's mind (we were standing in a circle around him), said to him as though he were speaking of some practical everyday matter (the Arab house was an island in a great landscape of sand):

"You are the commanding general of our forces. I come up, covered with blood, and report to you the outcome of the battle. Put yourself in that situation, Captain. Pretend it's true."

Pilli assented, and walking to a high point nearby, stood there waiting (already the ideas of Rank and Supreme Command were swarming through his mind with enormous rapidity; already the abstract splendor of Military Hierarchy had consumed him with its blaze).

The other officers watched in amazement, puzzled both by Pilli and by the man who had made the proposal (who had gone off in order to reappear "panting and drenched with blood" before Pilli).

The soldiers in the company, who knew about Pilli's departure and who had commemorated him constantly that evening, laughing at him, describing him, etc., were looking on from a distance.

The lieutenant who had made the proposal came running up, pretending to be panting, snapped to attention before Pilli and cried with what seemed genuine emotion:

"General, on our right wing the enemy has been completely defeated. Our best men have fallen. Our flag waves over the field."

The men at last gave up.

There was no longer any interest in it for them. Pilli was

no longer C.O. He aroused no terror. Everybody could understand him now.

The majority renounced the malicious joke and their revenge. It was not this man who had abused them, if there had been abuses; it was Oscar Pilli, and for Oscar Pilli there were no laws.

With tremendous pride, the blood rushing to his face, with great rapidity, Pilli immediately raised his arm and in great sincerity cried out: "Continue the struggle until victorious!"

The lieutenant saluted and then we heard his footsteps beat away into silence as he ran off.

Then another officer, as though he had grasped, or been overcome by the spirit of the game, went off. We waited, in silence, and then he reappeared, panting, sweating from the battle, ran up to Pilli and shouted:

"The third battalion has been destroyed. Our lines still hold!"

Pilli cried out, "Resist until victory!"

There he stood on that high point of the ground. On his face glowed that same burning light, both serious and comic, that he had when saying Mass, but this time the light was brighter because of the tumult of battle, the lightnings of power, the extraordinary abstract blaze of obedience, the smoke of glory that rose from the field.

The others standing near him, who looked on or participated in that comedy, were merely men. He displayed his chest blazoned with ribbons; he had unfurled the flag of another world.

Present and past no longer existed. Oscar Pilli was a star, and the others, dull satellites, revolved about him.

We had to enter into his world, into his orbit, to be happy. Another man ran up "panting and drenched with blood."

We lost a man like Oscar Pilli.

CARLO CASSOLA

CARLO CASSOLA, THE SON OF A LOMBARD JOURNALIST AND A
Tuscan mother, is regarded as one of the most distinguished
writers of the Italian younger (i.e., fortyish) generation.
Commonly classified as a Tuscan writer—most of his stories
are set in southern Tuscany, in the triangle between Volterra,
Massa, and Siena—he was actually born in Rome (March 17,
1917) and lived there until he was twenty-three. Intended
for the practice of law, he turned to literature when he was
eighteen, and published his first collection of stories in 1942.
But the crucial experience of his life, both as a man and a
writer, was his participation in the Italian Resistance movement in the Volterra area; and it is no accident that much
of his subsequent fiction has been set in wartime or postwar
Volterra and is overtly concerned with the nature and quality
of political commitment. At present Cassola lives in the small
provincial center of Grosseto—his dislike of urban literary life
is both conviction and temperament—where he earns his
living teaching history and philosophy. Apart from his stories
and novels, he has published a diary of a trip to China and
collaborated on a study of the miners of the Maremma. In
1960, his novel *La ragazza di Bube (Bebo's Girl)* was awarded
the Premio Strega.

His chief writings are: *La visita* (1942); *Alla periferia*
(1942); *Fausto e Anna* (1952); *I vecchi compagni* (1953);
Il taglio del bosco (1954); *La casa di via Valadier* (1956);
Un matrimonio del dopoguerra (1957); *Il soldato* (1958);
La ragazza di Bube (1960).

THE CUTTING OF THE WOODS

by Carlo Cassola

translated by Raymond Rosenthal

[1]

AFTER MONTECERBOLI THE TRAVELERS WERE REDUCED TO FIVE:
a young boy, two women, a child, and a man.

The conductor rubbed his hands together. "We're really
cozy this evening, a regular family," he said, satisfied.

The man at the back smiled. Then, though nothing could
be seen in the darkness, he began staring out the window.

The man looked about thirty-seven or thirty-eight years old.
He wore a jacket with a fur collar that was frayed by use,
and combed his hair so that it rose slightly over his forehead.
He had a thin face, a straight nose, firm lips, large-boned, ro-
bust hands.

The bus came nearly to a halt at the start of the hill; after
changing gear it continued to climb, snorting. The man seated
at the back asked that they stop at the store.

"Stop at the store," the conductor repeated, relaying the
order to the driver.

In the store's doorway a woman already along in years was
waiting for the bus. She sharpened her eyes to make out the
traveler but failed to recognize her nephew until he was a
few paces away.

"Oh, Guglielmo," she said. "How are you? I couldn't see
you in this dark."

"How goes it, Lina?" the man replied.

"All right, and how is Caterina? But it's cold; why don't
you come in?"

A bulb hanging at the end of a wire constituted the room's
only light. The furniture was just as sober: a bench placed
against the wall, two tables drawn up to it, four or five

243

stools; this was all the shop offered its customers. The goods were piled up behind the counter. There was the usual stock, of course, though not much of any one thing: food, tobacco, spools of thread, notebooks, pen points, postcards. Some stale biscuits were also on display in a box with a glass cover. From one summer to the next the bunches of herbs used to keep away the flies had hung forgotten on the walls, and a small kerosene lamp was kept permanently lit under a print of the Sacred Heart of Jesus.

"Do you want to go back into the house?" his aunt asked.

"No," Guglielmo answered. "I'll eat a little soup and then I'll go."

Without taking off his hat, he sat down at the empty table (the other one was occupied by two men playing cards) and remained there, motionless, his gaze lost in the void.

"Is it cold?" one of the card players asked.

Guglielmo shook himself. "It is," he replied.

"It'll take just a few minutes," his aunt said, coming back from the kitchen. Guglielmo nodded his head to show that it was all right.

"Have you been away from home for long?" his aunt asked.

"No . . . only since Monday," the man replied.

"Where have you been?"

The man made a gesture in the direction of the door.

"To Massa," he said, "I went there to buy a stand of timber," he added, anticipating the woman's question.

"But why on earth so far away?" the woman insisted.

Guglielmo smiled. "It suited me," he said.

"And you'll go to cut it?" His aunt went on with her question.

"Of course," Guglielmo replied. "With the usual crew."

The woman's curiosity seemed satisfied. Changing the subject, she said that she hadn't seen Caterina for months.

"I'm old and I don't like to walk. And I can imagine all the work those children give her."

He agreed with a nod of his head.

"That girl's an angel," the woman concluded.

"That's just what she is," he said.

"You see, Guglielmo, in your misfortune you've had at least this good luck: a sister who can take care of the girls. . . ."

"Yes," he replied. "I can call myself lucky on that account at least. I don't know how I could have managed. . . . I would have been forced to marry again."

The woman disappeared behind the curtain that hung at the back of the room, returning after a couple of minutes with a bowl of clear broth in which a few grains of rice were floating. Then she put half a loaf of bread and a pint of wine on the table. The man picked up the bread and began to tear it into small pieces. Then he poured some wine into the bowl. Finally, energetically working his spoon, he mixed everything together, broth, wine, and bread, and began to eat.

His aunt stood for a while watching him; then, seeing that he didn't lift his eyes from his plate, she went behind the counter and sat down again.

Guglielmo also ate some bread and cheese, drank another glass of wine, and then asked how much he owed.

"One lira, forty centesimi," his aunt replied.

Guglielmo took his watch out of his vest pocket. "Eight-fifteen," he said. "I'll find them all in bed," he added, as though talking to himself.

"Give my regards to Caterina," his aunt said. "And kiss the girls for me. And take care of yourself."

"Don't worry," Guglielmo replied.

He said good night to the card players and went out. It was no longer as dark as an hour ago, though the moon was hidden behind a bank of mist. Guglielmo stopped to light a cigarette, then began walking quickly.

After a few hundred yards of level ground, the road began to descend. The fields came to a stop, and the road burrowed into a wood. Guglielmo threw away his cigarette butt and quickened his pace. He kept reviewing the business deal he had concluded the day before, re-examining every detail. He made his calculations all over again and always reached the conclusion that he should earn not less than seven thousand lire. Certainly he had taken a chance, buying it without being sure of the going seasonal prices. . . . Thinking of his business affairs, he didn't notice the road. Almost without being aware of it, he walked over the small bridge, and still walking quickly, climbed the slope that led to the village. But gradually he slowed his pace and his thoughts went off in another direction. He passed a half-ruined little stone house and remembered the old man who used to live there and his tales of witches, magicians, devils, enchantments. . . . Guglielmo was still not averse to believing such stories.

Walking past the small cemetery, he glanced sadly through the gate and said a requiem for his poor wife. It was exactly three months since she had left him. He forced himself to hasten his steps and again to think about his business deal. At last he reached the village. At the entrance to San Dalmazio, he stopped at a store also owned by a relative of his. While he was waiting to be served, he took off his hat and mopped away the sweat with a handkerchief.

"You're sweating in this cold weather?" the woman asked him.

Guglielmo muttered that he was, not particularly wanting to go into explanations. The village was sunk in silence and darkness. At that hour all the women and children were already asleep. Guglielmo took the badly paved road that climbed steeply to a point above the village, where his house stood.

Trying to walk quietly, he went into the kitchen, but his sister woke up and shortly afterward came in to ask if he wanted anything. Guglielmo told her that he had already eaten.

"We didn't expect you tonight," his sister said, almost as though excusing herself for not having been awake.

"I came back early," Guglielmo replied.

"The girls are all right," Caterina said, though her brother hadn't asked. "Were you able to settle the deal?"

"Yes. I'll go down on Monday."

"Are you sure you don't want anything?" his sister insisted. "I can light the fire in a minute and heat something up for you."

"No. Go back to bed or you'll catch cold."

Left to himself, Guglielmo drank another glass of wine; then he sat down at the table, lit a cigarette, and pulled out a thoroughly crumpled notebook and a pencil stub. He wrote down in a column his expenses for the day; before adding up the figures, he thought for a while to be sure he wasn't forgetting anything. He had the habit of writing down even the smallest expenditure, and at the end of the month it was rare for his accounts not to balance perfectly down to the last centesimo. He crushed out his cigarette butt on the floor, put the wine bottle back into the cupboard, placed the glass on the sink, and went to his room.

The moon was shining on a strip of the floor. Guglielmo turned on the light. The room was only dimly illuminated. It was a small room with a tile floor and a ceiling crossed by naked beams. The large bed, the closet, and the large chest of drawers occupied almost the entire space. Guglielmo removed his jacket, went to the chest of drawers, took out his watch, and laid it on the marble top. His glance fell on his wife's photograph but he instantly looked away.

In the morning at half past five he was already up. He put on his pants over his nightshirt. Then, pouring water in the washbasin that rested on the sink, he began to wash. He used laundry soap. When his sister came in, in her petticoat, he was drying himself.

While Caterina was heating the coffee, Guglielmo wrote down in his notebook the expenditures that he would have to make that morning. Before going out, he told his sister that he hoped to be home for lunch, but in any case she shouldn't wait for him.

Once outside, instead of going down through the village, he took a short cut along a dirt road that bore to the left; and then he followed a path across the fields. In fact, he had in mind a visit to his chief woodcutter, Fiore, who lived at the bridge beside the Cecina River, an hour's walk from San Dalmazio. Since they were already agreed, Guglielmo could have waited till the next morning, Sunday, when Fiore came to the village to get his customary Sunday shave, but he was too anxious to finish the hiring. From Cecina he would reach the provincial highway in time to take the bus for Pomarance. At Pomarance he had to buy a billhook, tar paper, candles, tobacco, matches, and rope.

He returned just before noon. Adriana, the younger of the two girls, ran out to meet him; she wrapped herself around his legs so tightly that Guglielmo had a hard time getting free of her clutch. The older girl was shy with her father, however, and held off. Guglielmo kissed her too, and gave each of them a stick of taffy. Adriana showed her happiness by shrieking and jumping about and then quickly popped the candy into her mouth. Her aunt stepped in and took it away from her because she had to eat. The child started wailing but stopped almost immediately.

"And you?" Guglielmo said to Irma, who was looking at him silently. "Haven't you anything to say to me?" he added with a smile.

The child lowered her eyes in confusion, and Guglielmo stroked her hair. Then he took off his jacket and hung it over a chair; he washed his hands and sat down at the table. While waiting, he took out a newspaper that he had bought at Pomarance. A So-and-so, whom he didn't know, was dead; the Agricultural Association had made available a quantity of seed potatoes. His sister put the soup bowl on the table. Guglielmo folded the newspaper carefully and put it back in his pocket. He uncovered the soup bowl, and immediately a thick steam and a sharp smell of cabbage struck him. First he served the children, then his sister; he filled his own plate last. Caterina picked up her bowl and went to sit beside the fire to watch the pot in which the rabbit had almost finished cooking.

The two children chattered away, while Guglielmo and his sister ate in silence. Guglielmo served out the rabbit, giving himself the head. He ate a good deal of bread, then licked the small bones clean. Two or three times he told Adriana to stop talking and eat, but said nothing other than that. With his last piece of bread he wiped his plate clean and the meal was over, since they ate fruit only on Sundays. Guglielmo lit a cigarette and took out his notebook and pencil.

The younger girl began imitating him; she puffed out her cheeks and pretended to be blowing out smoke. Guglielmo noticed, barely smiled, and returned to his calculations. His sister was resting, waiting while the water for the dishes was heating.

Now Adriana, the younger one, wanted a piggyback ride. "Don't bother your father," Caterina told her.

But the child insisted and Guglielmo compromised by putting her on his knee. Then, thinking that the older girl might be hurt, he pulled her next to him, encircling her waist with his free arm. Happy, yet visibly embarrassed, the child held herself rigid, staring at a point in the floor.

The next morning, as a Sunday indulgence, Guglielmo rose a little later than usual. He dressed himself in his dark clothes, put on a pair of high boots without hobnails, and immediately went out for a shave. The barber worked only on Saturday afternoons and Sunday mornings; on the other days he labored in the fields. His kitchen served very well for a barber shop. Guglielmo was the earliest riser among his customers; while he shaved him, the other people of the house were washing and eating breakfast. After being shaved, Guglielmo went to Mass, then returned home. The children hadn't gotten up yet, but he could hear them talking and laughing. His sister came in, set her shopping bag on a chair, and put the fresh bread on the table.

After breakfast, Guglielmo picked up a bouquet of flowers that his sister had kept fresh in the sink and went out again. It was a beautiful morning. Guglielmo crossed the village and took the road that sloped gradually downhill, to the cemetery. The brilliance of the sun, the smells of the countryside, the confused noises that filled the air, all contributed to putting him in a pleasant frame of mind. The months of hard work and big profits which he had before him were a heartening prospect. Guglielmo was glad that he had decided to buy the stand of timber without waiting for the regional auctions. "I'm in the dark about the going prices, but so what? It could be a good thing or a bad thing. Maybe in fifteen days I could have made a better deal; but it doesn't matter—the essential thing is getting to work again. My God, if I had to live another fifteen days without doing anything, I'd end up in the madhouse! The work will distract me; it will help to cheer me up. Already I feel different, it seems." He stood before the gate, pushed through it, took off his hat, and crossed himself. The small cemetery was deserted. An iron cross and freshly turned earth marked the place where his wife was buried. Guglielmo remained standing beside the mound. He would not be able to return there until Christmas, so he tried to collect himself and concentrate his thoughts on the dead woman. But it was hot, there was a rustling in the air, everything seemed to distract him. For a while he followed the flittings of a hornet among the crosses, the mounds, and the weeds. Then, with an effort of will, he returned to meditation. But there was an emptiness in his mind. Then he got to work; he walked to the small shed in the corner, found the spade, and again turned over the earth on the grave. He felt happy again, with the work of filling the flowerpot and arranging the flowers. Finally he stood once more before the mound, more composed this time. But he still could not succeed in concentrating. When he felt that he had remained there long enough, he crossed himself and left.

On the way back he realized that he had better walk more slowly if he didn't want to start sweating. When he reached the village he stopped in the small piazza, which was already fairly crowded. Triangular in shape, the piazza was enclosed by the church, the store, and, on its longest side, by a low stone wall. Below the wall there was a steep drop some three hundred feet down, at the foot of which a small stream flowed.

Guglielmo leaned against the wall and stayed taking the sun. He smoked several cigarettes and exchanged a few words with his fellow villagers who were spending their Sunday morning in the same fashion. About noontime, there was not a single space left along the low stone wall.

Immediately after dinner, his sister got ready to go out with the children.

"You come too," she said to Guglielmo.

"Yes, come, Daddy, come," the girls started pleading.

"It will be such a long time before you see them again," his sister added.

"No, I can't come," Guglielmo answered, and the irritation showed in his voice. "I have something to do in the village," he said a moment later.

Guglielmo waited for them to leave, then walked down to the end of the village. He entered a store and stood where he could watch the card players. Standing there behind the players' shoulders, he followed their game. A little later an itinerant singer arrived, and before long everybody stopped playing cards in order to listen to him. He was a handsome old man with a white beard, lively eyes, carefully tended hands, and elegant manners. He wore a brown corduroy suit and woolen stockings of the same color. A thin, small voice sang the story of the brigand Tiburzi, and at the close of every stanza he plucked the strings of his guitar. It was almost an hour before he reached the end. Guglielmo and the others listened to him with great attention. At the end they all gave him some small change, and the owner offered him something to drink. The old man thanked them and asked for details about the shortest way to Pomarance. They told him that Monday was market day at Pomarance and that he would make out well there. He thanked them over and over again and finally left. Without a word, the men returned to their cards.

The sun was setting behind the hill in front of San Dalmazio when Guglielmo left the store and started walking reluctantly up the steep path that led to his house. He was just about to go in when he heard someone calling him. He turned and saw the two little girls running toward him up the small side road. Both of them had their arms loaded with wildflowers. His sister was behind them.

"Look how many I've got, Daddy! Look how pretty they are!" And they showed him the flowers, their faces shining with pleasure.

"We picked them for Mama," Irma added.

"Good girls," Guglielmo said, and they preceded him up the stairs.

Then Irma wanted to show Papa her schoolwork. Guglielmo examined the notebooks hastily and said merely that she had been a good girl.

Immediately after dinner, Caterina put the girls to bed. But before they went, one at a time, they hugged and kissed their father. Not very long afterward, Caterina and Guglielmo also went to bed.

"Don't forget, write every week," Caterina said.

"I will, don't worry," Guglielmo replied.

"Then good-bye until Christmas," Caterina said, embracing him. "Take care of yourself, Guglielmo, and—"

She couldn't go on because she started to cry. Guglielmo loosened himself from her embrace and went to his room. "Tomorrow night, God willing," he thought, "I shall sleep in the hut."

[2]

At five-thirty they all met as arranged in the village piazza. In an hour they reached the store where, on Saturday afternoon, they had agreed to gather the greater part of their equipment and provisions.

Fiore, the crew boss, was close to fifty. Short, stocky, with gray hair cut in a brush, he was anything but an easy man to manage; but his great experience and his ability to work steadily made up for his faults.

Francesco seemed to be much older than Fiore, though he was not. He had not always worked as a woodcutter: he had been a wandering peddler, a cook, a wagoner, an artisan. He was not a good worker, but his inexhaustible supply of stories and anecdotes helped to pass the long winter evenings and the days of rain when woodcutters are forced to remain idle in their hut.

Amedeo, the same age as Guglielmo, was also his first cousin. He had no particular attitudes or characteristics. Finally there was Germano, by far the youngest of the group, since he had just reached twenty.

In two hours the bus brought them to Massa. Here there should have been a buggy waiting to carry their equipment, but it wasn't there and they had to hire one. Then after they reached the landlord's farmstead, Guglielmo couldn't find the overseer, with whom he had talked and come to a very clear understanding, and his irritation increased. To relieve the boredom of waiting, they showed him around the farm. It had been built along the most modern lines and consisted of a series of white buildings, all, except for the silos, in the same low, elongated style. One after another, Guglielmo visited the model stable, the model hayloft, the model manure pile, the model dovecote, and so on.

To make amends for his forgetfulness, the overseer invited Guglielmo and his crew to eat with him. He came from the north and seemed very conscious of his position. He said that he got along very well with the landlord, who was a man of liberal views, while the peasants, ignorant and conservative, didn't want to collaborate in the reforms.

The older men went to bed early. They were settled for the night in a small hayloft next to the stable. Germano stayed up, attracted by the presence of a young peasant girl. At five in the morning, Guglielmo had to give him a good shaking in order to waken him. Grumbling and cursing the fate that had caused him to be born a woodcutter, the boy got up and got his gear together.

Guglielmo was also in a bad humor. He had slept very little; his head felt heavy and his bones broken.

Outside there was a beautiful sky, stars everywhere. Not a breath of wind was blowing. The peasant with the two mules needed to transport the tools and provisions was waiting. Germano took no part in the work of loading; he was still asleep.

Finally they started out on foot.

For a while the mules' hoofs resounded on the brick paving. Then the sound was muffled on the hard-packed earth of the country road.

Germano brought up the rear. He was walking with his hands in his pockets and his head sunk down between his shoulders; although the weather was chilly, his body still kept the heat accumulated during sleep. He stumbled forward like an automaton, and when they left the road to take a short cut, tripped several times on the stones and nearly fell. He decided to watch his step, but after they returned to the road he fell back into his dozing.

Even at the head of the line, they walked in silence.

The dawn light was just beginning to break. The road cut along the winding, luxuriant course of a stream. Thickets of briers, meager scrub, and isolated small trees grew along the banks. On either side of the stream for short stretches extended plots of land where wheat was grown; farther ahead the terrain rose sharply, becoming barren and eroded. From the few houses on the surrounding heights, there was not a sign of life.

The little group continued its silent march. To the east, above the line of low hills, the sky had begun to brighten.

"Dawn," said Amedeo.

That superfluous remark succeeded in lifting their spirits. As if waiting for it, Guglielmo pulled out a cigarette, and immediately Germano copied him. Francesco stopped to light his pipe. Then the conversations interlaced, Fiore ahead talking with the muleteer, Guglielmo with Francesco and Amedeo. Germano was walking alone at the rear, but now his cigarette had fully wakened him and he was whistling, content.

"A woodcutter's life," Amedeo was saying, "is better than a peasant's. . . ."

"It's better to be rich and do no work at all," Germano joked, behind him. "I mean, at least you see a little of the world."

"I saw enough of the world," Francesco began, "when I was a peddler. From Massa to Volterra, there's not a town I haven't been in. And I used to go to the big fairs in those days, at Florence, Siena. . . ."

The climb was so gradual that they hardly noticed it. They walked at a good clip, talking and smoking; they would willingly have gone on walking that road forever; it seemed it never wanted to end. At every curve a new stretch of straight road rose before them, and the landscape gave no sign of changing. Always the same tracts of level land on either side of the stream and the low hills that abruptly obstructed the view to left and right.

"Not sleepy any more?" Guglielmo asked Germano.

"Not sleepy now. Just hungry."

"You make out O.K. last night with the girl?" Amedeo asked.

Germano frowned. "She was stupid," he finally said. "I tried to get her outside but she wouldn't take the hint."

"Or pretended not to," Amedeo said.

"Then you'd have been better off getting some sleep," Guglielmo concluded.

"You hear that?" asked Germano. "Those are partridges."

And in fact they could hear the crying of the partridges. By this time the birds had already begun their morning search for food. What with the stream, the wheat fields, the underbrush, and overhanging ledges, the place was perfect for partridge. And Germano, who was a passionate hunter as well as Don Juan, felt himself filled with the sacred fire.

"If I had my gun with me, I'd start shooting on that side over there and I'd bring back something to eat," he said, pointing to the steep ledges, thick with underbrush, on their left.

"You couldn't do it anyway; this is a private game preserve," said Amedeo.

"If I had my gun, I'd show you how much I care about them and their signs," Germano retorted.

The muleteer's abrupt change of route brought the talk to an end. They left the road and turned up a path, which, after crossing a field, started to climb in zigzags along the side of a hill. There the earth was barren and crumbled underfoot. The driver anxiously watched his mules to see that they didn't slip or fall. The men followed in Indian file. Germano, who was obviously in bad shape, was muttering curses at that damned climb that threatened to last forever.

"Some forests they've got here!" he grumbled angrily. "I haven't even seen a blade of grass."

All their faces, recently serene or even happy, again turned dark, almost gloomy.

At last the slope leveled off and the view began to open up around them. They were out of the clay country. In fact, beyond the last rounded clumps of hills there arose, still very low on the horizon, a large, dark pyramidal shape.

They stopped in a ravine to eat breakfast. The food, the wine, and then a smoke put new life into them. Only Germano remained grumpy; but he had adopted that pose and now he had to keep it up.

"Is the whole Maremma like this?" he said. "You walk, and walk, you never meet anybody, and you never get anywhere."

Amedeo laughed. "And where do you want to get to?"

"And as for Massa," Germano continued, ignoring him, "I always hear them talking about Massa, Massa, but Pomarance is paradise compared to Massa."

Germano was a local patriot. He felt it his duty to support both the village where he was born, San Dalmazio, and the commune to which it belonged, Pomarance. Which didn't prevent him from constantly lamenting the fate which had caused him to be born in a place where there was nothing to do but be a woodcutter or a peasant.

Guglielmo was the first to rise; he was now beginning to experience what first the darkness and then the work of walking had kept muted: the desire to get to his stand of timber, to take possession, to start working. He regretted that the first two days would be lost in building the hut. He had in fact already discarded the notion of using an existing hut on the slope across the way from the stand because, what with the crossing back and forth, even more time would have been wasted.

As he climbed the last hill, he thought that if it hadn't been for that mix-up at the farmstead, they would have been there the evening before. And when he reached the summit and saw the splendor of the rising sun shining behind the swollen, fretted clouds that rimmed the horizon, he was overpowered by a feverish need to walk, to act, to recover the time that had been lost.

As the hill rose higher, the slopes were more and more thickly covered with brush and small trees.

"Is it much farther?" asked Germano.

"See up there?" Guglielmo said, stopping for a moment and pointing to a high point on the wooded ridge. "Where you can just make out those three tall trees? It starts there and stretches down on the other side, all the way down to the Sellate."

"Fine! It'll take two hours to get there," Germano remarked, persistently sour.

Actually, it took much less. In fact, after crossing the brook below, they began an almost continuous steep climb, and in three-quarters of an hour they stood beside the three isolated trees that marked the start of the stand of timber.

The sun, by now high on the horizon, flooded the valley beneath them, at the bottom of which the Sellate flowed.

On the low ground, layers of mist still hung over the stream, and the air was simultaneously luminous and heavy with mist. Guglielmo breathed in deeply, filling his lungs; he felt his chest expand with energy and a sense of well-being. He stood contemplating the timber stand with a sense of legitimate pride. Finally he roused himself and turned to Fiore. "Here on the left," he said, "the stand follows the path except for two places where it cuts in. On the right it cuts down along the gully; and then there's something like a ravine, which gets gradually wider as it slopes down to the stream. Stand where I am so you can see better," and he gestured energetically to show Fiore the exact limits of the stand. "As you can see, the best part is up here on high ground. Lower down, of course, it's mostly brush and scrub, and just above the stream there's hardly anything. But a three-acre stand of pine and four and a half acres of copse, almost all good quality, and at the price I told you"—only Fiore had been informed of the price—"it's practically a steal. In our part of the country I would have paid twice as much."

By "copse" the woodcutters mean woodland under twenty

years old, in which the trees ordinarily do not exceed twenty to twenty-five feet in height. The good-quality wood is arbutus, ilex, oak, and bitter oak; the poor quality is hornbeam and ash. The higher grade furnishes the best charcoal. Pines are cut when they are twenty-five to thirty years old and twenty-five to forty-five feet high, and the wood is used for timbering and planking the mines.

The woodcutters listened attentively to Guglielmo's explanations, although whether or not the purchase was a good one didn't concern them since they didn't work on a percentage basis. Only Germano insisted on showing his lack of interest. Sitting down a few steps away from them with his back to the timber stand, he had lit a cigarette and seemed to be intent on his smoke.

"There's a lot of work here," Amedeo said, since Fiore had not yet managed to speak.

"Five months' at least," Guglielmo said.

"At first sight, you'd think it was a forty-year-old stand," Francesco said, alluding to the pine grove.

"And you can cut it easily," Amedeo said, "at least up here."

The favorable judgments of Amedeo and Francesco flattered Guglielmo; but he felt the weight of Fiore's continued silence. Fiore was standing stock still, his head cocked slightly on his shoulder. He kept staring at the stand, as if his expert eyes were capable of perceiving factors for judgment that had gone unobserved by the others.

"So?" Guglielmo asked him. "What do you say, Fiore?"

"It's a good buy. At least it seems to be."

And after delivering this laconic and noncommittal judgment, Fiore immediately started down the path that bordered the stand of timber on the left.

"Hey, are we going back again?" Germano cried to his disappearing back.

But nobody paid any attention. Fiore trotted on ahead; the muleteer was occupied with his mules, since the descent was very steep. Guglielmo was talking with Francesco and Amedeo and every once in a while they would stop to look at something.

The path became even more precipitous and was hemmed in everywhere by impassable woods. When he looked back, Fiore could no longer make out the others, though he could hear their voices above him. At last he emerged into the open, in the bed of the stream, which was wide and filled with worn boulders. Down the middle of the channel there was only a small trickle of water.

From here they climbed up the opposite slope to the hut that would house them during the first days. They unloaded the tools, the big brass cauldron, the provisions and blankets, and then sent back the mules. Francesco, in his capacity as cook, was the first to start work; Germano helped him. At noon the pot of polenta stood steaming on the table, and they ate slices sprinkled with goat's cheese. In the afternoon they began constructing the new hut, placing it approximately in the middle of the stand. They started by felling two pines so as to give themselves space; then they carefully cleaned away the underbrush and cut some young trunks and thick branches, chiefly of ilex, for the framework of the hut. When Francesco's sharp whistle sounded from the opposite slope, they quit work.

Guglielmo was tired and sat down outside the hut. The hillside across the way stood completely in shadow. The timber stand took the shape of an isosceles triangle, the stream forming its base and the three isolated trees its apex. His eye took in the whole stand with a sweeping glance, then ran its length, finally concentrated on its confines. He went up the path again, mentally straightening out all those places where it cut in and leaped across the rocky ravine, running his eye along it to the point where it fell sheer to the stream. The dark clumps of ilex delighted him no less than the threadlike white trunks of the hornbeam and ash and the light green of the pines; the reddish slash of the path no less than the damp, lichen-covered rocks in the ravine.

Then, gradually, all the colors darkened and fused. Guglielmo's happiness dissolved. He remained a few minutes more, sitting there before that dark shape as the night came down.

Going into the hut, he looked almost with desperation at the firelit faces of his crew and the bowl of polenta steaming on the table.

[3]

It took them three days to build the hut. After they finished the framework of branches, they covered it with sods, the grassy sides inward, so that from the outside it looked like a hut made of mud.

Inside the hut two large mounds of earth, piled with layers of twigs, served as beds; in the center, on a line with the door, was a fireplace and space for the table. Nothing else.

They spent the third day transporting and stowing away their provisions and tools. After eating, Guglielmo left for the farmstead, reaching it after dark. The overseer was not there. His wife, who was pregnant, was sitting idly in a corner of the immense kitchen. Somewhat embarrassed by the woman's presence, Guglielmo pulled out his notebook and re-examined his accounts, though there was no need for it. Then, excusing himself, he went outside. He wandered about the farm grounds, winding up in the stable, where he watched the milking—done, of course, with ultramodern methods.

After dinner the overseer detained him a long time with his talk, repeating his complaints against the backward and presumptuous peasants and saying that he was sorry he had left Piedmont. There was no comparison here with the satisfactions that the manager of a farm enjoyed up there—and he took particular care to emphasize this title, evidently annoyed by the word "overseer." Guglielmo slept in a small room adjoining the kitchen. At four that morning he started out on foot. His head ached irritatingly the whole way. Moreover, he hadn't eaten, and halfway back, climbing through the woods, he suddenly felt so weak that his legs buckled and he wanted to stretch out on the ground.

As soon as he saw the valley of the Sellate, he could hear the strokes of the axes ringing in the air. The pale dawn sunlight shone slanting on the wooded hills. A faint breeze, which had just risen, barely rustled the leaves. Guglielmo took long breaths of the crisp, fragrant air; he was filled with a sense of physical and moral well-being, and as he went down the path, he stopped again to listen to the blows of the axes. Down below they boomed deeply; higher up and to the right they rang sharp and clear. *Tock, tock, tack, tack,* they came one after the other, but he could not see the men wielding the axes until he was almost upon them.

Passing Fiore, he barely returned the man's greeting. He reached the hut, cut himself some bread and meat veined with fat, and bolted it down; he took a few swallows of tepid coffee and went outside in his shirt sleeves, carrying his ax and billhook. It was his job to give orders about the cutting, but he walked past the men without saying a word and began working along the path.

Tock! A wedge-shaped chip flew out under his ax. *Tock!* The white notch in the tree's trunk drove deeper. A few more oblique cuts, then Guglielmo started chopping laterally. With every blow of his ax, chips of wood went flying. The blade drove accurately into the triangular notch; Guglielmo wrenched it free, raised it again and swung down, striking at the same point. Ten, twelve more strokes, and the pine tree fell, still attached to its stump by a thin, fibrous tongue of wood. A few more strokes, and the tough fiber was severed. The pine settled to the ground. Straddling the trunk, Guglielmo trimmed off the branches and topped the tree.

He worked hard the whole day, paying no heed to what the others were doing. Every so often he straightened up to look around, breathed in the penetrating odor from the cut wood and listened to the strokes of the axes. Then he returned to his chopping.

Although he had been on his feet for fifteen hours, he was the last one to quit. He ate mechanically, staring fixedly at some point in the hut and mentally seeing the ax rise and fall, rise and fall, until the tree crashed. He was restless all night; dreaming or half asleep, he kept seeing the axes whirling.

The hut was built at the line that divided the pine grove from the copse. From this point they worked back up the hill.

Germano and Francesco chopped on the left, Fiore and Amedeo along the path. Guglielmo cut here and there, as he thought best.

Out of every ten pines, one was spared. In fact, in every acre of land a hundred trees were left standing, forming the seed trees, or, as they put it poetically, "the forest's dowry."

Frequently, whole days went by without the appearance of a living soul. At other times their contacts with the rest of the world were limited to seeing a muleteer go by. He went along the wagon road that coasted the stream, pulling two or three mules loaded with fagots, totally unaware of the woodcutters. He raised his head only when the chopping began again, but, misled by the echo, he looked over to the opposite slope. One morning, about noon, Germano was just giving the finishing blow to a thirty-foot tree when he saw, standing a few steps away, a man with a rifle slung over his shoulder.

"Is it far to ———?" the man asked, pronouncing a name that Germano couldn't quite understand, though he had never heard it anyway.

"I'm a stranger here," he replied. "Look out!" he added a minute later.

A few more strokes of the ax and the pine fell with a crash, sliding a few yards down the slope. Germano straightened up and mopped away the sweat.

"How was the hunting?" he asked.

"Bad," the man answered, and with an indifferent gesture pulled out a pheasant.

"Not so bad then," the boy commented.

"To walk all that way for this . . ." said the man, with a contemptuous grimace; and then, as though he felt the weight of all the miles he had walked, he sat down on a stump. He pulled out a pack of crumpled, gold-tipped cigarettes and offered one to Germano, who accepted. Taking it, he felt obliged to keep the man company, at least while he was smoking. And driving the ax into the ground, he squatted on his haunches beside the hunter.

"They said the hunting here was first rate . . ." the hunter began, leaving his sentence unfinished. "And what's it good for? Goats, that's what. Too damn much work," he added, as though talking to himself.

He was tall and rugged in build, his dark hair streaked with blond, and his face strongly creased with wrinkles. He dragged so often and so deeply on his cigarette that he had thrown away the butt before Germano had half finished his.

"But there are lots of pheasants here," Germano said. "Every morning until about nine, you can hear them calling. I was thinking I'd bring back my gun when I go home."

Without warning the man gave a sharp whistle. A minute later a dog came running up. Pushed away by his master, the dog sniffed at Germano's boots. The boy patted him.

"A pointer?" Germano asked.

The man nodded.

At that moment Guglielmo appeared. Germano jumped to his feet and picked up his ax; Guglielmo was about to say something but noticed the dog and the hunter.

"Morning," he said.

"Morning," the man replied.

He lit another cigarette and then asked Guglielmo the same question he had asked Germano.

"Yes, I've heard of the place," Guglielmo replied. He thought for a while and then said, "It's a couple of hours from here."

"God," the man said, "that's a fine fix."

Guglielmo invited him to eat with them. The man didn't have to be asked twice. In silence he ate the soup prepared by Francesco. The woodcutters hesitated to ask him questions or even to talk among themselves. At last it came out that the man was a tradesman from Florence. An enthusiastic hunter, he had been in the Maremma now for a week, with a friend; but the friend had fallen sick and stayed behind at a farm at ——— (again that incomprehensible name).

"Have some coffee?" Guglielmo asked. "You understand, it's not real coffee. . . ."

The man gestured as though to say it didn't matter; in any case, a hot drink was always welcome. Afterward he passed around his gold-tipped cigarettes.

"But there's only one left," said Guglielmo, pushing back the pack.

"I still have four more packs," the man replied, smiling and patting his pocket.

"If that's so," Guglielmo said, "I'll be glad to take one, though we're used to stronger tobacco."

"And what about *me?*" Amedeo said, laughing. "This tastes like straw to me."

Francesco had refused because he smoked a pipe. Fiore, who was smoking a cigar, took a cigarette and put it down on the table.

"Well," said the man, getting up, "thanks for the hospitality." He said good-bye to all of them and walked out of the hut.

"Go along with him," Guglielmo told Germano.

Germano went with him to the high point of the timber stand. From that vantage, the man oriented himself with a glance.

All afternoon Germano was thinking about hunting. He kept stopping his work and listening, trying to make out the cry of a pheasant from the valley below. Then, feeling the boss's eyes upon him and half sighing, he raised his ax again.

The next day was Sunday. About ten o'clock, Guglielmo and Germano went down to the stream to do the wash. Just as they walked out on the stream's dry bed, a pheasant flew up from a huge clump of trees. Germano cried out in mingled surprise and regret, "If I only had my gun! But when I go home for Christmas, I'll bring it back."

"The hunting season closes December thirty-first," said Guglielmo.

"That's right," said Germano. "I'd forgotten."

Since there had been no rain for a month, the Sellate had dwindled to a thin trickle of water in the middle of its bed, threading its way between white, polished rocks. But the pebbles at the edges of the stream were yellow and dirty.

As their washtub they chose a hollow in a great rock buried in the bed of the stream. Standing on either side of the hollow, they began rubbing and soaping the clothes vigorously.

Each had a piece of soap, and both used the same scrubbing brush. The water was clear and freezing.

"I pity the women," Germano said, looking at his reddened hands.

"So do I," said Guglielmo.

In their village the place where the women did the washing was just below the small piazza. It had not been roofed over, and when it rained the women sheltered themselves as best they could by setting the bundles of dirty clothes on their heads. Guglielmo remembered his wife when she came back from the washing, carrying the clothes basket balanced on her head. Just last winter she had ruined her hands. They were all raw and bleeding, and for a month she had not been able to do the laundry or even to wash up after meals. Luckily, with the good weather they had gotten better.

"Luckily . . ." Guglielmo thought immediately after. "Some good luck, seeing she died three months later."

"Women have their own work too," he said aloud, talking in order to dispel his sad thoughts. "And it's right that way. If the man works, the woman shouldn't sit around doing nothing."

"Work like a dog and my wife at home playing the lady," said Germano. "I wouldn't put up with that." Then he said that if he didn't have his military service to do, he would get married before the next summer was over. "How old were you when you got married?"

"Twenty-eight," Guglielmo said.

"A bad age," Germano said, smiling.

Guglielmo smiled too. "Oh, we don't have to worry about *our* women. . . ." Then he told Germano how after the war he had done a year's service near Venice. "You should have seen the girls there. Bold as brass. And the way they talked . . . It knocked us Tuscans over."

The slight current of the stream had pushed the soap bubbles to the margins of the basin. The men rinsed the clothes for the last time, rose to their feet, and energetically wrung them.

"Finished," said Germano.

He stretched the wrung-out clothes on a clean rock, wiped his hands on the sides of his pants, then took a cigarette and matches from his shirt pocket. Guglielmo did the same. Then they picked up the clothes again and started across the stream, their cigarettes in their mouths, talking of this and that.

When they got back to the hut, Germano was assigned to watch the caldron in which the polenta was cooking; Francesco had gone to the farmstead with Amedeo. This monotonous task gave the boy the leisure to immerse himself in his thoughts, which were not happy ones. He wanted to get married because the girls in his village were so strict and proper that his sensuality was frustrated. But getting married meant the beginning of a hard life. He would have to work more, eat less and drink less, and also deprive himself of even those few amusements that a tiny, isolated village like San Dalmazio offers.

"Especially if your wife gets pregnant at the start . . . I hope they send me up near Venice for my military service. If it's true the girls up there are the way Guglielmo says they are . . . But I wouldn't marry one of those girls and that's for sure. I'd have to give up wood chopping if I did; I'd have cuckold's horns so big I'd get tangled up in the trees."

And the boy laughed to himself.

Francesco and Amedeo returned late that afternoon. The meal was eaten in silence, and after dinner there was silence too.

[4]

Every evening after supper the woodcutters stayed up for an hour or two. As soon as they finished supper, they put out the candle, leaving only the fire in the middle of the hut. Then they settled down on the twig-covered mounds and had their smoke. Guglielmo's brand was Maryland, Germano's Moresco or Nazionale. Amedeo pulled out cigarette papers and a tin box containing very dark, almost black, tobacco; then in leisure he began to roll himself a cigarette.

"I don't know how you can smoke that stuff," Germano

would say. And he added, "That isn't tobacco; it's gunpowder."

Once or twice he had tried making a cigarette from Amedeo's tobacco; but after a few puffs he had to throw it away because it was too strong.

"Your stuff isn't tobacco, it's straw," Amedeo would come back at him. "Why, a hundred cigarettes a day as weak as yours wouldn't do for me."

"In my younger days," Francesco began, "I knew a fellow who smoked tobacco that would make Amedeo's taste like sugar. And it wasn't just tobacco; he'd mix in dried-up cabbage leaves, peppercorns, even loam."

"But I knew him too," Amedeo would say. "Wasn't that Beppino, the one who used to go fishing for leeches in the Cecina?"

"No," Francesco replied. "It wasn't Beppino. It was Beppino's brother." And he put his pipe back in his mouth.

"Beppino's brother? Did Beppino have a brother?"

But Amedeo's question went unanswered.

"When I was in the army," said Guglielmo, "I knew a man who smoked a hundred cigarettes a day, and that's a fact."

Guglielmo was always glad to talk about his memories of military life. Born in 1899, he had been just old enough to serve for a year during the First World War.

"In the army," Amedeo remarked, "you meet all sorts."

And then, as though struck by the profundity of this statement, he sat staring at the flames of the fire, his cigarette clenched between his fingers. At last he shook himself, unrolled his cigarette, rolled it again, licked it carefully, and put it back into his mouth. The tobacco with which Francesco filled his pipe was a little less dark but even stronger smelling. Fiore smoked the cigars called *toscani*. Since, after two puffs, he always let it go out, he would use up half a box of matches by the end of the day.

This fencing on the subject of tobacco, repeated every evening, started off the nightly sessions. Fiore rarely participated. Guglielmo, too, was rather quiet. Amedeo would make some strange observations and Germano amused himself by teasing

him. But the moving spirit of these nightly conversations was
Francesco. It seemed that that old man had lived twenty lives,
so many were the things he knew and the adventures he had
had.

In general he told stories from his own life, not all of them,
to tell the truth, very credible, but no one ever questioned
their authenticity. Truthful or not, they were what was needed
to get through the interminable winter evenings. At times he
would tell them stories from history: the Inquisition in Spain,
the Crusades, Alexander VI, the Borgias. Here too there was
no great respect for strict truth. Or he simply told them
stories.

When Germano—it was usually he—asked him to tell a
story, Francesco began by fencing. "Time was when I knew a
lot of stories, but my memory's not good now. There was the
story about Porsella, the story of the goat Margulla, the Beauty
of the Sun. . . . That story about the Beauty of the Sun was a
long one, three evenings weren't enough to finish it."

"Then tell it, that's what we need. Start this evening and
you can finish the day after tomorrow."

"But I tell you I can't remember it."

However, he remembered it very well; and even if he had
forgotten some passages, his lapses didn't dismay him, for he
had the imagination and quickness to invent what he forgot.

"Oh, you remember," Germano would insist.

Finally, after a show of reticence, Francesco would suddenly decide to tell the story. He laid down his pipe, coughed
several times, made a sign to show he was about to start. Then
he cleared his throat again, and finally began:

"In the old days, the King of Portugal had a daughter, in
whose honor he held a magnificent hunt. More than five hundred hunters began the chase at the crack of dawn, on a preserve belonging to the King. If there were more than five hundred hunters, the boys used as beaters numbered more than
five thousand. As for dogs, suffice it to say that for this occasion they had collected every hunting dog in the kingdom. At
a certain moment the King's daughter, who was a skillful
huntress, saw a dove browsing on the grass in the meadow.

She spurred her horse and got within rifle shot of the bird. While she was taking aim, the dove flew away and settled down farther off. The King's daughter spurred her horse again and came again within shooting distance. But the second before she pulled the trigger, the dove flew off. Annoyed by the bird's behavior, the King's daughter persisted in following it; but every time the dove flew up just in time, and settled down a little farther away. Finally it disappeared altogether from the huntress' sight.

"In the meantime, evening had fallen. The King's daughter . . . but no, I'm wrong, it was the King's son. No, no, it was an ordinary groom. You see, I don't remember any more."

Germano was disappointed. Guglielmo smiled, knowing that this sudden amnesia was only a trick to excite the curiosity of the audience. In fact, a few moments later Francesco calmly resumed his story. "To his great dismay, Beppino—that's what the groom was called—saw that he was lost. He listened for the sound of the horns that summon the hunters when the sun sets; but he couldn't hear a thing. Meanwhile night had fallen and he had to make a decision. The place was utterly uninhabited, a wilderness. You can picture it by thinking of a place like this place here. 'I'll keep going,' thought Beppino, 'and perhaps I'll find someone who can show me the way.' He was also worried because the King would certainly notice his absence and fly into a rage, and perhaps when he got back he would be thrown into prison. For three hours he went on without meeting a living soul. Finally he saw a distant light, and started toward it.

"After three more hours he reached a magnificent castle. He dismounted and knocked at the gate; but no one came. After some hesitation, Beppino decided to go in. He called out, but no one answered. He walked through one hallway after another, went through room after room—and every one the size of a parade ground. There wasn't a living soul. At last he came to a room larger than all the others, in the middle of which was a table laid for two persons. And since he was ravenously hungry, Beppino sat down.

"The first dish was rice. Beppino, who loved rice, started

eating greedily. But at the same time he saw that the rice in the bowl across the table was vanishing before his eyes, as though someone were there eating with him. When he swallowed his last mouthful, the other bowl also stood empty.

"The second dish was tripe. You see, it was Thursday. Beppino liked tripe less than rice, but he was still hungry and so he ate it. And, little by little, as he ate, the tripe in the other plate disappeared.

"The third dish was fruit: loquats. Beppino didn't like loquats at all; nevertheless, he ate them too. And, little by little, as he put them into his mouth, the loquats in the other plate disappeared."

The story continued in this vein until, after a series of more or less incredible adventures, Beppino freed the Beauty of the Sun from a magical spell. She turned out to be the King of Portugal's daughter, and the tale ended with the inevitable wedding.

The story had not lasted three evenings, as announced beforehand, but it had taken up a good hour. Francesco knew the art of storytelling. Although his forms were conventional, he developed and embroidered them gradually in the telling, yet he never hesitated even for an instant. True, he often contradicted himself, but his listeners didn't point this out. They didn't mind.

His tales were all of a particular type, a strange mixture of the realistic and the fabulous, and they were not frightening. Actually, Francesco knew an extraordinary number of ghost stories, but he claimed they had all happened. According to him, not only did witches, wizards, and magicians really exist, but there was a large number of them in the countryside around San Dalmazio and Pomarance; even quite recently they had left evidence that they practiced both black magic and white.

The others did not question these assertions, except for Germano, who wanted to show that he was a skeptic in such matters.

One evening, conversation on this particular subject

stemmed directly from the talk about smoking, which formed an almost indispensable preliminary to the nightly palaver.

"This pipe," Francesco said, taking it up in his hand, "was given to me by a wizard, who used to use it for his enchantments."

But several evenings before, he had said that the pipe was left him by his grandfather, who had gotten it from Cavalier Serafini, the same man who had hidden Garibaldi in 1849, when the General had passed through San Dalmazio on his flight from Rome.

He turned the pipe over in his hand and added, "Gianni the Devil gave me this pipe."

"What?" said Amedeo, dumfounded. "Gianni the Devil is a wizard? That's news to me."

"Of course he's a wizard," Francesco said.

He put the pipe back in his mouth.

"If not, why would they call him Gianni the Devil?" he added after a bit.

Actually the nickname had been handed down from father to son and had no connection at all with witchcraft.

"Gianni the Devil," Francesco resumed, "can cure all kinds of sicknesses. Animals and human beings. Didn't you call him," he said, turning to Guglielmo, "when your wife fell sick?"

Guglielmo shook his head.

"What was wrong with her?" Francesco asked again.

"Something in her kidneys. An inflammation. But they didn't know what it was."

"I see," Francesco said.

"At first the doctor said that it was her kidneys, and later that it was something in her blood. But who knows what it really was? In twelve days she was dead. There you have it."

And he let the subject drop. During the day he was absorbed by his work; but at night the memory of his wife kept creeping into his mind.

It was Germano who broke the silence. He frankly expressed his doubts about the magical powers of Gianni the Devil. He knew the miller well; Gianni lived a stone's throw away from him, and he had always seemed to him a man like everyone else.

"How can you say that?" Francesco replied. "If you'd been at the Fosini farmstead—I'm referring to something that happened about ten years ago—you wouldn't be talking such nonsense now."

"What happened at Fosini?" Amedeo asked.

"Extraordinary things. We couldn't tell for sure what was happening."

"Flying donkeys, you mean?" Germano snorted ironically.

"Exactly," Francesco answered seriously. "Donkeys, horses, oxen, and every other sort of animal started flying."

"I heard about it too," Fiore said, joining in the conversation, an unusual thing for him.

"But how could such things happen?" Germano asked in an altered tone. Francesco's self-assurance had confused him.

"Because of witches," Francesco replied. "Come night they'd get on those poor beasts and ride them like crazy. They'd find the animals in the morning, completely drenched in sweat. . . . In a single night they'd ride to Rome and back."

"Why Rome?" Germano persisted.

"Sacrilege," Francesco replied. "Then they called on the man I mentioned a minute ago—the miller, Gianni the Devil —and from that time on nothing ever happened any more."

"Well, maybe," said Germano, not at all convinced.

"All right," said Francesco, "then listen to this. Do you know that I once saw a damned soul?"

Germano felt his breath fail him. Then, too, Francesco's face was very close to his, and he was staring at him fixedly.

"What is—a damned soul?" he finally asked.

"A dead man," Francesco replied. "A dead man who has no peace"—and his voice resounded solemnly in the silence of the hut—"and who takes his peace from the living." And at this point he seemed to sink back into his memories. He had put his pipe into his mouth again and was blowing out big puffs of smoke. "I was your age," he began, speaking to the boy, "when what I consider the most terrible adventure of my life took place. My father had taken me to the fair at Sasso.

After the fair we ate and then my father stretched out on the grass and told me that I should take a nap too. But I wasn't sleepy, so I started wandering around. There was a villa above us—a large villa, shut down tight. I went closer and noticed that there was a hole in the hedge.

"I squeezed through that hole and came out in the garden. It must have been a grand garden once, but now it was completely ruined. I walked around and then I found a little door, half open. I pushed it, went down a small stair, and started up a hallway.

"It was a damp, narrow hallway, but there was enough light to see by. As I turned the corner I found myself face to face with the damned soul."

Here Francesco paused to gauge the effect of his story on his audience. At last he resumed. "He had a skull instead of a face and he was dressed like a monk. He stretched out his arm, but I jumped back and managed to escape his grasp. Then I turned and started to run like a madman. I got out into the open, found the hole in the hedge again, and ran all the way down to my father. I woke him up and told him what had happened to me. And my father said it served me right, I shouldn't have been wandering around instead of taking my nap."

Germano said it was all a lot of nonsense and that he didn't believe in such things. But before they went to bed, they asked him to get a tool they had left in the woods and he refused to leave the hut.

Frequently they played cards at night. It was generally Germano who suggested a game. He was also the first to get tired of it, throwing down his cards, and asking that they quit.

When Germano proposed a game, Amedeo immediately agreed because he had a real passion for gambling. Francesco also agreed, but without much enthusiasm. He was extremely moderate in everything he did.

Though they would ask Guglielmo if he wanted to play, they asked out of courtesy, since his reply was invariably in the negative.

So the three of them played cards together, or forced Fiore to make a fourth.

"Haven't you ever played cards?" Francesco asked Guglielmo.

"Not once in my life."

"Why not? Don't you like it?"

"I prefer watching," Guglielmo answered.

Sometimes he explained that he didn't play cards on principle. He knew too many people who had been ruined by gambling.

"You're right," Francesco would say. "I knew some people who used to have money and now they're begging in the streets. But we play for nothing."

"But that's just it; I don't play on principle."

"If that's the way it is, then . . ."

"Come on, deal," Germano would break in.

The game was punctuated by the usual ritual expressions. Certain expressions could make them all smile. Whatever card he was playing, Francesco would pronounce its name lingeringly, slurring it: a king, a crone, a hunchback, an ace. . . . Fiore played rather well, but he seemed to get no pleasure from it. Usually, at the end of a game, Germano would argue with his partner because he accused him of playing badly. Sometimes he even slammed his cards down on the table. But the others were usually more tolerant.

Guglielmo carefully followed the progress of the game, seldom taking part in the arguments.

Sometimes they would start playing at six o'clock and finish only at eight or eight-thirty, the hour they went to bed; but more often interest would slacken off after a few games, and finally Germano would say he'd had enough. Francesco usually delayed by playing a few hands of solitaire, and finally the cards were put away. These were the worst evenings because, after the game ended, the time dragged on in general silence, almost as though the card game had somehow halted their thoughts and frozen their tongues.

One evening it was exactly seven o'clock, the cards were put away, and there was a long silence. Sitting still there in the darkness, the men felt overcome by sadness, gloom. Guglielmo arose and walked out of the hut. He took a few aimless steps along the slope. He went over his accounts in his mind; then he remembered that for two Sundays he had received no mail from home. But he suddenly was struck by the strangeness of what he saw.

The grassy slope was drenched in light. It was as though an invisible hand had bathed it in some precious liquid. The slanted shadows of the hut and the trees that the woodcutting had spared stood out black as ink. On the opposite ridge each tree stood out sharply, isolated, so clearly that you could count them, up to the point where they blurred and formed a continuous black line. At the bottom of the hill wound the shining ribbon of the Sellate.

As always when his thoughts turned away from his work, his wife came back to his mind. Not that he remembered the cemetery; this never happened; nor did he ever think to ask himself where his wife might be now, at the very moment he was thinking of her. Although he was a believer, Guglielmo had never put to himself the problem of the next world. He would assent without conviction when he listened to the usual talk: that his wife was certainly in heaven; that if *she* didn't merit it—she who had been so good, who had never harmed anyone—who did have the right to go to heaven? And they would point out, taking all the necessary precautions against the evil eye, how healthy the girls were, how well they were growing up. It was a sign that the dear departed was up above watching over her children.

Such talk slid over Guglielmo's mind without leaving a trace. Thinking of his wife, he did not see her grave again nor did he feel her spirit near at hand. He remembered her as she had been alive. But especially he remembered her when she was sick. He remembered every detail of those terrible days. He had been helping the charcoal burner who was burning the last remnants of the season's woodcutting when, one afternoon at four, a boy from San Dalmazio arrived to tell him to come immediately, his wife was sick. He, who two days before had left her in perfect health, had walked for three hours with his mind in a tumult. Finally entering the room, he had seen his wife turn her face toward him with a sad grimace that she intended to be a smile. Never would he forget the impression she had made on him; she seemed to have turned gray. But it was only because of that suffering face.

"I thought I would die while you were away," his wife said to him. For five minutes he stood bent over her, incapable of making a gesture, of saying a word. Without finding out what had happened, he sat down beside the sick woman's bed and, together with his sister, watched over her for two days and nights. The poor woman tossed in her bed with a fever of more than 104. She was delirious. Then the fever suddenly disappeared; the doctor declared that the danger was past. Guglielmo went back to work. Saturday afternoon he set out for home again; on the road he was happy, the season was over, during the summer he would stay at home. He was sure that he would find his wife out of bed, but it was not to be that way. Guglielmo returned to a nightmare. His wife was very weak; she didn't eat and even her character had changed: she became angry over trifles, treated her sister-in-law badly, fretted when the children were noisy. Caterina began to weep hysterically and said, "Don't you think something will happen? My God, Guglielmo, I'm so frightened." As a man, Guglielmo believed it was his duty to show that he was hopeful; actually, he was crushed under the burden of inescapable fate. And when, that Friday, his wife again had a high fever, he was not surprised; he had expected it. His wife didn't speak to him any more, but often looked anxiously toward the door, as though she feared to see someone enter. . . . Or, for a long, long time, she stared at her husband and seemed to want to say something; then, as though distrustful and fearful that she would be misunderstood, she turned her face to the wall and two silent tears ran down her cheeks. Guglielmo came close to her, dried her cheeks with his handkerchief, tried to get her to look at him again . . . but she persisted in looking at the wall. . . .

"But what did she want to say to me?" Guglielmo wondered. It was an intolerable question. He hurried to go back into the hut.

"Been out to get a breath of fresh air?" Amedeo asked.

"Yes."

"How was it?"

"Fine, but now I've got a chill."

"When it's cold like this," Francesco pronounced, "I mean a dry cold, you can stand it easily."

"But *you* never leave the fire," Germano observed.

"And where is Fiore?" Guglielmo asked.

"Asleep," Amedeo replied.

"Already?"

"What else is there to do?" Germano said. "We're really cut off from the world here. Sunday I'm going to the farmstead," he added, as though speaking to himself. "It's always better than staying here."

Since Francesco had stretched out, Germano and Amedeo lowered their voices. Fragments of their conversation reached Guglielmo's ears.

"I can't wait to do my military service."

"What do you expect?"

"Better than here."

"Don't complain, boy. I wish I was twenty again."

No one bothered to feed the fire, which was going out.

"Just get up every morning at five—"

"In the army they'll get you up at four."

Lying side by side, Germano and Amedeo continued talking in low tones. Francesco began to snore. Fiore had been sleeping for some time. "But what did she want to say?" Guglielmo thought. At last he fell asleep.

[5]

Christmas was approaching and the men made ready to leave for home. Since Christmas fell on Saturday, they would have two days to themselves. But Fiore said immediately that he wouldn't go. That's how he was—more comfortable in the woods than at home. Amedeo used to say that he should have been born a bear.

At the last moment Guglielmo also gave up the idea of leaving.

"Tell my sister that I was afraid the trip would tire me. Tell her that I didn't like to leave Fiore alone."

"But," Amedeo couldn't keep from saying, "if your wife was alive, you would have gone home."

"Of course," Guglielmo replied.

"You can't disappoint a wife," Amedeo concluded.

"Tell that to Fiore."

Amedeo began to laugh. "You see, though, what a man that Francesco is," he said. "He has nobody in this world, so he could just as well spend his Christmas here."

In fact, Francesco, though he came from San Dalmazio, had no relatives in the village. He lived in two tiny rooms above the parish house, and he prepared his own meals. Yet it looked as though solitude did not trouble him and there was never a time when he seemed melancholy or ill at ease. He used to say that, even if he had it to do all over again, he wouldn't raise a family; he was completely satisfied with the vagabond life he had led.

They left on Friday at noon in order to be in time to catch the bus, which left Massa at five-thirty. In the afternoon Guglielmo and Fiore continued working at the timber stand. Then Fiore made supper. After eating they had a smoke; then they stretched out side by side and went to sleep.

During the afternoon they had not exchanged more than ten words, but the work had made up for the lack of company. The next two days were worse, because they wanted to observe both Christmas and the sabbath.

Faced by the prospect of an entire empty day, Guglielmo rose as late as possible on Christmas morning. After drinking their coffee, the two men remained for hours seated on the edges of their beds, opposite each other, stealing hasty glances at each other but not saying a word. Every so often Fiore would poke the fire. Guglielmo smoked three or four cigarettes, but an incipient headache—he was becoming subject to them—compelled him to stop. And it was barely nine o'clock in the morning.

"I would have gone home gladly, but after what happened to my wife . . ." he began.

Fiore's response was a kind of grunt, which discouraged Guglielmo from continuing.

The fire was dying out. Guglielmo tramped down the ashes all around its edges, then went outside; he yawned and walked a short distance through the wood. There was really nothing to do, nothing to think about.

At about ten he went down to the Sellate to wash up, a little more leisurely than was his habit during the workdays. Taking off his shoes and stockings, he washed his feet. The water was absolutely freezing. After washing his face, neck, and arms, his hands became hard as wood.

The distant days when he had been a soldier came to his mind. At Cividale, in 1919, they had had to wash in the open, and in the mornings the water was invariably covered with a crust of ice. At times it was so hard that they had to break through it with the points of their bayonets. The men from the Veneto didn't seem to mind but it had been torture for the Tuscans. If he had had company, even Fiore, Guglielmo would have talked freely of his memories of military service; but he had to be content with mulling them over alone.

Later, while they sat outside the hut enjoying the pallid winter sunlight and waiting for the water to boil, he asked Fiore how many months he had served as a soldier.

"Thirty-six months, during the Great War," Fiore responded. "I was a mule driver," he added, replying to another question.

Under the spur of further questions, it came out that he had served in the front lines, employed in transporting ammunition; that on one occasion a shell had killed the mules and had wounded him rather badly, since he had spent forty days in the hospital; and that after Caporetto he had been taken prisoner. Guglielmo had been working with Fiore for ten years; they had spent innumerable evenings together in the hut, when the silence, the darkness, and the heat of the fire make for confidences; and he had slept in the same room with him more often than with his own wife; yet he had known nothing about Fiore's wound or his having been a prisoner. And, in fact, the wound, the prison, the war had passed over Fiore's existence without leaving a trace; just as it seemed that the death of his only son, which had taken place two years ago, had not shaken him in the slightest. He was at work the day after the funeral, as conscientious and rude as ever. There was nothing that interested him outside of the timber stand and the making of the charcoal; he could talk of nothing but pine groves and copses, first-grade and second-grade timber, cords of wood and the forest's seed growth. The only feeling that animated him was professional pride.

When in turn Guglielmo began talking about his war experiences, Fiore sat listening with indifference, not even taking the trouble to nod in agreement every now and then.

"Well," Guglielmo said, when they sat down before the soup of beans and spaghetti—the Christmas meal was no different from that of other days—"we're far enough ahead with the work, don't you think?"

"Uhm," Fiore replied. "Could be farther."

But Fiore had no wish to go into details. He enjoyed giving terse and obscure answers. It was the most irritating aspect of his whole personality.

"Up till now the woodcutting's gone well," he said a little later, "but how will we get started in the copse? Half the time will be wasted cutting away the underbrush."

"It won't be worse than last year, at Caiani."

"No? Three times worse."

"But it was soaking wet there," Guglielmo burst out.

Fiore held firmly to his opinion. To hear him, the copse at Caiani was as dry as this one was wet. In order not to cause bad feelings, Guglielmo let the discussion drop.

But he had to vent his feelings somehow; and so, as soon as he had finished eating, he walked with long strides down to the bottom of the stand. Leaving the path, he dove into the copse. Naturally, the grass, bushes, and brambles were damp, but the trunks of the oaks seemed perfectly dry. "And *this* is what that stubborn mule calls a sopping-wet wood, worthless even for making charcoal twigs." Of course, until then the weather had helped them; they had had a November and December such as are rarely seen; and perhaps, taking the weather into account, it had been a mistake not to start chopping trees from the bottom; but in any case you couldn't even compare it with the copse at Caiani. Getting himself completely soaked, scratching his face and hands, Guglielmo feverishly pushed his way through a good part of the copse.

Afterward he shaved himself in front of a piece of mirror stuck into the mud of the hut. Fiore, seated next to him, was calmly sharpening the axes and pruning hooks.

"You going to the farmstead tomorrow?" Guglielmo asked.

"No."

In the misty air at the end of the valley, they could make out a village. "What place could that be?" Guglielmo thought. Then it made him think of something else: "In what direction does our village lie?" He couldn't quite orient himself and so he couldn't decide with certainty.

Now he thought of the illness from which his wife had died. What kind of disease was it? The doctor hadn't been able to give it a name, and when people asked him for an explanation he found himself embarrassed and couldn't answer.

If they tell you "It was pneumonia, or cancer," you don't accept it because of that, but it's better than nothing. In the village they said that his poor wife had been bewitched. This too was an explanation, but Guglielmo had not accepted it, though he was not averse to believing in enchantments. Placing his hand on his shoulder, the priest, Don Mario, had told him that he should set his heart at peace, it had been the will of God. . . .

The sun had already set. Guglielmo stood up. "And this day too has gone by," he said.

He went into the hut and lit the fire. The pine boughs sputtered and the flames burst through with a hissing noise. Guglielmo sat down on his bed and held out his hands to the flames. Fiore was preparing their supper.

After supper he took a short stroll through the stand, stopping now and then to look at the lights of the village trembling in the darkness. He could even imagine it was his own village. In the past the sight would have given him pleasure. At that hour his wife, his sister, and the little girls would be sitting down to eat, and Guglielmo used to have the habit of following mentally the course of the meal. The wood might be dark and inhospitable, perhaps with a wind blowing and rain pelting down, but he had the comfort of thinking that in his kitchen the light shone neatly on the spick-and-span sink and the laid-out table. His family was sitting at the table, clinking their cutlery, the conversation of his wife and his sister and the chatter of the girls rising in the intimate atmosphere of the room. Now supper had ended, Irma was beginning to get sleepy, but the little girl seemed to become even livelier and more restless. Seated opposite each other, the two women were resting before washing up and putting the girls to bed. It was thanks to his work that his family led such a comfortable, tranquil existence; so Guglielmo did not complain of the hard life he was forced to undergo during the greater part of the year.

But now, if he thought of his home it pained him, and the sight of the distant lights, which recalled those family images, weighed on him intolerably. He went back to the hut. Fiore was already lying on his bed, though Guglielmo could not tell whether he was sleeping or not. Better to follow his example. Better to behave as Fiore did, to stretch out in the dark and let his eyes follow the half-spent flickerings of the fire and his thoughts travel at random wherever chance took them. And hope that sleep would come quickly.

To plunge into the darkness of sleep was the best thing left him. When Guglielmo felt sleep coming on he was happy, because for a few hours he would be freed from all thoughts, because another day had gone by. One by one the days passed, and the months and the years piled up at his back.

He was already thirty-eight; the forty-year mark was not far off and, once it was passed, he would be a mature, almost an old man. The day of his misfortune was also, slowly, moving farther away. Guglielmo only hoped that time would fill the gulf that had opened in his life. In any case it was a good thing that the time passed. The years would slide away one after the other, his daughters would get married, and he would become an old man almost without realizing it.

So Christmas passed, the first Christmas that Guglielmo had spent away from home. "I should have gone home," he thought in the morning. Another empty day yawned before him. Guglielmo felt strongly about customs and traditions, so it did not even occur to him that he could get through Sunday by working.

The monotony of the day was broken by a visit: a woodcutter from the Apennines near Pistoia, who spoke with a markedly Emilian accent. In the Maremma one often came across camps of woodcutters from the mountains around Pistoia. The mountaineers arrived in the autumn and left again late in the spring. They spent Easter as well as Christmas in the woods. Their camps could be recognized immediately by the presence of women and by the characteristic form of their huts, which were rectangular rather than oval-shaped.

The man belonged to a camp an hour's distance by the road. He had come to ask the loan of a few pounds of cornmeal. He said that there were eighteen of them, all from the province of Pistoia, and that their camp got its supplies from a farmstead at Marsiliana. But Guglielmo had never heard of this place before. Fiore took a great interest in the newcomer and asked him several questions of a professional nature. They could not understand each other very well, however, because the terms they used in their work were not the same.

"We'll bring it back the day after tomorrow," the man said, loading the sack on his shoulder.

Guglielmo told him not to put himself to any trouble. "We'll come ourselves and visit you next Sunday."

"Do you know the road?" the man said, and he repeated the directions.

"Perhaps I'll find the charcoal burner I need," Guglielmo explained later to Fiore. Charcoal-burning is a difficult trade, handed down from father to son. There are no charcoal burners in the Maremma. They all come from the Apennines near Pistoia, from Garfagnana or Montemignaio.

"You'll need one who knows his job, with that wet wood," Fiore said; but Guglielmo ignored the allusion.

Germano, Francesco, and Amedeo arrived at midnight. Guglielmo woke up immediately.

"How's Caterina?" he asked Amedeo.

"She's fine. She was sorry you didn't come."

"You explained to her . . ."

"To tell the truth, I didn't give her many explanations. She understood by herself."

"Yes," Guglielmo said. "Did you see the girls?"

"I saw the older one."

"Everybody well at your house?"

"Thank God, yes."

Then the three men lay down on the mounds, wrapping themselves in their army-type blankets. Germano complained that the twigs were harder than a mattress, but two minutes later he was sleeping. Amedeo and Francesco, who for their part were weary too, quickly fell asleep. Fiore had not even awakened, or at least gave no sign that he had.

But Guglielmo found it hard to go back to sleep. He felt almost remorseful that he had not gone home. It seemed to him that he had failed in his duty toward his sister and the children. "My God, I'm becoming worse than Fiore," he thought.

But, after all, that wouldn't be so bad. Fiore at least felt nothing. He had not even felt the death of his son. Much better to be like Fiore; or like Francesco, who had nobody in the world.

[6]

After two days of inactivity, Guglielmo was delighted to start working again. At dawn he was already up and about. The job was to chop down the last remaining pine trees on the hill. Guglielmo got to work quickly, followed by Fiore, who had no ups and downs in his work habits. The others, however, were tired and half asleep, especially Germano. The boy did not conceal his ugly mood. After the interval at home, the work in the woods seemed particularly hard to him.

"You were better off yesterday, eh? Walking arm in arm with your girl," Amedeo said.

"And you in bed with your wife," the boy snapped back.

"That's life," Amedeo said. "You have to work from the moment you're born, unless you're born rich."

"But Christian work," the boy answered between ax blows, "not this. It's all right for Fiore. Or for the boss," he added, lowering his voice, "who gets a few thousand lire when he's done. Not for us poor devils."

"You should have been born a boss," said Amedeo ironically.

"Try to finish by this evening," Guglielmo shouted at them.

By working late into the dusk, they managed to finish chopping down the pines. Last of all they cut down the three large ilex trees that formed the highest point on the slope. It was already dark when they gathered up their tools and went down the path to the hut, where Francesco had prepared supper.

They did not stay up that evening. Amedeo proposed a game of cards, but nothing came of it. And nobody wanted to talk. By seven o'clock they were already stretched out on their beds, most of them asleep.

The next morning they began chopping trees in the scrub. It rose before them like a continuous curtain; Guglielmo assigned each man a section about thirty paces wide. Now the job was more complicated, for they had to clear away the brush under the trees before chopping them down. Yet it didn't require half the time Fiore had predicted. In fact, an experienced woodcutter, by using his billhook, could quickly clear away the underbrush. The brambles would become an obstacle only farther down the slope.

During the morning Guglielmo worked awhile with Germano, who lacked experience in cutting scrub; then he returned to his strip, the last on the right, bordered by a kind of rocky crevice or channel, which gradually widened out until it formed a real cliff of stone jutting over the Sellate.

It was very hot and the sky was completely empty of clouds.

The patch of scrub was dry. Guglielmo had to interrupt his work every so often to mop the sweat.

"It's too hot," he thought, and the thought made him look up.

The sky, utterly limpid, could not deceive an expert like him. Behind the serene surface a knowledgeable eye can detect the clouds, as behind the clouds it discerns the clear sky. Until then they had been exceptionally lucky in the weather, but it couldn't go on indefinitely. If December had been clement, January, in all probability, would be stormy. Guglielmo sensed that the season of the great winter storms was near, when the woodcutters are forced to remain idle, shut up in their hut, and a man is lucky if the weather clears long enough for him to rush down and draw the water. He knew well those long, monotonous days when the rain beats down uninterruptedly on the tar-paper roof, and inside the hut the men yawn and look at their watches every five minutes. And all the time the nostalgia for home grows stronger and stronger. During those days Francesco's presence would prove really useful, with his imperturbable good humor and his inexhaustible supply of conversation, tales, and anecdotes. You might say Guglielmo had hired the old man solely for this reason.

"It will last another week," he thought, giving the weather a searching glance.

It was not the boss in him speaking, fearful of having to pay his workers even for the days of enforced inactivity and thus seeing his earnings reduced. He feared those days for himself, knowing from experience that only work could drive away the thoughts that tormented him.

The good weather lasted another week, as Guglielmo had predicted. During that week the men worked furiously, almost as though they had a presentiment that they would soon be forced to stop.

Sunday afternoon, right after eating, Guglielmo and Germano left for the camp of the Pistoian woodcutters to fetch the flour. They went down to the Sellate and walked along it for some distance. The wagon road crossed and recrossed the dry bed of the stream.

"This way," said Guglielmo, and they turned up a path that climbed through the wood.

The Pistoian woodcutters' directions had been sketchy, but they were sufficient for a man who knew the woods as well as Guglielmo. The forest grew thicker and thicker and the path became a narrow fissure between two walls of trees. Many times the path came to a fork, but Guglielmo was guided by a freshly broken branch at the beginning of the right path.

After a good half hour, they reached the first hut; Germano had never known Pistoian woodcutters before, and he was struck by the unusual shape of their hut. They went to the doorway, but no one was there. They continued along the path and, after a hundred yards, found another clearing with two huts. Outside there was a woman; she was squatting on her heels, mixing something in a steaming pot. She glanced at them and then turned back to her work without saying a word. She wore a pair of pants and a man's jacket; she was squat and rather fat. Her hair looked gray, but perhaps it was only dusty. All in all, her masculine clothes and the coarse, hard lines of her face made her a very unfeminine creature.

"Where are the men?" Guglielmo asked.

"Ahead," the woman replied.

As they continued walking, Germano expressed his surprise at finding a woman in the woodcutters' camp.

"Didn't you know?" Guglielmo said.

And then he explained that Pistoians stay for several months on end in the woods and so they bring their women with them; the women not only do the washing and cooking but also help out with the chopping and charcoal-burning.

"Their women," Guglielmo concluded, "look like men."

"I saw," Germano said. "They even wear pants."

"And they smoke."

"But do they all sleep together, men and women?"

"Of course," Guglielmo replied.

"Well, it can't be a bad life," Germano said, excited by the thought of such promiscuity.

They found the men in another clearing, busy building a hut. Here too there was a woman, dressed like the first, and she too was of uncertain age. The frame of the hut had already been built and now they were covering it. They had formed a chain and were passing the sods along while two men on ladders were setting them in place on the roof. The woman was working in the line just like the men.

"Good afternoon," said Guglielmo.

The last man in the line was the one who had come to get the flour. He recognized Guglielmo immediately, stopped working, and came forward to meet him.

"I see you're building another," Guglielmo said.

"It's for a work team from my town. They should arrive this week," the man replied. "Come along, come and have something to drink," he added, after a moment.

They walked back up the path with the man.

"Bring us something to drink," the man told the woman, still crouched over the pot of polenta.

The woman obeyed quickly. She went into the hut and came out with a half-empty bottle of wine and gave it to the man, who offered it to Guglielmo.

"Well, here's to you," Guglielmo said, and he drank straight from the bottle. He passed it on to Germano. The man drank last. He wiped his mouth with the back of his hand and asked, "Have a hard time finding us?"

"Oh, no," Guglielmo answered, smiling. "We're familiar with these woods by now."

"Come from these parts?"

"Not right here. From San Dalmazio. Pomarance," he added, seeing that the man did not recognize the name of his village.

"Oh, yes, Pomarance," the man said. "I once did some chopping there."

While Guglielmo talked with the man, Germano curiously watched the woman's movements. She had picked up an ax and was splitting some wood for the fire. The boy went up to her and offered to help. The woman answered in a few words of dialect that Germano couldn't understand, but from her rude tone he realized that she was not pleased by his offer.

"I also came to hire a charcoal burner," Guglielmo said.

"There are some good ones in my town. When do you want him?"

"The second week in February."

"Good. Don't worry," the man replied.

"About the pay . . ." Guglielmo began.

"Oh, you'll come to an agreement," the man said.

And with these few words the deal was concluded.

The man wanted them to stay for supper, but Guglielmo asked for the flour and then, together with the boy, started out for home. Germano was excited by what he had seen and kept talking about it.

"We think we live like animals, but they're even worse. Did you see that woman? You could only tell she was a woman by her hair. And the way they talk! I couldn't understand a word."

"They're poor people," Guglielmo said. "We're rich compared to them." ·

At one time the Pistoian mountaineers had seemed to him to be really poor people, deserving his pity. He had met them everywhere, in the woods of Castelnuovo, Serrazzano, Monterontodo, Montieri, Casole, and they had always struck him as miserable, brutalized people. He was especially struck by the fact that the women were condemned to the same life of hard labor as the men. The sight of those unfortunates always suggested, by contrast, his own good fortune. He always used to think of his home, where his wife and children led a quiet life and lacked nothing. This time, too, he thought of his own home, but, alas! his wife was no longer there. She was dead; she had disappeared forever. No matter how hard the life of those people was, it was still less hard than his. No, in his condition he could not afford to pity anyone.

[7]

In the dead of the night Guglielmo was awakened by the

hurricane. He listened for a while, thinking of nothing. The noises outside absorbed him completely. He heard the roar of the wind growing louder and louder until the gusts struck with astonishing violence against the side of the hut; and the hut, its tautened joints groaning, seemed to bend beneath them. Then the wind disappeared and you could hear the rain again, pattering faster and faster on the roof.

At a certain point, from a movement next to him, he knew that Fiore was awake too.

"You hear that rain, Fiore?" he whispered.

"I'm not deaf," Fiore replied rudely.

"Now that it's started, who knows how long it will last."

"It'll soak everything," Fiore said.

"You couldn't really expect . . ." Guglielmo began, but he didn't go on.

When they woke in the morning, the music was still the same. The others were up too, exchanging comments on the storm.

"I thought it would blow everything away, hut and all."

"Weather for wolves."

"What a terrible night."

"You'll see, tomorrow we won't even be able to stick our noses outside."

Germano woke up last and found it hard to grasp what was happening. Evidently he had slept right through it.

Amedeo started laughing. "A bombardment wouldn't wake you."

"Blessed youth," another commented.

They stayed in bed, for there was no reason to get up. The violence of the storm, which gave no sign of diminishing in intensity, excited them and made them almost happy. Then Fiore got up, lit the fire, and put the coffee on to heat.

Amedeo cursed shortly and immediately after began laughing.

"What's the matter with you?" Germano asked.

"A raindrop fell right on my cigarette, *plaf*, and put it out."

"It's true—it's raining into the house, men," Germano said, shifting his position quickly.

Obviously the roof was waterlogged and the rain was filtering through. But this too only heightened the excitement and gaiety.

They got up from bed to drink the coffee. And the long day shut up in the hut began.

Germano immediately proposed a game of cards. Amedeo made a wry face. "What? In the morning?"

"And what difference is there between morning and evening?" Germano asked. "Here it's always night now."

And it was true, from the moment when they could no longer open the door.

They lit the candles and the game began. It was Germano and Francesco against Fiore and Amedeo. Guglielmo sat down behind Germano and set himself to follow the game.

Germano and Francesco won the first game by a large margin. Confidently, the boy said that he was absolutely certain of their final victory.

"You think so? With only seven points' advantage?" Amedeo said. "We've got plenty of time to catch up."

"This time it'll be fourteen points," said Germano, shuffling the cards.

Instead, Fiore and Amedeo won three hands in a row and were ahead by nine points. The game was nearly over, and except for a play that would sweep the board, there was no hope of improving their chances. Depressed, Germano made no reply to Amedeo's teasing, while Francesco smiled imperturbably.

Then he and the boy were dealt magnificent hands; they might actually have swept the board, but Germano made an error at the very last. It set off a wild argument.

"You should have kept spades, not clubs," Amedeo explained.

But Germano was unwilling to admit he had made an error and kept justifying himself for playing as he had; however, when Guglielmo intervened on Amedeo's side, he fell silent.

It annoyed him bitterly, that error committed in the very last hand, which had decided the whole game.

"Don't be upset," said Francesco good-humoredly. "Take revenge instead."

"Revenge, revenge," Germano cried, full of life again, and he began shuffling the cards.

Guglielmo was no longer following the game. He had pulled out his notebook and pencil and was doing his accounts. The price of charcoal was going up; the deal was proving better than it had seemed at the beginning; he was certain to make nine thousand lire. But Guglielmo had even bigger deals in view. Next year he would contract to cut wood on several stands at the same time. He was tempted to become a wholesale charcoal vendor. By now he possessed a little capital and was in a position to extend his activities.

Yes, he had gone far since the days when he was just an ordinary woodcutter and used to receive wages of ninety centesimi a day! He had gone far, but . . . "Why do I think about these things? Why do I add up all these figures? What do I care if I earn a thousand lire more or less? If only she were alive, I'd go back to being an ordinary woodcutter!"

About ten o'clock it stopped raining and they could stick their heads out. Large drops of rain carried by the wind slashed at the five men as they stood outside the hut, breathing in the fragrant, sharp-smelling air.

"Go get some water," Guglielmo told the boy. "But hurry, it's going to start again soon. We've got to strengthen the roof covering," he added, turning to the other men.

While Germano went to the stream to fill two pails and a canteen, Amedeo brought a ladder and climbed up to the roof. There he saw the damage caused by the storm. A sheet of tar paper had been torn loose and its edges were in tatters. The whole roof was crumpled and torn and in the hollows small puddles of water were lodged. Amedeo brushed away the water, patched the tar paper as best he could, and stretched another sheet above it, nailing its edges carefully to the transverse logs that formed the roof's frame.

Germano had just returned when, exactly as Guglielmo had foreseen, it began to rain again.

"It might at least have given us time to cook our food," Francesco grumbled.

He had to resign himself to cooking inside the hut. It takes a long time to cook polenta, and the air soon became unbreathable. They had to open the door, so the wind dashed the rain inside and soaked part of the floor and the pallets on which they slept. But the activity helped the morning to pass rather swiftly. At last they closed the door again, threw sawdust on the wet floor, and sat down to eat.

After the meal, Francesco settled himself comfortably on his bed, pulled out his pipe, filled and lit it, and then sighed with satisfaction. These days spent shut up in the hut did not displease him in the least, and not because he lacked the will to work. Francesco worked slowly, in keeping with his quiet nature, but nonetheless always managed to get his work done. He preferred the sessions in the hut to working because then he felt himself the center of general attention and respect. The boss was Guglielmo; on the job Fiore also gave orders; but who, except Francesco, could keep the conversation going? These palavers were the center of his existence, and nothing gave him more pleasure than sitting down in the middle of a circle of listeners and holding their attention with his stories. This was not the case with the others, first of all because they lacked his talents, and second, because their world was their families. For Francesco, the hut, the sputtering fire, and the attentive faces of the woodcutters took the place of a family.

That afternoon he brought out an extraordinary number of riddles and conundrums. Germano tried hard, but failed to solve a single one.

"Well, listen to this, then," Francesco said. "Listen, it's easy:

"You are not a blackbird,
You are not a thrush,
So who are you?"

Germano pondered the riddle for a long time but to no effect.

"A toad," said Francesco.

"A toad?"

Francesco nodded.

"But it could be—anything," Germano protested. "How could I guess that?"

The next morning the wind had stopped and throughout the day a fine drizzle came down, which left them feeling bleak and depressed. Through the partly open door the men gazed outside. Behind the veil of rain a pine tree that they had spared was barely visible. Down below, they could hear the deep roar of the stream in flood. Every so often the weather looked as though it were about to clear and they could see the slope on the other side of the valley, but the rain never stopped, even for an instant. Germano put a sack over his head and ran down to the stream; but he filled only the pails because the water was muddy. And so that day they drank their wine unwatered.

They looked out the door, stared at each other, yawned, and sighed. But it was worse for Guglielmo than for the others. The man who is bored, who labors, who suffers, can console himself by thinking of other times in his life; he remembers the cherished moments of his own past life or looks forward to the prospect of a better future. Guglielmo was denied this consolation. The future held no attraction for him, and he avoided thinking about it; as for the past—there had been many happy moments in his life, moments which he had once remembered with pleasure. Hadn't the time when he was engaged been happy? He used to come back from the timber stand on Saturday evening; Sunday morning he dressed up in his best clothes, shaved, and saw his fiancée in church, at Mass. He saw her from a distance because in church the women stayed in front, seated on benches, and the men behind, standing. In the afternoon he would fetch his fiancée and go for a stroll with her along the highroad. They walked on beyond the point at which promenades usually ended, strolling to the cemetery and even farther. Usually,

Guglielmo's sister Caterina accompanied them. Caterina was young and extremely vivacious. They sat down on a bank; the two girls would start talking to each other, Guglielmo only rarely joining in the conversation. Once he had tried to speak his mind on the new fashion of short hair, which had started to spread even at San Dalmazio, but his sister had broken in, shouting him down: "What do you know about it, you wild bear?" And his fiancée had started laughing and then looked at him and gently ran her fingers through his hair.

Hadn't his wedding day been happy? There were twenty-four guests at the dinner table and the two of them seated at the head, she gay and relaxed, he embarrassed and happy. . . . And hadn't all the years they had lived together been happy? And now he might have been able to console himself by thinking that, after all, ten years of his life had been happy; there are some people who never have a day's happiness in their entire lives. But actually these memories were no longer happy for Guglielmo; he found no pleasure any more in them. His happiness had been a lie, a happiness founded on ignorance and deceit. For those years that seemed to be the best of his life were the very ones that had prepared his misfortune.

"What time is it?" Germano asked.

"Ten o'clock."

"Ten? I don't know how we'll ever manage to get through this day."

"You can get through a life and you think you can't get through a day?" said Francesco.

He had put on his glasses, taken out a needle and thread, and was mending a shirt, humming in a low voice:

> "I want to go to California
> Where life is free of care. . . ."

"Would you really like to go to California, Francesco?" Germano asked curiously.

"Why not? I was going to go to America when I was a little boy; then I got sick and couldn't go. But if they said to me right now, 'Let's go to America,' I'd be ready to take my chances. . . ."

In the afternoon the conversation became lively when it touched on one of the woodcutters' favorite topics: bandits. Francesco had at his fingertips the stories of Tiburzi, Stoppa, Fioravanti, Menichetti, and the other famous bandits of the region; besides, when he was young, he had known Moriani in person, and spoke of him with great admiration.

"He was killed here," he said, "together with his brother, while Breccia, the third member of the band, was captured alive."

"What? Here?" Amedeo intervened. "You mean near Castelnuovo."

"No, here, right here where we're chopping."

"Go on," said Amedeo. "He was killed above Castelnuovo. My poor father was there and saw him. They kept the body on show for two days."

"They killed him at the Three Trees. You know that much, don't you?"

"Yes," Amedeo answered, "I think the place was called something like that."

"And the Three Trees were precisely those three ilex trees we chopped down a few days ago. You may not have noticed it, but there were still bullet marks in the trunks."

"But I've always heard—"

But Germano interrupted him. "Let him finish telling about it."

"It was a spy who did it," Francesco said, "otherwise they wouldn't have caught him in a hundred years. When they saw they were surrounded—there were more than a hundred *carabinieri*—each of them took cover behind a tree—there were exactly three of them—and they started shooting. And you know, they didn't miss a shot. Moriani in particular was a great marksman. But none of the *carabinieri* were killed because the bandits were content to wound them in the legs. Well, after some time had passed, Moriani ran out of ammunition, so he turned to his brother and asked him for some. But when he turned, he showed himself and got wounded in the shoulder. When the other two saw that he was wounded, they gave up and started running away through the woods. Moriani's brother was cut down by a volley; Breccia reached the Sellate, but they spotted him when he was crossing and wounded him in the leg. As for Moriani, they warned him several times to give himself up, but not on your life. They had to finish him off with their rifles, but they didn't get the satisfaction of taking him alive."

At nine that evening, Francesco was still holding forth with his stories.

Guglielmo slept through the night. When he awoke he was struck by the silence outside.

Had the good weather returned? He lit a match and looked at his watch, which he kept hanging on a nail above his head. It was still too early to get up. But after a quarter of an hour, unable to stand it any longer, he got out of bed. Although he tried to get up softly, Germano woke up.

"What time is it?" he grumbled.

"Still early," Guglielmo whispered. "I'm going outside to take a look."

But the door wouldn't open. Guglielmo was puzzled. "What the devil's happened?" Finally, mustering his strength, he succeeded in shoving it open.

"What the devil is it?" he muttered again, and then immediately realized why the door was stuck. It was snow. It was barely dawn yet, but Guglielmo was able to see that during the night there had been a heavy snowfall. Five inches of snow lay on the ground.

He walked about at random, stepping on the soft, yielding carpet. He didn't know whether to be glad or not, but the novelty of it soon filled him with pleasure and excitement. Forgetting the difficulties that the snowfall would eventually create, he walked around the hut, buried his hands in the snow, shook a pine branch; when he felt the freezing snow slide down his neck, he laughed.

Germano meanwhile could not go back to sleep and lay there listening. Not a sound came from outside the hut. Guglielmo's cry reached him, but it was muffled. What the devil was going on? In the wink of an eye he had slipped on his boots and was outside. His reaction to the snowfall was openly enthusiastic. Following the tracks furrowed in the white sheet of snow, he ran after Guglielmo.

Finally everybody was awakened by the excited voices of Germano and their boss. The news of the snowfall put them all in a state of feverish activity. In a flash the fire was lit and the coffee heated. The hut became the center of festive and noisy excitement.

Germano's appearance struck Amedeo, who said, "What with that thing on your head, you look like—like a Turk. No, I don't know what you look like."

Germano was wearing a black cloth cap without a peak. His pink face, his shorn head, that strange head covering, and his shoulders white with snow made him look like a young Russian peasant, but certainly not a Turk.

Although the snow made the woodcutting much more difficult, they all considered it a pleasant change. At every blow of the ax, the tree would shake and answer with a small shower of snow. So they all got thoroughly soaked. And the drops of snow down their necks, which then slid down the ridge of their spines, caused a great deal of gay cursing. At the end they were all completely wet but in good spirits. As they were returning to the hut, Amedeo and Germano even started a snowball fight.

Before eating, they made arrangements for drying themselves. They built a great fire and stripped off their clothes.

"Hey, Francesco," cried Germano—Francesco was outside the hut watching over the cooking of the polenta—"come and see, there's a bear in the hut."

He was referring to Fiore. A thick, grayish mat of hair covered the woodcutter's chest and back. Everybody laughed, but Fiore took the remark in good part. Crouched on his pallet, he turned first his chest and then his back to the flames, until he was completely dry.

"You talk about Fiore, but not yourself," said Amedeo to the boy, and began pulling at the hairs which grew thickly in the hollow of his chest.

"Ouch! You're hurting me," Germano cried. "Keep your hands to yourself. I'm no woman."

[8]

During the following days it started to rain again, and the snow turned to mud. Especially outside the hut, where the ground was most trampled, keeping one's balance became a problem. Germano, who had greeted the snowfall with such enthusiasm, was the first to curse its consequences. "Look at them, they must weigh forty pounds apiece," he said, as he pulled off his boots. "Damn this stinking weather."

Then came days when the north wind blew, freezing the sweat on their bodies, and these were the most painful; every few strokes, they would leave the ax blade sticking in the trunk and warm their stiffened hands by blowing on them. Germano got chilblains; the pain was so intense that sometimes tears would come to his eyes. And he had to bear Amedeo's sneers, who said that only women and children got chilblains, but a man, especially a woodcutter, was a weakling if he succumbed.

Guglielmo's trouble was even worse. One evening he ate hardly anything and went immediately to bed.

"Aren't you even going to have a smoke?" said Francesco.

"I don't feel like smoking."

"Uhm. A bad sign."

A little later he went up to Guglielmo and put his hand on his forehead.

"You've got a first-rate fever," he said.

The next morning Guglielmo was so ill that the woodcutters were alarmed and talked of going to Massa for a doctor. But Francesco said that in his opinion, since the patient was not coughing, the lungs were not infected; for the moment there was nothing to fear.

Guglielmo for his part felt no fear whatsoever. On the contrary, he felt extremely well. For the first time since his misfortune, the thought of his wife did not cause him pain but rather a sense of well-being and calm. Secretly he hoped to die. It did not even occur to him that his children, the children she had brought into the world and had nourished and raised at the price of so much pain and sacrifice, would be left without support.

Moreover, under the disturbing influence of his fever, his mind was in no position to reason. He lay there half asleep, half awake, content to surrender himself to the flux of unfinished thoughts and fleeting images.

Because he kept his eyes closed, he did not distinguish between day and night. At one moment the thought flashed into his head that perhaps it was the same disease from which his wife had died. It had started, hadn't it, in the same way, with a very high fever? With all his soul Guglielmo hoped it was. He too would lose the ability to speak, he would no longer answer his friends when they asked him how he felt. In turn he would want to say something, but the effort would be vain. . . . And so he would come to know what she wanted to tell him when she had stared at him so insistently. Not being able to know that had been for him the worst of torments.

In forty-eight hours the fever disappeared. Guglielmo began to eat, and in a few days he had recovered completely.

February, on the whole, was fairly clement. Toward the middle of the month, the charcoal burner appeared. He was a tall, straight man, with gray hair, his cheekbones and hands veined with the bluish streaks that came from his long exposure to the charcoal dust.

The firing of the wood is a very delicate operation, which demands great experience. The charcoal burner begins by building a wooden egg, about three yards high, lining the bottom with sods, which are placed over a layer of dry leaves and loam. As he piles the wood, he takes care to leave an oven about fifteen inches deep in the center of it. Then he sets fire to it from on top; the charcoal kiln starts smoking immediately. After twelve hours or so, the burner begins to open up vents in the pile, which he then widens or closes, depending on how the wind is blowing, so as to ensure a uniform draft.

The firing lasts three days; if it has been done according

to the rules of the craft, the charcoal takes on temper; that is, it reacts to dampness by spitting out a white resin.

The woodcutting was nearing its end. They were working above the stream, encountering difficulties in the steep slope of the terrain and the brambles that covered the trees.

March lived up to its reputation; there was not a day in which a shower of rain did not come down or a sudden gale start blowing. The changeable weather hindered the work of loading the timber. The muleteer from the farmstead was given his job of transporting the timber to the provincial road. From there, by means of truck, the logs were to be carried to the mine at Boccheggiano, where they would be used for propping up the shafts.

When the job of transporting the wood was finished, the work with the charcoal began. The bundles of wood were carried by the men to the wagon road alongside the Sellate. Here they were loaded on a cart pulled by three mules, and then transported to the farmstead.

The bad weather got worse; there were three days of almost uninterrupted rain and wind; it seemed that winter had returned. On the fourth morning the sky was utterly cloudless, the air warm, and a gentle breeze carried with it sharp odors of the forest. The wooded ridges were steaming, drying in the sun. Guglielmo was walking down with the men to the low ground near the stream when he heard Amedeo say, "Spring has come."

He was struck by the rightness of the observation. It was indeed the first morning of spring. Deeply, he breathed in the air, which seemed heavy with the smell of flowers. His eye was caught by a bee buzzing around a tuft of primrose, and the creature seemed, in its buzzing, to be expressing its joy at the coming of spring.

And for an instant Guglielmo too felt his heart fill with joy. The spring had come, and for him especially it meant a great deal, for with the spring the hardest part of the work ended and he would be able to get home now and then to be with his family. . . . But suddenly the realization that this year would be utterly different stabbed him with anguish. The rebirth of nature had begun but there would be no rebirth for him. Let the bee, the flowers, the other men, and all nature enjoy the spring; he, Guglielmo, was forbidden to share in that joy.

Preoccupation with the work distracted Guglielmo from his thoughts; but during the next days, whenever some aspect of the general rebirth of nature struck him, he felt a sudden, piercing pang.

He was saddened too by the sight of his crew and their delight in reaching the end of their work. Amedeo and Germano, especially, he could see, were happy to be going home. Once he heard them joking with each other.

"You think you'll find your girl waiting for you?"

"If I don't, I'll find another. But you'll have your own worries."

"Why?" asked Amedeo, laughing.

"Because your wife won't recognize you with that beard of yours."

"Don't worry. I'll shave it off before going home. I'll shave and I'll make a new man of myself. I'll look like a dummy in a store window."

Germano was young: it was his right to be happy and carefree. So Guglielmo thought. But he couldn't rid himself of a feeling of rancor toward Amedeo. It seemed to him almost as though Amedeo had robbed him of something.

Amedeo, Germano, Francesco, and Fiore left one afternoon immediately after luncheon. The day before, the last charcoal kiln had been lit, and Guglielmo was staying to watch it.

"Stop and tell Caterina that I'll be home too the day after tomorrow," he said to Amedeo.

After he had said good-bye to his crew, he remained standing at the door of the hut. He heard their happy voices disappearing in the distance and picked out Amedeo's voice from the rest. Damn it, but Amedeo had every reason to be happy, happier than anyone else. Is there anything better than going home to your family after so many months? And Guglielmo followed in his mind's eye his friend's homecoming. There he was, just coming into the village, saying good-bye to the others and going on alone through the deserted street, in the moonlight. Most of the village had gone to bed at that hour, but someone was still awake at his house. . . . A few more steps, and he climbs the stairs and enters the bright kitchen. He embraces his wife, kisses her on both cheeks, and then she helps him to take off his pack. "Sit down," she says to him, "the soup will be ready in a minute." He sits down at the table set for him, looks around, and rubs his hands with satisfaction. And his wife is standing at the stove, she looks at him with an affectionate smile. The man is slightly embarrassed; he has spent too many months in the forest, and so, just to have something to do, he breaks off a piece of bread and starts to chew it. . . .

Guglielmo went down to the charcoal kiln.

[9]

He stayed up all night helping the charcoal burner. It was the most delicate phase of the firing, complicated by a strong wind that had risen, so that it was necessary to adjust the draft vents constantly. Actually the charcoal burner did not seem much pleased by Guglielmo's assistance. From long experience Guglielmo knew that charcoal burners are jealous of their trade, suspicious and proud, and that they surround even the simplest operations with an atmosphere of deep mystery, as though they were gifts from heaven. They look with a cold eye on the outsider who approaches the charcoal kiln. But since Guglielmo had had nothing to do all day, he was not sleepy; in the circumstances he had no wish to go and shut himself up in the hut with the wretched thoughts that inevitably assailed him when he was alone and idle. The small amount of work that watching the charcoal kiln gave him provided a useful distraction. Gradually, as the time passed, he felt less and less sleepy and at a certain point he decided to stay up all night.

But he began to feel hungry and at about two o'clock he went back to the hut to get some bread and cheese for himself and the man. The moon lit up the timber stand as though it were full day. The two men sat opposite each other while they ate; afterward Guglielmo offered the charcoal burner a cigarette. But the man preferred his pipe. Until that moment they had exchanged only a few words, in every case about the work in hand. But now that the draft had been adjusted, there was a pause in the work and a kind of conversation began. Guglielmo asked him how many years he had been working at his trade.

"Forty years," the man replied. "I began to work with my father when I was eleven."

The trade was handed down from father to son, but his only son had refused to take up his father's trade. After his military service, he had married a girl in the Veneto and had remained there, working as a farm laborer. As for his girls, one was dead, the other, who had gone to work as a maid in Modena, had married in that city.

"Then you've been left alone with your wife," Guglielmo said.

"I've been left completely alone. My wife died last year."

Guglielmo looked at him. Then the man said, "It's a bad thing to be left alone, especially at my age."

He added that for him there was no difference now between working and staying home. He was alone at work, he was alone at home. He made all his own meals, month in and month out. Easter and Christmas too. He had been left alone like a dog, at the age of fifty-one.

"My house is outside the town and if someday I suddenly took sick, nobody would notice it. Just as though it happened to me here in the woods. And then I'm full of aches and pains and I have no one to rub me down. It's different for you," he said. "You're young; you can get another woman."

Guglielmo said that he didn't feel like giving his children a stepmother. He himself had known what it meant to have a stepmother, and he couldn't in all conscience make his children undergo the same experience.

The man listened to him quietly, then asked, "How old are you?"

"Thirty-eight," Guglielmo replied.

"I wouldn't be afraid if I were thirty-eight. Certainly it's a terrible misfortune; but nothing compared to what it is when a man is old."

Guglielmo said nothing, but he felt that the man's judgment was unfair. After all, he had lived for twenty-five or thirty years with his wife, while Guglielmo's wife had died after nine years. This was the difference, entirely to the charcoal burner's advantage, and Guglielmo could not take any other differences into consideration.

"A charcoal burner's life is hard," the man began. "You woodcutters, what do you know? Think your life is worse, do you? You never have to stand on your feet for seventy-two hours at a stretch. Working in the woods is the worst fate that can befall a man, but between the woodcutter and the charcoal burner there's a difference. Yours is still a life for a Christian. It's hard work, but you work together and in the evening you gather around the fire and talk a bit. Look at my hands. Yours are raw and cracked but they're clean. But look at mine. You see? The charcoal has worked under the skin and won't ever go away. There are even cases of charcoal poisoning; you keep breathing in the charcoal and finally your body gets poisoned. Forty-eight hours later you're dead. That's the fate that's always hanging over my head. And what happens to you woodcutters? At the worst an ax slips and you cut a foot or a hand."

"I know a harder trade," Guglielmo said. And since the other man looked at him questioningly, he continued; "Miner. I was in the mine at Boccheggiano the other day," he continued, "and saw how those men come out of the pit."

"But how long do they work?" the charcoal burner answered. "How long does the shift last?"

"Eight hours, I think."

"And what's eight hours compared to seventy-two? They do eight hours' work and rest sixteen. We do three days' work and rest one. That's the difference."

"I still say that working underground is the worst thing there is. At least if you have an accident here, you're in the open air."

"There's no life worse than a charcoal burner's," the man replied stubbornly.

And he started to fill his pipe with his very dark, almost black tobacco.

Guglielmo recalled what Germano always said when teasing Amedeo. "That's not tobacco," he said, "that's gunpowder."

The man smiled complacently. "There aren't many people," he said, "who can smoke tobacco like this. But, you see, a lighter tobacco wouldn't satisfy me. What do you expect? We're used to breathing charcoal dust, so to us your cigarettes would taste like stuff for girls."

One could see that despite everything, the man was proud of the hard life he led, proud of the exhausting vigils beside the charcoal kiln, the charcoal dust that had lodged forever under his skin, and that tobacco of his, strong as gunpowder.

A long pause followed.

"We have time to think," the charcoal burner said at last. "We charcoal burners don't do anything but think."

Guglielmo nodded assent, though without really having understood what the man meant.

"And what is there to think about except home? In thirty years the only thing I've thought about is that. You work alone beside the kiln and you think about your home, your wife, your children. . . . You know, we come down from the mountains after the first crop of chestnuts and we go back at the beginning of summer. And in all those months we seldom exchange a dozen words with another human being. They say that we're like bears; but it's the work that makes us like that. Until now I didn't complain because, you see, I had the memory of my home and my chestnut trees to keep me company. Now, instead, I try not to think about it. There's no one waiting for me up there. That's the whole difference between my life before and my life now. I try not to think about it," he added, after a moment, "but what else can I think about?"

Guglielmo looked at the man and all at once felt an enormous compassion for him. Poor man! To have been left alone in the world, to have to make his own meals, with no one to take care of him if he falls sick. "I think I'm miserable," he thought, "but there's still somebody who loves me, who looks out for me."

"How clear it is!" said the charcoal burner suddenly.

Guglielmo turned in surprise and saw that the man was looking at the sky.

"And how many stars there are!" the charcoal burner went on. "Has anybody ever had the idea of counting them?" He started to laugh. "Only a charcoal burner would ever think of such a thing. We're the only ones who know the night that well. That's the way it is," he said then, "if you're a charcoal burner, you become . . ." He did not finish his sentence. He stood up and returned to his work.

Guglielmo followed his movements for a while and then began looking at the sky. How many stars there were! How many distant and unknown worlds! Don Mario had once told him that the stars were millions of times larger than the earth. Were they inhabited too? Was there work, suffering, death, pain up there too?

The stars were beginning to fade. The dawn rose, gray and leaden. Chilled, Guglielmo got to his feet and took a few steps around the kiln. He muttered good morning to the man and returned to the hut.

At noon he reappeared with the pot, the bowls, the bread and wine. But the daylight was not suited to confidences and so they ate and smoked in silence. In the afternoon Guglielmo helped the muleteer load the sacks of charcoal. The muleteer would return the next morning for the last load. And then, good-bye.

He was tired that evening. Immediately after supper he wrapped himself in his army blanket and waited for sleep to come and close his day. It was the first night he had slept alone in the hut, and it would also be his last. The next night he would be sleeping at home. He sighed, turning on his side.

Outside, the charcoal burner stayed awake all night, thinking of his mountains.

[10]

The driver whipped up his mules briskly and they started off. Guglielmo said good-bye to the charcoal burner and took his last look at the timber stand. He would probably never see that man again, nor come back to that place.

They arrived at the farmstead at one o'clock in the afternoon. Guglielmo ate with the overseer. The overseer talked and talked, this time about politics; he said that the war in Spain had been won by now, and that after that Italy would send an ultimatum to London and Paris, and London and Paris would bow their heads. So Italy would become mistress of the world.

Guglielmo barely listened. He felt a strange feeling growing inside him, a feeling of apprehension, disquiet. Was he afraid of going home? Was this it?

"And so," the overseer said at the moment of farewell, "you'll be glad to get home, I suppose."

Guglielmo muttered in agreement. The apprehension was growing, growing. . . . With his heart aching, Guglielmo waited for the bus to leave. Throughout the trip he gazed obstinately out the window, even when it turned dark and he could no longer see anything.

He got off at the shop.

"Oh, Guglielmo, is it you? It's been such a long time," his aunt exclaimed, coming gaily to meet him.

"Good evening, Lina," Guglielmo replied.

His aunt looked at him smiling, but his face was tense.

"I wanted . . . a drink," he said.

His aunt poured him a glass of wine and asked him if he wanted to eat.

"No," Guglielmo answered, and emptied the glass.

His aunt was watching him closely.

"How are things, Guglielmo?" she asked.

Guglielmo leaned against the wall, pushing back the brim of his hat. "Oh, God, Lina . . . Worse and worse."

His eyes glistened, and the tears welled up and ran down

his cheeks. The two stood there like that for a few instants, facing each other. Then his aunt placed a hand on his arm. "Go home, Guglielmo," she said gently. "You've been gone for five months. You'll be glad to see the girls again, won't you?"

"Yes," Guglielmo replied in a barely audible voice.

He dried his face with the back of his hand, then picked up his sack, and without another word, started on his way.

He had set the sack on the ground and stood leaning against the gate of the cemetery.

He had never felt so hopeless, not even during the days of his wife's illness. For a moment or two he completely lost his head; he thought of stretching out on the ground and dying.

"Rosa," he murmured. "Rosa," he said in a loud voice. "Rosa, help me! Rosa, send me a little resignation!"

The sound of footsteps made him turn. He could make out the burning tip of a cigar and a hazy figure coming up the road.

"Do you want a hand, Guglielmo?" the man said, passing near him.

"No, thanks," Guglielmo replied. "I'll manage myself."

He waited until the man had gone, then put the sack back on his shoulder and started walking again.

He was thinking that Rosa would have to help him. He could not go on like this. From up there in heaven she had to send him the strength to live.

He looked up at the sky. But it was completely dark; there was not a single star.

ITALO CALVINO

ITALO CALVINO WAS BORN ON OCTOBER 15, 1923, IN SANTIAGO de Las Vegas, a small village near Havana, Cuba; he grew up at San Remo on the Italian Riviera. Born into a professional scientific family—his father was a geologist and a professor of agronomy, his mother a botanist—Calvino tried to interest himself in science but quickly renounced it in favor of literature. During the German occupation he joined the partisans and fought in the Garibaldi Brigade. For Calvino, as for so many Italian writers, it was a crucial experience, maturing him as a man and shaping his political concerns for years to come. After the war he resumed his studies at the University of Turin, where he wrote his thesis on the novels of Joseph Conrad. It was in Turin that he first began to write fiction and came under the decisive influence of Pavese and Vittorini. He also took an active and passionate part in politics and contributed frequently to left-wing journals and newspapers. After working for some time as a salesman for the publishing firm of Einaudi, in 1947 he joined the firm as an editor, a position which he still holds. He is currently coediting with Vittorini the distinguished literary review *Il Menabo*. Hailed by the critic Elena Croce as "the most interesting young writer of his generation," he won in 1959 the Premio Bagutta for his collected stories and novelettes.

His most important works are: *Il sentiero dei nidi di ragno* (1947); *Ultimo viene il corvo* (1949); *Il visconte dimezzato* (1952); *La formica argentina* (1952); *L'entrata in guerra* (1954); *Fiabe Italiane* (a scholarly collection of Italian folk tales), 1956; *Il barone rampante* (1957); *La speculazione edilizia (A Plunge into Real Estate)*, 1957; *La nuvola di smog* (1959); *Il cavaliere inesistente* (1959).

A PLUNGE INTO REAL ESTATE
by Italo Calvino

translated by D. S. Carne-Ross

HE RAISED HIS EYES FROM THE BOOK (HE ALWAYS READ IN THE train) and rediscovered the landscape piece by piece. The wall, the fig tree, the quarry with its chain of buckets, the reeds, the cliffs—he had seen them all his life but only now, because he was returning, did he really become aware of them. Every time he came home to the Riviera, Quinto renewed contact in this fashion. But he had been away so much, come back so often, the thing had been going on for years; what was the fun of it when he already knew the scene by heart? All the same, he still hoped for some chance discovery as he sat there with one eye on the book and the other on the landscape. But now he was simply confirming familiar impressions.

Yet every time there was something that checked the pleasure he took in this exercise and made him look down at the page on his lap, something irritating that he couldn't quite pin down. It was the houses, that was it, all these new houses that were going up, apartment buildings six or eight stories high, their massive white flanks standing out like barriers propping the crumbling slope of the coast and putting out as many windows and balconies as they could toward the sea. The Riviera was gripped by a fever of cement. An apartment building here, the identical window boxes of geraniums on every balcony; there a building that had just gone up, the windows still marked with white, waiting for the Milanese families who wanted a place by the sea; a little farther on, some scaffolding, and below, the cement mixer in action and a sign advertising the local real estate office.

In the little towns on the terraced hillsides the new buildings played piggyback with one another, while in their midst the owners of the old houses added another story and craned their necks to see out. The town where Quinto lived had once been surrounded by shady gardens of eucalyptus trees and magnolias, where retired English colonels and elderly spinsters leaned over the hedges and exchanged Tauchnitz editions and watering cans. Now the bulldozers were churning up the soil with its rotting leaves and its gravel from the garden paths, picks were demolishing the two-story residences, the ax was at the broad-leaved palm trees, which fell with a papery scrunch from the sky so soon to be filled by the desirable, three-room, all-convenience, sunny homes of tomorrow.

When he came home, Quinto had once been able to look out over the roofs of the new town and the poorer quarters down by the sea front and the harbor. In between were the crowded houses of the old part of town, with their moldy, lichenous walls, lying between the hill to the west, where the olive groves clustered thickly above the gardens, and to the east, the green swarm of villas and hotels stretching beneath the bare flank of the carnation fields, glinting with greenhouses as far as the Point. But all he could see these days was a geometrical arrangement of parallelepipeds and polyhedrons ranked one above the other, corners and sides of houses, clustering roofs and windows and blank walls pierced only by the ground-glass bathroom windows, one above the other.

The first thing that always happened was that his mother took him up to the roof terrace. Left to himself, with that idle, vague nostalgia of his which faded almost as soon as it came, he would have gone away again without troubling to go up there. "I'll show you what's new since you were last here," she said, and started pointing out the new buildings. "The Sampieris are adding another floor, that's a new house built by some people from Novara, and the nuns, even the nuns . . . You remember the garden with the bamboos that we used to be able to see down there? Just look at all the digging that's going on there now; heaven knows how many floors they're going to have with foundations like that! And the giant Chilean pine in the garden of the villa Van Moen—the finest on the Riviera it used to be—well, the Baudino firm has bought up the whole area and the tree's been chopped down for firewood. What a shame it is; the authorities ought to have stopped them. Of course, they could hardly have transplanted it; goodness knows how deep the roots went. Now come over to this side, dear. They couldn't take away any more of our view to the west than they've done already, but just look at that roof that's popped up over there. I tell you we have to wait half an hour longer every morning for the sun!"

Quinto would say, "Oh, good Lord, my dear, you don't say!" and things of that sort, mere grunts and chuckles. He couldn't manage anything more. Sometimes he said, "What can one do though?" and sometimes too he felt a positive satisfaction at a particular piece of damage that was quite beyond repair, some residue of a boyish desire to *épater* stirring in him, or perhaps it was the shrugging assumption of wisdom on the part of the man who knows there's no use fighting against History. All the same, Quinto was offended by the spectacle of this landscape, *his* landscape, being overwhelmed by cement before he had ever really possessed it. Basically, though, he was historically minded, anti-nostalgia. He'd seen a bit of the world: hell, what did he care? He was quite prepared to create far more havoc himself, and in the field of his own life. He almost hoped that, as they stood there on the terrace, his mother would minister to these perverse inclinations, and he found himself trying to catch in the resigned denunciations that she accumulated from one visit to the next the note of some feeling more violent than regret for a treasured landscape that was dying. But the reasonable tone of her complaints kept clear of that acrimonious slope that waits for all complaints too long repeated and leads, in its lower reaches, to mania. The disease is revealed by little tricks of speech, the habit of calling the builders "they," for example, as though they were in league to destroy one; it shows in expressions like "Just look what they've done to us now!" of things that damage a great many other people besides oneself. But no, his mother's serene melancholy provided no foothold for that contradictory demon of his, and the longing to stop being merely passive and to take the offensive grew all the sharper in him. The thing stared him in the face. The district, *his* district, that amputated part of himself, had taken on a new life, abnormal and graceless perhaps, but *for that very reason* (such are the contradictions that operate in minds brought up on literature) it was more alive than ever before. And he was excluded. Bound to the place by no more than a thread of nostalgia and by the devaluation of a semiurban area with no further claim to a view, he was only hurt by what was happening.

These reflections had prompted the remark "If everybody's building, why don't we build too?" He had thrown this out one day in conversation with Ampelio. The Signora had overheard it, and putting her hands to her head, had cried, "Oh, no, my poor garden!" His remark and her response had set in train an already lengthy series of discussions, calculations, inquiries, negotiations. With the result that Quinto was now coming home to try his hand at real estate.

[2]

But as he thought the matter over by himself in the train, his mother's words came back to him and he felt a sense of discomfort, even remorse. She was lamenting the loss of a part of herself, something she was losing that she knew she would not get back again. It was the bitterness older people feel when every general injury that touches them in some way seems a blow against their own individual life, which has no longer any means of redress; because when any one of life's good things is taken away, it is life itself that is being taken. Quinto recognized in the resentful way he had reacted the cruelty of the *coûte que coûte* school of optimism, the refusal of the young to admit any sort of defeat since they believe that life will give back at least as much as it took away, so that if today it destroys some dear spot, the tone of a particular scene, something charming and beautiful but hardly to be defended, or remembered, on the grounds of its "artistic" value—well, tomorrow it will undoubtedly give you something else in exchange, something that will be destroyed in its turn but that can be enjoyed meanwhile. And yet he felt how mistaken the cruelty of youth is, how wasteful, and how much it bodes the first unseasonable taste of age; and at the same time how necessary it is! He understood it all, God help him! He even understood that basically his mother was perfectly right. Without anything of this sort in mind, she was quite understandably upset. She simply told him, each time he came home, about the way everyone was adding to their houses.

The result was that Quinto hadn't dared tell her what he had in mind. It was this project of his that was now bringing him home. It was all his own idea; he hadn't even discussed it with Ampelio, and indeed only very recently had it come to figure in his mind no longer as a possibility, something that might or might not be done, but as an urgent decision. The only thing that had been agreed—with his mother's resigned consent—was to sell a part of the garden. They had reached the point where they had to sell something.

It was the period when taxation was pressing hard. Two particularly savage taxes had burst at almost the same time, after his father's death. (Signor Anfossi, grumbling and almost too scrupulous, had always looked after these things.) One was the estate surtax, a graceless, vindictive measure passed during the immediate postwar period, which bore particularly hard on the middle class. It had been delayed by the laborious procedures of bureaucracy only to explode now, just when one least expected it. The other was the inheritance tax; it looked reasonable enough from the outside, but once you found yourself face to face with it, you couldn't believe it was true.

Quinto was prey to a variety of emotions. He was worried by the fact that he couldn't raise even a tenth of the money needed to pay the two taxes. And stirring inside him was an ancestral hatred of the tax collector inherited from generations of frugal Ligurian farmers who disapproved of government as such, combined with the irrepressible fury of the decent citi-

zen at being singled out for fiscal massacre—"while the rich,
as everyone knows, get away scot free." Added to this was the
suspicion that somewhere in those maddening tangles of figures was an obvious trap, clearly visible to everyone except
himself. All these sentiments, which the tax collector's pallid
communication arouses in even the most innocent breast, were
crossed by the feeling that he was an incompetent landowner,
unable to make the best use of his property, the kind of person
who, in a period when capital was in continual, speculative
use, a period of swindling and paper credit, sits back with his
hands in his pockets and lets the value of his property de-
crease. It came to him that this unreasonable malice on the
part of the nation against a family without means was the
beautifully logical expression of what in official language is
known as "the legislator's intent": the intent to strike at unproductive capital. And as for the man without capital, or
without the will to exploit it, why, God help him.

Whenever one made inquiries at the tax office or the bank
or at one's lawyer's, the answer was always the same: Sell.
Everyone is selling now—they've got to, to pay their taxes.
("Everyone" obviously meant "everyone like you," that is,
property owners whose property consisted of a few unproductive olive trees or some houses with fixed rents.) Quinto's
thoughts had at once turned to the piece of land known jocu-
larly at home as "the flowerpottery."

The flowerpottery, which had formerly served for raising
vegetables, was a small plot of land at the bottom of the garden. On it stood a shed, formerly a chicken coop, now full of
flowerpots, tools, potting soil, and insecticide. Quinto regarded
it as a marginal addition to the property; he was bound to it
by no childhood memories, since everything he remembered
about it had gone: the coop where he used to watch the lazy-
stepping hens, lettuce seedlings fretted by snails, the tomatoes
craning up their slender sticks, the zucchini snaking along under cover of their leaves, which spread out over the ground.
In the middle, queening it over the rest of the kitchen garden,
there used to be two succulent plum trees, which, after oozing
gum and darkening with ants through a prolonged senescence,

finally dried up and died. The need for a kitchen garden had gradually lessened, what with the children away at school and then at work, the older generation dropping away one by one, and finally Signor Anfossi, tireless thunderer to the last—and when *he* went, the house really seemed empty. So Signora Anfossi had moved in with her flowers and turned it into a kind of clearinghouse, a nursery, using the ex-hen house for storing flowerpots. The soil had proved to be moist and exposed to the sun, hence particularly suited to certain rare plants, which, having been granted temporary accommodation there, proceeded to make themselves at home. The spot had acquired a mixed air, devoted at once to horticulture, science, and elegance. It was there rather than among the gravel paths and flower beds of the garden proper that Signora Anfossi liked to pass her time.

"We'll sell it," Quinto had said. "It's a good building site."

"Oh, is it?" his mother had replied. "And where, pray, am I going to move my calceolaria? There isn't another place in the garden. And what about the pittosporums, which are *so* high already? Not to mention the espalier of plumbago, which will be ruined." She paused as though an unexpected fear had struck her. "And what happens if once we've sold the land, they decide to *build* there?" As she spoke, there rose up before her eyes the gray cement wall crashing down onto the green spaces of her garden and transforming it into a bleak back yard.

"Of course they'll build there." Quinto felt irritated. "That's why we're going to sell it. Why would anyone want to buy the land if they couldn't build on it?"

But in fact it wasn't easy to find a purchaser. The builders were looking for new sites near the sea, with a view. The district was already overbuilt, and it was scarcely to be expected that people from Milan or Biella who were looking for a neat little apartment would shut themselves up in a hole like that! Moreover, the market was showing signs of saturation and a slight downward curve in the demand for houses was expected. Two or three firms that had gone ahead a bit too fast found themselves neck deep in unpaid debts and went bankrupt. The price originally fixed for the site had to be lowered. Months went by, a year, and still no buyer appeared. The bank was no longer willing to extend further credit required by the unpaid taxes, and threatened to foreclose. Then Caisotti showed up.

[3]

Caisotti came with the man from the Superga agency. Neither Quinto nor Ampelio were at home, so Signora Anfossi had to show them around the site. "He's quite uncouth," she told Quinto afterward. "He can scarcely speak Italian. But that chatterbox from the agency was there and he talked enough for two."

While Caisotti was busy measuring the borders of the site, the sleeve of his jacket caught on a wild-rose bush. "I don't want you to think I start by taking away what doesn't belong to me," he said, laughing, as she patiently freed his coat from the thorns.

"That would be too bad, wouldn't it?" she said. Then she noticed that there was blood on his face. "Oh, dear, you've scratched yourself."

Caisotti shrugged, and putting his finger in his mouth, rubbed his cheek with spit. There were traces of blood at the corners of his mouth. "Come up to the house and let me put something on it," the Signora said. Gradually the note of severity she had given to the interview, the figure below which she could in no circumstance go ("Anyway I shall have to speak to my sons. I'll let you know definitely one way or the other"), the strict clauses about the maximum height of the building, the number of windows, and so on—all this began to give way before Caisotti's easygoing way of putting things on a conciliatory basis, of making everything a matter of more-or-less, and what's-the-rush?

Meanwhile the fellow from the agency talked ceaselessly. He was a big man in a white suit; he came from Tuscany. "As I was saying, Signora, it's a real pleasure to put through a deal with a friend like Caisotti. Signor Caisotti—believe me, I've

known him for years—is a person one can always do business
with. He'll meet your terms, you'll see, Signora. You'll find
yourself thoroughly satisfied, I promise. . . ."

I'd be more satisfied still, she said to herself, returning to
her constant preoccupation, if we didn't have to sell. But what
else was there to do?

Caisotti was a countryman who had gone into the building
business after the war. He always had three or four jobs under
way; he would buy some land, put up as large a building as
the local regulations permitted, and stuff it with as many tiny
apartments as it would hold. He would sell the apartments
while the building was still under construction and then, with
a tidy profit to show, at once buy some more land and repeat
the process. Quinto turned up promptly in response to his
mother's letter, in order to see the deal through. Ampelio sent
a telegram saying that he was busy with certain experiments
which made it impossible for him to come, but urged that they
should not go below a certain figure. Caisotti didn't try to go
below this figure, and Quinto found him strangely easy to deal
with. He commented on this afterward to his mother.

"Yes, but what an untrustworthy face the man has! And
those tiny little eyes!"

"Of course he's untrustworthy," Quinto said. "So what?
Why should he look honest? An honest face on him—that
would really be dishonest!" He broke off, realizing that he was
speaking more warmly than he had intended, as though
Caisotti's appearance was what principally mattered.

"Well, I wouldn't trust him," she said.

"Of course not," Quinto agreed, "neither would I. And he
doesn't trust us. Didn't you notice the way he hesitated at
everything we said and how slow he was in replying?" He
liked this relation of spontaneous, mutual distrust between
Caisotti and themselves and he was sorry that his mother
didn't appreciate it too. This was the proper relation between
people who look after their own interests, between men of the
world.

Quinto was at home when Caisotti paid a second visit to
conclude the negotiations. He came into the room as though he

were in church, his lips curled back. He was wearing a khaki cap and took his time about removing it. He was a man of about forty-five, fairly short but solidly built and broad-shouldered. He had on an American-style checked shirt, which followed the curve of his belly. He spoke slowly, with that plaintive, questioning whine peculiar to the Ligurian hill country.

"As I said to the Signora, sir, if you'll take a step to meet me, I'll take one to meet you. You know my offer."

"Your figure's too low," Quinto said, though he had already decided to accept it.

The man's big, fleshy face seemed made of a stuff too formless to retain its lineaments or expressions; they at once tended to subside as though engulfed not so much by the deep folds at the corners of his eyes and mouth, but by the sandy, porous texture of his whole face. He was snub-nosed and there was an unusual distance between his nostrils and his upper lip, which made him look either stupid or brutal, depending on whether his mouth was open or shut. His lips were thick and fleshy in the middle, but they disappeared altogether at the corners, as though his mouth ended in two deep slits in either cheek. This gave him rather the look of a shark, a suggestion heightened by the slightly receding chin above the broad throat. But the oddest thing was the way his eyebrows moved. When Quinto said dryly, "Your figure's too low," it seemed as though Caisotti were trying to draw his scanty eyebrows together in the middle of his forehead, but all he succeeded in doing was to raise the skin above the bridge of his nose by a fraction of an inch. The skin corrugated tentatively until it resembled a navel, and this upward thrust communicated its motion to the brief canine brows, which instead of drooping did their best to stand on end, trembling with the effort to keep stiff. The brows in their turn affected the eyelids, which curled up into a fringe of tiny, quivering folds as though they were trying to make up for the missing brows. Caisotti sat there with his eyes half closed, looking like a whipped dog, and said plaintively, "All right, then, you tell me what I ought to do. I'll show you the estimates, I'll show you what figure I can hope to get for the sort of building one can put up there, with no view and no sun. I'll show you everything and you can tell me if I'm going to make a profit or if I'm going to be out of pocket. I'll put myself in your hands entirely."

Caisotti's pose of docile victim had already made Quinto feel uneasy. "All the same," he said, in the effort to be conciliating, "it's a good central position, you know."

"Yes, central is central," Caisotti agreed, and Quinto was glad that they had found some common ground. He was relieved to see the fold on Caisotti's forehead smoothing out and the eyebrows being hauled down from their unnatural elevation. But Caisotti carried on in the same tone of voice. "Of course, it won't be a particularly fine building," he said, giving what Signora Anfossi called one of his horrid laughs. "You realize I can only have it facing this way." He gestured with his thick, short arms. "It won't be anything very fine, but you say it's central and I agree with you."

The phrase about the building "not being particularly fine" had revived the Signora's anxieties. "We'd want to see your plans first," she said. "After all, we'll have to look at the place every day of our lives."

Quinto's expression during this exchange was a blend of fatalism and arrogance, the expression of a man who knows that the last thing to be hoped of the building was beauty and that, at best, it might achieve a mean anonymity indistinguishable from the anonymous structures all around. This at least would serve to keep it quite separate from the villa.

"But of course," Caisotti said accommodatingly, "of course you'll see the plans. It'll be a four-story house like every other four-story house—that's the maximum height the building code allows. I have to draw up the plans and show them to the engineers in City Hall for approval, and once they're passed, I'll show them to you so that you can tell me what you think." The submissive voice was taking on a threatening edge. "I'll bring everything up here and you can tell me what to do. . . . I'll even let you see what all this is going to cost me and what profit I can make. You're educated people, you understand these things better than I do. . . ."

"It's not a question of being educated," Quinto said, suddenly irritated, as always, by any reminder of his status as an intellectual. "You know perfectly well how much you can offer just as we know what's the least we're prepared to take."

"If you're already thinking of the least you're prepared to take," Caisotti said with a laugh, "what are we talking about?" As he spoke, he shook his head backward and forward, and Quinto noticed the thick, bull-like nape, which seemed to be subjected to a continual strain. The corners of his mouth went up and he was a shark, or bull perhaps, a bull snorting through its nostrils. His grimace might have been meant for a snigger or else an expression of anger. And at the same time he was also a poor wretch who says to himself: What's the use? They're just taking me for a ride, saying one thing and meaning another. I'm bound to fall into the trap.

Quinto felt that after his remark about "the least we're prepared to take," he ought not to say anything more, so he concluded simply, "Anyway, we'll reach some agreement . . ." slipping back into the vague formulas in which Caisotti liked to deal.

But Caisotti wasn't satisfied with this either. "Oh, yes, we'll reach an agreement," he said with the sorry little laugh of the man who knows he is being taken advantage of. "You mean you'll tell me what I've got to do, and we'll go on like that, putting things off from one day to the next and if I don't get my work done in the summer, I'd like to know when I can get it done. I can do precious little building once the wet weather comes."

His eyes were blank, his mouth gave nothing away; all his expression was in his cheeks; they alone were unguarded. The left cheek, just above the gravelly expanse where he shaved, still showed the spot where the rosebush had scratched him. It gave a suggestion of fragile innocence to the leathery face, a suggestion intensified by the way his hair was cropped close on his nape, by his plaintive tone of voice and the bewildered way he looked at people. Quinto again found himself wanting to be nice to the man, to protect him, but this image of Caisotti as a little boy did not march with the other image, that of Caisotti as shark, outsize crustacean, crab, which was how he

appeared as he sat there with his thick hands spread out loose-
ly on the arms of the chair. Quinto went ahead with the negotiations in this fashion, indulging now the one image, now the
other. But one thing was becoming clearer all the time: he
positively *liked* the man!

[4]

"We've found a buyer."

"About time."

Quinto had gone to school with Canal, his attorney. A small
man, he sat buried in the big armchair behind the desk, his
head sunk into his shoulders. Spasms of fatigue flickered across
his expressive face.

"He's a contractor," Quinto said. "I came to ask if you knew
anything about him—whether he's honest, solvent, that sort of
thing."

For years Quinto and Canal had not managed to sustain a
conversation and on the rare occasions when they met in the
street, they found nothing to say to each other. Their manner
of life, professions, politics were all different, if not antagonis-
tic. But now they had something concrete to discuss. Quinto
was delighted.

"What's his name?" Canal asked.

"Caisotti."

"Caisotti!" Canal sat up sharply, bringing his hands down
on the table. His air of fatigue was gone. "You've picked a
choice specimen."

It was not a promising start. But although he had already
decided to stand up for the man, Quinto made an initial con-
cession to his mother's way of thinking. "Of course you've only
got to look at his face to see the sort of fellow he is. All the
same . . ."

"It's not his face. It's that every time he makes a deal, every
time he puts up a building, there's trouble. I've taken action
against him in several cases. He's the biggest swindler in
town."

Quinto was delighted to hear that Caisotti was such a

scoundrel. The charm of business, it was just coming to him, was precisely that it brought one into contact with people of all sorts. It meant dealing with crooks and knowing that they were crooks, making sure that they didn't cheat you, and indeed, if the opportunity occurred, cheating them. What counted was the "economic moment"; nothing else mattered. All the same, he felt alarmed at the possibility that Canal's information might be so unfavorable that he would have to abandon the project.

"But in an affair like this," he said, "how can he cheat us? If he pays for the land, it's his, if he doesn't, that's that. Has he got any money?"

"Everything has gone well for him so far," Canal replied. "He came down from the hills in patched pants—he could hardly read or write—and now he's setting up construction jobs all over the place. He's making a lot of money. City Hall is eating out of his hand."

The rancor in Canal's voice was familiar to Quinto. He represented the old middle class, conservative, honest, economical, undemanding, without much go or imagination, rather inclined to be stingy. For the last half century this class had witnessed changes that it had been unable to resist and had seen a new, traditionless class take the field. On every occasion it had had to give way, affecting an air of indifference but with teeth clenched. But wasn't Quinto moved by the same sense of resentment? The difference was that he reacted by going to the other extreme and embracing everything new, everything that did violence to his feelings. At this very moment, as he was coming up against a new race of raw, unscrupulous contractors, he felt something like a scientist's interest in an important new sociological phenomenon, and at the same time a positive aesthetic satisfaction. The squalid cement invasion bore the shapeless, snub-nosed features of the new man, Caisotti.

"How much is he offering?" the lawyer asked.

Quinto described the initial negotiations. He had got to his feet and was standing by the window. Canal's office was in a smart street, but it faced the rear of the building. The roofs and terraces and walls belonged to the windy, sunlit city as it had been in the nineteenth century; but there too the scaffolding was sprouting, the newly painted walls, the flat roofs with the elevator shed on top.

"Given the state of the market, it's a good price," Canal said grudgingly, gnawing at his lower lip. "In cash?"

"Part cash down, part in installments."

"He's made his payments all right so far, I believe. But he's just put up a house; he ought to pay cash."

"That was what I wanted to find out. Now that I know where I am, we can close with him."

"Of course, if it were a question of having him do some work for you or of buying from him, I should have urged you not to go ahead. But in a case like this, I can't see that it matters whether you sell to him or to someone else. . . . So long as he pays up. You'll need to take a good look at the contract, though, the maximum height of the building, number of windows, that sort of thing."

Canal went to the door with him. "Are you staying here awhile or are you off again?"

Quinto shrugged. "Who knows? Off again, I expect."

"How are things with you, your work . . . ?" Canal took care to leave his questions quite general. Quinto was always moving from one job to another, and he was afraid of appearing out of touch.

Quinto's reply was equally vague. "I've got a new thing in hand now, with some friends. It's too early yet to . . ."

"How about politics?"

Here again it was difficult to answer. They were on different sides of the fence and since they respected each other's position, they didn't want to get involved in an argument. But this time Quinto was a little more definite. "I've dropped politics nowadays."

"Yes, that's what I heard. Someone . . ."

"What's the political situation here?" Quinto asked.

Canal was a Social Democrat and served on the City Council. "Oh, you know, the usual sort of thing."

"You're well? Your wife?"

"Yes, thanks, we're all fine. What about you? Still a bachelor, eh. No projects in that line? Ah, well. Look, you get in touch with me again when you've had a word with Bardissone."

[5]

Quinto emerged from this exchange of pleasantries with his nerves on edge. He had to traverse a stretch of the main street that he normally avoided on account of its crowded confusion. When he came home, he liked to walk in the countrified outskirts of the town or along the sea front, where he could still recapture the pulsations of the past, the marginal deposits which memory had preserved. But today he felt no nostalgia for a passing order. Seen from these sidewalks, the aspect which the city offered was the same as ever, appallingly unchanged, and what new elements there were—faces, young people, stores—didn't count; his adolescence felt disagreeably close. Why in the world had he come back? All he wanted at the moment was to see the thing through quickly and be off. The idea of staying there filled him with disgust.

He noticed a man on a bicycle propped against the curb; his face seemed familiar. A stringy old fellow in a sweater, his sunburned arms resting on the handlebars. He was a carpenter, Quinto now remembered, a Party member who must have been on the committee in the days when he served on it himself.

He was talking to someone. Quinto walked by, supposing that the old man hadn't recognized him, but he didn't look away because he did not want to give the impression that he was cutting him. But the carpenter had seen him, for he said to the other man, "Why, it's Anfossi!" waving to him in a friendly way. Quinto waved back with equal friendliness, but didn't stop. The carpenter, however, put out his hand and said, "Good to see you, Anfossi. So you've come home for a while, eh?"

They shook hands. Quinto had always liked the old man's somewhat owl-like face, with those tortoise-rimmed glasses and the crew-cut white hair; he liked his voice too, with its broad northern vowels, and his strong, soft handshake. All the same, on this occasion he would have been happy to dislike him; a response to the old man's warm humanity did not fit in with his present frame of mind, which was leading him to feel well-disposed toward Caisotti. And anyway he didn't want to stop. He wanted to stop even less when the carpenter (Quinto was irritated at not being able to remember his name since he felt that he could only reply in the right tone of voice if he called him by his first name) began saying, "We've been following your career, you know, all those articles in the national press. The national press!" he repeated for the benefit of the other man.

Quinto shrugged and tried to explain that he was no longer writing articles, but the carpenter wouldn't listen. "No, no, it was fine work! One could see you meant what you said."

He pointed to the other man, whom Quinto didn't recognize in the least, and said, "You remember him, don't you?"

"Of course," Quinto said. "Good to see you again."

"But it's Comrade Martini, don't you remember?" the old man insisted, as though Quinto had confessed to not recognizing him. "Comrade Martini of the Santo Stefano Section."

"You held a meeting at Party Headquarters in Forty-six to explain the Amnesty to us," Martini said.

"Yes, yes, I remember," said Quinto, though he remembered no such thing.

"Those were the times, though!" said the man called Martini. "Things looked hopeful then, eh, Masera?"

Quinto was much relieved to find that he remembered the carpenter was called Masera, and as though the end of his search for the man's name meant the end of his sense of guilt, he managed at last to look at him in a friendly way. He now recalled a windy evening when they had bicycled together along a road by the sea, which at the time was partly blocked by potholes. Masera's bike had been as rusty and broken-down as the one he had now. They had been going to a meeting. It was a fine, warm memory.

"Everything looked hopeful then," Masera repeated, but in

the manner of someone who takes a pessimistic line in order to be told by a better-informed comrade that "things still look hopeful now, more so than ever. The struggle is on. . . ." But Quinto said nothing, so that Masera was forced to add himself, "And they still look hopeful now, eh, Anfossi?"

"Ah," said Quinto, stretching out his arms.

"But it's hard here, I'll say it's hard! Men being fired—ah, the dirty bastards! What are the comrades saying where you are?"

"It's hard there too," Quinto said.

"Times are hard everywhere!" Masera laughed, as though this solidarity in hard times made things a bit better.

"Tell him . . ." Martini whispered something to Masera, of which Quinto managed to catch only the word "lecture."

Masera nodded, smiling understandingly and at the same time doubtfully, as though he had had the same idea himself already but dismissed it as hopeless. "Are you still against public speaking?" he asked, turning to Quinto, "or have you finally turned into an orator? Now that you're here, you see, we were thinking that if you could come to Headquarters and give a talk—well, the comrades would certainly appreciate it."

"No, no, I have to leave almost immediately, and anyway I can't make speeches, you know that, Masera."

"Still the same, eh?" said Masera, laughing and slapping him on the back. "Hasn't changed a bit, has he?" he said to Martini, whom Quinto still didn't remember ever having seen before. "Not a bit," Martini agreed. They were honest, friendly people, but Quinto had no desire to feel himself among friends. Quite the contrary, these were the days of every man for himself, pistol at the ready—the kind of relationship you had with businessmen, contractors, wide-eyed men who knew what was what.

He compared Masera with Caisotti: Masera, trusting, expansive, prepared to find everything in line with his dream; Caisotti, wary, reticent, untrustworthy. No doubt about it though, it was Caisotti who was in touch with his time; he was accepting the conditions of the age, shirking nothing, you might say, whereas poor Masera, with all that stuff about being decent, pure in heart, and so forth, was really an escapist. He wasn't living in the real world at all. Quinto shook off the burden of guilt with which Masera's straightforward social conscience threatened him. You were still doing your duty too by taking part in private enterprise and dealing in land and money; it wasn't an epic sort of duty, maybe, in fact it was rather prosaic, rather bourgeois, but hell, he *was* a bourgeois. How on earth had he ever supposed he was anything else?

Quite reassured now about his bourgeois status, Quinto felt the uneasiness he had experienced with the two workingmen give way to a generalized, almost casual good will. It wasn't altogether insincere: now that he was saying good-bye, he really wanted them to think well of him.

[6]

Nowhere were the reports on Caisotti favorable. As a result, Quinto found himself taking the man's side. He was being victimized, the whole city was out for his blood, all the stuffed shirts were against him, and yet the poor bricklaying peasant, armed only with his shy, uncouth nature, was standing up to them.

The point was that these negative judgments still left Quinto free to go ahead. People disapproved, but they didn't warn him off altogether. He was the sort of person who liked doing things that were moderately controversial but would never court head-on disapproval, and he found himself supplied with approval and disapproval in exactly the proportions that his temperament required.

Moreover, since he still had to fight down a certain personal uneasiness in the first place, he was reassured by the thought that he was in professional contact with his fellow citizens. He felt he had finally returned to the ranks of the traditional middle-class element in the district, united in the defense of its modest interests, which were under attack. And yet, at the same time he realized that every step he was taking was helping the rise of Caisotti and his like, the new shifty, graceless middle class that matched the graceless, amoral age they were living in. Let's face it, Quinto said to himself; you people have lost every round! And with this his hostility shifted from the small society of his home town, from his mother and Canal— and from Masera the carpenter. His opponents were now his friends in the big cities in northern Italy, where he had lived all these years, years spent discussing the shape of the new society, the role of the workers and of the intelligentsia. Caisotti has won, Quinto told himself.

He couldn't wait to give his friends there a demonstration of his new position. He got on the train and next day he was lunching with Bensi and Cerveteri in the usual modest restaurant in Turin.

They were talking about starting a review to be called *The New Hegel*. The waitress was trying to get their order; it was her third attempt, but they were too deep in conversation to pay any attention.

Bensi looked at the menu and read the list of dishes, but apparently nothing took his fancy.

"Why not call it *The Hegelian Left?*" he said.

"In that case, why not *The Young Marx?* More punch."

"Are you going to order?" The waitress was still at it.

"I propose *The New Rhine Gazette.*"

"What about getting hold of the actual heading of the *Neue Rheinische Zeitung* and using the same characters?" Quinto suggested. His remarks were never quite to the point, but they had a casual, professional air about them. He still hadn't found an occasion to reveal his disagreement with the group, though this suggestion was intended to open the way.

"All right, the title is *Encyclopedia,*" Bensi said in a different tone of voice, as though up till then they had been joking, and Quinto's proposal was therefore quite irrelevant. "Or maybe that can be the subtitle. The point is to make it clear from the title down that what we are aiming at is a general phenomenology subsuming every kind of conscious activity within a single body of discourse."

This brought Bensi and Cerveteri into conflict, and Quinto was uncertain whose side to take. If everything was to be subsumed within a single body of discourse, should the paper only print what was already included within that body, or should it also print stuff that was still outside? Cerveteri wanted to include the stuff that was still outside. "I'd like a column called 'A Politician Dreams,'" he said. "We'll invite leaders from all political parties and ask them to tell us what they dream. Anyone who refuses has obviously got something to hide."

Bensi was overcome by one of his paroxysms of maniacal laughter. This involved bringing his face down to the level of the tablecloth and covering his eyes with one hand, as though to indicate his pained amusement at the sight of a friend losing himself in a maze from which only he, Bensi, knew the way out. "We go from ideology to dreams," he managed to say, "not from dreams to ideology." And then, as though succumbing to a malign temptation, he added, "All your dreams are pronged on the ideological spike like moths on a pin."

Cerveteri looked baffled. "Moths?" he said. "Why *moths?*"

Bensi was a philosopher, Cerveteri a poet. Poet Cerveteri was a premature gray; his long, spectacled face provided a battleground on which melancholy Semitic features fought a well-matched engagement with more expressive Florentine traits, whether erudite or plebeian it was difficult to determine. The outcome was a face including both aggression and concentration, but which somehow remained deeply inexpressive, like a cyclist, say, or like someone trying to concentrate on one point in the center of an indefinite series of points. "Why did you say moths?" he repeated. "I dreamed of a moth last night. I was sitting here, in this very restaurant, and they brought me a huge moth, on a plate." And he gestured in the manner of one raising the wing of a huge moth.

"Christ!" said the waitress, who had come to see if they wanted dessert.

Bensi laughed with exaggerated bitterness, the laughter of a man tired of adversaries who give themselves up unarmed. "Dream symbolism is always a deification," he remarked. "That's what Freud failed to understand."

Quinto greatly admired the incessant intellectual activity of both men. (His own mind inclined rather to relapse into a state of sleepy indifference.) And he was impressed by their breadth of cultural reference. Uncertain which part to take in the argument, the terms of which he only vaguely understood, he decided as usual to back the side most opposed to his natural inclinations, namely Bensi's rigidly mechanistic philosophy, and to resist the appeal of Cerveteri's fluid play of sensation. He turned ironically to Bensi and said, sneering at the poet, "Why not go the whole hog and call it *The New Freud?*"

The philosopher was still in the grips of the convulsion of laughter provoked by Cerveteri and he brushed off Quinto's joke like an irrelevant fly. It appealed to the poet, however, who took it up enthusiastically. "That's it," he cried. "Let's call it *Eros and Thanatos!*"

Bensi brought his hands together and rubbed them till they creaked, while his face contracted in a clenched laugh that made him turn purple. "Do you think you're going to checkmate history with those two? The dialectical process pops out between them like a cuckoo from a clock."

Bensi had a round, cherubic face, like the face of those people from the hills who never really grow up. His forehead, under the babyish wave of curly hair, was so convex that it seemed about to explode. It was marked with little bumps and scratches, as though the pressure of thought made it butt into things. Bensi led with his forehead, holding it forward like a millstone, always grinding, grinding, or like a wheel, setting off a complicated system of gears, driven by an inadequately synchronized central force that made it waste itself in countless secondary motions, as for example the incessant quivering of his lips. During the discussion Quinto found himself looking now at Bensi's eyes, now at Cerveteri's. They both squinted, but the philosopher's squint was extroverted; his eye seemed to fly in pursuit of ideas just on the point of vanishing from the field of human vision into some oblique, unrecognizable perspective. The poet's was an inner squint. The pupils of his close-set, restless eyes seemed to strive to register the effect produced by external sensations in some secret, interior zone of consciousness.

"Let's make an anthology of obituary notices," Cerveteri suggested. "We might make it a regular feature. Better still, what about a whole number filled with nothing but obituary notices?" And he ran his finger down the black-barred column of the obituary page in the folded paper he was holding.

Bensi shrugged. "We're just about to house the conscience of mankind in an electronic brain."

Cerveteri's answer was a lengthy quotation in Latin.

"Saint Augustine?"

"Lactantius."

Quinto's attention wandered and he found himself trying to overhear what people were saying at the nearby tables. There was a family to the right, or perhaps they were two different families, country people who had come in to town to meet. A woman was talking about the damage done by rain to the alfalfa fields. She obviously owned land. She was not young, but she was still of marriageable age, and as she spoke the men nodded agreement, their faces blurred with wine and food. They were farming people, perhaps, from different regions, meeting to settle the terms of a marriage. The woman was showing, in the presence of the man's family, that she was a mature, competent person, as though to outdo the other women there by this evidence that she was much more than a mere housewife.

Quinto felt sharply envious of everything that these people represented: the sense of interests at stake, the attachment to things, concrete and in no way ignoble passions, the desire to better oneself in more than a material sense, and in addition there was something placid and earthy and solid about them. There was a time, Quinto reflected, when you could live the life of the mind only if you owned land. But in detaching itself from its economic basis, culture had paid dearly. It depended on privilege in those days, certainly, yet it was still firmly rooted. Nowadays the intellectual belonged neither to the bourgeoisie nor to the proletariat. For that matter, even Masera could do nothing better than ask him to give a lecture.

At another table a waitress was flirting with a couple of men in bow ties who couldn't keep their hands at home. In between the jokes addressed to the girl, Quinto could hear words like "Italian Gas," "General Electric," and stock-market quotations. A pair of stock-market agents, obviously, smooth operators. At any other time he would have disliked them intensely, but in his present mood he found that they embodied his ideals: expedience, cunning, quick functional intelligence. A man who isn't trying to make money doesn't count, Quinto said to himself. Why, even the workers have their trade-union struggles. But we intellectuals make a distinction between the larger historical perspectives and our own interests and in the process we have lost the taste of life. We have destroyed ourselves. We don't mean anything.

Cerveteri had gone back to his dream. "A large moth," he was saying. "It had big wings with minute gray, wavy markings, like a black-and-white Kandinsky—no, a Klee, perhaps. I was trying to lift these wings with my fork and they gave out a fine dust, a kind of gray powdery stuff, then disintegrated between my finger and thumb. I tried to lift the fragments to my mouth, but they turned into ashes and spread over everything, covering the plates, sinking into the wineglasses. . . ."

My superiority over these people, Quinto reflected, is that I still have the bourgeois instincts that they have mislaid in the wear and tear of intellectual fashion. I shall stick to these instincts and in so doing save myself, while they'll crumble away. But I've got to start making money. Selling some land to Caisotti isn't enough. I must start building too. I'll use the money I get from him to put up another house next to the one he is building. . . . Quinto concentrated on the possibilities of the site that had not yet been exploited, on the ways of putting it to the best use.

Cerveteri's hands fluttered over the tablecloth, which was littered with crumbs, cigarette ashes, stubs crushed on plates or ashtrays, bits of orange peel tortured into strange shapes by Bensi's nails, match sticks shredded away by Cerveteri's fingers, toothpicks dislocated by Quinto's hands and teeth.

I must get into partnership with Caisotti, he said to himself. We'll speculate in real estate together.

[7]

Quinto had an idea. Adjoining the land they were proposing to sell was a bit of garden with a bed of forget-me-nots in the middle. It was fairly level and about the same size as the flowerpottery. It too offered an excellent site for a small apartment building. But he realized that once Caisotti's building was up, it would lose all value as a site since the law did not allow houses to be constructed right on top of one another. It's clear, Quinto said to himself, that whichever site we sell, we're going to reduce the value of the one immediately beside it. So the only thing to do is to go into partnership with Caisotti and build together. Let him have both sites and put up a single large building there; in return we'll take a certain number of apartments, which will remain our property. I must talk this over with Ampelio at once.

Quinto and his brother did not live in the same town. Their rare meetings took place in their mother's house and it was there that they had now arranged to meet to discuss the sale.

"I've got an idea," Quinto said to Ampelio the moment he arrived. On their way from the station they stopped at the fish market and bought half a pound of limpets. When he got home, Ampelio kissed his mother hurriedly and told her about the limpets that he had bought. He had been away for six months. He was a university instructor in chemistry, and though he earned a wretched salary he hardly ever came home, not even during vacations. He had at one time been more tied to his home town than Quinto, but now he seldom showed his face there. He no longer seemed to take any pleasure in his familiar haunts and in the life he used to lead. Nobody in fact knew what his tastes were nowadays, except insofar as they were revealed by small, unexpected gestures—like this business of the limpets, for example—and even then it was hard to tell how far they were sincere.

Quinto began telling him about the negotiations with Caisotti. As he explained, Ampelio went into the kitchen and Quinto followed him, talking. Ampelio undid the paper in which the limpets were wrapped and picked up a knife and then a lemon. He stood by the sideboard, opening cupboards and pulling out drawers with quick, confident gestures as though he had left everything in place the day before. He cut a slice of lemon and sprinkled it on the limpets without taking them out of their paper. He made a gesture indicating that Quinto was to help himself; Quinto rejected the offer vigorously—he couldn't stand shellfish—and went on talking.

Ampelio said nothing, giving no sign of either agreement or disapproval. Several times Quinto broke off under the impression that his brother wasn't listening, but Ampelio would say, "And what then?" and Quinto carried on again as though nothing had happened. Ampelio had always been like this, even when he was a boy. The only difference was that in those days, Quinto, being the older brother, would lose his temper, but in time he had got used to it. Ampelio sat there at the polished kitchen table, still in the overcoat and scarf that he had been wearing even though it was late spring. He had a small black beard and was already balding; his eyes were concealed behind the thick lenses of his glasses. Quinto watched him ease the limpets out of their shells with the point of his knife and with his other hand raise the shells fringed with seaweed to his lips. The soft flesh of the limpets vanished between his lips framed by the dark beard, with a sound of breath being sucked in or else blown out, it was hard to tell which. Then he put the empty shells one on top of the other in a little pile.

Quinto had unrolled a map. Still chewing, Ampelio glanced at it out of the corner of his eye. His mouth, surrounded by beard, was like a sea urchin turned upside down, the mouth moving among the black spines. Quinto had explained the present phase of the negotiations and told Ampelio what he had found out about Caisotti. Now, his finger on the map, he said, "I see it like this. If we build in area A, we preclude the possibility of selling area B or of building on it. This means that if we sell area A to Caisotti for its value as a building site, which I call X, we deprive area B of its value of Y. So what it comes to is that if we sell at X, we lose the chance of a possible X + Y. Or putting it the other way, we now own A + B; if we sell A, we are left with only B — Y."

Quinto had been mulling over this little algebraic demonstration for several days, hoping to impress his scientific brother.

Ampelio got up, went to the sink, drank from the faucet, rinsed his mouth, and spat—one after the other. Then he said, "Obviously we've got to use the flowerpottery as capital to invest in any building we erect on the second site. And since the regulations don't permit two buildings to be put up so close to each other, we must think in terms of a single large structure occupying the two plots, to be built by Caisotti, half for himself, half for us."

This was precisely the plan on which Quinto had been racking his brains as though it were the knottiest problem in the world. And here was Ampelio coming out with it as though it followed naturally from the facts of the situation! Quinto didn't know what to say next. Ampelio sat down and started covering the borders of the map with figures, every now and then asking for additional information, which Quinto was never able to provide quite accurately. What was the maximum height allowed by the building code? How many apartments did Caisotti intend to put in? What was the price of cement? Quinto realized that his brother couldn't know any more about building estimates than he did, yet there he was, rapidly jotting down figures with a confidence that Quinto envied deeply.

"Let's reckon eight apartments, plus a couple of shops on the ground floor," Ampelio said, calculating the annual rents and the time it would take to amortize their capital.

"But what about the money we need right away to pay the taxes?"

"We'll apply for a loan and use the prospective building as security."

"Oh, God!" Quinto screeched in desperation. Ampelio, as always, was composure itself. He didn't laugh, no wrinkle creased his massive brow. For him, everything was in the sphere of the possible.

Signora Anfossi came into the kitchen. "Well, boys, have you figured it all out? Is it all right?"

"Yes, yes. We're going to lose though, either way."

"Oh, that Caisotti, with his nasty dishonest face!"

"It isn't Caisotti's doing, poor man. But we're going to be in the red, all the same."

"Then why not drop the whole thing?" the Signora suggested. "That's it, we'll tell him we've changed our minds and that we're not thinking of selling at present. As for the taxes, we'll have to ask the bank again."

"No, no, Mother, look, we were just saying that what we must do is propose something much more complicated to Caisotti."

"More complicated? Heavens!"

"Yes, yes, something very complicated. In the long run we'll make a handsome profit."

Quinto bent down to talk to her, gesturing in a nervous, combative way, trying at the same time to convince her and to start an argument. Ampelio stood beside him, tall and serious, his dark beard thrust forward. He looked like a judge whose only task is to pronounce sentence.

"Now, Mother, listen. You know the forget-me-not bed. . . ."

[8]

Quinto and Ampelio went out together. They walked rapidly along the familiar streets, talking in a way they hadn't done for ages. It was as though they had never left home, two brothers playing a busy part in the town's economic life, controlling a whole network of interests: brusque, practical people, with both feet on the ground. They were play-acting and they knew it, since they were both very unlike the characters they were assuming at the moment. In the normal way, before the afternoon was over they would have relapsed into skeptical inertia and then gone their separate ways, Ampelio back to his laboratory and Quinto to his intellectual disputes, as though these were the only things in the world that counted. Yet for the time being their present roles seemed feasible. And how fine it would have been, two brothers against the world together! So many things would have been within their grasp, they could have done so much—what exactly, they would have been hard put to it to say. Here they were, for example, on their way to Caisotti to put the proposition to him, to explore the situation, to ask him—well, to ask him something or other. Hell, why make things difficult? At present they were sizing him up. They would decide later what course of action to take.

Caisotti did not have a telephone. He had an office upstairs: CAISOTTI BUILDING COMPANY. They rang the bell and a girl opened the door. It was a small, low room with a typewriter and some blueprints on the table. No, Caisotti wasn't in; he was always out and about, on the job; he was hardly ever in his office.

"When will he be back?" Shrug. "Where can we find him?" "Try at the Caffè Melina, just over there, but it's a bit too early." "We have to see him at once." Shrug. "I suppose you could leave a message with me."

"Well, thanks anyway, Miss Shrug." Ampelio produced this witticism, greatly to the surprise of Quinto, who had never heard his brother employ such a sarcastic, confidential tone in his family circle. He took a look at the girl. Not bad.

Not more than sixteen or so, she had the look of a country girl, with her pink-and-white complexion, her eyes dark under the well-marked brows, and two soft, black braids of hair falling onto her ample breasts.

"You must be the Anfossi brothers," she offered.

Cunning little bitch, Quinto said to himself, false as hell, with her nose in the air and that butter-wouldn't-melt expression.

Ampelio's joke might have seemed designed to pave the way for an improbable exchange of pleasantries with the girl, but he at once resumed his usual dry manner as though he had gone too far. He asked about the building sites where Caisotti might be found, said good-bye and went down the narrow stairs. But at the bottom he produced one more unlikely witticism. "*Ciao, bella!*" he cried.

On his way down, Quinto turned around and saw that the girl had not yet shut the door. She was looking down through her heavy lashes and smiling in a curious way. He had the impression that behind that country-girl face of hers, Caisotti was staring at them in his enigmatic fashion.

"Not bad, the girl, eh?" he said, wanting to talk about her.

"Mmm," Ampelio said, as though avoiding an indelicate topic.

They went to one of the places she had suggested, where Caisotti's firm was putting up a new house, or rather adding new floors to an existing two-story house. It was in one of the main streets and the addition would fill the gap between two large buildings.

They went in. There were mounds of cement all over the place, but no sign of men at work. The staircase was not in yet, so Quinto and Ampelio had to climb up on some sloping planks. "Hey! Anybody about? Caisotti! Is the boss here?" Their voices re-echoed between the bare walls.

On the third floor two workmen were crouching down, banging away at chisels. They had the air of people doing something they know to be useless. The two brothers at once stopped shouting and asked, almost in a whisper, "Isn't Caisotti here?" "No." "Hasn't he come yet?" "We don't know." "Is the foreman here?" "Next floor up." Quinto and Ampelio went up.

On this floor the walls were in place, but the roof and the floor were lacking. The doors opened onto empty space. A kind of wild gaiety came over the pair of them. *Haie!* they whooped at each other, *haie!* as they climbed along the planks of the scaffolding with arms extended, like tightrope walkers.

There was a noise of scraping shoes. A narrow plank spanned the open floor of a room, resting on the doorsteps at each side. And there, outlined against the doorway, as though in hiding, was Caisotti.

They calmed down, feeling rather silly. "Ah, Caisotti, hello there, we were just looking for you." The man's heavy bulk blocked the frame of the doorway on which the narrow plank lay. He stood there with his hands in his pockets, giving no sign of recognition. Quinto went forward a few steps along the plank, then paused as he felt it bend beneath him. He was waiting for Caisotti to do something, at least put a foot on his end of the plank to keep it steady, but no, he said nothing, did nothing. Suspended there in space, Quinto, simply to break the silence, said, "I want you to meet my brother, Ampelio." Caisotti took one hand out of his pocket and bringing it up to the peak of his cap, struck it with the flat of his hand. Quinto turned around toward his brother, slowly, so as not to start the plank wobbling, and noticed that he was responding to Caisotti's gesture with precisely the same gesture. They both looked serious.

"Don't go there; you'll fall," Caisotti said slowly. Then: "If you'll both go down, I'll be with you."

They went to the Caffè Melina and sat at a noisy table on the sidewalk. Caisotti wanted to buy the drinks. "A Punt e Mes?" Ampelio took Punt e Mes. Quinto, who suffered from stomach trouble, ordered a *rabarbaro*, though secretly convinced that *rabarbaro* was bad for him too. Ampelio offered Caisotti a cigarette. Quinto didn't smoke. The two men were perfectly at ease with each other and Quinto felt rather jealous.

Caisotti was repeating to Ampelio everything he had said to Signora Anfossi and Quinto, interjecting remarks like "As I had the pleasure of saying to your mother," or "You're an engineer, sir; I don't have to explain this to you." Ampelio had his degree in chemistry, but he raised no objection. He listened in silence, the cigarette dangling from his black beard, eyes half shut behind the thick lenses. He asked a question now and then, but casually, as one professional to another, and not, or so it seemed, with anything of Quinto's nagging compulsion to show himself well informed and on his guard.

Indeed, when Quinto raised an objection, Caisotti turned to Ampelio with that plaintive air of his, as though he were asking for protection. "Of course you understand that your brother's point—"

"No, no, Caisotti!" Quinto broke in, to cover himself. Ampelio's only response was a broad gesture, brushing the surface of the table as though to clear away side issues and get back to the heart of the matter.

Caisotti would obviously have liked to go on playing the victim, but his heart was no longer in it. Instead he remarked, still to Ampelio, "You're the elder brother, sir, and you understand—"

"No, look here, I'm the elder brother," Quinto interrupted, feeling slightly embarrassed. Caisotti nonetheless continued to treat Ampelio with markedly greater respect.

"And if you tell me that on your side you want a space between the floors, fine, I'll see you have your space."

"It's you who need the space," Ampelio said, "to avoid dampness in your ground floor."

"I need the space, certainly I need it, but tell me this, please: won't I sell the ground floor just as well without the space, whereas if you should decide one day to build on the site next to me, you'd find the space very handy."

Quinto looked at Ampelio. Slowly he blew a cloud of smoke. He waited until the smoke had drifted away, then said, "And what if we were to build together?"

There was a tiny movement of Caisotti's fingers as he knocked the ash off his cigarette; his eyes were moist, like someone looking into the distance to banish some remote excitement, but at the same time they came to a sharp point and the wrinkles thickened around his lids.

"I'd say we could get along very nicely."

[9]

Ampelio considered that they ought not to let themselves be influenced by unfavorable reports on Caisotti. "You know how it is here. All you ever hear about people is gossip. Someone new makes his mark and gets ahead, and at once the whole pack is tearing him to bits."

Canal came near to doing just that. "Go into partnership with Caisotti? You two, your mother? With that crooked, loose-living peasant! The way he drags that girl around with him. . . ."

"We saw the girl," Quinto said, instantly distracted by a facile curiosity. "What about her? Who is she? She looks as though she came from the country." He glanced at Ampelio as though asking his support. I told you what they're like, Ampelio's expression seemed to say.

"She does," Canal said. "He brought her with him from the village where he used to live—he's got a wife and children up there."

"You mean . . . ?"

"I don't mean anything, I don't know anything about them and I don't want to. There's something dirty about the whole setup."

Quinto described his impression, on first seeing the girl, that there was some resemblance between her and Caisotti, all the more disturbing because it wasn't a physical or external resemblance.

"I wouldn't doubt it," Canal said.

"How do you mean? The idea of him and that girl . . . she's barely sixteen . . . with a man who might be her father. . . ."

"Oh, he's got lots of children. He left home because he'd filled the whole valley with his bastards."

"You think she's his illegitimate daughter?" Quinto said, but he felt that the moment had come to react against this gossipy curiosity and show himself in his true colors, a man of the world with no provincial prejudices. "And what if she is, what's the harm? All right, so he's got an illegitimate daughter, and instead of abandoning her he finds her a job and keeps her with him. Is that any reason to stick your knife in him?"

"Oh, I know nothing about it, I assure you."

"And if she were his mistress and not his daughter, what would be the harm in that? He likes girls, they get on well together. . . . Why do you people always have to split hairs?"

"It doesn't matter to me what she is. She may be his daughter or his girl friend—or both at the same time, for all I care!"

"How about getting back to the contract?" Ampelio suggested.

It was a bright, cool afternoon, the kind of weather that makes you feel ready for anything. After their meeting with Caisotti, the two brothers had gone at once to see Canal, their lawyer. They had had to wait since Canal was busy with clients, but this in no way diminished their excitement and they had sat in the waiting room putting the finishing touches to their project. They spoke in broken snatches to prevent anyone understanding what they were talking about. From Canal's office came the sounds of a noisy argument in dialect; he had taken over an old-fashioned clientele of country people, small proprietors doggedly pursuing trivial, interminable suits concerning wills or disputed boundaries. For the first time Quinto did not feel guilty at the distance between himself and this ancestral world; he belonged now to another world from which he could look back on the old one with a superior irony. He was one of the new men, who had thrown off the old-fashioned prejudices, who were used to handling money.

Canal, however, had no sooner heard their schemes than he sat up in his chair in alarm. "But you're crazy! You and Caisotti? Why, he'll spit you like a pair of thrushes!"

Quinto smiled. "Steady, now. Let's wait and see who's going to be the thrush, shall we? The deal is entirely in our favor."

"And Caisotti agrees? You don't say!"

Quinto kept on smiling. "Caisotti agrees. We've just seen him about it."

"But you're mad. Go into business with Caisotti! You and your mother!" And so it went on.

"Listen," Quinto said. In explaining the affair to Canal he had adopted an air of indulgent patience, like a grown-up son explaining something to his father, who thinks he is still a child. Resentment at not being taken seriously is never, on such occasions, far below the surface.

Quinto explained that Caisotti was prepared to buy the two sites, paying partly in cash (which would allow them to settle their back taxes) and partly in apartments (which would mean turning an unproductive asset into a profitable source of income, at no cost to themselves). Quinto appeared to be more and more amused by Canal's objections, and even to go out of his way to provoke him. Every new angle that came up made the game more difficult and exciting, and served to put their skill to the test. Quinto had great confidence in Canal and was delighted to give him so complicated a case and to see how skillfully he handled it. Ampelio, on the other hand, was irritated by the way the lawyer kept raising difficulties; it struck him as mere defeatism. It was not that he trusted Caisotti or that he thought their project foolproof, but rather that Canal's scruples went against the brisk, almost aggressive spirit with which he had thrown himself into the affair. He was convinced that it was one of those things that you either handled resolutely, in the way people do who set a dozen such deals going every day and then let them take their own course; or else you got bogged down in ifs and buts, and then the whole thing became an interminable bore. And in that case, God, why start it in the first place?

He was on his feet, smoking, and from the dry, ironical way he spoke he seemed to have grown more pessimistic about the affair than Canal, and he started attacking Quinto. Deprived of his brother's support, Quinto began to hesitate. Of course, if the outlook was really so uncertain, perhaps the best course was to back out and return to their original project—sell the flowerpottery and leave it at that.

But now it was Canal who wanted to go ahead. As he studied the clauses of the proposed contract, he began to enjoy the prospect of anticipating all the ways in which Caisotti might wriggle out of his obligations and to arm himself with more involved clauses, precautions, restraints, guarantees of every description. He was grimacing and rolling his eyes, running a hand through his disorderly hair, speckling the papers on the desk with marginal notes. "I'll draw you up a contract designed especially for Caisotti, one that won't give an inch. He won't have a hope in hell of getting out of it." He giggled as he sat there bent double, imagining a contract as spiky as a porcupine.

Then, with a skeptical shrug, he added, "Insofar as contracts ever really hold, of course."

[10]

It began during the period of plans, blueprints, estimates. The key man now was Travaglia.

Travaglia was one of the busiest construction engineers in town and he couldn't spare Quinto and Ampelio much time. They conducted their business through brief, harassed sessions while construction plans were unrolled and spread out on the table and Travaglia answered the telephone and cursed his surveyors.

Travaglia did everything by fits and starts, now issuing a spate of orders, now sitting at his desk tracing lines with a ruler, now scrapping everything and making a clean start. But then, every so often, he would raise his clear eyes, smile, stretch his arms down his heavy body, and be perfectly at peace, as though vistas of endless leisure stretched out ahead of him. He was a fat man, but he sat perched on the high swivel stool by the drawing table; he laughed, staring into the distance. "Do either of you two have the faintest idea what a construction contract is?" His manner was protective, contemptuous, artful. His weight and his early baldness gave him an air of maturity, an authoritative appearance which he put to full use. The Anfossi brothers, who lived from hand to mouth and pursued vague ambitions quite out of their reach, represented in Travaglia's eyes a way of life which he had rejected at the start of his career: the life of art, of science, and to some extent of political ideas as well. And he'd been right to reject them, he assured himself as he looked at them: never getting ahead, making no sort of position for themselves. Quinto, a man still without arts or parts; Ampelio, a dishwasher in some university laboratory who might get a chair at the age of sixty. A pair of failures, there was no longer any doubt about it. As he looked at them, he felt more than ever satisfied with himself, and in dealing with them he paraded his own philosophy of life, that of the practical man who puts first things first. But there was something else in his attitude, a note of violence, a sort of aggressive irritation which the Anfossis always aroused in him. "Because, after all, damn it, I like the poor devils! And I'm the only person who understands them."

They were looking at some accounts. Travaglia raised his head and studied the pair of them, then broke into one of his tired, silent laughs. "Tell me," he said, "just tell me one thing: who put you up to this?"

"You don't need to say any more—you've had enough of us for today. We'll be back tomorrow. We'll tackle the question on our own." The Anfossis were on their way to the door.

"Hey!" cried Travaglia, running after them. "You don't think I'd let you go it alone! That fellow Caisotti would swallow you in one mouthful, you poor innocents. You stay where you are. Let's see now, where were we?"

They had to send the surveyor to ask Caisotti about something marked on the plan. His office was not far from Travaglia's. The man returned with the news that he wasn't there. "I asked the girl—"

"Ah, the girl. . . ." Travaglia sniggered.

"She said she didn't know."

"That girl doesn't even know where her— But she was there when we saw it. Go back and tell her it's on the table; it was there this morning and it must be there now."

Ampelio had been sitting in his raincoat, his beard sunk on his chest, not saying anything. Suddenly he stood up and said, "I'll go."

Travaglia gave another of his silent laughs, another stare at nothing, as though he had something in mind that he couldn't put into words.

Quinto was confused. After a while, he said, "I don't understand; you wanted Ampelio to go there to . . ."

"What?" Travaglia was already thinking about something else. They started checking the figures.

Ampelio was back in twenty minutes. He stood there stiffly without saying anything.

"Well?"

"We'll have to go to the site. There's a mistake in the plans."

In the end they all went. The flowerpottery and the part of the garden with the forget-me-not bed were in a state of confusion; Signora Anfossi had started to transplant her flowers. It was a fine day and under the warm sun flowers and leaves took on an air of luxuriant gaiety. Quinto had never realized that so intense and various a life flourished within that narrow space, and now, at the thought that it was all to die and be replaced by a structure of bricks and girders, he was overcome by a sense of sadness, a fondness even for the weeds and nettles, which was almost repentance. The other two, however, seemed merely to be enjoying the pleasant weather. Travaglia had been wearing a hat, but feeling the heat he had taken it off and was carrying it in his hand; it had marked his forehead with a red, sweaty line. Before long he began to feel the sun on his bald head and he put his hat on again, but on the back of his head, which gave him a gay, Sunday air. Ampelio had finally removed his unseasonable raincoat and was carrying it, neatly folded, over one shoulder. They were measuring a section of the site where the boundary line curved in. Quinto left them to it. Travaglia, although he was working, was in one of his periods of contemplative calm. "What are these called?" he asked Ampelio, pushing aside some plants with his fingers. Ampelio answered with an air of vigorous authority that surprised Quinto, who had not realized his brother took any interest in flowers.

There was a sudden movement among some dahlias in pots, and who should emerge, peering at them through her thick lashes, but Caisotti's secretary. She was wearing a lightweight suit. "Oh, you're here," she said. "I was looking for Signor Caisotti."

"Certainly we're here," Quinto said, for some reason suddenly furious. "This is still our property; the contract hasn't yet been signed."

Shrug. "I don't know about that. He said he'd be here, with a gentleman—" She broke off and covered her mouth with a letter she was carrying, as though she were embarrassed at having said too much. She stood there stiffly in her close-fitting jacket.

"That's it, he's not yet bought the site and he's already selling apartments, even though they're not built yet," Quinto said, turning to the other two, denouncing the man and at the same time forced to admire him.

Travaglia and Ampelio weren't listening. They had turned toward the girl. The engineer stood with his head inclined to one side, his eyes half shut, laughing in his tired way. Ampelio, one finger in the pocket of his jacket, his coat still draped sideways across his shoulder, his eyes hidden behind his thick glasses, looked like someone from the nineteenth century. "Ah, mail," he said, reaching toward the letter that the girl was holding. She quickly hid it behind her back, as though they were playing a game. "It's not for you, it's for Signor Caisotti." "Is it so urgent?" Shrug. "How should I know?" "Do you or don't you know," Travaglia broke in, "that Caisotti's measurements are all to his advantage?" "Oh. . . . Well, where the land slopes it measures less." "Oh, so you know that, do you?" Shrug.

Travaglia laughed. "Does Caisotti tell you every morning what you've got to say or only what you're *not* to say?"

The girl blinked and tossed her hair over her shoulders. "How do you mean? Caisotti never tells me anything."

"Fine sort of secretary you must be."

The discussion was becoming playful. They were walking up and down together, the girl between them. She had picked a flower and was holding it between her lips. Ampelio brought out a pack of cigarettes, offering them to the girl first. "No, thank you, I don't smoke," she bleated, the flower still in her mouth.

"A girl with no vices, eh?" Travaglia said teasingly.

"So what?"

There was a rustling sound from the terrace above and Signora Anfossi looked over the hedge. She was wearing a big straw hat and garden gloves, and carried a large pair of scissors, with which she cut some roses. Travaglia noticed her first; he took off his hat.

"Hello, boys, who is this with you? Oh, Signor Travaglia, it's nice to see you. Have you come to take a look at the site? Do please put your hat on. What do you think about this great project of ours?"

Travaglia replaced his hat carefully. "We'll try to do a good job, Signora, you can count on that."

"And who is the charming young lady? Wait a moment, I think we've met," the Signora went on, sliding her sunglasses down to the tip of her nose. "Yes, it's Lina."

Quinto, for some reason, said dryly, "No, no, mother, you don't know her."

"But I do," she insisted. "She came here the other day to get the draft of the contract. Her name's Lina; she's the contractor's secretary—our partner's, I should say."

The girl had drawn back a little when Signora Anfossi appeared, and was looking the other way. Now she stepped toward the hedge. "Yes, it's me, Lina. Nice to see you."

Quinto and Ampelio were both irritated and wanted to put a stop to the proceedings. Ampelio made a start by asking Travaglia about the slope of the ground. "There must be some way of allowing for it, surely?"

But Travaglia continued his conversation with the Signora. "I see you're doing a little gardening," he remarked.

"I'm trying to save what can be saved."

They all went about their business, the Signora to her roses, Travaglia and the two brothers to measure a corner of the site again, while the girl, Lina, stood a little way off, by herself. Travaglia's mind was not on the job; he was bubbling into laughter again.

"You poor jerks!"

"Why?"

"Because of what you're doing to your mother, making her call Caisotti your 'partner.' Your mother's partner."

"You're mad. We've never called him our partner. She was the one who used the word just now, heaven knows why.

Partner, my ass! Anyway, what has that got to do with it? What's more, this is our affair and we'll finish it ourselves."

"You poor, poor jerks!"

They were going on like this, out of temper with each other, measuring the ground and exchanging sarcastic remarks, when they heard a mumble of voices behind them. They turned around and there was Caisotti, standing beside Lina. He said something to her in an undertone, the slack lines of his face stretched tight with anger, but the girl stood up for herself. He had snatched the letter out of her hand; apparently it enraged him, for he read it several times, spelling it out to himself, syllable by syllable. He put away the letter, stuck his hands in his pockets, and walked on, taking no notice of the rest of them. Apart from the impression of brutality and obstinacy, Quinto was conscious again of something weak and defenseless in this solitary man who made an enemy of everyone. He was striding up and down, his face contorted with anger, his eyes wrinkled. Quinto had never seen him quite so badly dressed. He was wearing a shrunken jacket buttoned over a checked woolen shirt, shapeless yellow pants, and a pair of old shoes spotted with cement. He really looked like a bricklayer now; he needed only the cocked hat made out of newspaper.

With Caisotti, Quinto noticed, the girl dropped her usual air of reserve and looked almost brazen, ready to argue the toss with him. She walked a few steps behind, a little frightened but still aggressive, as though there was a rage against him deep inside her which she'd never let out.

Caisotti continued to walk up and down, looking tense and irritated. Then he turned to the Anfossis and nodded toward them as though they were meeting by chance in the street. "We're here to measure this bit of the site where the ground slopes," Quinto said, then at once regretted that he had spoken, for he caught in his voice a suggestion of apology for their being there at all, although the land still belonged to them. To correct this impression, he turned on Caisotti aggressively. "We're here because your measurements won't do, you see, they're all wrong!"

Caisotti peered forward as though he were looking at Quinto on the horizon. His eyelids were red, his eyes watery, his lips moist like someone in a towering rage, or like a child liable to burst into tears at any moment. "What's this new trouble you're trying to make?" Clearly he could hardly wait to start working off his temper. "You go and do your job and leave me to do mine," he shouted.

"Just a moment, Caisotti." Travaglia stepped forward with the air of someone just then arriving on the scene. "You're a contractor, that's your job, I'm an engineer, that's mine. Right? Well, then . . ." And he began explaining the whole thing to him. Caisotti listened to him, but he kept his eyes on the ground and shook his head, as though to say, Yes, all this is fine, I could get on with you, you know your job, but these two are impossible, you never know what they'll want next, and anyway it's clear they've got it in for me.

"No, no, Caisotti, just listen to me." Travaglia smiled blandly, sleepily, in the manner of someone who understands this sort of situation and knows there's no good getting worked up about it. "But what am I going to do? Just tell me what I'm expected to do!" Caisotti opened his arms wide and his cadences became more plaintive than usual, one long, unending whine, and even Travaglia's vowels grew broader and broader, as though to say, Take it easy, we'll find a way. As they spoke, they both seemed to be trying to lull one another to sleep. Quinto felt excluded from this softly voweled game; he felt expressly singled out as a person who simply didn't count, and not only him but his whole family—as though being property owners and having dictated the terms of the deal, as Quinto was convinced he had done, had no importance whatever. He didn't know whose tone irritated him more, Caisotti's or Travaglia's. This was exactly the occasion when Ampelio should have intervened in that disconcerting way he had; Quinto turned around, but he wasn't there. He was a little way off, at the bottom of the garden where it was greenest. Quinto saw his back, a dark shadow against the sun; Lina was facing him, with that willful little air of hers, twisting a lock of hair around one finger. They were speaking in undertones, and every so often he took a step forward and she stepped back. At a certain point, still with his back to the others, Ampelio said loudly, as though he had been listening to everything the contractor said:

"All right, Caisotti, if that's the way you want it. We're still prepared to drop the whole thing. The contract hasn't been signed yet."

"Drop the whole thing, what do you mean?" cried Caisotti, his voice angry and bitter again, but in the middle of this outburst he changed tactics and forced a laugh. A Caisotti laugh, not pretty to look at, a clenched, gap-toothed kind of laugh. He was looking at the others to see if they agreed that Ampelio had said something absurd. "Drop the deal, you say. Then what are we all doing here?" He laughed again. "We're here to make a deal, right? A friendly deal, that's what we all want, right?"

The Signora looked over the hedge again. "Drop the deal, you say? Oh, dear, my poor plants, pull them up, put them back again, pull them up. . . ."

Caisotti was waving his arms now, laughing; he was at his most expansive. "No, no, Signora, we're all friends here; we're going to do things in a friendly way. Don't you worry, we'll do a good job, you'll have nothing to complain about. And while the workmen are here, are there any little improvements you'd like made in the garden?"

"No, no, on no account workmen in the garden."

"Then we'll have no workmen in the garden! We'll have a path here; they can pass in front."

"That wall that'll be facing us—perhaps if it had a few creepers on it . . ."

"What's that, creepers, eh! Fine, we'll have some lovely plants, just whatever you want. You'll see, we'll get on fine."

As he stood there gesturing clumsily, he knocked down one of the dahlias. "And he didn't even say he was sorry," Signora Anfossi remarked afterward.

[11]

Oddly, when it came time to sign the contract, Caisotti didn't make a fuss about the points where trouble was expected. He picked on quite trivial points where it was easy to meet his objections. Quinto was positively disappointed. It was a tricky, involved contract, prickly as a thornbush; Canal and the notary had really outdone themselves. Everything was there: the construction contract, the date for final payment of the total sum, as well as date and amounts of the regular installments; the dates when the completed apartments were to be handed over; and the whole thing was tied to a "reversion clause," which meant that if the contractor failed to meet any of his obligations (as specified in the contract), the property reverted to the owners, together with any buildings constructed on it in the meantime, in whatever state they were then in.

"If he signs this," Canal said to Quinto, "you're safe—he won't be able to touch you."

Caisotti had signed, he had let them have their way as though the business of a contract was a mere formality. He came to the notary's by himself, without a lawyer or anyone —"an economy measure," they said, or else, "because every time he hires a lawyer he ends up quarreling with him." The meeting was attended by the three Anfossis, the Signora and her sons, as well as by their lawyer and their notary. As Caisotti came into the office (the atmosphere of the place in itself was presumably calculated to intimidate him) and saw all those educated people writing away, he looked around like a trapped animal who instinctively tries to escape but knows it's no longer any use. Daniel in the lion's den, Quinto said to himself, always ready to see the man in a favorable light. But this image of Caisotti as victim gave him no satisfaction; he needed to see him as some wild, savage beast, a lion, for example, and his own party as a den full of Daniels surrounding the man—relentless, virtuous Daniels goading him like jailers with forked, contractual clauses.

Caisotti took a chair near the notary's desk, while the others sat or stood around; he listened attentively as the contract was read, his mouth half open, every now and then silently repeating a phrase to himself. Quinto found himself wondering if the truth of the matter was that the man was simply stupid. But in fact he was concentrating in order not to miss anything, and every so often he would raise one of his big hands and say, "Stop," and the notary would go back and read the passage again, enunciating very deliberately. At times it looked as if Caisotti was on the point of rejecting the whole thing, as if he thought this was all a trap. Quinto half expected him to jump to his feet and say, You're crazy! and slam the door behind him. But no, he waited for the notary to finish, and then nodded to indicate his approval. When he did raise an objection, it was in some part of the contract where no one had expected trouble; he was particularly concerned with the technical details and there was some business about gravel which led to endless argument, all the more so since Ampelio seemed to think it was a matter of principle and refused to budge an inch, even though Canal advised him to let it go.

Quinto was bored, and since everyone was concentrating on the discussion, he went over to the window and looked out at the street, bright in the spring sunlight, and tried to work up some feeling for the place and for the deal, which was going ahead nicely; but he felt as if the whole affair was now really over and that this adventure in real estate was merely a matter of administration, of long, boring discussions. It no longer interested him or excited him and his only hope was that from now on Ampelio would stand by him.

The ground was easy now and everything seemed to be going smoothly; it was at this point that Caisotti succeeded in deferring the date on which one of the payments was due, or rather two of the three payments, and also in lowering the total by two hundred thousand lire.

They had not yet reached the point of signing the contract when Ampelio looked at his watch and said that he had to go if he was to catch his train.

Quinto had had no idea he intended to leave. "What do you mean? The thing hasn't been signed yet. . . ." Suddenly he felt furiously angry with his brother. "Why do you have to go now?"

"I have to go, that's all there is to it. Who's got to be in the laboratory tomorrow, you or me?" Ampelio's voice was insulting.

Quinto felt thoroughly fed up at the idea of having to stay and look after everything himself; he had got it into his head that Ampelio was going to handle the matter, which would leave him free to regard it with a certain detachment. He had hoped that from now on it was going to be like this. They began to argue in a rapid undertone, in front of Caisotti and the notary. "You never said you'd have to go. Leaving me here like this . . ." "It's practically finished. Mother has power of attorney; she can sign and then everything is settled." "No, there's still lots to do. We haven't agreed on anything. . . ."

"But if Ampelio has got to be at the laboratory tomorrow . . . ?" Signora Anfossi broke in.

There's more money to be made this way than in all his laboratories put together, Quinto was on the point of saying, as though he were playing the part of an elderly businessman who doesn't want his sons to go to college. But he checked himself, and what he in fact said was, "Yes, but we ought to reach some agreement, so that when one of us is away the other is here."

"If you have to leave too, don't worry," Caisotti said suddenly. "Go ahead. At this stage, if necessary, the Signora and I can settle the rest of what there is to settle."

Quinto remembered something that Canal had said—greatly to their annoyance, at the time—and which Travaglia had repeated in almost the same words: "I tell you what'll happen. You start this wretched business going and that's the last that'll be seen of you. You'll leave your mother to pull the chestnuts out of the fire."

"As a matter of fact," the notary said, "it would be convenient if one of you did stay. There are still some papers to see to."

"I'm staying, of course I'm staying," Quinto said quickly. "I've no intention of going." He was furious because he had really wanted to stay, though admittedly he had had half an idea of going to Milan. Bensi and Cerveteri had called a meeting to set the editorial policy of their new review, and though he didn't really want to go, since he disapproved of their position, he would have quite liked to be there, just by accident as it were. One way and another, he was furious.

Ampelio had left. Everything was dealt with rapidly—the signatures, the promissory notes, and all the rest. As Quinto and Caisotti walked down the stairs, chatting about the time when building would start, Caisotti said, "Everything depends now on getting the green light from City Hall. We'll have to put up the proposal to the technical office, wait till they hold a general meeting, and then if everything goes well—"

"But . . . how long will that take?" Quinto suddenly felt alarmed. "I thought everything was settled."

Caisotti snorted. "With those bureaucrats? Not on your life! They can hold us up for months. And if there's something they don't like, oh, that means headaches, I can tell you!"

"But the work?"

"The work doesn't start till we get the green light, that's for sure."

Quinto stopped on the stairs. "Look here, Caisotti, you've just signed a contract committing you to handing over the finished apartments to us by December thirty-first."

"Take it easy!" Caisotti took a step forward. Quinto had not seen this expression before, a look of sullen fury quite different from the occasion when he had lost his temper in their garden. "Take it easy! The contract says I hand over in eight months. And eight months means *eight months after I get the authorization.* Right?"

"The hell it does! Look, Caisotti, the date is on the contract. You're required to let us have the apartments on the last day of December this year."

Yes, and then again, no. December 31st, agreement, contract. . . . It appeared that in one place the contract stated that the apartments were to be ready in eight months, and in another, "by December 31st." However, legal opinion was that they needn't worry, since there was no reason to suppose it would take long to get the affair approved. Moreover, they said, Caisotti is the kind of man who always gets his way. He'd got his hooks into the boys in City Hall.

Quinto and Caisotti said good-bye as they left the notary's office. Quinto was already wondering if he hadn't slipped up somewhere.

[12]

Work started late. There were a couple of men on the job; they were digging the ground in preparation for the foundations. One was a lean, dark, bad-tempered fellow who wore nothing but a pair of shorts, with a handkerchief tied around his head like a pirate. He was a born idler, always taking time off to smoke or play around with the maids. Every now and then, with a heavy sigh, he would pick up the shovel that he had left sticking in the ground, first spitting on the palms of his hands. The other was a great bull of a man with red, cropped hair; he kept his head down as though he didn't want to see anyone or hear anyone, though in fact he was a good-looking fellow, in spite of his savage, bewildered expression. He laid on with pick or shovel as though he were a bulldozer, and if he replied to the other man's witticisms, it was only in sullen, inarticulate grunts. "A fine worker," commented Caisotti, who paid a visit now and then to see how things were going. This was in answer to Quinto's objection that with only two workmen the job would take a year. "He does the work of three men. Keeps at it for hours on end, without a break. Only wish I'd got a few more of his sort."

The main events of the summer were these: A dispute with Caisotti about the mounds of earth that were blocking the road. A two-week break in the work when he had to transfer all his men to another site, where he was badly behind schedule. And his failure to meet the first payment.

Quinto was enjoying himself. He was always on the move; seeing Canal to get him to write a warning letter to Caisotti;

seeing the notary about details of the registration of the contract—there was always something not quite in order; seeing Travaglia and getting him to the site to check that everything was going according to the terms of the contract—in fact, the foundations were hardly laid; seeing Caisotti to hurry him on or complain about something. Quinto's professional friends were always ready to lend a hand, and though they didn't take him too seriously they were amused to see him finally face to face with practical problems. Travaglia did not spare him a good deal of ironical witticism, the notary provided tactful advice, and Canal, all professional rigor, stuck his heels in and wouldn't give an inch.

Relations with Caisotti were more difficult, more indirect, but when Quinto did manage to get hold of him, he felt that he was enjoying the richest rewards that the project had to offer. *Moral* rewards, that is, since the question of the material rewards due to follow was shot through with an anxiety, a shiver of danger, which Quinto recognized—now that he was experiencing them for himself—as the spice of private enterprise. He felt morally rewarded when, for example, an exchange of phrases with Caisotti revealed the mutual respect between capitalist and contractor—the meaningful look rewarded him ("we're in this together"), the flicker of confusion on Caisotti's face, which meant that he had played his cards well. Their approaches were brusque. "Look here, Caisotti," Quinto would open aggressively, bearing down on him while he was sitting alone at his usual sidewalk table in front of the Caffè Melina, scowling at a coffee cup or an empty glass (business was obviously going badly), "what's this all about, eh?" Caisotti would reluctantly bring Quinto into his field of vision, then look away again as though he'd rather not have seen him. Quinto, rising a little self-consciously to his theme, would then proceed to justify his complaint. Caisotti would continue to look straight ahead of him, biting his lips as though he were keeping back a violent outburst and just managing to transform it (by means of the jerky movements of his head that followed next) into a general sense of discouragement and distrust. His replies were always wide of the mark, but loaded with an absolute lack of esteem; they were often so insulting as to preclude all further possibility of discussion. The gloves were off now, and the cups and saucers rattled as Caisotti's fists, compact as small footballs, pounded on the table. In these exchanges, Quinto noted with satisfaction, it was Caisotti who seemed anxious to keep his voice down and prevent anyone from overhearing what they were arguing about. Then they would both calm down and act as though the barrier separating them had been removed. They talked about the future, about what they both had to gain from going ahead with the venture. They talked like partners, like equals. The motley, busy crowd that filled the street pressed up against their table. From where they sat, they looked across a gay, vulgar flower bed down to the sea front.

Quinto would go home and find the red-haired workman busy at the foundations—the other man had left ahead of time; he was digging away like a madman.

The appearance and the color of the site were changing. The dark, wet-smelling undersoil was being brought up into the light. The living green of the surface soil was disappearing under shovelfuls of soft earth and big, doughy clods heaped up along the trenches. Tangles of dead roots, snails, and worms showed on the walls of the trenches. Signora Anfossi would stand among the clustering plants and the flowers she was leaving to wither on their stems, the tall bushes and the branches of mimosa, and peer over the hedge to watch the mounds of earth growing day by day more numerous in the waste land which had once been her garden. Then she would turn back to her green.

[13]

"In the meanwhile, if you find anyone looking for an apartment or a shop, you can send him on to me," Quinto said to the man in the Superga agency, after paying him his commission.

"Send him on to you. . . . How do you mean?"

"It'll take a few months still, of course," Quinto said. "The apartment building on my land—the one Caisotti is putting up. It'll be ready by December."

"December? Oh, sure." The agent laughed.

"Yes, December—it's in the contract. We've got a reversion clause, you know!" Quinto was by now resigned to the fact that the apartments wouldn't in fact be ready by December, but it annoyed him to hear it put like this, as a matter of course, by this individual who had nothing to do with the affair. "Caisotti has to hand them over by the end of the year."

"Sure, sure, the end of *next* year, eh! No good counting on dates when you're dealing with a guy like Caisotti!"

"Bit late to tell me this now, isn't it? Who recommended Caisotti to me in the first place?"

There was a woman waiting in the office, dark-haired, lean, tanned. "Did you say apartments?" she asked. "In what part of town? How many rooms?" She was about thirty-five, a Milanese or anyway from Lombardy. In her tight-fitting summer dress she looked too thin, even a little wasted, but there was a suggestion of energy, of impulsiveness, in her expression. Quinto looked at her. There was a certain refinement, a harmony of line, in her face and breasts and her bare arms.

"No, no, Signora," the agent said, "they're not ready yet. Anyway, you want to buy an apartment and I gather these are to be rented." He looked at Quinto.

"That's so, yes," Quinto said, and the subject was closed.

"Now, that new house I was telling you about, Signora," the agent went on.

"Good-bye," Quinto said, going out. He was irritated by the way the man at once ruled out the possibility of the woman being interested in one of his apartments. He felt furious, suddenly, at not being able to discuss the matter with her: the number of rooms, the way they were laid out, the conveniences, etc. At his abrupt good-bye, she had looked at him questioningly, a hint of a smile on her face. An interesting woman, not good-looking perhaps, but interesting— very much a woman. What Quinto would have liked was not so much to talk to her about the apartments, but simply to talk to her. And in fact he had not moved far from the agency, as if he was waiting for her to come out. She did appear a moment later, and he went up to her. "Excuse me," he began, "I just wanted to say—about those apartments, if you had thought at all about that part of town, the question of sale or lease is something we could discuss."

"Oh, thank you," she said, "I really don't know yet. As I was saying to the man, I simply wanted to get a general idea of the possibilities. We haven't decided whether to take a place here or in Rapallo. My husband . . ."

They walked along together.

"You're from Milan?"

"Well, Mantua really."

"Ah, Mantua. Which part of the beach do you go to?"

"Near the Serenella. Do you know it?"

"Yes, I go there every now and then."

"Well, whenever you're next there, my umbrella is the one nearest the pier."

Quinto went there the next day. There was not much beach and it was packed with people. She was sharing her umbrella with a group of friends, among them a colonel. Quinto had to sit down and join in the conversation, which was a great bore. He was sorry he'd come. She was nothing much to look at in a bathing suit and she didn't interest him the way she'd done the day before. The sea was rather rough and no one wanted to swim, but finally they decided they ought to go in and splashed about in the breakers, making a great deal of noise. There was a rope, half rotten and slimy-green with seaweed, hanging from a row of iron posts. Nelly was nervous and kept close to the rope. As each wave came, Quinto held her by the arm, from behind, to support her. A wave that looked as if it was going to be bigger than the others was just on them, and Quinto managed to get his hands on her breasts. It was in fact quite a small wave. She laughed and did not remove his hands.

They spent the night together. To find a room, Quinto had to spend the whole afternoon searching; it was August and hotels and pensions were all packed. Finally he managed to find a place where they only asked to see the man's papers. The room overlooked a busy street and Quinto, used to his cool house up on the hill, was hot and couldn't get to sleep. It was not a proper double bed and they had to lie close together. They were naked, the sheet was sweaty, and the light of a street lamp shone through the open window. Nelly was sleeping with her back to him and he had to lie on the edge of the bed if he wasn't to be pressed right against her. He thought about waking her up. Being the first time, their love-making hadn't amounted to much, and he felt that perhaps it was up to him to start again. He would only have needed a little encouragement, but she was asleep and he was lazy and it suited him to think that she was the kind of person who didn't mind much one way or the other—not at all the sensual woman he had at first supposed. He looked at the back of her neck; her skin was no longer fresh and her shoulder blades were bony. For years Quinto had gone only with women who slightly repelled him physically. This was a deliberate program: he was afraid of ties, he only wanted casual affairs.

He started thinking about the project, about Caisotti, about the payments. . . .

[14]

There was no cement. That month, apparently, the usual deliveries had not been made and all the building jobs in the district were idle, or so Caisotti said. Travaglia did in fact confirm the story when Quinto went to ask him about it, but then he started to laugh and implied that while cement was not to be had in certain circumstances, in others—well, there was cement. It was a question, in short, of being willing to pay for it. A good many crews had suspended work, but only for a few days; most of them were now busy again. Only Caisotti had no cement; and this was the time to start laying the foundations.

"A put-up job, you say! This is the last straw, with all I've

got to put up with—you people coming here to give me hell!"
Caisotti turned on Quinto aggressively when he came to
inquire what was happening; but then, as usual, he calmed
down and started being sorry for himself. "You think this
is my idea of a joke?" he whined. "Keeping my men idle,
machinery rented for nothing, losing the best time of the year,
missing my delivery dates. . . . If they won't let me have the
cement, what the hell can I do?" Lately the man had become
quite impossible to deal with. He had got it into his head
that because he hadn't yet been able to meet the first payment,
the Anfossis were going around setting people against him.

"Look here, Caisotti, you don't pay us and you try and put
the blame on us!"

"Hell, man, I'm having a hard time. Happens to everyone,
see. And you go and bring the lawyer into it. He hates me,
that guy does; I've known it for ages. And you have to tell
the notary all about me, and he blabs it to half the town. Yes,
and your mother, she goes around saying that Caisotti doesn't
pay his debts. Then what happens? They all start pestering
me and I don't get my cement."

"So it's true then. . . . You don't have the cement because
you haven't paid for it!"

Caisotti waved his fist in Quinto's face. "Watch your step,
mister," he yelled. "I've had enough! I don't pay for it, eh. . . ."
They were standing in the most chaotic part of the site,
amid piles of earth and planks left here and there. From the
tool shed the red-haired workman emerged and stood, towering, behind Caisotti, his back slightly bent, his face expression-
less, a cross between an angel and an orangutan.

"Put your hands down, Caisotti, do you mind?" Quinto
said. "Starting a fight will settle nothing." Never had the man
appeared to him so much an unarmed hero in a hostile world,
taking them all on single-handed. He was pleased with himself, too, for having responded to Caisotti's brutal outburst
with only a sense of cold superiority; he was aware all the
time that he was the one who had the situation under con-
trol. And in fact Caisotti quickly put his hands in his pockets,
as though ashamed of his outburst, and muttered something

under his breath. Then he turned his anger against the big workman, finding some excuse to bawl him out. The man stood there in silence, listening, head down.

Quinto remained master of the occasion. But Caisotti neither paid up nor did he push the work ahead.

Then there was the argument about the pipes. They had been uncovered during the digging and then left lying where they were. According to the terms of the contract, everything recovered from the site belonged to Caisotti. But Signora Anfossi, seeing the pipes apparently thrown away and left to get rusty, leaned over the hedge one day when he was there, and asked him if he meant to do anything with them.

He was in one of his black moods. "What do you expect me to do with your pipes?"

"Well, then," she said, delighted, "if you're not going to do anything with them, they'd be useful to me in the garden. I'll send someone to get them." And so next day she sent the gardener for them and got him to fix up a system of pipes to water a bed of narcissus. This had happened more than a month previously. Then one day she had looked over the hedge (she heard Caisotti moving about on the other side) and she made some comment or other about his failure to meet the first payment or the work being behind schedule. In her quiet, composed way, she never lost an occasion, as she moved about the garden, looking after her flowers, to make some little wounding remark. He had mumbled something, not wanting to be drawn, and they both kept on with what they were doing. That seemed to be the end of it, when suddenly Caisotti started shouting furiously, "It's theft, Signora Anfossi, theft, I say! I'm going to report you to the police! That'll teach you to go about stealing people's pipes! First you sell and then you steal back what you've sold. Fine way for the gentry to behave!"

"You must be mad," Signora Anfossi said, shaking her head.

That was the day Ampelio came home. He had been attending a conference of chemists in Germany. Quinto was upstairs; he heard him talking to their mother, then go out again. She came up to Quinto's room. "Quickly, you must go after Ampelio and stop him. I'm afraid he's going to do something silly. I told him that our nice Signor Caisotti had reached the point of calling me a thief, and Ampelio said, 'Where is he, where is he, I'll bash his head in!' And he went off to look for him."

Quinto ran out into the road after his brother; he was some way ahead, walking fast. "Ampelio, Ampelio," he shouted. "What's the matter with you? Mother's frightened. Where are you going?"

Ampelio kept on walking, not bothering to turn around. "I'm going to bash his head in."

"Look, do we really have to take everything Caisotti says seriously? He's quite irresponsible. . . ."

"I'm going to bash his head in."

"That won't help, Ampelio. I nearly poked him myself the other day. The bastard's trying to create difficulties in order to put off the deadline. If you start a quarrel, you'll be doing him a favor."

"But in the meantime I'll have bashed his head in."

This might have been the moment to raise a different type of objection, namely that Caisotti had a pair of shoulders like a brick wall and fists to knock down a calf, while Ampelio was a university teacher who didn't weigh much over a hundred pounds. But neither of them raised this point; it probably didn't even occur to them. Quinto, puffing along behind Ampelio, developed a different line of argument. Their relations with Caisotti were in a delicate phase, he said; they had to use tact, diplomacy, pay no attention to his tantrums. The great thing was to be flexible. . . .

"Flexible!" said Ampelio. "Paid off pretty well so far, your flexibility, hasn't it? There's not one brick on top of another."

It was Quinto's turn to lose his temper. "God! I like that! I've been chasing Caisotti for months and now you suddenly turn up and start taking a strong line! Hail the conquering hero!"

"But I've been at Frankfurt!"

"What the hell's that got to do with it?" But Quinto had paused to think before replying, and now he had lost steam.

They walked on for a little while in silence. It wasn't clear where Ampelio expected to find Caisotti, and Quinto didn't ask him. Then, suddenly, as they were crossing the square, they heard the noise of an engine starting up and there the man was, behind the windshield of a small, three-wheeled truck. The body work projected in front like a torpedo; Caisotti was sitting stiffly in the saddle, grasping the shuddering handlebars. He was wearing a cap fastened under his chin and a windbreaker. Turning to Ampelio as though they had been talking a few hours ago, he said, "They've let me have my cement! I told you you only had to be patient, didn't I? Now I can get the work going again; I'll put on all the men I can. You give me a few days' grace and I'll settle the payment with interest. Right?"

Ampelio was calm and friendly. "Fine. When do you start laying the foundations?"

"Saturday."

"This Saturday? Couldn't start sooner?"

"Saturday will be time enough. The cement will dry over the weekend, then on Monday we'll start work."

"What about the payment? The second one is almost due, you know."

"You'll just have to be patient for a while and I'll settle the two together. That's for sure—I know where I am now. I wouldn't say that if it weren't so."

"We're counting on you, Caisotti."

"We'll beat all the records this time! 'Bye now, and my respects to the Signora." And with a volley of sharp reports, the machine was under way.

Quinto didn't know what to say. "You see?" Ampelio remarked.

"See what? He's played one more trick on us, I see that."

Ampelio shook his head briefly as though excluding this possibility altogether. "No, no, this time he'll keep his word."

"Grow up, won't you! You don't know him. Start laying the foundations on Saturday, hell! You don't realize what state the work's in; go take a look. He's just playing with you. And this business of putting off the payment again, as though it didn't matter! And you stood there calmly and let him get away with everything!"

"What about you? You never opened your mouth all the time."

"I wanted to watch you handle it. But I never expected—"

Ampelio shook his head. "You don't understand the situation. He's going through a difficult period right now, but he's got a chance of recovering. If we're always on his back and start taking legal action, we'll start a panic among his creditors and the next thing we know, he'll go bankrupt. Now the question is this: is this in our interest or is it in our interest to back him up? If he goes bankrupt, there'll be the suit about the proceeds, with all the creditors. . . . We'll have to hand the project over to another firm, and God knows on what terms. On the other hand, if Caisotti can put his affairs in order, we're all right too."

Quinto wrung his hands. This was his own reading of the situation, reached after much painful thought; he had been trying to explain it to his brother a minute back. And now . . . "I thought you wanted to bash his head in," he remarked.

"It wasn't the psychological moment. I realized that at once. And then don't you see, Caisotti has given ground; all that talk of his was intended to make amends, even his final 'My respects to the Signora.' He changed his position in a flash."

They were on the brink of a quarrel. Quinto had only to come out with, "All your doing, eh?" which was on the tip of his tongue; Ampelio had only to give way to the temptation to add, "It only needed a bit of energy," and they would have come to blows. But they kept quiet. After a while, as though there were no other point to raise, Quinto said, "And we should have told him that the first thing to do is buttress the soil on our part of the site, where they've knocked down the wall. They've dumped everything there. The first rain we get, we'll have a landslide on our hands."

"We can leave a note about that in Caisotti's office," Ampelio said. "First things first. That's a secondary matter."

They stopped by his office. Quinto went in alone; Ampelio had gone to buy some cigarettes. The secretary was more

evasive than ever. "You can leave the message with me. Oh,
all right, put it in writing if you want. If Caisotti comes. . . .
I haven't seen him for a couple of days." Suddenly she smiled
and gestured lavishly. "So! The traveler returns! Got a present
for me?"

Ampelio was standing in the doorway. He clicked his heels
and bowed low. *"Gnädige Fräulein,"* he murmured.

[15]

The town's most widely read newspaper was *The Financial
Forecast,* a fortnightly published by the Chamber of Com-
merce. Modest in format, it consisted of only four pages, occupied exclusively with debt failures and defaulters. The
names were listed in alphabetical order, with the addresses
and the amount of money owing. Sometimes, with an air of
reticence or excuse, an explanation was added like "Traveling,"
"Sickness," "Address Unknown," and often, with something
like a gesture of extenuation, "Insufficient funds." A world of
small projects and ambitions and failures floated in these
columns of faded type: packers and mail florists, ice cream
dealers, builders, people with rooms to let. . . . And the small
fry whose financial designs were impossible to make out, people trying to clutch on to the banks of the great money river,
people trying to get ahead in spite of their debts, condemned
to bear the shame of the paltry sums they owed.

Quinto had now caught the *Forecast* habit too, and every
two weeks, when he saw people with the new issue, he hurried
to the newsstand to get his copy and studied it in the street
like all the others who wanted to check the financial position
of the people they had business dealings with, who were
looking for the first signs of a crisis or a bankruptcy, or who
were simply curious to take a look inside their neighbors'
pockets. There was one name Quinto was looking for, *that*
name. . . . And then one day, there it was: Pietro Caisotti.
Two loans for 300,000 lire defaulted. Here was the slope
that all too many firms had not been able to remount. The

payments, the deadline for the apartments, everything was now problematic. Everything hung by a thread.

It was a ticklish moment. Even Canal, who had made some preliminary soundings himself, recommended calm. In this crisis Caisotti showed his ability; he at once went to see the lawyer, tacitly warning him not to take immediate steps. He explained that his failure to make payment, even though the notice had just appeared in print, was in fact out of date; it referred to the situation of two weeks back, which he had just about got in hand. He was on the point of concluding certain deals, and what's more he was owed money by various people himself and before long he'd be in a position to meet his obligations in full. It was learned through Canal's inquiries that Caisotti was in fact due to collect a certain debt; they succeeded in discovering the date and the amount of the sum. It wasn't a great deal and they would have to hit him quickly if they wanted to collect their debt before anyone else got at him. Caisotti was due to be paid in the morning, and it was arranged that Quinto should make a surprise visit in the early afternoon, promissory note in hand, before he could pretend that he had no money.

Quinto rang and rang again; he was about to go away when the door opened. It was the inevitable Lina, sweating just a little (it was a hot August day); she was now wearing her long black hair in a ponytail. "You're looking for Caisotti? I don't know if he's in." "What do you mean, you don't know?" The office consisted of only two rooms. As Quinto stood there, a door opened down the narrow corridor. It was dark, and in the darkness, wary as a lizard, Caisotti peered out. He looked as if he had been asleep in his clothes; his shirt was sticking out, his belt was undone, his hair was rumpled. He seemed helpless, as though he couldn't see or hear and only wanted to get the gummy taste of sleep out of his mouth. Then he turned about, and going over to the windows, threw open the shutters. The light flooded the room, leaving him blinder than before. It was the familiar office, which, apparently, served as a bedroom as well. The bed, a straw mattress spread on the floor, was behind a screen; there was an iron washbasin. Caisotti went to the basin, and pouring some water from the jug, splashed it over his face, then dried himself. His face still dazed with sleep and his hair wet, he went to the desk and sat down. Quinto took the chair facing him. Lina was no longer there. Outside, the town was lying in the heavy noonday heat shot through with the elusive, tangy smell of burning sand from the beach. Quinto felt as though he'd already said everything he had come to say, even though he'd not opened his mouth. The light had not yet penetrated Caisotti's gluey eyeballs.

He began to talk, slowly, sighing, as though they were in the middle of a conversation. "You know, when things get to a certain point, I give up, I let them do what they want." He carried on in this strain. The light bothered him and he closed the shutters. What a headache it was, he went on, trying to build houses, with everyone putting spokes in your wheel! City Hall wouldn't let you do this, the state hit you for taxes, you have to depend on a dozen people for everything you need. Quinto noticed that Caisotti's complaints were all phrased in such a way as to make it impossible for him to disagree; and it was a special kind of agreement they elicited, being addressed not so much to the business colleague or the creditor, but rather to someone holding the political views which he held himself, or had formerly held.

"And it's the same with the cement," Caisotti continued. "A hell of a situation that is. They've got us by the throat, there's no way out; it's a monopoly. . . ." And he began complaining about the big cement companies, quoting instances, restrictions, violations, mentioning places where it would have been easy to get all the cement he wanted if they hadn't been taken over and closed down by the all-powerful cement companies. He showed more skill than Quinto would have expected in identifying the causes of his difficulties and in setting individual facts within a general frame of reference. All the same it was wearisomely familiar, the old, old story about the little man being crushed by the big monopolies that turned up inevitably in every discussion of the Italian economy. Quinto found it particularly irritating since he was not at the moment disposed to consider the situation from this point of view. Not that he didn't agree; Caisotti's case was, in its broad outline, undeniable. But Quinto's role was now that of the owner of real estate and he wanted to look at things the way real estate owners looked at them.

Caisotti described an attempt to start a stone quarry in his village, where he owned a small piece of land; the land was valueless, just a heap of stones, but these stones, according to Caisotti, were perfect for making cement. He'd spent a lot of money on the project, he said, and then the cement companies stepped in and prevented him from going ahead. This reference to "a small piece of land" made Quinto (real estate owner) prick up his ears; this property constituted, in Canal's eyes, a kind of final guarantee, since a foreclosure could be put on it. Now it appeared that it was all stones, the right kind for cement maybe, but useless because the monopoly had succeeded in stopping the project.

"Ah, it's a struggle, it's a struggle," Caisotti said. "Who would have thought, Anfossi, *in those days,* that it was going to be still like this? Remember?"

"Mmm," Quinto murmured. He wasn't sure whether Caisotti's reference was to particular memories or simply to common knowledge.

"We thought that once we'd come down from the hills and chased *them* away, everything would be all right. And now look. . . ."

It appeared that Caisotti had fought with the partisans and indeed in the very outfit to which Quinto had belonged. He had been an inspector in the commissariat, with which Quinto had never had much to do, since the different units of the brigade had been spread out in different parts of the valley and in different valleys. But now it was coming to him that he had once seen the man, wearing a khaki shirt and carrying a Sten gun slung over one shoulder; he had been raising hell about the requisitioning of some beef. Caisotti was much better informed about Quinto and remembered the units to which he had been attached and reminded him of the places where they had bivouacked. Quinto had forgotten the names, but obviously they would be familiar to Caisotti, who came from those parts.

He had gotten up and was standing in a corner of the room. "Do you see this?" High up on the wall, half hidden by a cupboard, was a picture; it was one of those composites with the pictures of all the men of a particular city or formation who died in the war, a white, red, and green ribbon around one corner and underneath, the inscription: "In Memory of the Men of the ——th Brigade who Gave their Lives for Freedom." What with the indistinct light and the dirty glass, the picture was hard to make out. Quinto stared at the tiny faces of the fallen, but he didn't seem to remember any of them. He had known so many men who had afterward lost their lives. He was still easily moved by the memory of how even on their last evening he had eaten baked chestnuts with them from the same pot and slept beside them on the straw. He found himself looking for a particular face, a man he had scarcely known who had been killed, stupidly, almost as soon as he arrived. They had been out on patrol together, and it was just chance that one took one side of the road, one the other. He thought for a moment that one of the tiny photographs looked like him, but then he saw another that could just as well have been him. The pictures had been taken ages ago; many of the faces were those of schoolboys, others were men in uniform with their berets and insignia. It was impossible to tell one from the other. Quinto sighed deeply. What was there to say now?

Nothing was settled. Caisotti asked for a deferment on the first payment; he had to finish another building already under way. Once he'd finished it, he could concentrate all his material and all his men on the Anfossi site and complete the work within the stipulated time—which, he reminded Quinto, was to be figured from the date the contract was approved by City Hall, not from the date when it was signed. To make things more difficult for him at this stage, he said, would hurt them as well as him.

Quinto went home in a foul temper. It was not only his failure (once again) to make Caisotti pay up, but also the discovery that he was an old comrade in arms. A fine turn Italian society had taken! Two partisans, one a peasant, the other a student, who had taken up arms together in the belief that they were building a new Italy. And look at them now! Both accepting the world as it was, both chasing money. And they didn't even possess the old bourgeois virtues; they were simply a couple of real estate sharks. It was no accident that they were in partnership and, of course, trying to swindle each other.

However, Quinto reflected, Caisotti had at least retained the habit of looking at his difficulties as part of the social struggle. Whereas in *his* case . . . ?

[16]

Shrouded in scaffolding, a chaos of planks, ropes, buckets, sieves, bricks, splotches of sand and lime, the house began to grow in the fall. Already its shadow was falling on the garden; the windows of the villa were shut out from the sky. But it still seemed no more than a temporary structure, a mere obstruction, something that would be pulled down the way it had been put up. That was how Signora Anfossi tried to see it, concentrating her displeasure on transitory symptoms like the objects that fell from the scaffolding onto her flower beds or the piles of planks in the road. She refused to look on it as a *house*, something that would always be there staring her in the face.

Caisotti proposed that in place of the first payment, he should increase the number of rooms to be handed over to the Anfossis. Negotiations were prolonged; during the discussions about the size of the additional rooms, it was discovered that Caisotti had made them all narrower than the contract stipulated so he could squeeze one extra room into each apartment. He was stealing their property, as it were, and proposing to pay them with what he had stolen! Canal spotted the trick in time and a supplement to the contract was drawn up; several clauses of the original contract were revised and the reversion clause was strengthened and extended to cover the delivery of the new apartments. This was fine, but they were still no nearer getting any money out of him, still no nearer the day when the building would be completed.

Ampelio paid a two-day visit during these negotiations. Both he and Quinto were at home, when who should suddenly turn up but Lina. She was bringing some papers: Caisotti wanted her to check some facts before entering the contract on the books at City Hall. Why Caisotti was being so scrupulous was far from clear, since he had never troubled himself about this sort of thing before. Signora Anfossi, as it happened, was out; this was unfortunate since it was always finally up to her to find the papers and accounts which Quinto, as he rushed frantically about, left scattered all over the house. Whenever information was needed, the Signora was the person to see.

Quinto and Ampelio sat down in the study to go over the papers while Lina sat opposite, looking softly at them. "Wait a moment while I look for the account we drew up the other time," Quinto said, and went off next door to ransack his drawers. He turned half a cupboard upside down and hunted through a dozen files, but couldn't find what he was looking for. When he returned, Caisotti's papers were still lying on the desk, but there was no sign of either the girl or Ampelio. She must have left, Quinto supposed. She would be back for the information tomorrow. He called, "Ampelio!" but there was no answer. He hadn't gone out, because his beret was still on the hatrack; he was balding and never went out without it. Perhaps he was upstairs. Quinto went up to the next floor and looked into a number of rooms, calling his name; he even went into the bathroom and from there into his brother's room.

Lina and Ampelio were in bed. The girl at once pressed her face into the pillow; her black hair spread out and around, a pink shoulder emerged from the sheets. Ampelio raised himself up on one elbow; the ribs were clearly visible in his lean, naked body. Mechanically he reached for his glasses on the side table. "Christ," he said. "Do you have to stick your damn nose in everywhere?"

Quinto shut the door and went downstairs, black with rage. He could have killed the man. To start an affair of this sort, here in the house, with somebody in Caisotti's pay—just when their business relations were in such a delicate phase . . . To go upstairs at the double with that sanctimonious little tramp . . . Ampelio didn't give a hang for the project. He left him all the responsibilities and headaches, and when he did show up, he started criticizing. And there he was upstairs, having himself a good time, leaving his fool of a brother to ransack his drawers. They were probably laughing at him, sending him to look for papers that quite likely had no importance whatever! He didn't put it past that slut. Always "Yes, sir," "No, sir," with him, demure as could be, but when Ampelio showed up, it was *hoop-la!* Or maybe Caisotti had sent her, to fool them. If so, it was clear why he hadn't told her to try her tricks on him; she wouldn't have had a hope in hell there! But even so, loosing her on Ampelio wasn't really very clever. It was a filthy trick though, a filthy trick. And what was he supposed to do? Turn down the sheets for them?

Quinto was on his way out when the doorbell rang. It was Caisotti. He needed some details, he said; they wanted them at City Hall. . . . But was it really so urgent? There was something furtive in his manner that was unlike his usual wariness; he seemed anxious, unsure of himself. Quinto took him into the study and showed him the papers that his secretary had brought; he told him she had been looking for him. "Oh, she was here, was she? Where is she?" "Why? Didn't you send her?" "Of course I sent her," Caisotti said, "but she had some other things to do as well. There was something I wanted to tell her. Where is she?" Quinto shrugged. "How do I know? I suppose she's gone back." "In that case, I'd have met her." Caisotti looked around toward the other rooms and the staircase, like a baffled animal.

"I suppose she went another way. Where do you imagine she is?"

It looked in fact as though Caisotti had followed her up to the villa, and not seeing her reappear, had come after her. He made one excuse after another to stay; his tone was conciliating, he made concessions, and even went so far as to propose some improvements in the building—at no extra cost. And all the time with that wary, uncertain look, searching Quinto's

face as though waiting for him to give himself away. At times
it looked as though the uneasiness that kept him there was going to harden into some barely controllable violence. The slack
muscles of his pale face grew taut, the blood showed through
his clenched knuckles, the shark mouth twisted into a nervous,
ingratiating grimace that seemed the prelude to some wild
outburst. Quinto was annoyed at being stuck there with
Caisotti and having to shield his brother and that tart upstairs.
His resentment against Ampelio made him side with Caisotti;
and at the same time he was aware that this was the right moment to force him to make important concessions. He was
never going to have the man in his hands again like this, but
on the spur of the moment he could remember nothing useful
to ask him. Irritated at not being able to show that he was on
his side, he could think of no way out except to persuade him
to come and take a look at the site to see how the work was
getting on.

Caisotti went with him reluctantly, taking care to keep the
villa, and especially the garden gate, well in sight. They
climbed up the gangplank, onto the second floor, where the
cement was still wet. Quinto examined the angles of the walls
and the doors. "This wall ought to be thicker, Caisotti," he
said, his voice booming through the empty space. "Here, do
you see what I mean?"

Caisotti didn't move. He was looking furtively through the
bare brick frame of the window, across the dense green of the
garden, which Quinto scarcely recognized from that unfamiliar
vantage point. "Thicker? Yes, of course, but wait till it's finished, with the mortar, you'll see. . . ."

[17]

Caisotti's stock was starting to go down, among his own following too. Even the red-haired giant—his name was Angerin
—burst suddenly into revolt.

Angerin lived on the site in a wooden shack used as a tool
shed and night watchman's hut; he slept on the ground, like
an animal, never taking off his clothes. First thing in the morn-

ing, his face blank and bewildered, he would set off down the hill with that ambling, apelike gait of his to buy a roll of bread, a blood sausage, and a tomato; he would come back chewing, his mouth full. He appeared to live on this, though every now and then he was seen cooking something in a dirty pot balanced on a couple of bricks. Caisotti, apparently, owed him a couple of months' wages. The man was hunger itself and yet, being immensely strong and obedient, he was given all the heaviest work. The other men insisted on being paid regularly; otherwise they would go off and work elsewhere, for jobs were easy to find in the building trade. So Caisotti economized at the expense of Angerin—who was docile and incapable of taking any steps on his own—treating him like a slave. When he first arrived, he had been a frightening, bull-like figure, but he had lost weight, his shoulders curved in and his arms hung listlessly by his side. Lack of food, overwork, and sleeping on the ground were ruining him.

The only person who took any notice of him was Signora Anfossi, and Quinto learned about him from her. She would have him up to the villa and give him sugar and biscuits and old undershirts. She'd offer him advice and ask him about himself, a painful procedure for Angerin, this, since she couldn't understand his inarticulate dialect and made him repeat everything ten times. He was from the mountain hinterland, like Caisotti, who had brought him down to work. "I don't think he's ever had any god except Caisotti," Signora Anfossi said.

"He's probably his illegitimate son," Quinto suggested, laughing.

"Yes, I wondered about that. I asked him if they were related and he seemed confused."

"Him too. . . . What a man!"

"What do you mean?"

"Oh, gossip, gossip."

On the job, the other men laughed at him and played tricks on him. He exploded quite suddenly. From the villa they heard the sound of blows, the crack of planks thrown down on planks, men shouting. Quinto ran out, down to the site. The workmen were in the road, scattering in all directions; one had jumped from the second floor, right on top of the flowers. "Help! Angerin has gone crazy! Help!" The giant was up on the second floor, smashing everything. He sent buckets of mortar crashing against the walls, wrenched the scaffolding apart, toppled over ladders, blindly hurled bricks, cracking the walls and wrecking the fresh cement. The noise re-echoed in the empty building, grew enormous, and this obviously excited him still more. No one could get near him; he was making great flailing strokes with a shovel, which would have killed anyone on the spot. It was his way of working off his resentment against Caisotti—blindly, without caring whom he hit.

"Send for the police!" someone shouted. "No, no, send for Caisotti. He's the only person who can handle him." The foreman had in fact ridden off to look for him. Quinto stood and watched the skeleton of this house, which had risen so slowly and so painfully, being demolished before his eyes, watched the girders buckle under Angerin's blows and the window sills crack. He was already reckoning the time that would be lost in repairing the damage, thinking of all the places that would merely be patched up, all the arguments they would have to go through. . . .

Caisotti arrived in his three-wheeler. As soon as the sound of his motor approached, then stopped, the sounds inside the new building stopped too. Caisotti got out, looking pale and drawn, but quite calm. He pushed his way through the men without looking at anyone and went up to the building, then propping a ladder against the wall, he climbed up to the second floor.

Angerin was there waiting for him, shovel raised, tensing himself to strike. Caisotti climbed another step. He spoke quickly, in dialect, not raising his voice. "Angerin, you're sore at me?" The giant stared at him, wide-eyed, and started to tremble. At last he said, "Yes, with you." "You want to kill me?" Angerin hesitated a moment, then: "No." "Drop that shovel!" It didn't sound like an order, more like a question or a statement; or maybe an order to a tame dog. Angerin dropped the shovel. As soon as Caisotti saw that his hands were empty, he came up quickly, and here he made a mistake. Angerin was beginning to be afraid of what he had done, but now his rage flooded back; seizing a trowel, he threw it violently at Caisotti. It hit him on the forehead; it was only a glancing blow but it opened up a long cut, which quickly brimmed with blood. It looked as though Caisotti must be stunned by the pain, but no, he reacted quickly. It was his only chance. The giant would have finished him otherwise. He raised one arm, more as though he wanted to hide the sight of his blood from Angerin than to stop the bleeding, then hurled himself on top of him. They rolled over and it was difficult to see what was happening, then Caisotti was on top and Angerin was no longer trying to hit him but merely to drag him off and then not even that. Caisotti, his knee pressed against the man's chest, started to pommel him, one sledgehammer blow after another thudding dully on his back, his chest, his head, his bones.

"He's killing him!" said one of the workmen standing beside Quinto. "No, he won't kill him," someone else said, "but Angerin won't see a penny of his back pay. It'll all go to repair the damage." The thudding blows continued, then someone cried, "That's enough! He's not defending himself any more." Quinto recognized his mother's voice; she was standing by the hedge, very pale, a shawl wrapped around her.

Caisotti got to his feet and slowly came down the ladder. Angerin's outstretched body began to stir and then he too got up, first on all fours, then onto his feet. But his body was slack and bent and he started to limp about, picking things up and putting them back in their place.

Caisotti walked forward, holding a bloody handkerchief to his face; he pulled his cap over it to keep it in place; his eyes were full of tears. "It was nothing," he said in dialect to the men. "All right, you can go back to work now." "Work with that lunatic? The hell you say! Damn near killed us, he did. We're not going back, we're going for the police." "He won't hurt you; he wasn't after you anyway. He's all right again now. You're not calling anyone. Back to work!" And he got back into his three-wheeler, the bloody handkerchief slipping down over his eyes, and jammed his foot down onto the starter. He pushed for a moment, trembling with the putt-putt of the engine, blinded by the tears that were rolling down his cheeks. Then he was off.

[18]

Quinto spent most of the winter at Milan, working on the editorial board of the magazine that Bensi and Cerveteri had started. He would come home every now and then and stay a few days. He used to arrive in the evening and on his way to the villa pass by the site. The shadow of the building stood out in the darkness, still wrapped in its trellis of scaffolding, pierced with blank window spaces, roofless. The work was going ahead so slowly that it looked the same from one visit to the next. This, he felt, was as far as it was ever going to get; he couldn't even imagine it finished. So this was where his passion for concrete reality had led him, to this shapeless heap of bricks and beams lying there unused; it had been a mere caprice, something started and then dropped halfway. Only with Bensi and Cerveteri did he feel himself a man of action, and this helped him to overcome his neurotic sense of being less educated and intelligent than they were. There too he was acting in continual opposition to his own instincts, but this was a more manageable kind of opposition. What in the world had ever made him dabble in real estate? He no longer felt the slightest interest in the project and stayed away for months on end, leaving all the headaches to his mother.

As for Ampelio, it was no use relying on him for anything. He was always preparing for some exam or other, the dirty grind, and there was no hope of shifting him an inch from his chosen path. Every three or four months, he came to see his mother for a couple of days, and that was that. During one of these brief visits, it happened that Quinto came home too. They met in the morning. Quinto, who had arrived the night before, was in the bathroom, washing, when Ampelio came in. Quinto went at him at once. "Well, what have you been doing? Have you settled anything? Have you seen to having the property confiscated since the work hasn't been finished on time? And what about the foreclosure?" It was a relief to have someone on whom he could unload his own bad conscience and his resentment at the whole affair, which had seemed so straightforward at first and yet grew more and more involved as time went on.

Ampelio stood by the bathroom door; he was wearing an overcoat. His umbrella hung over one arm. No trace of expression was visible behind his glasses. "There's nothing to be done," he said calmly.

Quinto was in his pajamas. "What do you mean, there's nothing to be done?" he shouted, drying himself hurriedly. "What do you mean? We've got the reversion clause, haven't we?" He went back into his bedroom, shoving Ampelio out of the way. "Caisotti hasn't handed over the apartments. Right. So we take back the site and everything on it. We've got to get moving."

"Well, get moving then," said Ampelio.

When Ampelio took this tone, Quinto always lost his temper completely. He knew what his brother was like, he knew that the angrier he became, the calmer Ampelio's contemptuous irony would be; and yet he lost his temper every time. "So, you've been here five days. You should have been to see Canal and started legal proceedings. And what have you done? Nothing!"

Quinto was sitting on the edge of the bed, getting dressed. Ampelio stood in front of him in his overcoat, his hands on the handle of the umbrella, which was poking into the bedside rug. Ampelio's standing there fully dressed while he was half naked made Quinto feel even more uncomfortable. "You've been here five days," he went on, "and you haven't settled a single thing! Caisotti is selling his apartments before he's finished building them, and we sit here twiddling our thumbs. If we had some tenants who were due to take possession, he'd have to finish the work. Have you tried to find any tenants? Have you been to the agency?"

Ampelio always paused a moment or so before answering,

staring at nothing. After a while he said, "You've got the whole thing back to front."

"What do you mean?"

No answer.

"What do you mean?" Quinto shook him by the arm. "What are you talking about? Are you trying to say that I've been doing nothing myself and that I come here and take it out on you, is that what you mean? Is that it?" He continued to shake his arm, but Ampelio had nothing further to add. "All the months I spent here," Quinto went on, "trying to pull the chestnuts out of the fire—your chestnuts too, don't you understand?—sweating my guts out, you didn't take the faintest notice, you didn't even bother to thank me. Can you deny it? Just answer me: can you deny it?"

It was not Ampelio's way to explain himself. He would only have had to say: "You spent three months here on the beach," and Quinto would have been punctured; he wouldn't have known how to go on. But Ampelio would never do what you wanted, not even in a quarrel. All he said was, "O.K., give me my share, we'll divide the apartments between us, I'll sell my part of it just as it is, to Caisotti or to anyone who'll buy it; I'll take what I can get. I don't care so long as I don't have to go on having these squabbles with you. The only thing I regret is leaving Mother in your hands."

"What the hell are you talking about?" Quinto seized him by the wrists. "Don't you know that I've done everything so far, that I've done it for you too?"

Ampelio shook him off. "You're sick, your nerves are shot to hell. You ought to go see a doctor."

"Why do you treat me like this, why do you insult me?" Quinto yelled, and began pounding him with his fists. Ampelio fell on the bed and lay there without even trying to defend himself. He merely held his knees and elbows up so that Quinto's blows, which were passionate rather than powerful, hit only his arms and legs. He was still holding his umbrella, but he made no attempt to use it. His glasses had fallen off and were lying on the bed. He simply waited, hunched up, his beard in the collar of his overcoat, staring at Quinto without

resentment or anything else, only the lost look of the myopic
and a complete withdrawal.

Quinto stopped suddenly. Ampelio got up and put on his
glasses. "Go and see a doctor; you're not normal." And he left
the room.

[19]

At the end of the winter Quinto found a job in Rome, working for a movie company. He left the editorial board of the review after quarreling with Bensi and Cerveteri. The Roman
world was lavish and uninhibited; the producer was a man
who managed to lay his hands on hundreds of thousands of
lire from one day to the next. It was a convivial sort of existence, with ten-thousand-lire notes flying around as though
they were small change. In the evenings they all went off to
eat together at a restaurant, then on to someone's house to
drink. Drinking made Quinto ill; nonetheless, this, finally, was
life. He had not yet laid his hands on much actual money, but
he was on the way at last.

His mother's letters, full of maddening little details, went
into everything exhaustively, and nearly drove him crazy.
They had lost a possible tenant because the apartments
weren't yet ready; Caisotti had now got the roof on, but the
elevator shed on top exceeded the limits permitted by the
regulations. Travaglia was supposed to come and note the violation, but he was nowhere to be found. Quinto was now living in another world, where everything was possible, everything could be fixed, everything was done quickly; even so,
he was unable to wash his hands of the project, if only because he found that in the movies, the more he earned the
more he spent, and it wasn't enough. He was after a French
girl who was part of a Franco-Italian coproduction team, and
he was always on the go. It was a rootless life.

And more and more the thought of that cursed apartment
building nagged at him.

As soon as he had a few days off, he went home. I'm going
to take the affair in hand and settle everything in quick order,

he said to himself. He felt he had adopted the style of the
movie world. But one look at that muddy, cluttered site, at
that squalid cement structure standing there half finished, and
he felt his bustling efficiency draining away. He didn't even
know where to start. He listened to his mother listing the
principal subjects of dispute (for example, the interminable
argument as to whose responsibility the drinking water and
electricity connections were), and then to Caisotti, who no
longer troubled to conceal his contempt for partners so helpless and distracted.

The man was now selling or leasing apartments, in defiance
of the contract, which gave him no rights on the property until he had delivered their part of the building to the Anfossis.
He would finish an apartment hurriedly and still be putting in
the fixtures and giving it the last coat of paint when the occu-
pants were due to arrive.

"You can finish your apartments when you want, but we
have to wait for ours! Is that it, Caisotti?"

"You don't even have any tenants waiting to come in."

Quinto had expected this answer. He had looked for tenants
and put the matter in the hands of the agencies, but it was
quite clear that nothing was going to be ready in the summer.
Someone did come up the hill to have a look, but finding
the building still under construction and the whole place covered with mud, went back to the agency to complain that he
had been given the wrong address. The only thing ready was
a shop on the ground floor, a kind of storeroom, which he
hoped to rent to a flower shipper, since the flower market was
nearby. He went there early one morning, when business was
at its briskest, to explore the possibilities, but the season was
already in full swing and no one was going to think of moving
at such a time.

One Sunday, the day before he was due to return to Rome,
he was passing by the site when he saw someone examining it
with interest and then walk inside. Quinto followed him. He
was a small, elderly man wearing an overcoat and a hat. He
went up the cement steps (still without marble) to the second
floor and peered through the blank doorways. "Excuse me, is

there someone you want to see?" Quinto shouted up the stair-
well. The old man passed from one apartment to another, taking care not to trip over the cans lying around. "No, no, I'm
just looking."

Quinto went up to the second floor himself and looked
everywhere for him; finally he saw him come in from a balcony. "Do you want a place to rent?" Quinto asked. The old
man was already on the way to the next floor. "No, no, just
looking." Quinto went up to the third floor. "If you want an
apartment, the ones to the right are ours. We can discuss
terms," he shouted into space, for the man had disappeared
again. "We've got three-room and four-room apartments—"
Realizing that the visitor was on the floor above, he ran up.
"Three-room and four-room apartments," he repeated.

Even if he decided against doing so, the fact remained that
the man had come to look for an apartment. Otherwise, why
should he be sticking his nose in everywhere as though he
wanted to examine every room and every detail of the construction? Everything depended on being able to persuade
him now, so that he did business with them and not with
Caisotti. "It's a mess just now," Quinto said, "but if you want
an apartment, we can have it ready in a matter of days. You
can start putting your furniture in . . ."

But the old man wasn't even listening. He was checking
the washbasins and the sewer lines. Perhaps he was deaf? But
no, he had answered promptly enough at the beginning. "If
we agree on terms now, you can move your furniture the first
of the month," he cried, but the man was gone again—and
the stairs joining the fourth and fifth floors weren't yet in
place. Quinto had a fright. He was such a nosy old devil. Had
he managed to fall down the elevator shaft?

But no, there he was, balancing on the cornice of the flat
terrace roof, which as yet had no parapet. He had climbed up
there on the planks that the workmen used, and was inspecting the water tanks. He was coming down now, keeping his
balance carefully, knees slightly bent, arms thrust forward.

Quinto went to give him a hand. "Look, will you please tell

me. If you don't want to buy or rent, why exactly are you so interested in this place?"

The old man, refusing his help, had now reached the landing and was starting to go down the stairs. "It's nothing. I was just taking a look at the building because I have to foreclose."

[20]

During the spring the film company moved to Cannes for the outside scenes. Quinto went to and fro between Rome and Cannes and sometimes stayed at the French producer's villa at Juan-les-Pins. The journey took him near home, but he didn't stop; he couldn't spare the time, and the transition from the rhythm of moviemaking to that of Caisotti's building firm was too much for him. Financially and intellectually, he was used to living a quiet, modest life and he was finding this new and in every sense of the word extravagant existence a continual strain. The French girl was proving difficult. He was leading a life that seemed to carry every possibility of happiness; and yet he felt miserable.

The situation at home was more and more involved. Someone had bought a garage in Caisotti's part of the building, and then hearing that his ownership was liable to be challenged, had rushed off to Signora Anfossi to ask what the situation was. She advised the man not to buy from Caisotti until he had fulfilled his obligations. There was a fearful squabble when Caisotti heard about his, and he was threatening to sue the Signora for defamation. How could he meet his obligations with the Anfossis slandering him and doing their best to ruin his business? Canal, meanwhile, had drawn up a claim against Caisotti for failure to fulfill the terms of the contract, for damages sustained by his clients due to loss of rents, and for his violation of the clause relating to the height of the building. Unless Caisotti gave satisfaction within a month, he was going to prosecute. But Caisotti now had a lawyer of his own and he too was drawing up a claim: he accused Signora Anfossi of repeated defamation of character, of violation of the contract (failure to drain the cesspool within the agreed time), and even of theft. This referred to the business of the pipes the year before; it continued to crop up whenever there was a quarrel. Caisotti's charges made no sort of sense, but if Canal presented his claim, Caisotti would answer with his. It would at least serve to confuse the issue and drag the thing out. They were at present negotiating in order to try and find some way of reaching an agreement.

In the thick of all this, Quinto was catapulted from Cannes back to Rome. The French producer was withdrawing, the Italian company was neck deep in debts. They shot a few inside scenes at Cinecittà, then the crisis took a turn for the worse and the whole project was suspended. Signora Anfossi wrote to say that she had at last been able to find a tenant for the shop: a certain Signora Hofer, a florist, who exported gladioli to Munich.

In September the Italian producer went bankrupt and the movie was bought by a new company, belonging to a big building-site speculator, which finished it rapidly on a shoe-string budget. Quinto was no longer needed, since his job of "production assistant" was considered superfluous. He thought he still had some money due to him, but they were able to show him that according to the terms of his contract they didn't owe him anything. He had already broken off with the French girl at Cannes. He came home without a job and without a penny.

His mother was now mainly involved with Signora Hofer. She didn't pay her rent, she didn't answer letters, and she was nowhere to be found. Apparently she had gone to Germany. She turned up, finally, when Quinto was at home. She was nearly six feet tall, an energetic, handsome woman, a little heavy perhaps, but well built; her suit did not conceal the generous breasts; her legs were a shade masculine, but slender and shapely. She had a hard, plain face, but it showed a kind of pride, the pride of a woman who knows her business. Her blond, curled hair was fastened in back by a quite inappropriate pink ribbon. Quinto was instantly drawn to this heavy German body and he couldn't take his eyes off her, but she addressed herself, impassively, to Signora Anfossi. She had a strong accent, but her Italian was coldly fluent. She told the Signora that she had had to remain in Germany longer than she had anticipated and had therefore not been able to pay the rent. But her affairs were now in order and she would return with the money within the week. And off she went, treading firmly in her mannish shoes. Quinto had not managed to catch her eye.

Toward the end of the week, his mother began saying, "No sign of Signora Hofer." He was stretched out on a chaise longue reading *The Confession of Felix Krull.* "Signora Hofer, eh? Signora Hofer . . . We'll make Signora Hofer pay up all right!" He went on playing, obsessively, with her name and her image until gradually he found himself summing up in her person everything he had missed, everything he had failed to bring off—his real estate plunge, the movies, the French girl. "Signora Hofer," he sniggered to himself. "I'll deal with Signora Hofer."

She was only in her shop first thing in the morning, with a couple of packers; this was when the flowers arrived from the market. She supervised the packing of the gladioli into baskets, which were then taken to the agent who made the trip to the airport at Milan. This done, she pulled down the shutters and left. Quinto got up late and he never saw her. She had, however, left her home address.

When a week had passed, he said to his mother, "Let me have the receipt form, signed, and the revenue stamps. I'm going to call on the Hofer woman and make her pay up."

She was living in an old house on the sea front. She opened the door herself. She was wearing a blouse with short sleeves and her arms were a little softer than Quinto had expected. Her expression was doubtful, as though she didn't recognize him. Quinto at once pulled the receipt out of his pocket and said that since she hadn't been able to find the time to visit them, he had come to her in order to settle their account. She opened the door and let him in. Her room, with its embroidered cushions and dolls, suggested a furnished apartment. On a chest of drawers there were photographs of two men, with some flowers in front of them. One was a German airman, the other was an Italian officer who, thought Quinto (always ready to suppose the worst), looked as though he were wearing the uniform of the Republic of Salò.*

"You really needn't have troubled, Signor Anfossi," she said. "I was coming to see you tomorrow or the day after." Quinto's glance was shuttling between her eyes, still remote and distracted, and the firm, full flesh of her body.

"But why don't we settle the account now? I've brought the receipt. . . ." Quinto's voice was trying to sound a little playful, a little suggestive—anything to get away from this dry, business-like relation. But it was no good; these delicate vibrations were wasted on Signora Hofer. "If I say that I am coming to see you tomorrow or the day after, Signor Anfossi, it means that it isn't convenient for me to pay until tomorrow or the day after." A fine nerve the woman had, taking this high tone when she was already a week late. It was not, however, on the field of finance that Quinto was resolved to conquer.

He gave a little laugh and said, firmly, "Signora Hofer, I don't like quarreling with a good-looking woman like you."

Plainly she was not expecting this approach, and there was a momentary glint in her eyes that was on the edge of irony. But Quinto, quick as a sexual maniac, was already reaching out to unbutton her blouse. She started back, indignantly, then stopped. "Signor Anfossi, what in the world do you think you're doing?" But his arms were already around her.

The woman was a tigress; he was no match for her. They lurched violently from one end of the room to another, but he never succeeded in getting her off her feet. He had no idea what he was doing; he wanted his revenge for everything—and this was it. In this state of frenzy, he almost passed out at one point and found himself lying exhausted, surrounded by dolls, on the couch. Signora Hofer was standing looking at him with a faint air of contempt. Not once had she smiled.

Quinto straightened himself, trying hard to keep his mind blank. She showed him to the door. Simply for the sake of

---

*The short-lived "Italian Socialist Republic," proclaimed by Mussolini in September, 1943, after the collapse of the Fascist regime.

something to say, he took the receipt out of his pocket. "Then you'll be coming . . ."

She reached out for the receipt, went to the bureau, opened her purse, put the receipt into it, went to the door and opened it. "Good evening, Signor Anfossi."

Quinto left. The days were drawing in. It was dark.

[21]

The woman whom Caisotti employed as his lawyer didn't seem quite to understand the nature of the dispute. He had to decide everything for himself and she merely tried to give a legal color to what he was saying.

"Come off it," said Canal from behind his desk. "Are you seriously proposing to accuse Signora Anfossi of theft? The judge is going to laugh in your face. You ought to advise your client not to play the fool," he added, turning to the lawyer.

Caisotti was sitting in an armchair, fists clenched, face dark and savage. The lawyer turned over some pages. "Let me see . . . Yes, here it is. On the eighteenth day of June, nineteen fifty-four, four metal drain pipes measuring . . ."

Canal did his best. He spoke sensibly, like a practical man, without flights of rhetoric, though there were moments when he had difficulty in controlling himself. He was fed up with all this deception and disgusted by the way the law could be used by scoundrels to protect themselves. But this was how things went and his job was to adjust them as best he could, and repair the damage done by swindlers who think they are smart and by starry-eyed dreamers who think everything should be done for them. They both end up by making the same sort of mess, he reflected. So he just went on trying to persuade the other side that there was really no point in dragging the affair out by introducing legal quibbles: the debt had to be paid, the apartments had to be completed and handed over. As for the exact amount of the sum owed, here there was room for compromise since his clients were aware that they had nothing to gain by ruining Caisotti's business. They therefore proposed a final figure. The alternative was to go to court—and this time they meant it.

It was Canal who had proposed these conciliatory tactics to Quinto. "What are we trying to do?" he said to him the day before the meeting. "You've lost interest in the whole affair, that's perfectly obvious. You're practically never here, you leave all the dirty work to your mother. She has every right to wash her hands of it, but instead she takes the thing seriously. As for Caisotti, it doesn't matter to him what happens; he's got no reputation to lose. He arrived here in patched pants, he lives like a beggar and carries on like a petty crook. It's impossible to corner him. You can't ever tell what he's going to do next. This is his system and he makes it work. He keeps his head above water; he's a person you've got to reckon with."

Canal announced the figure that he and Quinto had agreed on. The woman turned toward Caisotti, who screwed up his lips, then shook his head. "My client feels that this figure does not offer a basis for discussion," she said. Caisotti got up; she too got up, and stubbing out her cigarette, she gathered the papers into a brief case. Then she picked up her handbag, shook hands with Canal and Quinto, and hurried after her client, who walked out with his hands in his pockets.

"Oh, I know!" Canal said to Quinto when they were alone. "He's just a peasant, that's the trouble, and he's an idiot. Heaven knows what he thinks he gains at this stage by refusing to pay and dragging the affair out like this. But that's the way he is." And he stretched out his hand to Quinto to say good-bye.

Quinto would have liked to stay a while and talk about his experiences with the movies, but Canal was busy and he had to go. At last he could talk about something that everyone was interested in—Cinecittà, French actresses, and so on—unlike the days when he could discuss only politics and literature and never knew what to say to his old friends. But now the only subject of discussion was Caisotti.

Caisotti, Caisotti, Caisotti . . . He couldn't take any more of the man; he was through. Sure, he knew what sort of guy he was, he knew he'd win every round, he had known this before any of them! But how did they all manage to accept Caisotti as something normal? Oh, they criticized him, of course, but only verbally; they weren't concerned to destroy him, to *deny* him. All right, he, Quinto, had been the first to praise Caisotti —against the opposition of all the stuffed shirts in town. But at that time he had appeared in a different light; he had been one of the terms of an antithesis, part of a vital process. But now he was simply one aspect of a gray, uniform reality, of a reality which had either to be denied or accepted. For his part, he was not going to accept it!

The notary, Bardissone, for example, delivered a kind of panegyric of the man when Quinto went to see him. "He'll pay all right, believe me. Don't go by appearances; he's not a bad man. He's altogether self-made, remember, and now he's head of a considerable firm. It's a hard moment for everyone; we all have our ups and downs, you know. . . . But try and get on with him; he's a decent fellow, believe me."

Travaglia was much occupied with politics. The local elections were due the next year and it was said that he wanted to run for mayor. Quinto met him one day in the street and told him something of what went on behind the scenes at Cinecittà; he did his man-of-the-world act. In front of the Caffè Melina they ran into Caisotti. Since the meeting at the lawyer's, he and Quinto no longer spoke to each other, but Travaglia stopped and shook him by the hand. After a while, he said, "And what about this business with the Anfossis?"

Caisotti started to talk in his self-pitying whine, but he didn't go into details and Quinto made no comment beyond shrugging his shoulders now and then, Travaglia, however, tried to argue with him and convince him, but he put forward the Anfossis' case as though it were patently childish; one had to try to understand it, he implied, but there was no use pretending it made any sort of sense. Caisotti in due course came up with a proposal: he would pay the Anfossis a part of what he owed them, but they would have to let him run the apartments. Obviously *they* weren't going to be able to handle them. He would make it his business to look for tenants and collect the rents, and at the end of the year he would hand over a fixed sum.

This arrangement would leave them wholly at Caisotti's mercy; Quinto saw this clearly, but he also saw that it did provide a way of escaping from all this worry, at least for a year, and moreover it spared him the remorse he would feel at leaving his mother to struggle with the rents. Travaglia too understood that this proposal was not altogether to the Anfossis' disadvantage, and he supported it. Quinto tried to bargain and they ended up in Caisotti's office. There was a new secretary, a redhead, new furniture, and a new fluorescent lamp. Caisotti had them both sit down and offered cigarettes. A woman came in, a countrywoman, obviously, no longer young, with a little boy. "I'd like to introduce my wife," Caisotti said. "She's come to live here too now. She was just about my last link with home."

The understanding was that Quinto would discuss the whole matter with his mother and with Ampelio, who was due to come home for a visit.

He was walking up toward the villa, alone, when he saw the old carpenter, Masera. The man was going down the hill, on his bicycle; he braked when he saw Quinto and said hello.

"So you're home for a while, eh? On business? The building, I suppose. . . . It always seems to be in the same state every time I pass by. It must be driving you all crazy. Is it true that Caisotti hasn't paid you yet? Look, I've never liked to ask you, but sometimes I've seen you in the street looking a bit worried, and I've said to myself, I'll just have a word with him now. Then I thought, no, better not. . . . But we often talk about it, the comrades, you know. . . . How did you ever go and get yourselves in Caisotti's hands? Didn't you know the kind of guy he is? If I told you some of the dirty tricks he's played on us . . ."

Quinto's nerves were at the breaking point, and yet at the same time he felt a sense of relief. This plunge in real estate, which he had defended and exalted to himself, as though to protect it from the attacks of Masera and his friends, had now become something he could discuss calmly with them. They were on his side, they were behind him.

"Oh, I know you had to sell quickly, to pay your taxes," Masera went on. "And it was a good idea to go into partnership for your building—leave the work to others, for what that was worth. . . . But why didn't you come to Party Headquarters to ask us? We could have given you some advice. There are contractors who, even though they're not in the Party, are our friends, or at least they want to keep in with us. Then we've got a cooperative society too; it's a going concern. . . . Come down and talk things over with us one evening. We're planning a joint action to stop speculation, to stabilize real estate prices, to get the building code respected. It's just not possible to put up with the sort of things that are going on now, all this swindling. . . . We can fight back; there's plenty to be done. Look, you'll be needing tenants soon. Well, come and have a word with us. Every now and then we hear of someone; people write to us, from Turin and Milan, people in the Party—with money too, sometimes. If we can give them an idea of the price . . ."

Quinto walked home feeling as if he was carrying a corpse on his back. Strangled by Masera's well-meaning chatter, the daring individualism of the free-enterprise building contractor, he rolled romantic eyes wildly in the midday sun.

Ampelio was there. They shut themselves up in the dining room, and covering the table with papers, they went over their accounts from the beginning.

The Signora was in the garden. The scent of honeysuckle was in the air, the nasturtiums were an almost too vivid splash of color. If she didn't raise her eyes to the ranked windows of the apartment buildings all around, the garden was still the garden. She went from bed to bed, pruning the dead stalks, making sure that the gardener had watered everything. A snail climbed up the pointed leaf of an iris. She pulled it off and threw it on the ground. A sudden burst of voices made her look up. There, on the top of the building, they were laying the tar on the terrace. She thought it was nicer when they made houses with tiled roofs and put a flag up to show that the roof was on. "Boys, boys!" she shouted toward the dining room. "They've finished the roof!"

Quinto and Ampelio didn't answer. The shutters were drawn and the room was half dark. They sat with bundles of papers on their knees, calculating once again how long it would be before their capital was amortized. The sun was sinking behind Caisotti's building and the light that filtered through the slats and played over the silver on the sideboard grew weaker and weaker. Now only the upper slats were bright, and slowly the light died, reflected on the polished surfaces of the trays and the teapots. . . .

COOK'S

by
Sheridan H. Garth
and
William I. Kaufman

POCKET TRAVEL GUIDE TO EUROPE

GC•959/95c

New, compact,
comprehensive
reference books
that tell you how
to plan your trip;
how to go and why;
what to see,
wear and buy;
where to stay and eat.
With hundreds of
helpful suggestions,
useful tips and fascinating
historical details.
Illustrated with many maps

COOK'S

POCKET TRAVEL GUIDE TO THE WEST INDIES
INCLUDING THE BAHAMAS, BERMUDA AND THE SPANISH MAIN

GC•958/95c

PUBLISHED BY
POCKET BOOKS, INC.